A Stanley Burnshaw Reader

BY STANLEY BURNSHAW

André Spire and His Poetry

The Wheel Age

The Iron Land

The Bridge

The Sunless Sea

Early and Late Testament

Caged in an Animal's Mind

The Seamless Web

In the Terrified Radiance

Mirages: Travel Notes in the Promised Land

The Refusers

My Friend, My Father

Robert Frost Himself

A Stanley Burnshaw Reader

EDITED BY STANLEY BURNSHAW

Two New Yorkers

The Poem Itself

Varieties of Literary Experience

The Modern Hebrew Poem Itself

Stanley Burnshaw [signature]

A Stanley Burnshaw Reader

Introduction by Denis Donoghue

The University of Georgia Press   Athens and London

The author records his especial thanks for help to a number of
friends and colleagues, in particular to Arthur Casciato,
Stephen Corey, Susan Glassman, Karen Orchard, Jacob
Weissman, and Robert Zaller.

© 1990 by Stanley Burnshaw
Published by the University of Georgia Press
Athens, Georgia 30602

Set in Linotron 202 10 on 13 Linotype Walbaum by
Tseng Information Systems, Inc.
Printed and bound by Thomson-Shore
The paper in this book meets the guidelines for
permanence and durability of the Committee on
Production Guidelines for Book Longevity of the
Council on Library Resources.

Printed in the United States of America

94 93 92 91 90   5 4 3 2 1

Library of Congress Cataloging in Publication Data

Burnshaw, Stanley, 1906–
    A Stanley Burnshaw reader / introduction by Denis
Donoghue.
        p.   cm.
    Includes bibliographical references.
    ISBN 0-8203-1195-2 (alk. paper). – ISBN 0-8203-1196-0 (pbk. :
alk. paper)
    I. Title.
PS3503.U65A6   1990
811'.52—dc20   89-48330
                                                      CIP

British Library Cataloging in Publication Data available

Photograph of Stanley Burnshaw by Edie Yoder

IN MEMORY OF LEDA BURNSHAW

(1909 – 1987)

Manhood begins when we have, in a way, made truce with necessity; begins, at all events, when we have surrendered to it, as the most only do; but begins joyfully and hopefully only when we have reconciled ourselves to necessity and thus, in reality, triumphed over it and felt that in necessity we are free.

—Thomas Carlyle, *Edinburgh Review*, 1828

Contents

Introduction

DENIS DONOGHUE

According to W. H. Auden's poem "Who's Who," "a shilling life will give you all the facts," but we know it won't. It is hard to say what constitutes, in that regard, a fact. Is it the sort of thing that gets into *Who's Who* or, as in Auden's poem, the single telling thing, the clue, that doesn't? In Elizabeth Bishop's poem "Over 2000 Illustrations and a Complete Concordance" there is a line I have never been secure about: "Everything only connected by 'and' and 'and.'" Sometimes I construe it as saying that there ought to be, in anyone's life, richer and more diverse connections than "and" and "and." In another mood, I think she means to say that a string of "ands" is enough: why demand more? It would be bizarre to regard anyone's life as if it were without facts: it would be like thinking of a complex sentence without the punctuation that disposes its clauses; a wild speculation.

Stanley Burnshaw has not published an autobiography, so it is impossible for me to give all the facts; or even all the "facts." In the third Part of *The Refusers: An Epic of the Jews* (1981) he has told us enough about his father to convince us that the elder man was indeed a significant person, a visionary. Writing about his father, Stanley Burnshaw folds himself into the story. The only claim he appears to make is that he is his father's son. But there is more to be said, and I wish I knew enough to say it. It is possible to deduce from *The Refusers* and from many poems a sense of Stanley Burnshaw's work, and some of the events that have animated it. Perhaps we should be content with that, and set aside our demand for further chapter-and-verse. But it seems desirable, for worthier reasons, to list a few of the facts a shilling life would note.

Stanley Burnshaw was born on June 20, 1906, in a house at 150th Street and Broadway in New York. The house was an orphanage, directed by Stanley's father. The children it housed were survivors, displaced persons, many of them rescued from Czarist pogroms. The director came from Courland, a province of Latvia. He had set out for the United States upon discovering that, as a Jew, he could not enroll as a student in the Latvia Institute of Oriental Languages. New York City and, later, the state of New York became his home, haven too for the children he nurtured. In 1912 he moved the whole community of pupils and teachers to a farm of two hundred acres in Pleasantville, New York: twenty cottages, each to hold thirty children.

The history of this experiment in education is amply given in the third part of *The Refusers*, a narrative of such interest and bearing that it has also been published separately as *My Friend, My Father* (1986). So I need not comment further on Stanley's early life except to remark that he grew up and thrived in a happy family. His possessions included fresh air, cultivated parents, nineteenth-century *Lieder*, the heritage of German Romanticism—Goethe, Schiller, Lessing—and the destiny of being, in some hard-to-describe sense, a Jew.

It is my understanding that Burnshaw's life, in the years before he started trying to become a writer, was reasonably comfortable. He has not claimed the privilege of drudgery. He took a bachelor of arts degree at the University of Pittsburgh, and got a job as an assistant copywriter in a large steel mill outside that city. In May 1927 he and his wife set off for a year in England, France, and Italy. During that year he met the poet André Spire, author of *Plaisir poétique et plaisir musculaire*, a book that brings together several considerations which Burnshaw has developed in a wholly different way in *The Seamless Web* (1970) and other books. Not poor, Burnshaw saw enough poverty at large to turn him into a Communist: he was persuaded by the promise of a revolution according to Marx. For a few years it seemed to him that Communism provided the only hope for the wretched of the earth; for those who, as things stood, could "hear no music but the song of death." Burnshaw started sending his poems to congenial magazines and went to work for *The New Masses*.

Burnshaw's disenchantment with communism is an experience shared with many idealists of his generation: it is not news. I deduce from his fiction and poetry that from January 30, 1933, when Hitler was named Chancellor, Burnshaw's most acute concerns were also his father's: the fate of the victims of fascism in Hitler's Europe. Burnshaw's father was in communication with several Jews in Europe, who kept him informed of events which most people in Europe and the United States didn't learn for years and, in many cases, could not bring themselves to believe: Hitler's plan to exterminate the Jews.

If it is hard to say what a biographical fact is, it is virtually impossible to indicate what the word "Jew" means. What am I saying when I refer to X as a Jew or when I say that Isaac Bashevis Singer is a Jewish writer? A year or two ago I wrote an essay on this question in *The New Republic*, and received a gentle letter from Irving Howe, who maintained that I was in error; I had exaggerated the extent to which being a Jew is an issue of religious belief and observance. That, according to Howe, is merely one of the many meanings of the word. I am indeed an outsider in this matter, a Christian, a Roman Catholic. Howe was gracious enough not to make the obvious implication: what could I possibly know about Jews, or about the meanings of the word "Jew"? It is a question I must ask myself. It is true that I have long taken the word "Jew" to refer, in the first instance, to one's religious beliefs and practices; to one's relation to the Bible, the Torah, and the tradition of rabbinic commentary upon these. Orthodoxy, I have assumed, refers to a certain commitment, a conjuncture of belief, kinship, and observance. I have also assumed that these beliefs are transmitted; that no modern Jew has invented them. Even if one's relation to this body of belief, observance, text, and commentary is heterodox, it depends on the orthodoxy it questions or even rejects. Irving Howe's sense of the matter is different. He maintains that "to be a Jew" may indeed mean holding those beliefs and piously observing them, but that it need not involve these commitments. A Jew, according to Howe, is a person who shares, in one degree or another, the familial and ancestral memory of exile. If, say, your grandparents escaped from a ghetto in Poland and made their way to New York or Chicago and established a family, and if you accept the inherited memory of that experience, you are a Jew.

It would be improper on my part to go much further into the question, or to concern myself with current disputes in Israel about the legal definition of a Jew. Even on Howe's terms, however, questions would remain: do I cease being a Jew by electing to ignore my family's ancestral experience? Or am I in Howe's sense a Jew whether I like it or not? It is not necessary for me to say anything further. Let it be agreed, then, that a few million people are Jews in Howe's sense; they participate, willingly or not, in a communal memory, passed on by lore from one generation to the next. I am aware that there are people who think of themselves as Jews of a completely secular kind. Burnshaw's father seems to have been such, and indeed now Burnshaw himself. On a recent visit to Israel I met a woman who regards herself as a Jew but has no interest in Judaism or any other religion. For her, being a Jew means being a socialist, taking part in a great social and political experiment which she identifies, nostalgically indeed, with Ben-Gurion.

I will venture one deduction, and then have done with the theme. I assume that Stanley Burnshaw's relation to Judaism is most certainly not that of orthodoxy: further, that in his attitude toward the founding texts of Judaism he is a pluralist, perhaps a latitudinarian, perhaps a sceptic. The first section of *The Refusers* is called "Moses," and it bears a certain relation to the life of Moses as we read it in Exodus, Numbers, and Deuteronomy. The relation is based on an appalling notion, that Moses refused to accept the God given him and invented a God according to his own sense of what his people needed. "He is Pure Idea —invisible as a wind, unseizable as a wave." I cannot see the merit of a God who is available to any reader of Hegel. Moses's God seems to me a mere hyperbole of Man. The only force he has is whatever Moses gives him. Moses is the first of Burnshaw's refusers. I cannot warm to him, except in one respect. His Yahweh, like Wallace Stevens's Supreme Fiction, is only an idea, even if Pure Idea. I feel a certain tenderness toward the desire the projection of such an Idea appeases, despite the vanity it also consorts with. I feel far more warmly toward the second of Burnshaw's refusers, Uriel da Costa, even though I cannot condone da Costa's apostasy. He was a Portuguese Catholic who converted to Judaism and in 1615 settled in Amsterdam, where he refused Judaic orthodoxy even to the extent of being excommunicated. The third refuser is Burnshaw's father. His refusal, like his son's, brings the story nearly to our own time. I begin to feel that a Jew is characterized by his inability—his refusal, rather—to leave certain stories alone. But I find in Burnshaw's work, especially in his fiction and poetry, a further implication: the experience of being a Jew is indeed susceptible to historical description, but it defines itself by way of ethical interrogation. The particular way in which Jews refuse to become like other people is by bringing God endlessly to the bar of justice. The world, to Jews, is a tribunal in which God stands accused of indifference.

It is not clear to me how God as Pure Idea can be accused of anything. If we need a culprit, I accuse Burnshaw's Moses. In the poems, however, Burnshaw resorts to a more traditional God than that of his Moses, and especially to certain founding and consequential narratives. One of these is Genesis 22, in which Abraham is commanded to sacrifice his son Isaac: at the last moment the command is rescinded, and Abraham is allowed to substitute a ram for the boy. Christians construe the event as prefiguring God's sacrifice of his son on the Cross; this time, there is no reprieve or substitution. Genesis 22 is of particular moment in Burnshaw's work. The poem "Isaac" is used again in "Mirages," the epilogue to *The Refusers*. Of the story of Abraham and Isaac, Burnshaw writes: "They think it again and again / Through forty centuries." Several familial traditions are invoked in a few lines:

> Even my own father
> One morning of my longago childhood helplessly
> Watched his thought slip through the Hegelian chain
> With which he wrestled the world, to relieve the curse
> *Thou shalt not raise thy hand . . .*

Narrative is a mild word for a story of such provenance. When a story is recited generation after generation for the cohesion of the community to which it is addressed, we call it a myth: its truth is a primary consideration within the community, but of no account outside it. Or rather: those outside the community have no standing in this matter, they are mere transients, *peregrini*. In "Isaac," Burnshaw speaks of "the blind obsessive tale," and I suppose he thinks those who continue to recite it would be wise to drop the whole case. In "A Coil of Glass" the condition of being "mythless" is represented as indeed a trouble, all the more disturbing for being, apparently, inescapable. It is my impression that he despairs of the ancestral stories, and has come to think they can't hold:

> A book might be the lens of pure hard tears,
> The coil of glass that sights whatever sleeps
> In time—gone light of earth holding the crumpled hours.
> Focus the glass at will: look at the man—
> Adam, Arthur, Christ. Look at the woman—
> Lilith, Iseult, Helen. Light up the brain
> Of the priests and kings, the file
> Of heroes set on the seeded steps of time.
> Then watch these idols crash on the floor of your mind.
>
> Mythless your heart breaks
> On the edges of days revived. Nothing can heal
> The wound until you learn the lens, until you know
> Builders of myth were men whose hungering minds,
> Cutting through shells of sense, needed to image
> The fact they hoped to see.

As a Christian, I am bound to find this passage shocking. I cannot speak of Christ and Arthur in the same breath. The story of Arthur is a fiction, even though it has been recited for nationalistic purpose in Britain; it is not a myth. The life, death, and resurrection of Christ is for Christians a founding myth: it is not composed of idols, nor do we see them crashing on the floor of our minds. The Christian myth is not something dreamed up by a few hungering minds: the Gospels bear witness to a life; they do not, like Burnshaw's Moses, invent one. Burnshaw is tender toward such pieties, but he makes light of their differences and their fortunes.

Burnshaw's position, so far as I can deduce it from the published evidence, is that no story, no founding myth, can bear the burdens placed upon it. Inevitably we see it crashing on the floor of our mind. Instead of a myth, therefore, he proposes a description of human life as such, founded upon the best discoveries of modern science and art. To use a formula he shares with Kenneth Burke: whatever else may be said about us, we are bodies that learn language. Or, more elaborately, we are bodies that use symbols. To sustain this emphasis, and give it the force of an axiom, Burnshaw (like Burke again in this respect) elects a metabiology or a metaphysiology rather than a metaphysics. If the metabiology blurs the distinction between men and cats, all the better: we are to accept ourselves "as above all else a creature bound by the laws that control all other creatures." The gist of Burnshaw's "creature-knowledge" is to recommend this acceptance. So he delights to find evidence of organic continuity; multiplicity issuing from unity at a primordial source. As in the poem "Blood":

Would we could know
The way men moved
When thought was only
A great dark love
And blood lay calm
In a depthless dream.

I am less convinced by the argument than by the sentiment that adheres to it. Any argument that urges me to start again, and start from the indisputable scratch of being a body that learns language, is persuasive; but I fear it's just a matter of postponing the evil day of division. "It is very unhappy," Emerson writes in "Experience," "but too late to be helped, the discovery we have made, that we exist: that discovery is called the Fall of Man." Burnshaw is not asking us to pretend that the Fall never took place, but to establish as the ground of our beseeching—I use T. S. Eliot's phrase—the life we share with cats and dogs and trees. I am not sure what, in the end, is gained; though I see the merit of postponing the anatomies of our differences and conflicts. In "Poetry: The Art," Burnshaw says:

> The poetries of speech
> Are acts of thinking love

but I can't see that the sentence would be the less true if "love" were altered to "hate": poetry, like speech, is found in both characters.

On the argument, Burnshaw and I will hardly come to an agreement. As to the writing that animates it, the nuances of care and affection and concern from one occasion in his work to the next, we cannot quarrel. What I admire most warmly in his work is the plenitude of the culture from which it comes and to which it returns. I have said a few words about the inheritance that culminates in *The Refusers* and in *The Modern Hebrew Poem Itself,* an anthology he edited with T. Carmi and Ezra Spicehandler. But I have said nothing yet about the range and catholicity of Burnshaw's European sources and relations. I take it for granted that his work emerges, at least in one respect, from Romanticism and from the version or development of Romanticism which we think of as French Symbolism: Nerval, Baudelaire, Rimbaud, Verlaine, Mallarmé, Laforgue, Claudel, Valéry, Apollinaire, Perse, Aragon, Éluard, and Char, poets I list in the order in which they appear in Burnshaw's remarkable anthology *The Poem Itself.* I call it an anthology, but that is a misnomer: it is the book which exemplifies Burnshaw's theory and practice of translation, the best of its kind, tested upon a representative selection of poems in French, German, Spanish, Portuguese, and Italian.

Nor have I said anything about Burnshaw's distinctive way with words. He has poems like "To a Young Girl Sleeping" which are Elizabethan in their grace and delicacy; poems, too, like "Thoughts of the War and My Daughter" which make a perennial poetry. There are poems like "End of the Flower-World" which make you feel that the whole tradition of English poetry that crowds the mind in Hardy's work is as strong as ever.

When I first read *The Refusers* and Burnshaw's poems I was puzzled by one feature of his language: his recourse to compound words.

It seemed that his feelings often required, for adequate expression, not the subordination of adjective to noun or adverb to verb, but a more exacting justice, as of two or more words given equal attention in the one context. Perhaps I should list a few of them: wisdom-warmth, snow-world, leaf-world, mist-shadows, shadow-mists, more-than-glance, more-than-turn, upgathered-dispersed, the mother-once sea, poison-flowers, creature-innocence, justice-hope. I now think I understand these revisions. Sometimes, Burnshaw is willing to take his occasions and themes as they come, and to see them as they seem to want to be seen. But more often he elects to see things in the light of the justice for which he is prepared to take responsibility. He is an instance of what Philip Wheelwright in *The Burning Fountain* calls "the Stylistic Imagination," the imagination that "acts upon its object by distancing and stylizing it." Some years ago it was common to quote Edward Bullough's essay "Psychic Distance as a Factor in Art and an Aesthetic Principle" to elucidate such a stance. I am not sure that the maintaining of psychic distance always works in the cause of justice, but in Burnshaw it does. Like his compound words, it stands back a little from the hot gates, and composes the constituents of every experience in favor of those who need such care. Burnshaw can be immediate when he pleases; as in "Florida Seaside." But in such poems as "The Terrified Radiance" and "Caged in an Animal's Mind," he has a more demanding task, an occasion requiring notable powers of survey and abstraction. The justice of it pleases.

A Stanley Burnshaw Reader

My Friend, My Father

Opening chapter of *My Friend, My Father* by Stanley Burnshaw with an introduction by Leon Edel, Oxford University Press, 1986. First published as Book 3
of *The Refusers: An Epic of the Jews*, Horizon Press, 1981. Copyright 1981 by
Stanley Burnshaw.

This is his greatest day, they were telling me. Aren't you proud of your
father? Think of it, son! The man from the White House in Washington! The president coming this afternoon to visit us here. What a great
honor, boy, for your father! Aren't you proud?

I nodded hard with my six-year-old smile, but all I could think of
was Giant. How big can he be—President Taft? Four hundred pounds,
some said from his pictures, and tall. They had already opened the
double doors, but maybe, I hoped, they'd have to break down a wall . . .

Where did this happen and when, you ask? Nineteen twelve—where
we lived—a place called Pleasantville. Thirty miles from Manhattan.
My father had built up a paradise world for orphans rescued from
Europe. It was famous by now. People were coming from Germany,
Belgium, France—even Japan—to see what this immigrant Jew had
made from his dream.

A dozen trustees and their wives, clothed in their summer best, kept
milling around our verandah, restless, half afraid that the Man mightn't
come. Not my father. Certain that he could count on the President's
host, he moved about through the waiting group, spreading assurances,
lavishing courtesies. Then he noticed me propped on a pilaster, with
my baseball mitt and bat. He walked toward me slowly, winking his
light blue eyes. Looking down, he beamed, "Run off, if you want to!
Take your ball and bat, but not too far. I want you here when the President comes with our friend Mr. Lewisohn." He turned toward two of
the dressed-up men who were watching. "Gentlemen," he announced
with elaborate whimsy, "I want you to meet my only son in America."
It was one of his favorite pleasantries, at which I never failed to grin
though the humor was past my reach. It appeared, for a moment, out

of his hearers' also, till his reassuring twinkle explained he was teasing the brink of propriety.

Soon, with all the others who filled the hall, I watched the Man on the podium, heard grandiloquent phrases, clapped with the crowd, and fidgeted in my seat. William Howard Taft's great bulk disappointed, but I saw from the look on my father's face that this odd stranger, twice his cubage, had flooded his heart. To be sure, as I later realized, none of the tributes revealed the least comprehension of what this "Institution" on which the President poured his praises meant for the man who had shaped it. Nor had it troubled anyone else in the hall, to judge from their words. Nor eminent visitors who came and would come from all over the world. Nor me—till I neared the age that my father had reached at the time: his forty-third year.

Weeks after it entered my mind, I decided to question him. He was happy to talk about all the events that my letters had led him to think of. In his characteristically organized way, he told the tale of his youthful years and the ones that followed, without broaching or even skirting the question. Indeed if it hadn't opened my eyes on this man and his world—and my own—I shouldn't be writing these words. Only one other person, so far as I know, had a glimmer; and he covered it over quickly. But whether he said it aloud I'm unable to tell, since never in all his replies did my father mention the matter. Had it dropped too deep inside him to bubble up to awareness? Within the range he envisioned, there were bounds beyond which presumptuousness might not venture. He knew, he was sure, what his strivings had sought and won. But he didn't suspect he was—how shall I put it?—teaching a lesson to God.

Madness, you say? Hardly. Hold on for a moment! Accuse him of anything else—he was Reason itself—he was Moderation's advocate. Like many other young scholars enthralled by the Greeks, he'd been awed by the workings of hubris. Mention Odysseus and out of his mouth came the hero's speech to the nurse, warning of insolence, unrestraint, and the costs of excessive pride, followed with explanations. As I think back now, it was never far from his thought—nor from my own.

What would you guess he proposed when my teacher told us to letter a proverb to hang on a wall? "Just two words," my father beamed, "but the best to remember. Here!"—he wrote out FESTINA LENTE— "Latin for 'Make Haste Slowly.' You know what that means: before you act in a hurry, stop and take time to think. *Festina* means hasten; *lente*, slowly. A splendid rule of the Greeks." Then he uttered some sounds that I'd never heard. Seeing me gape, he chuckled, "That's how they said it in Athens. Would you like to learn—?" I shook my head. "But your very first words were Greek." I nodded, mumbling the line from Homer with which I had greeted the world . . .

Of course, some said he was pushing knowledge too far. But coming from where he'd come and being the person he was, did he have a choice? Does anyone? If you go back early enough in a life, fate seems to put out branches in different directions. He was lucky—or so he believed . . .

Stopping again? Another attempt gone wrong? What you've written is faithful enough. On with it! tell what's crowding your ears. Shut out the clashing voices! You've more than enough to recount my life from all that you saw and heard. Why hesitate now? It's really no earth-shaking story or the universe would display the signs.—True, though: it's left some marks on a score of lives—or hundreds. The number's no matter. What counts is the passing of time with its shadows that hide and devour meaning. The longer you wait, the worse: whatever pattern you found won't deepen, for all your probings. I, your father, was born; I lived, strove, fought when I had no choice—what else is a life? Besides, you know the wherefores and whys as well as anyone cased in another man's skin could imagine.—*Imagine!* That's the trouble that freezes your fingers, harsh as you've been on your brain to stick to the truth— my truth—as though any man could *know* another man's story . . .

You were probably right to stop attempting what can't be done. Yet you'll never give up, so fixed you are on its "meanings." Maybe there's still a way. You must let me speak through your mouth . . . unless that would mean defeat to you after your starts and surrenders.—No! Allow me to speak through my *own*, for a while at least. The risks will be mine. What can you lose by my telling? Besides, whenever you're ready to have me stop, I'll leave. Meanwhile stand by quietly, son, while I take your task. Put down pen and pencil and hear! I'll even talk in your manner. Listen! . . .

Your ancestors—yes, I'm aware you're not avid for history, but this is a link with your French friend Spire, whose people had come from Speyer, not fifty miles from Worms-on-the-Rhine, where our forebears lived for years. In 1648, with the Peace of Westphalia, families took to the road: Spire's for France; ours for da Costa's Holland. A call had reached my father from one of the Baltic provinces: Courland, literally "chosen country." It was always changing sovereigns. At the time I was born and reared, it was solidly German, but before I finished school Czar Nicholas turned things upside down. To most Courlanders— Lettish peasants: Germans mixed with Slavs—the shift from German teachers to Russian meant very little: they were still enslaved by the barons. But for "my circle" the change was a shocking blow. Suddenly we were ordered to spurn the German Romantic ideals that nourished our hopes: to exchange our excited faith in the Sun of Enlightment for the gloom of the Russian steppe.

We learned quickly to manage, even to giving a hand to the Russian teachers, who reeled at their tasks. Faced with youths trained to outGerman the Germans, the bumbling pedagogues did their miserable best. Besides, we were young, proud, cocksure; and Mitau, long the capital seat of the Dukes of Courland, well lived up to its sobriquet "God's little country." And so we went on with all that we'd done before but with double the fervor, our reading circle proudly declaiming Schiller, Goethe, and Lessing till the halls of the Russified college rocked with Enlightenment's paeans to Man.

Yet life in the charming town on the Lielupe River, with its pine forests and meadows, all but closed us off from the world outside. Blissful provincials, none of us spoke of the turmoils plaguing people in Europe, news of which, if it came, escaped my ears. As Jews, our numbers were limited to families known to have lived in the city for years. And I never knew antisemitism. On the contrary, the feeling between ourselves and the Letts was closer than friendly, since Jews had helped in their struggle against the barons' attempts to wrest the Republicans' power.

And of course everyone knew of my father's profession. To work as Associate Rabbi in a city of 20,000 was to be a public figure. Synagogue tasks were his occupation and yet, for reasons I can't explain, he had also amassed some wealth. We always seemed to be living in more than comfort—all five brothers and sisters—and to keep a kind of open house for relatives, friends, and neighbors. This ease combined with my native ebullience may perhaps explain my innocence when, having passed the state exams for the graduates of the Gymnasium, I applied at the Lazarevsky Institute.

I entered the Rector's office and showed my credentials. "Training to teach, young man?" He eyed me carefully.

"Not at all, sir."

"No? Then what?"

"To enter the diplomatic service."

"You?" he blasted. "Didn't your father tell you it's closed to Jews?"

"Then you give me no choice but to serve some *foreign* country?" He gaped at me in amazement. "Thank you, Herr Rector," I said and turned on my heels.

By the time I was home, I'd decided to leave for France. "France," my father began, "Why?"

"The land of Enlightenment, Freedom, Justice," I cried, "where the Declaration of the Rights of Man was—"

"Yes. Quite so," he replied rather strangely. "Your brother Friedrich will meet you there." He paused thoughtfully. "Nothing for you in Mitau. After a year, if you change your mind, go to London. Your brother Max will be there. Talk with him, then decide! He comes next month."

"Of course," I agreed, but, proud as I was of this brother—he had won a medical post on a prince's estate—I had made up my mind on France. All my heroes of Progress and Reason—Voltaire, Diderot— all who had fought for the causes I prized had come from this land. Besides, nearby was Italy, cherished by Goethe. I would lose no time fitting myself for sharing that world.

In the months ahead I often found myself brooding about the scene with the Rector. What did being a Jew have to do with my competence? Jewish lawyers, doctors, businessmen came and went as they pleased —I had never heard of a "problem." Why had *my* Jewishness set me apart? My father's? All sorts of men sought his advice, Gentiles as often as Jews; and not on religious matters. People spoke of his breadth of knowledge, tolerance, fairness. To be sure, we belonged to the synagogue, kept the holidays, said the prayers, though our family's way of expressing religion was music—singing . . . Thus I kept pressing my brain, but it left me staring in space, bereft of even a semblance of justification.

I decided to talk things out with Eugene Thal, my closest companion. We had started the reading circle together, holding discussions of new ideas till the sun went down. For all his devotion to books, I considered him much more worldly than I if only because his father, a wealthy merchant, had made himself known as an atheist. If any among my friends could end my bewilderment, it was Thal.

When I knocked at the door of his house there was no one home. Nor had anyone seen them depart. One week later they all returned, solving the mystery. Father and Mother Thal and their eight children, who had left Mitau as Jews, were now officially Protestants, baptized in the Lutheran church at Königsberg. Eugene denied it all when I asked, "How could your atheist father do such a thing to his son?"

"But it didn't happen, I tell you."

Months passed. Brother Max returned for a visit, planning a study-year in Berlin before embarking for England. Sooner than I could believe, my twenty-first summer had ended: I would leave in late October. Never once as I gazed through the train window did I think to ask if my eyes would ever again behold the faces smiling goodbyes. Of course, I'd be back for an August visit—probably with my brother, who'd help me settle in Paris.

On the trip from Mitau to Königsberg I was unexpectedly thrown into contact with dozens of Jewish immigrants who had boarded the train at St. Petersburg and Moscow. For the first time I learned of the terrible hardships forced on these men and women, who had lived for years beyond the Pale prescribed by the Czars. My heart went out to these brave and resolute people who, despite their inhuman treatment at the hands of corrupt officials, hated to leave their birthplace.

When the train stopped at the frontier town of Eydtkühnen, a delegation of German Jews, led by a well-known scholar, boarded the coach. They had come to help the immigrants pass through customs, check their papers, and prepare them for their voyage across the ocean. Because I spoke both languages, the Russians asked me to help reply to the detailed questions the German delegates presented to every household. Words I could scarcely believe came out of their mouths. I looked at the delegates' sober faces: they had heard such accounts before. As for myself, long before the last of the immigrants answered, I'd abandoned the thought of France.

I approached the delegates' leader. "If you were I, Herr Hildesheimer, would you throw in your lot with these people?—go to America?"

"If I were you? No question."

"Unfortunately I haven't money for passage."

"Neither have they. If you're ready, sail with my blessings! Shall I put your name on the list?"

"How explain," I began to stammer, "to my father? to my mother?"

"Say that you took the advice of a cautious scholar who would do the same if he weren't three times your age."

On the cattle boat *Virginia* bound for New York I spent four crowded and troubled weeks. Much of my time was given to "mastering" English with the help of three small books I had bought in Hamburg: *A Student's Grammar of English, A Christmas Carol* by Dickens, and the same in German translation. Reading the two versions was simple enough, but not the pronunciation or spelling, neither of which seemed to follow logic or rules. I appealed to the ship's doctor, who tutored me for an hour each day. To judge from the number of times he laughed, his labors were well rewarded, though he urged me on for "doing well for a brand-new immigrant." He also took me down a peg when I said I was certain to find a job at once as a teacher of Latin or Greek.

I had other tutors as well—among the immigrants. Some at first were unable to bear my ignorance, others refused to believe it. I did my best to explain. As a rabbi's son, I had known our people had suffered because of the Church. From the bloody Crusades through seven centuries, Jews had been chased from country to country—Britain, Spain, France, Germany: pillaged, tortured, walled into ghettoes even in lands of refuge. And yet such things, we had firmly come to believe, belonged to human prehistory. The Christian nightmare was ended. Great revolutions had flooded light on the world. Ghettoes were shattered. Freedom, justice, emancipation proclaimed the Bright New Future for all. Life was teeming with hope. We would live to be part of the golden Brotherhood of Man . . .

My Russian shipmates stared at each other in horror. "Courlander Jews!" they groaned. "Nobody ever spoke of the Easter pogrom? Elisavetgrad . . . Kiev . . . Odessa . . . Christmas in Warsaw in 1881 . . . ?"

"Never. Not in my presence." I shook my head. "Maybe they wanted to spare me. I was ten years old—no, eleven."

"So was my son, but he knew."

Before the *Virginia* arrived in New York I had learned as much as the people on board would tell me. Some were reluctant to speak or mocked when I questioned; others glared with distrust. Scrambling among the ones who would talk, I was able to piece together enough to darken my days and nights. For the first time, I began to think of my father with doubts, questionings. How could this sage of my youth withhold the facts that were part of our birthright? How could he calmly let us depart for the world unarmed for its hazards? Out of fear? Self-protection? Ignorance? Shame?—of the shame we might suffer once we learned? Father Thal must have weighed the costs of contempt before the Königsberg baptism, but his sons at least were alerted.

Rage, pain, confused with self-accusation hovered above my head as I stared at the ocean, eyes bulging with scenes my shipmates had witnessed. The Easter pogroms kept gnawing my mind. What could our people have done to have earned such suffering? By now the whole world knew the attacks had been planned, carefully planned in a hundred towns by the Czar's police: Cossacks driving the natives to pillage, plunder, rape, kill—and the Poles matching the Russian feat with a torrent of Christmas blood for their holiest time of the year. Nothing had stopped the butchery. People of power and fame—Victor Hugo in France, Gladstone in England—denounced the "unheard-of barbarities" only to learn of renewed attacks in April that followed—and again and again in the next two years. The victims, after the first pogrom, set out for Lessing and Schiller's land but were barred from entering. The vast tide had to look elsewhere for shelter.

Among the friends I made on board was a teacher of history who had spent some time with a man sent over by HIAS—the Hebrew Sheltering and Immigrant Aid Society, formed in New York to facilitate emigrations by providing funds for travel, hostels, and shelters. From one of their Hamburg agents, my teacher-friend had gleaned some remarkable facts. Since 1881, he was told, about 75,000 refugees had found their way to Palestine, Argentina, and South America, roughly a third to each, with another 10,000 to Canada. But the overwhelming numbers had gone to America: some 700,000—from Russia, Poland, and Austria-Hungary—more than five times as many as during the decade after the first pogrom in Odessa.

Jews all over the globe were helping their fellows. The world was watching the starkest test of brotherhood, and much of the world was moved by proofs of the bond. Jews, from the rich to the poor, gave what they could. Men of wealth, themselves safe from the dangers, were bringing forward stupendous sums to assist their people. This very year, from his palace-home, Munich-born Baron Maurice de Hirsch had set aside 500,000 British pounds to enable Russian victims of persecution to establish themselves on the soil of friendly lands. And this act was but one of many. Other groups in a number of countries were standing guard for the safety of their brothers.

Terrible as the forces of hate had become, there were deeper, vaster strengths in the human heart—so I reasoned. Evil was more than counterweighed by the good that inhered in man. Hope had kept faith —havens of welcome were showing the way. And for all the blood on his history, man would not die into blackness—least of all in civilized lands where every person could raise his head with pride. While Russias and Polands raved in barbarity's nightmare, the sun that had dawned on the West glistened, and I—I was on my way to a country of light. What counted now were my days to come in that land.

My head rang with these wondrous words and my heart believed as I strode from Castle Garden's gates into my newfound city. Fortune struck on my very first day. One of the horse-drawn wagoners, waiting for immigrants, dropped me off, without saying why, at a house on Rutgers Street. When I entered the hall, I noticed a dark-eyed girl gracefully perched on the landing, watching the new arrivals. I smiled at her as I made my way to my room. Before two days had passed, we were greeting each other.

[The next hundred pages picture the private and public life of the son of the Great Enlightenment from his early working years as a scholar and teacher to the sudden change caused by a random event: winning first place in a national contest for educators. Giving up, almost against his will, his hope of serving the world at large, he accepted the task of shaping the lives of hundreds of orphaned children in a wholly sectarian setting. Then, twenty years later, having achieved his goals, he applied himself to remaking the welfare procedures of a large midwestern city. The words that follow—the last of the chronicle—come from the lips of the son of "My Friend, My Father," who is now spending his aging years in directing yet another venture in teaching, 3,000 miles away from his daughters and son.]

All the while I brooded over the birthday letter I planned to send my father in May. Freed from livelihood tasks, he had time to view and compare all he had hoped to achieve at the start with all he had done, and to find *by studying both together,* the paradigm of our epoch: the young idealist Jew who was well on his way toward fulfilling his mission, only to witness all he believed in, fiendishly menaced . . . I pointed out that he alone was able to write such a work, since nobody else could know both sides of the story. His answer was simple and prompt: "If to find one's joy in re-living the past is the mark of age, count me as being far from old, though in fact I'm going on seventy." I replied that re-living was not my proposal, but rather re-seeing the twofold story against the backdrop of seventy years and into the present. "Much too busy," his postcard said, "even to think of weighing the pros and cons, but I'll give it the careful thought it needs once my school is in order: after September. N.B. Despite myself, I've made some notes both pro and con your 'paradigm.'" He added the date: Los Angeles, May 6, 1939.

Earl Browder, head of the Communist party, addressing a crowd of the faithful on the eve of the Russo-German Pact (August 23), gloated in triumph, "Hair will grow on the palm of my hand before the Soviets talk of peace with the Nazis." As he raised both hands for all to see, the New York audience screamed in applause. Nine days later Hitler invaded Poland. In forty-eight hours Britain and France were at war with Hitler.

> Keep this *confidential* [my father wrote at the end of September]. One of my friends of many years has a "nearby friend of a friend of a friend," as it were, who receives sporadic reports from a kind of "underground." Whether or not my guess is right—that it's part of a network in touch with Hasidic Jews —the fact remains that tales we dismissed as preposterous proved to be true . . . among them the Russo-Nazi Pact. However, the latest, reported yesterday, simply defies belief: that Hitler has ordered Himmler and Heydrich to round up every Jew, Marxist, and other enemy; work the "productive" ones to death in newly constructed labor camps and annihilate the rest . . . Conceivable? . . . One bright note to help us maintain our sanity: Erica has moved to the south of France. P.S. Your excellent "Heritage" book arrived —what a treasure!

An almost undecipherable P.P.S. retailed the "latest rumor—Hitler's partner in crime will reap his share of Poland before November."

The underground prediction was off by a month, and the Nazi attack on Denmark and Norway had escaped their ears or my father would have forewarned me. After the fall of Holland I asked for a word of his Dutch nephews. I received no answer.

A month's spell of mild but discomfitting illness explained the silence, in a letter meant for my birthday, which arrived late—June 22, 1940— the morning that France surrendered. Most probably, his difficulties in writing by hand rose from his anxious haste to touch on all that had happened, from the brilliant retreat to England under an air umbrella of hundreds of thousands of stranded soldiers at Dunkerque, to cryptic news of his nephew Sigmund's flight from Paris, to questionings of the whereabouts of my old French poet, Spire. He had also taken the time while convalescing "to reconsider in depth the autobiography project." Someone "with more perspective"—meaning myself—should do the writing; he would furnish full accounts in seven installments. In fact, he was on the trail of a stenotypist who, he hoped, might come to his home after working hours.

Surprisingly, he had failed to mention the new Nazi technique of lightning war, the *Blitzkrieg*, that stupefied enemy armies. I supposed he saw no need to bemoan what everyone knew. That the spectacle of a Hitlerized Europe never left his mind suddenly struck me when I read the card that followed his letter:

> Rummaging through my ancient lecture notes on Heine, I found these words from the man who wrote *Die Lorelei*, which the Nazi textbooks attribute to Author Unknown. The passage was written a hundred years before Hitler: "The day will come when you will hear the storm of German lightning . . . German armies will plow through Europe mercilessly and tear up the roots of the past, reviving the forces of paganism." N.B. Vide your Professor Prescott on Poets as Prophets in your bible, "The Poetic Mind."

Lying awake in the dark for the midnight airwaves to bring in words from abroad, I realized how our dreads and hopes, griefs and joys, sank and leaped with the changing fate of numberless faceless strangers miles from our shores. We were being lived by their lives—much of the time, not all, for everyone did his workaday tasks as before, drawn by needs of the moment. Nor did I bother to ask how my father spent his hours; what mattered most was its thought, which sprang to life from his words. They were few, rarely touching on happenings widely known. Typical was the way he dealt with my glee at the failure of Nazi daylight raids over London:

> I lost all feelings of warmth toward Britain after I learned through our under-ground what the head of her Foreign Office Refugee Section said last week when the steamboat bound for Turkey with 200 Jews from Bulgaria (a third

of them children) sank in the Sea of Marmora: "There could be no more op-
portune disaster from the point of view of stopping this traffic." It could make
one almost proud of Zionist terrorists. P.S. We had better gird ourselves
for more of the same. When struggles worsen, people grow less humane.
Dec. 10/1940.

Cousin Erica's letter in March, mailed from Nice, though it said
nothing of Sigmund, offered, between the lines, reassurance concerning the lost Dutch nephews. I probably shouldn't have followed it up
by telling my father that André Spire—two or three years his senior
—was coming by ship "with a brand-new middle-aged wife who had
espérances," for he wholly ignored the news, even my added "Pseudo-
cyesis?" All that he sent in reply was a postcard: "Am mailing Installment One, which will raise some questions. How could I tell how
much you recall of my early years?" His packet arrived May 10th, as
it happened, a crucial date in the war. Hitler, faced with England's
defeat of his airforce and with Churchill's refusal to listen to peace,
aimed his killing machines in a changed direction: Greece, the Balkan
countries, Yugoslavia. Six weeks later his troops invaded the U.S.S.R.
Newsmen readied themselves for defeat on a scale too large to envisage: 3,000,000 well-trained Germans poised over 2,000 miles of front
versus 2,000,000 Russians whose fighting skills had never been tested.

Perhaps it was simply the shock of the *Blitz* on Moscow or the suddenness of Japan's attack, or both that made my father take stock with
a "Balance Sheet as of January 1942." In paired columns, he entered
items he judged as Pro or Con, adding numbers to give the relative
force of each. He had made this kind of picture before, at critical moments, "to clear the fogs from my eyes." Anxious to check his natively
hopeful bent, he decided, before concluding, to undervalue the Pros
—"and yet," he wrote, "the net prognosis is comforting, even omitting two facts: (1) that Japan's reputedly 'sneak attack' did more to
unite Americans than 1,000 rallies at best could have done; (2) as for
Hitler's *Drang nach Osten*, even Napoleon gave up the quest." Cau-
tiously self-convinced, he resumed his usual tasks, keeping a watchful
eye on his school, making notes for the new "Installments," answering
two or three HSGS* alumni who had sent him belated greetings.

Soon, he announced with unusual eagerness, he and his new wife,

*Acronymn for the Hebrew Sheltering Guardian Society, the institution for destitute
orphans that he directed for fifteen years.

Ethel, were going to do "their bit" for the cause. Quite as suddenly, his joyous elation changed. He received a tersely worded letter from Erica. Nazi officers, aided by turncoat Frenchmen, finally ferreted Sigmund, his wife, and children out of their hiding place. Only eleven days ago did she finally learn they had all been herded in deportation trains bound for German "detention camps," the meaning of which nobody knew. Two or three hopeful words ended her letter: Maurice, a cousin, agreed to take her daughters (twins) "to Mexico first." It was well arranged. We might hear from him "soon." Also about the family from Alassio. Nothing had changed . . .

> You can use a distraction [I wrote]: I'm sending a book I'm proud to have published: writings by Negroes from Frederick Douglass to Richard Wright, edited by my old-time friend and professor-poet, Sterling Brown. Yesterday I offered it to your former HSGS club-leader Harry Scherman as a choice for his Book-of-the-Month Club. He answered: "A book of writings by *Negroes?* . . . for *our* membership? Out of the question." It did no good to quote the Sunday Times and others that call it "a great book."

It did no good to urge it upon my father. Although, as he put it, "no one can doubt its importance," his overriding concern was the plight of Jews. Somber reports of mass killings had rumbled through London late last year: they fell on deaf ears. A Vilna girl swore she had seen thousands of corpses in a ditch twenty miles from her ghetto. No one believed her—no one wished to believe her—except one man, the underground said, who sent out a call for "arms and is now a Partisan leader roaming the Polish woods."

A week later my father sent a note that surprised me:

> Your friend "the part-time operative," as you call him, is here, doing his best these days to make me a Zionist! Of course the Jews need a haven, but he calls for a full-fledged nation, which would drain unbelievable sums from Diaspora pockets. To which he replies with a searching argument: antisemitism in other places would lower or disappear if the Jews had a land of their own to go to . . . Of course England will have to honor the Balfour commitment, even though last September, Eden (reportedly) said that he "loves the Arabs and hates the Jews." . . . I pointed out to your friend that the Jews inhabited the Promised Land only 550 years out of 3200. . . . I hope I shall live long enough after this war to see what comes of Herzl's dream. . . .

I had never heard him speak in this vein before. Nor had I viewed him as old. The possibility of his being "cut off before his time"—whatever his time might be—stopped me. On the other hand, so long as I could recall, he had been a model of health, confident strength, inexhaustible energy—patterned, as my mother once said, on his octogenarian father.

Installment Three arrived July the 3rd, one day after the British had halted Rommel's "invincible force" at El Alamein. Experts announced that "the tide of the war had turned for the world's future." It had also turned for my father's, at least in my eyes, for whatever fate or caprice might do, it was now too late to rob him of knowing that Light and another chance for Justice would triumph. A scribbled line on the typescript read "One of these days I'd like to look at your 'paradigm.'" When, I wondered? Safer of course to wait till after his last Installments, but what if he asked for it now? He had more than a right to know before going on. I had nothing on paper to send him. Clearing my desk, I pulled out a sheet and started:

The story of this immigrant Jew of exceptional gifts and achievement—one of whose "realized dreams" had brought him the kind of renown reserved for the few—stands for vastly more than a New World success. His career is a paradigm of the modern idealist Jew who starts out life as a son of the Great Enlightenment, a believer in its One Universal Religion, in the power of Education, in the irreversible Progress of Man toward a shining future ruled by Reason and Brotherhood . . . only to witness in later life the advent of Nazi savagery and its frenzied battle to root out civilization and all that man had achieved . . . but then, at last, in the blackness, to see the glimmering rays of the dawn of a world self-rescued, of the triumph of Light, of a new future for Reason, Justice, even Compassion.

Offered the choice in his thirtieth year of a brilliant public school career versus the ever uncertain prospect of salvaging children victimized by misfortune and persecution, he cast his lot with the second, thus launching himself on a lifelong future in which his conception of education broadened into a species of Biblical social mission: to do for victims of "fate"—orphans, at first, then people of all ages who were disadvantaged in varying ways—what a just and merciful Deity "ought to have done." So at least in his private, agnostic hours he defined his role, and was able as well, in times of reversal, to find consolation, while at other moments upbraiding himself for the possible "sin" of teaching the Lord a lesson by preempting his role. The next decades he spent in putting to work for entire Jewish communities the innovative proposals that the world of welfare had come to expect of one who still held fast to his faith in the endless human potential for reason and brotherhood . . . till Germany set all Europe on fire in a conflagration of hate.

I read the page quickly. Too many nouns with capitals, yet the draft such as it was would do as a start—though something was missing: the ever-worsening rumor-reports from unknown sources, including the friend of a friend of a friend. "Fantasies," people had called them— "morbid projections of fear." I wondered what the undergrounds sought to accomplish. More than once, fragments that first appeared in their tales surfaced later in news reports as facts—a phenomenon hard to ignore though scarcely conclusive. And yet . . . there was Erica's note on Sigmund: why the quotation marks for "detention camps" unless she was trying to tell more than she dared? . . .

Some of my father's friends took their cues from the *Jewish Frontier*, a monthly founded a decade ago, which was widely known for its "balanced judgments." Thus when the Socialist Polish Bund's London report of May reached its desk in August, one of their editors noted, "After reading this detailed account of the functioning of the Nazi extermination centers, we rejected it as a macabre fantasy of a lunatic sadist." I had never seen the journal; only clippings my father had sent from time to time. Hence my enormous surprise when I found the "Special November" double-issue outside my door that more than atoned for the journal's errors.

In the occupied countries of Europe a policy is now being put into effect whose avowed object is the extermination of a whole people . . . This issue attempts to give some picture of what is happening to the Jews of Europe. It is of necessity an incomplete picture because reports have to be smuggled out and evidence has to be pieced together. Consequently, we have hesitated to include any material whose authenticity was in any way doubtful. The information we print is vouched for by sources of unimpeachable authority. The best test of the credibility of these reports is furnished by the statements of the Nazis themselves, whose repeated public utterances make no secret of their intentions . . . The tempo of this planned slaughter is being speeded up. Unless it is checked, we are faced with the possibility of the murder of a whole people. . . .

The editors' six-page account of "The Plan of Destruction" preceded "German Police Testifies." The largest section, on Poland, published part of the London Bund report that the editors, two months earlier, had attributed to "a lunatic sadist." Articles dealing with Germany, Rumania, Lithuania, Czechoslovakia, France, and Holland completed the issue.

I tried, vainly, to telephone to my father—not that I had any message; I thought I might learn from his voice what the revelations had done. The next day's mail brought me his letter, "Now we know." He added a single sentence: "Half of Europe's Jewry have already met their doom in the German death camps—so Secretary of State Welles informs my friend Stephen Wise."

The news flashed over the world. Frantic appeals for Allied air raids to stop the slaughter brought no response. John J. McCloy, Assistant Secretary of War, twice vetoed the pleas of Weizmann and Shertok to bomb the Auschwitz death-camps, which lay within five miles of his target, I. G. Farben. Nor did Roosevelt's officers alter their plans in response to the protests, meetings, memorial services, rallies, and demonstrations that swept the country from coast to coast. I explained my failure to reach my father by telephone by his presence at some such meeting. How wholly misled I was, his letter made evident:

> You no longer need to send me your 'paradigm.' Mine has been looming in front of my eyes for the last three days—and even after I've dozed to sleep, it's there when I wake.—I must do something quickly to drive it away. How, I wonder? Not many options left at my age, as we're both aware.—Meanwhile a sentence dear to my father—not his words but Rilke's—hums in my head . . . almost as though the corpses of Babi Yar were shouting up from their pits and commanding ruthlessly in the mute shrill voice of the dead *Du musst dein Leben ändern!* What I'm saying here seems mad, but this has been going on for days. No need to answer this letter.

I strove to absorb the phrases. Once or twice I thought of calling my sisters, but stopped when I raised the receiver. Friends dropped in; without explaining, they made their visits brief. When they left I felt relieved, though for no reason other than wanting quiet. As the afternoon wore on, I lay on my bed, stared into the ceiling, while chimes from the neighborhood church bells numbered the hours.

I must have slipped away in a waking dream, for my father's screams were bursting my head: "Moses, what if the Goodness you brought is a lie?—if the Power that peopled this earth mocks at the agonized screams of people trying to force their pitiful will on the chaos?—even hurling their precious first-born into the flames as a final plea for the

Mercies? . . . What of your truth, Moses? Answer! What must we do? Murder ourselves or defy the fiend by creating out of our helpless hands what your Promised God should have done? Can you swear it, Moses? swear it is not a lie? Then swear it, Moses! Swear it, swear it!—"

Steady telephone ringing pulled me suddenly out of wherever I was. By the time I seized the instrument, it had stopped. Streetlamps flooded up from the pavements into my window, till the dark inside my room exploded in blackness, uttermost blackness—a hollow abyss blocking out every glimmer of possible light. I rushed to my desk, copied the paradigm notes I had scribbled off months before. Though Hitler's empire roared from the heights, I mobilized every positive sign, whatever its source: Allied landings in Africa—Algeria, Morocco—"that had turned the tide for good"; Russians fiercely counterattacking from Stalingrad, "the Germans' defeat now a certainty"; France's sudden turn-about, sinking its fleet at Toulon . . . "Nothing," I shouted, "could hold us back now. It was time to summon up arms for saving the unblemished good from the hells of war—for guarding forever against man's future destruction!"—I was overstating, knowingly, yet utterly sure that my affirmations' claims would in time prove true . . . Even more certain that the paradigm's victory-light had erased the abyss.

At about this time, a friend of my sister Marie, who accompanied her to all HSGS alumni events, called on her—unannounced—to broach the idea of a gala party "as a tribute to your father. It will keep what he stands for alive for the new generation—they don't even know his name. But how go about it? We want it to be a great surprise, yet we also have to make sure he'll attend. There's time, of course, and we've picked the date: May 4th, his birthday. Two full years away—he'll be seventy-five. We'll have to prepare soon, and we'll need your help, if you like the idea. Perfect time for making sure that all that he gave us won't be forgotten."

"Write to him now," Marie cried out. "He's had about all he can bear with the death-camp news, and his nephews seized by the Germans . . . If you write him now of your plans, he can start enjoying them now —he could live with them over and over again, long before the event. That's how he's been, living things over and over again in advance . . . But, of course, no matter how you decide, count on me! And please think of all that I've said . . . I can almost see him walking on clouds." A good many days would pass before the alumni group would act. Long before, I sent them my thanks, also offering to do whatever might help.

During these weeks I decided to ask my father's advice about a book we were trying to plan—one that might "make a difference—helping the so-called intelligent citizen to grasp the *political* difficulties that the Allied Powers would have to face when the fighting ended." We exchanged ideas—the challenge delighted him, even the working title and my fanciful roster of "ideal writers." Only a person of broad knowledge and high regard could serve the needs of this project. He would act as the General Editor and, as such, the responsible author, though the planning of every page and the writing itself would be done by other hands, under the guidance of one of my closest friends, whose grasp of world affairs was surpassed by no one I knew.

In the midst of our lively correspondence, newspapers startled the world with reports of an unbelievable armed attack by Warsaw's Jews on the Nazi soldiers surrounding their ghetto. On April 19th, when the battle broke out, less than 40,000 were left of the once 600,000 men, women, and children herded behind brick walls into hideous streets under constant Nazi surveillance. Ranging themselves into 22 units, 600 fighters (men and women), armed with 60 pistols and paltry munitions, launched their attack by day, fleeing below at night to their bunkers and cellars to celebrate the Passover. Utterly stunned by the storm of home-made grenades and flaming benzine bottles that ruined their tanks, the Nazis counterattacked with unheard-of fury. Every ghetto house was set on flame. Yet the rebels replied with bullets from smoking barricades, while others climbed through sewers and drains to attack from behind the enemy lines. Given three days to crush the rebellion, the Germans stopped the engagement, leaving their wounded and dead on the streets. The battle continued through six more weeks, some of the rebels carrying on for another month. As the end approached, all but four of them chose to die—by their own hands. The survivors made their way to Partisan units in Poland's forests. . . .

Good luck seemed to shadow my steps as I strove ahead with the book idea I shared with my father. Sumner Welles, my choice for editor, not only gave his agreement to all I proposed but also offered not to "do anything else till this most important volume has seen the light." He even approved my title—*An Intelligent American's Guide to the Peace*—which I feared might ring in some ears like a play on Shaw's primer for women, though there the resemblance ended; for "the Welles book" would introduce any literate man or woman to the multiple opportunities—and complexities—awaiting the victor nations. The project seemed important enough for the *New York Times* to contribute the use of its maps, one for each of our chapters.

Two "great" pieces of news [my father replied in the same day's mail]—Yours about Sumner Welles and a wonderful invitation from the HSGS Alumni. They're planning a gala event for my birthday-after-next. I've already started to make some notes about what to say. . . . I hope I'll be able to recognize at least some of my former "boys and girls," though it's been so long—more than twenty-five years.

A third surprise would greet him soon. My sisters Pauline and Marie and Marie's daughter had been planning a California trip for the summer to come. When their letter arrived "it sounded too good to be true," he told them by 'phone that evening. "I wish my oldest daughter and youngest son could join our reunion, and I know they will if they possibly can. Meanwhile nothing delights me more than the thought of being together. I'll be counting the days."

From all I was able to learn, the eight-week visit surpassed all hopes. Hasty letters and postcards gave me at least a notion of how they were spending the visit:

Our days begin late in the morning—after we've had our swim—Pop and Ethel arrive by car at our Santa Monica place; then we start out driving —a little while—though by now we've been over hundreds of miles of this countryside. After lunch, back to our place "to relax" and prepare for the routine hiking excursion. He's still an incredible walker, but there's more. To get to the Palisades (our route high over the ocean) you must climb 110 steps. What a picture he makes, counting off ten at a time (in German) and rarely losing his breath . . .

We have dinner together each night, often with some of his friends, and a musical evening weekly—German *Lieder* of course, the ones we were nursed on. Modern music: *verboten*.

You asked if we talk of the war. Of course we know of the Landings in France and the German missiles in London; but the only ones who bring up such things are his cronies. Without having made a pact, we steer quite clear of whatever might stand in the way of our goal—to live these weeks as joyously as we can. He himself has set the tone, with his avid talk about traveling all through Mexico, after the big celebration next May with the HSGS alumni. . . . If I tried to describe his state, I'd say it was resignation overlaid by a firm desire to gather the most from whatever time he has left, though nobody mentions *that* subject. One topic of course is taboo—the fate of the hunted in Europe . . .

But in fact he tried each day to learn the whereabouts of his niece's two young daughters, who, Erica wrote, would be taken to western Mexico. Nothing came through. Had their mother told them to sail back home, now that Paris was freed? Would he hear from Erica? . . .

After my sisters' departure he began again to send me handwritten notes by means of which, for seven whole years, we had kept in close touch with each other. I showered him with journals and clippings after he wrote that he now had taken "to scanning scores of books in the local stacks"—and "for no good reason," he added. That his new habit reflected some striving need, I was certain. Yet I couldn't seize on the reason, which seemed to dart in and out of his letter that came in October:

> Yesterday, while visiting friends, I happened to cast my eye on the books, as I usually do. Don't ask me why it lighted on Tolstoy's *The Kingdom of God Is Within You*, except that the title (a paperback) seemed unfamiliar in English. I mention this now because of something I found in the introduction, written by one of your poet-friends. The passage struck me at once—I reread and reread it again. I copy it off for you now, for reasons you'll see when you read it. If you give me your friend's address, I'll send him my thanks. "The mature man lives quietly, does good privately, assumes personal responsibility for his actions, treats others with friendliness and courtesy, finds mischief boring and keeps out of it. Without this hidden conspiracy of good will, society would not endure an hour."

There was no gainsaying the words. Taking them one by one, then all together, I felt myself oddly relieved—yet also disbalanced, and quite at a loss to understand my response. All I was certain about was a sense of closure; but of what? for how long?—Answers, I once believed, might emerge in dreams, but then some "scientist proved" that dreams merely kept a sleeper from waking. As I lay in bed, sleeping, the message seemed to sail high over the earth: a glistening banner-of-words that clouded the aeons of "civilized knowledge" below. In the morning when I awoke my head still reeled with pictures of hurrying people racing through hundreds of ages, each of them wildly searching about for a voice's answer. I looked for the current address of the poet-author of those lines, Kenneth Rexroth. He could never suspect he had written the coda words for my paradigm.

"Mirabile dictu!" my father wrote in November. "Erica's girls are here, though 'here' is 70 miles from the border. Ethel must handle the whole affair since I'm much too busy—more than in years. I have to make sure my address to the HSGS Alumni will be worthy of such kind honor." Hurried postcard-notes that followed brimmed with ebullience: "Living my early years again—part of my preparation. Makes me forget where I am: though my body's in California, my thought's in the East! Filling up pages of notes, more than I need. Can't seem to stop." And a day or two later: "One thing's decided. Near my conclusion, I'll quote the 'Hidden conspiracy' adage. My thanks for the author's address." I urged him to hold onto all the notes. He answered at once that he'd take them along in the spring, adding, "Happy news! Erica's girls may be here for New Year's—the one success of my family-rescue mission—with a saga past belief, which I'll save for the spring." Three days later another note: "Just to tell you, before I forget, that I'm making special plans for our coming reunion. Secret plans.—We shall more than make up for your absence here when we're *all* together in May. Don't try to guess what I have in mind! It's a real surprise.—P.S. I'm thinking about a Pleasantville trip. The maple trees we planted when you were six years old should be glorious in the spring."

Ethel, who served in the United Service Organization recreation center, had volunteered to run the party on Christmas Eve, so her Gentile colleagues could have their holiday free. Returning long after midnight, she found my father tossing about, racked with pains he had struggled against for hours. His cure-all—walking—brought no relief, and by early morning a doctor was summoned, who took him at once for tests. After a day under oxygen, he started to act like his usual self, despite his nurse's insistence that he hold off questions about his heart and quietly rest instead. Smiling and shaking his head, he began to sing as she left the room. When she returned he was dead.

The body was flown for burial beside my mother's grave in the hills of Westview, and we ordered a granite boulder to set near the one I had sent by freight from Maine thirteen winters before. What of the text for the plaque? The same that his daughters and son in their early years had heard him repeat, never failing to add that, despite the injustice around them, men for their sanity's sake must assert its belief. Although the source had been long forgotten, the will of the Psalm cried on: *I have been young and now I am old but never have I seen righteous forsaken or his offspring begging for bread.* In the war's last winter the words were too bitter to bear, but within a year the derisive overtones quieted as the salvaged nations, their triumph secured, buried the rest of their dead.

Stevens' "Mr. Burnshaw and the Statue"

Originally published in *The Sewanee Review* 69(Summer 1961):355–66, as "Wallace Stevens and the Statue" by Stanley Burnshaw. Copyright 1961 by the University of the South. Reprinted by permission.

Like others interested in Wallace Stevens, I try to read what I can about his meanings, for despite the zeal of his commentators, I still find it hard to understand some of his most attractive poems, especially one directed to me that appeared a quarter-century ago. I first learned about "Mr. Burnshaw and the Statue" from an editor of *The New American Caravan,* who telephoned out of the blue to announce, with great glee, that I had just been immortalized: Stevens had sent him a wonderful poem written as a reply to a review of *Ideas of Order* which I had published in *The New Masses.* The poem was magnificent; I was sure to be delighted; and, best of all, it would appear between the same covers that had already made room for a slight lyric of my own. Not yet in my *an trentiesme,* and frankly overwhelmed that the author of *Harmonium* had even bothered to read what I had written, I awaited the heralded poem with a certain awe. But when I finally got hold of the text, its meaning eluded my efforts. And twenty-five years later, whenever I finish a discussion of the poem, I wonder if it will ever be adequately explicated.

It will not, so long as critics fail to interpret the originating circumstance *from within* its period context. Trigant Burrow once horrified his fellow social scientists by showing why they would never understand a system so long as they remained on the outside. His warning has equal point for literary critics, particularly those who write about books of the desperate, guilt-ridden thirties from the blasé and serener standpoint of our decades. Obviously both the review and Stevens' reply were of a piece with the period in which they appeared: they are nothing more nor less than actions of their time. Judge them out of their context and they become grotesques.[1] But it is never easy for a critic to shed his assumptions, and it is especially difficult for an American, in our anti-Marxist midcentury, to give up, even temporarily, the attitudes that compose his security. Yet unless he is able to do this, he will never understand the writings of the thirties for what they were.

Some reporters of the episode make out the onlie begetter to be a meaner relative of Belloc's anti-Chesterton Don; some are more charitable; and occasionally the controversy is discussed with unexceptionable clarity (as by Louis Martz, in the *Yale Review*, Summer 1958). But there is always a suggestion of oversimplicity. Frank Kermode, for example, introduces the affair by stating that the reviewer "criticized Stevens' apparent indifference to what was going on in the world,"[2] which is exactly what the review did not do. Mr. Kermode writes in England, where a 1935 issue of a foreign periodical may be a trouble to obtain; but can one write several pages of respectable first-hand criticism by referring only to what others have said? And will the next discussant carry on from this newest authority? Obviously there would be no point in arguing with Mr. Kermode or with anyone else who has had his say on the subject. What is needed, rather, is light and more light upon a literary decade that is becoming increasingly darkened by myth. If Martz is right in stating that the critique was "so largely true" and "left the mark," it may be worth knowing something of its genesis.

To begin with, then, a few facts about the reviewer, with due attention to the pranks of selective memory. He was young and little known. Such reputation as he had came not especially from poems he had been publishing in avant-garde journals (*Dial, Transition, Poetry*, etc.) but from a book of essays and translations (*André Spire and His Poetry*, 1933) which had been widely reviewed and vastly overpraised. What value it possessed lay in its technical study of syllabism and accent in French prosody and the origins of *vers libre*. Like Stevens, he had been deeply involved with the Symbolist poets by night and with a business job by day; but unlike Stevens, he quit a remunerative career for the hope of teaching. When his first book appeared, he was writing a thesis on the relationship between poetry and mysticism, at Cornell University, where he had gone in order to study with F. C. Prescott, author of *Poetry and Myth* and *The Poetic Mind*. Armed with a graduate degree but unable to find a teaching job, he returned to New York (1933) with the notion of living by his pen. Apathy greeted him everywhere except in the office of an impoverished journal, which accepted some of his "proletarian" verse and offered him books for review.

He had arrived at his peculiar political position through seemingly inevitable stages. Born into a comfortable middle-class family, he had never given a thought to social problems until he found his first job —in a milltown outside Pittsburgh (1925). What he witnessed there of human misery and degradation was enough to convince him that something was terribly wrong with a social system whose "haves" could splurge à la Fitzgerald while others suffered without hope. He had no solution of his own other than to expunge the dark satanic mills, and even he recognized its absurdity. Hence his response, a few years later, to the one shining program of concrete action for ending want and suffering. Some fifty serious writers had already endorsed Earl Browder's 1932 presidential platform. Though Prescott had told him that a radical was a liberal in a hurry, he had also hastened to add that one doesn't play the violin when the house is on fire.

When in 1934–35 he found himself writing about books and plays, he knew he was practicing criticism of a very special sort, its attitudes and emphases determined by a particular moment in time. He was writing for a new *New Masses*, directed at the same audience to whom *The Nation* and *The New Republic* appealed, but from a wholly radical point of view.[3] How speak to such an audience? None of his associates was quite sure; there were no precedents to turn to in American journalism; and, as the managing editor never tired of reminding them, they were blind men leading the blind. But tentativeness and humility were unthinkable: the world was separating into two enemy camps and time was running out! One had to act in behalf of mankind, and for anyone with a brain there could be no choice. Like the rest of the intellectual Left, they moved in the serenity of certainty, naive examples of what Mann calls "the automatic tendency to believe that the intellect, by its very nature, takes its position . . . on the 'left,' that it is therefore essentially allied with the ideas of freedom, progress, humanity . . . a prejudice which has often been disproved." That "the intellect can just as well take a position on the 'right,' and, moreover, with the greatest brilliance" was inconceivable except to a few of these people—and their days of service were numbered.

As it turned out, the days of every seriously literary Marxist critic were numbered, for this was a criticism for the time-being-only. And the more perceptive practitioners recognized the temporal limitation, if not soon then before long. The overriding test—social amelioration —was quick to wear. After one applied it to a novel or poem or play, how much farther could one go in depth and range into the work of art itself? It was like any other extraliterary consideration—the psycho-analyst's, the historian's, the religionist's; once he had exhausted its possibilities, the critic would soon find himself carried into the literary structure; into a concentration upon form, which, as Stalin later made clear, was simply a bourgeois' basic desire for decadence. Inevitably, therefore, the critic dedicated to literature was foredoomed to give less and less attention to the very concern that accounted for his presence within the Left. Someone else would eventually have to take his place —until he too tired of the task (and a task it was, requiring deliberate effort) of looking at books in a certain way: the way of ultimate social welfare.

But for the time being—and until the unthought-about day of his departure—the critic could see some results of his contributions. More and more writers, some from the most unexpected places, were knock-ing at the door and asking to be let in. In 1934–1936 *The New Masses* printed work by Hemingway, MacLeish, Saroyan, Dos Passos, Elmer Rice, Erskine Caldwell, Richard Wright, Waldo Frank, Rolfe Hum-phries, Nelson Algren, Samuel Putnam, Edward Dahlberg, Horace Gregory, Kenneth Burke, to list some of the names that are especially familiar today. Controversies raged; the world of books had suddenly come alive with excitement. Audiences crowded into theatres and often argued out loud. Literature was reaching sectors of the population that one never regarded as part of the reading public. And better still, they seemed to care.

This startling experience, this sense of direct relationship with one's readers, was not only new in American letters; it could go far to sus-tain those writers within the Left who were wrestling with their private angels. The reviewer of Stevens, for example. In his darker moments, he would confront his own misgivings about the glory of the life-to-come in the stateless utopia. It would be ushered in, of course, by the Goddess of Industrialization whose handiwork he had already observed in a grim milltown. Little wonder he could not feel the thrill that others felt as they read a remarkable American poem about a new Soviet hydroelectric plant, with its climactic line: "billions and billions of kilo-watt hours." If he was certain of anything about the future, it was that in the long run economic improvement could do little for human beings unless a comparable change took place in the spirit of man.[4] And what was he doing here anyway, in this world that worshipped the logic of dialectics, he who valued above all else the gifts of the intuitive mind? How far would he be able to go, in the days ahead, in applying to his criticism the multiple-meanings principle he had learned from Prescott, or the fact that often "the real poetry will be between the lines"? True enough, he had already been laughed at for his academic concern with the golden scales and absolute literary worth—but he had countered with an unMarxist line from Marx, on the "eternal" charm of Greek art. He had also been advised that formal analysis could lead to futile complexities, and that a too-temperate stance was simply a foolish timidity. And yet, nobody had tried to speed up his slow political "development" by flashing a party-membership card under his nose. And none of his words had ever been corrected by the red pencil of a commissar. He could do as he pleased—for he *would* do no wrong. Like the others around him, he deeply believed in the necessity for promoting the Ultimate Good, whatever the circumstances. But within a year after writing the Stevens review, his private angel had pinned his shoulders to the ground. Until his departure, however, he continued to do as he had done, without wavering from his public position, perhaps hoping unconsciously that the very act of repeating beliefs might make them unquestionable for him.

I have described one case because I know it best, but other cases could serve equally well to suggest the absurdity of the unhistorical view. For to think that the Marxist critics were an undifferentiated right-thinking Left-minded phalanx is to create a monster that simply did not exist. Not only were the wars within the compound frequent and fierce. Even more important: any number of these writers were troubled or torn, each for his private reasons; but the tendency was to keep one's reservations under control, for what mattered was the task at hand—ending the material miseries of the many, extinguishing the dangers of Fascism. The basic economic problems of our society had to be put to rights so that one could go back to the business of living. Was the "final conflict" a glorious prospect? It was a tragic, an unnecessary class war: if only the Opposition would see how fine things would be if . . . As for enforced comradely associations, it was often possible to wriggle away from the nonsense, the piety, the dreariness; and when Marxist togetherness became too cozy to bear, one could always get conveniently ill.

The discomforts, the discipline, even the inner conflicts could be borne so long as these writers felt that they were responding to something greater than an organizational alignment of time and place. Mann put it best when he called Communism "an idea which is badly distorted in its reality, but whose roots reach deeper than Marxism and Stalinism and whose pure realization will again and again confront mankind as a challenge and a task." One could accept official membership, or continue in voluntary association, or remove oneself completely, depending upon the value he attached to the current carrier of this "idea." That so many stayed for so brief a time suggests the judgment that they had to make: the traffic in and out of the literary Left was surely the heaviest in American cultural history. Some departed in quiet and others shouted "I have been deceived." Still others crept into corners to lick their wounds.

The review that follows, reprinted only because of its documentary relevance to the Stevens poem that it evoked, is offered without the slightest pride of authorship—indeed, with much relief that it is less incomprehensible than other reviews from the same pen. Certain words and assumptions, however, may bewilder readers unfamiliar with reviews of the Left in the midthirties. For their benefit, then, the following minimal gloss:

1. The world, so pleasingly simple, is divided according to one groundplan only: We (Left), They (Right), and You (Left, Right, or Middle), with the Escapists in limbo. Reading the opening paragraph, one squirms at the trade-jargon current twenty-five years ago, as possibly others will squirm at the trade-jargon of our own decade twenty-five years hence.

2. Caveat with respect to irony: Marxist critics were often stupendously literal, earnest, humorless. To find "ambiguity" here is to do creative reading of the most misleading kind. To be taken straight.

3. Re final paragraph: these critics held the naive belief that a book could and would affect directly and even shape the minds of readers; hence, in a war between classes, each "nonconfused" book was an instrument for either the Left (*read* Good) or the Right (*read* Bad). Today we are much wiser; even sociologists have armed us with their construct of the "intervening variable" (prefigured by a few Marxist critics as a "seepage" of ideas, from the opinion-making illuminati to the benighted). Both sociology and life were simpler twenty-five years ago. One could take bearings and know where everyone stood pro tem. Authors of "Middle-ground" books were, of course, confused and in

need of direction, which was often generously offered by the reviewer. It requires no expertness in Freud to perceive that the present reviewer's concern with Stevens' confusion was at least in part a projection of his own.

4. At times one might make broad statements which one would not normally make, simply because they were supposedly required by the Ultimate Good. To add qualifications was to please one's petty pride and, besides, such impedimenta would weaken the march of mankind toward excellence. The overriding concern—the greatest good for the greatest number—was also a principle whose morality was beyond question, regardless of what might be required in its name.

5. Tone: not to be viewed as a separable element or as something injected to add power. If, as Martz says, the review was written "with a condescending tone," it was not for lack of visible provocation. *Ideas of Order* was offered to the reading public of the thirties by a man not in the least ignorant of the issues or, for that matter, of the controversies and the codes—after all, he had been reading *The New Masses!* Hence, when Stevens used a certain tone, he did so with full awareness. One example (not mentioned in the review): he could not help knowing that the word "nigger" was scrupulously avoided by white people who had now become acutely aware of its extreme offensiveness. Yet the longest poem in the book is called "Like Decorations in a Nigger Cemetery." Whether the title is actually essential to the poem, is beside the point. If Stevens had entitled another piece "Like Decorations in a Sheeny Cemetery," even his worshippers might have squirmed.

6. Comparative data: *The New Republic* (literary editor, Malcolm Cowley) devoted sixteen lines to *Ideas of Order* and twice as much to *Pittsburgh Memoranda*. Theodore Roethke, after remarking that "the times and a ripened maturity have begun to stiffen Mr. Stevens' rhetoric," concludes: "It is a pity that such a rich and special sensibility should be content with the order of words and music, and not project itself more vigorously upon the present-day world" (July 15, 1936).

TURMOIL IN THE MIDDLE GROUND

Among the handful of clichés which have crept into left-wing criticism is the notion that contemporary poets—except those on the left and extreme right—have all tramped off to some escapist limbo where they are joyously gathering moonshine. That such an idiot's paradise has existed no one can deny; but today the significant middle-ground poets are laboring elsewhere. And the significant trend is being marked by such writers as Wallace Stevens and Haniel Long: poets whose artistic statures have long been recognized, whose latest books (issued in middle age) form a considered record of agitated attitudes toward the present social order. Like all impressive phenomena of the middle ground, *Pittsburgh Memoranda* and *Ideas of Order* show troubled, searching minds.

As a matter of record Haniel Long has been struggling for a "solution" ever since his singular stories and poems appeared in the liberal magazines a dozen years ago. [*The next six paragraphs deal exclusively with Long.*]

Confused as it is, *Pittsburgh Memoranda* is a marvel of order alongside Wallace Stevens' volume; and yet to many readers it is something of a miracle that Stevens has at all bothered to give us his *Ideas of Order*. When *Harmonium* appeared a dozen years ago Stevens was at once set down as an incomparable verbal musician. But nobody stopped to ask if he had any ideas. It was tacitly assumed that one read him for pure poetic sensation; if he had "a message" it was carefully buried and would take no end of labor to exhume. Yet he often comes out with flat judgments and certain ideas weave through the book consistently:

The magnificent cause of being,
The imagination, the one reality
In this imagined world

underlies a number of poems. Realists have been bitter at the inanity of Pope's "Whatever is is right," but Stevens plunges ahead to the final insolence: "For realists, what is is what should be." And yet it is hard to know if such a line is not Stevens posing in self-mockery. One can rarely speak surely of Stevens' ideas.

But certain general convictions he admits in such a poem as "To One of Fictive Music." Bound up with the sovereignty of the imagination is his belief in an interfusion of music among the elements and man. And "music is feeling . . . not sound." This trinity of principles makes the business of living to him a matter of searching out the specific harmonies.

Harmonium, then, is mainly sense poetry, but not as Keats's is sense poetry, because this serener poet is not driven to suffuse sensuous imagery with powerful subjective emotions. This is "scientific," objectified sensuousness separated from its kernel of fire and allowed to settle, cool off, and harden in the poet's mind until it emerges a strange amazing crystal. Reading this poetry becomes a venture in crystallography. It is remembered for its curious humor, its brightness, its words and phrases that one rolls on the tongue. It is the kind of verse that people concerned with the murderous world collapse can hardly swallow today except in tiny doses.

And it is verse that Stevens can no longer write. His harmonious cosmos is suddenly screeching with confusion. *Ideas of Order* is the record of a man who, having lost his footing, now scrambles to stand up and keep his balance. The opening poem observes

> . . . This heavy historical sail
> Through the mustiest blue of the lake
> In a wholly vertiginous boat
> Is wholly the vapidest fake. . . .

And the rest follows with all the ironical logic of such a premise. The "sudden mobs of men" may have the answer;

> But what are radiant reason and radiant will
> To warblings early in the hilarious trees . . .

Sceptical of man's desire in general, there is still much to be said for the ordering power of the imagination. But there remains a yearning—and escape is itself an irony. "Marx has ruined Nature, for the moment," he observes in self-mockery; but he can speculate on the wisdom of turning inward, and a moment later look upon collective mankind as the guilty bungler of harmonious life, in "a peanut parody for a peanut people." What answer is there in the cosmic law—"everything falls back to coldness"? With apparent earnestness he goes a step beyond his former nature-man interfusing harmony:

> Only we two are one, not you and night,
> Nor night and I, but you and I, alone,
> So much alone, so deeply by ourselves,
> So far beyond the casual solitudes,
> That night is only the background of our selves . . .

And in a long poem he pours out in strange confusion his ideas of order, among them:

> If ever the search for a tranquil belief should end,
> The future might stop emerging out of the past,
> Out of what is full of us; yet the search
> And the future emerging out of us seem to be one.

Paraphrase, always a treacherous tool, is especially dangerous when used on so *raffiné* a poet as Stevens. Does he talk of himself when he explains that "the purple bird must have notes for his comfort that he may repeat through the gross tedium of being rare"? Does he make political reference in declaring "the union of the weakest develops strength, not wisdom"?

Asking questions may not be a reviewer's function, but uncertainties are unavoidable when reading such poets as the two under review; for the texture of their thought is made of speculations, questionings, contradictions. Acutely conscious members of a class menaced by the clashes between capital and labor, these writers are in the throes of struggle for philosophical adjustment. And their words have intense value and meaning to the sectors within the class whose confusions they articulate. Their books have deep importance for us as well.

Of course, objectively, neither poet is weakening the class in power—as yet they are potential allies as well as potential enemies—but one of them looks for a new set of values and the other earnestly propagates (however vaguely) some form of collectivism. Will Long emancipate himself from his paralyzing faith in inner perfection? Will Stevens sweep his contradictory notions into a valid Idea of Order? The answers depend not only on the personal predispositions of these poets but on their full realization of the alternatives facing them as artists.

(The New Masses, Oct. 1, 1935, p. 42)[5]

NOTES

1. Note that Stevens cut the poem and changed its title to "The Statue at the World's End" for the Alcestis Press edition (1936); that he made other revisions for the version in *The Man with the Blue Guitar* (1937); that he omitted it altogether from *Collected Poems.* (The original version of "Mr. Burnshaw and the Statue" appears in *Opus Posthumous.*)
2. *Wallace Stevens* (New York, 1961), p. 63. See below: Gloss, Item 5, and penultimate paragraph of the review.
3. Differences in critical judgments were, however, frequently tenuous. See, for example, "Two Kinds of Against," a review by Kenneth Burke of *No Thanks* by E. E. Cummings and *Poems* by Kenneth Fearing, *The New Republic,* June 26, 1935. See also conclusion of Burke's review of *Pittsburgh Memoranda,* by Haniel Long: ". . . it unquestionably suggests the magnitude and the quality of the philosophical issues arising from the confused ways in which capitalism both stimulates and frustrates ambition" *(The New Republic,* August 28, 1935).
4. *The Bridge* (New York, 1945), a play in verse drafted at this time but not completed for several years.
5. Mr. Burnshaw made, in a letter to the editor, some further comments that are added with his permission: "I have probably omitted a few things of possible relevance—I had never had any direct contact with Stevens, either in person or by letter; I have never been consulted by any writer on the episode;

I am personally unacquainted with all of them. The sole intermediary, if he can be called that, was Alfred Kreymborg, to whom Stevens had given the long poem for publication in *The New American Caravan*. Kreymborg told me that at the time he received the MS, he had given Stevens a 'marvelous description of' me; but as to Stevens' response, I learned nothing. Once or twice, when Stevens was still alive, I had thought about paying him a visit. But his reputation for dealing with uninvited guests discouraged me. Needless to add, I often regret my lack of courage, and now that I've written on the subject of our 'exchange,' I find myself wishing that he could read it.

"My own questioning as to the importance of the whole affair subsides when I realize that despite what Stevens later did with the poem, the scholars concentrate upon the original (uncut) version and have made it part of the essential study of Stevens. Samuel French Morse includes the uncut poem in *Opus Posthumous*. More important, William Van O'Connor judges 'Owl's Clover' (of which 'Mr. Burnshaw and the Statue' is Part II) to be Stevens' 'finest long poem.' I disagree with O'Connor, but my opinion can hardly count for anything in this instance."

A Future for Poetry: Planetary Maturity

For James Dickey

This chapter consists of notes for a lecture delivered at the universities of California, Minnesota, and Texas and first published in the "Stanley Burnshaw Special Issue" of *Agenda*, London, 1983/84. The author and publisher gratefully acknowledge the following publications in which poems quoted in this chapter previously appeared: From Eugenio Montale, *The Storm and Other Things*, translated by William Arrowsmith (New York: W. W. Norton and Co., 1985), reprinted by permission of the publisher. "Nudities" by André Spire and "Bread" from *In the Terrified Radiance* (New York: George Braziller, 1972), copyright 1972 by Stanley Burnshaw, reprinted by courtesy of the publisher. "Lovers in August" from *Selected Poems* by Miroslav Holúb, translated by Ian Milner and George Theiner (Penguin Books, 1967), copyright 1967 by Miroslav Holúb, translation copyright 1967 by Penguin Books. "The Fiend" is reprinted from *Buckdancer's Choice* by permission of James Dickey and Wesleyan University Press; copyright 1965 by James Dickey. "Ode to Hengist and Horsa," copyright 1963 by Donnan Jeffers and Garth Jeffers, reprinted from *The Beginning and the End and Other Poems*, by Robinson Jeffers, by permission of Random House, Inc. Excerpts from "To Robinson Jeffers," copyright 1988 by Czeslaw Milosz Royalties, Inc., from *The Collected Poems, 1921–1987*, first published by the Ecco Press in 1988; reprinted by permission. "Nature's Questioning" and "Dead 'Wessex' the Dog to the Household," reprinted from *The Complete Poems of Thomas Hardy*, edited by James Gibson (New York: Macmillan, 1978), by permission of the publisher; the latter poem copyright 1928 by Florence E. Hardy and Sydney E. Cockerell, copyright 1956 by Lloyds Bank Ltd. "Neither Out Far Nor In Deep" is reprinted from *The Poetry of Robert Frost*, edited by Edward Connery Lathem, by permission of Henry Holt and Co.; copyright 1936 by Robert Frost, copyright 1964 by Lesley Frost Ballantine. The quotation from Alberto Caeiro is reprinted from *Selected Poems* by Fernando Pessoa, copyright 1971, the fourth volume in the Edinburgh Bilingual Library. The quotations from the work of Umberto Saba are reprinted by the courtesy of New York University Press from *Modern Italian Poets* by Joseph Cary, copyright by the New York University Press. "The Far Field," copyright

"A future for poetry"—what do these words portend? I propose to single out a new attitude, a new point of view, a new state of being: it is all these things and more—which are with us already in some degree, and are sure to affect more and more people—and in time transform us, readers and poets alike.

How fine it would be to begin with a plain definition, then reel off examples, and end with a Q.E.D. But this new something I speak of only rarely is found in a "pure state." Usually it is intermixed with the old. The newness is missed—as often occurs when an art develops from one condition to another. But here the change is a radical one indeed: a movement away from what poems—with rare exceptions—have been in the past: *culture-bound*—hemmed in by the limits of purely human concerns and wishes, feelings, and laws, which, if viewed from a ship in space, would look so self-regarding as to seem myopic.

And yet most poetry, regardless of theme, has mirrored the culture of men and women, with the rest of creation a backdrop for their actions. The change that I aim to describe is *away* from poems that are culture-bound to something else . . . which will tend to define itself as we carry forward. But first, a warning. When I use the generic *Homo sapiens* or *man*, as I must for grace or brevity's sake, please take it as *shorthand only*, for male *and* female: both.

Let me start with a poem by a girl, Margie Twayaga. She wrote it in high school in Uganda. It's short and the title simple: "My Buttocks."

How useful are my buttocks!
And how helpful they are to me!
How then am I proud of my buttocks!
I am proud of their use to me.
They give me shape.

They help me when it is time for sitting.
I love my buttocks very much
Because they are so useful to me.
The trouble with me and my buttocks is
I love them very much
But they hate me more than I love them.
First, they hate me because I usually sit on them.
Then they hate me because
When I do bad things,
They are beaten!
I spend the day sitting on them and tonight
When I am thinking while sleeping,
I sleep *against* them.

Ha! my buttocks! my buttocks!
What can I do for you so that you will love me?
I love you more than any other part of mine.

The lines express something of the joy we feel to be stirring in a baby, kitten, or puppy as it suddenly discovers some new delight in its body. Yet this poem is *not* pure delight. More than half lists the "trouble[s] with me and my buttocks." Joy at the start, then uneasiness: where did it come from? Only one possible source: the culture that nurtured the speaker. It infused her—just as it does to us all—with notions of right and wrong . . . and consequent feelings of "trouble": guilt. My buttocks "hate me because when I do bad things / They are beaten" —and she then proceeds to think of the other ways in which she offends them. Rights and wrongs, punishments, rewards.—Now, when I speak of "the culture"—and I shall be doing so often—I do *not* refer to manners or breeding or receptiveness to beauty and humane feelings. I refer to "all those historically created designs for living, explicit and implicit, rational, irrational, and nonrational, which exist at any given time as potential guides for human behavior." "Potential guides for human behavior"—the anthropological view.

"My Buttocks" of course is a poem of self-discovery within the purview of the culture. What happens when self-discovery cannot go further? We know nothing of its course with other creatures, but with people, self-contemplation deepens and darkens till it comes to a stop . . . resolving itself into any number of forms: ineffably joyous faith at the hopeful extreme to suicide. Most of us settle somewhere between on the spectrum, but long before, we do what Margie Twayaga does: we celebrate ourselves *while we also* condemn ourselves. There are wonderful poems, as you know, on our self-celebration but few that temper delight with pained awareness. When you think in these terms, it is not a great leap from our young girl's poem to the one John Davies wrote in the 1600s. It is called "Affliction." Anthologists frequently print just the last two stanzas. I give you three-and-a-half:

> Myself am centre of my circling thought,
>> Only myself I study, learn, and know.
>
> I know my body's of so frail a kind
>> As force without, fevers within, can kill;
> I know the heavenly nature of my mind,
>> But 'tis corrupted both in wit and will;
>
> I know my soul hath power to know all things,
>> Yet is she blind and ignorant in all;
> I know I am one of nature's little kings,
>> Yet to the least and vilest things am thrall.
>
> I know my life's a pain and but a span,
>> I know my sense is mocked with everything;
> And to conclude, I know myself a man,
>> Which is a proud, and yet a wretched thing.

Is there nothing more to be said about being human? Not if one's view is circumscribed by the culture, where man is the center of all. A good many people no longer can bear that view. Faced with our decade's menaces—nuclear war, pollution, famine, genocide—they are forced to approach the world from a vantage point *outside* the culture, which reveals *Homo sapiens* as being, above all else, a *creature;* and despite his spectacular gifts and works, as much "in thrall" to the laws of existence as every other creature. The awesome burden that fell on us when we made ourselves able to kill *all* life upon earth compels us now to look at all life with *responsible* eyes. It is forcing on us, even against our wishes, the humbling condition of "planetary maturity."

Planetary maturity: *accepting* ourselves as above all else creatures bound by the laws that control all other creatures. What have such things to do with a future for poetry? Everything! So it seems to me —so it may seem to you as we read some verse from our country and other countries. I call them "creature poems," in part or in whole. What is a creature-poem? To paraphrase St. Clement and Samuel Johnson, it is easier to say what it is *not* than what it *is*. For one thing, most well-known poems about birds, fish, or animals are anthropomorphic expressions—Shelley's "Ode to a Skylark": not a creature-poem at all. As for Margie Twayaga's "My Buttocks," it begins in a creaturely way only to break its promise, and John Davies's "Affliction" is a wonderfully clear example of a culture-centered poem. Let us take off, then, in the other—the future—direction! . . . with complete short poems or relevant fragments, arranged into three main groups . . . arbitrary but useful.

I call them LOVING and DYING and SEARCHING. LOVING and DYING need no explaining; SEARCHING includes *all* things an inquiring mind might care to pursue or consider. We begin with LOVING—poems about any act that propels the life of a creature onward—loving in the broadest sense—*all* modes of sex as well as of reproduction. At once we run into conflict with the scientists, who declare that each has a different function: enhancing variability in one case, propagation in the other. My first example disagrees. It's a well-known lyric by the late Eugenio Montale. Like our other translations, this one will give you the sense, but not the sensation, of course, of the foreign poem. For our purpose, however, the sense will suffice. The poem is called "L'anguilla," "The Eel"—a celebration of the dauntless, tremendous drive of a creature that is, for Montale, the very symbol of *fertility* which he *also* calls "the arrow of *love* on earth." And so that we can't mistake his intent, he capitalizes *love*—or rather *Amore*. The poem is addressed to a woman —the translation is William Arrowsmith's:

The eel, coldwater
siren, who leaves the Baltic behind her
to reach these shores of ours,
our wetlands, marshes, our rivers,
who struggles upstream hugging the bottom, under the flood of the
    downward torrent,
from branch to branch, thinning,
narrowing in, stem by stem,
snaking deeper and deeper into the rock-core
of slab-ledge, squirming through
stone interstices of slime until
one day, light,
exploding, blazes from the chestnut leaves,
ignites a wriggle in deadwater sumps
and run-off ditches of Apennine
ravines spilling downhill toward the Romagna;

eel, torchlight, lash,
arrow of Love on earth,
whom only these dry gulches of our burned out
Pyrenean gullies can draw back up
to Edens of generation;
the *green soul* seeking
life where there's nothing but stinging
thirst, drought, desolation;
spark that says
all things start when all seems
ashes and buried branches;
brief *rainbow,* twin
of that other iris shining between your lashes,
by which your virtue blazes out, unsullied, among the sons
of men floundering in your mud: can you
deny your sister?

If this poem is obscure, the cause is the poet's love of compression. Note the ending, where the light-streaked rainbow-colored body of the eel is called "brief *rainbow,*" twin-sister to the one that you set in-between your lashes—the iris of the woman's eye. The Italian word *iride* means both rainbow and eel. Montale's poem exalts the sisterhood of two species of earthly creatures: womankind and eel in a celebration of the driving power of *Amore*—arrow of love on earth. Shall I reread it? A show of hands will guide me.

My next poem comes from France, where I heard it in 1927—years ago at a Sorbonne lecture. The poet is André Spire and the title "Nudities." The work has two parts. In the first a woman reasons with a man; in the second, he shouts his reply. The epigraph, from the Talmud, reads, "Hair is a nudity." But first some background to point out a strange irony. The poem appeared in a France still shaking with anti-semitic furies stirred by the Dreyfus Affair. The woman says: she has come to the man as a comrade; they're both comrades working to find a haven for victims of persecution. She's firm about this comradeship, insisting, "I am your equal and not a prey."—Hear, then, the poem, whose only recondite word is *chignon,* a round bun or coil of hair worn at the top or the back of a woman's head:

> *You said to me:*
> I would become your comrade:
> I would visit your house without fear of troubling you.
>
> . . . .

But do not let me see your eyeballs glitter
Or the burning veins of your forehead bulge!
I am your equal, not a prey.
Look at me: my clothes are chaste, almost poor!
You cannot even see the curve of my throat!

  I looked and I answered:
Woman, you are naked:
Your downy neck is a goblet of well-water,
Your locks are wanton as a troop of mountain goats,
Your round, soft chignon quivers like a breast—
Woman, cut off your hair!

You are naked: your hands now lie unfurled,
Open in nakedness across the printed page,
Your fingers, the subtle tips of your body,
Ringless fingers—that will touch mine any moment—
Woman, cut off your hands!

You are naked: your voice flows up from your bosom,
Your song, your breath, and now the heat of your flesh—
It is spreading round my body to enter my flesh—
Woman, tear out your voice!

Spiré has written other lyrics, one of which questions the scientists'
view that I cited before. In a poem about young men and women skat-
ing on a lake, he describes their interweavings, partings and meetings,
only to note at the end how male and female seem to be driven toward
each other by a force outside their willing—magnetized toward each
other in a civilized mating dance. The longer he watches, the more
deeply he sees *past* the persons themselves till the dancers-skaters—
faceless, clothesless, fleshless—appear to be merely "bearers, convey-
ors, of" "germs that yearn to merge."

Spiré was not a scientist, but Miroslav Holúb, a Czech immunologist,
has written an even more "clinical" creature-poem about loving. Unfortunately it's a difficult work to follow, with its references to entropy
and to Maxwell's demons. But its singsong refrain both before and after
the lovemaking act mark it with affirmation: "All this has happened before / All this will happen again"—once more I quote: "In the random
and senseless universe."

Your hand travelled
   the Aztec trail
   down my breast.
The sun popped out like the egg
   of a platypus
and aspens pattered
   their leafy Ur-language.
All this has happened before.

The jellied landscape
   was furrowed with happiness.
You worshipped me
   like the goddess of warm rain.

But in each corner of our eyes
   stood one of Maxwell's demons
loosening the molecules
   of rise and fall
back and forth.

And in and out, round and about,
   in and out,
through the cracked lens of the eye
   unendingly,
   surface behind glass
   entropy mounted
   in the random and senseless universe.

All this has happened before.
All this will happen again.

The first half is very simple description—the man speaking to the woman about their act of lovemaking. Your hand traveled, in ritual fashion, "the Aztec trail down my breast." The sun popped out like a duck-bill's egg, while trees pattered in their primeval language. The shimmering landscape was marked with joy as you worshipped me like an ancient goddess—and "all this has happened before." But—and now the scientist explains what happened next, as he alludes to the Laws of Thermodynamics. According to the Second Law, heat always moves from the hotter body to the colder one—and we presume this has happened here also. But it is the Third Law—about entropy—that he dwells upon till the end. According to this law, as energy decreases, entropy increases: as he says, "entropy mounts in the random and senseless universe." That is, entropy—or "heat-death"—leads to a universal state of inert uniformity. The speaker introduces entropy by an ironical reference to a theory of James Clerk Maxwell, the nineteenth-century physicist, who posited an imaginary agent—called "Maxwell's demon" —that could somehow stamp out entropy. But in the poem, the very opposite happens: "entropy mounts," it increases the general trend of the universe toward death and disorder . . . in which the love of these lovers must wane . . . And all this takes place in a "random and senseless universe." "All this has happened before. / All this will happen again." And no such scientific "Law" has ever stopped any lovers from loving. Nor will it do so ever.

I find this—despite the seemingly hopeless observation, perhaps even because of it—an essentially affirmative poem. For Holúb words speak out in a creature-acceptance of the way things are. By implication, it scorns any howling against fate and so on, in its calm, matter-of-fact, yet witty self-acceptance.

How far can acceptance go in such matters? I think as far as you wish. For it proffers freedom from culture's proscriptions, from all its "noes." Think of the difference in terms of seeing the world either with your naked eyes or through spectacles contrived by the culture. When you look through the lens of the culture, certain behaviors look right, certain others look wrong. But once you remove the spectacles, the distinctions vanish. And then such a work as James Dickey's "The Fiend" is a creature-poem about loving. And yet, if again you put on the culture's spectacles, what can the speaker seem—the "worried accountant . . . moodily passing window after window of her building"—what can he seem but a pervert, an obsessed *voyeur?* Please cast aside the spectacles while I read two specimen passages. The first comes after the worried accountant sits on a limb of an oak-tree, gazing:

This night the apartments are sinking
To ground level   burying their sleepers in the soil   burying all floors
But the one where a sullen shopgirl gets ready to take a shower,
Her hair in rigid curlers, and the rest. When she gives up
Her aqua terry-cloth robe the wind quits in mid-tree   the birds
Freeze to their perches round his head   a purely human light
Comes out of a one-man oak   around her an energy field   she stands
Rooted   not turning to anything else   then begins to move like a saint
Her stressed nipples rising like things about to crawl off her   as he gets
A hold on himself. With that clasp she changes   senses   something

Some breath through the fragile walls   some all-seeing eye
Of God   some touch that enfolds her body   some hand come up out of
    roots
That carries her as she moves   swaying   at this rare height.

And then—ten lines later:

By this time   he holds in his awkward, subtle limbs the limbs
Of a hundred understanding trees. He has learned what a plant is like
When it moves near a human habitation   moving closer the later it is
Unfurling its leaves near bedrooms   still keeping its wilderness life
Twigs covering his body with only one way out   for his eyes into inner
    light
Of a chosen window   living with them night after night . . .

And so on for many more lines. To the consternation of some, I read
"The Fiend" as a love-poem, much as Lionel Trilling read *Lolita* as a
love-story. If this seems perverse, I urge that you now recall that serious
thinkers in the Middle Ages conceived of love as a virtually physical
force that held the universe together. What *sort* of love? The question
is crucial. And I find the most sensible answer in Plato, in Lacordaire,
in Freud, each of whom thought in the encompassing terms, attributing its multiform manifestations to a *single generative power*. For the
Greek philosopher Plato, love "ascended" from sexual lust to desire
for all objects of physical beauty to a longing for union with beauty of
mind and soul. For the French theologian Jean Lacordaire, it was love
of God. For the Viennese psychoanalyst Freud, instinctual impulse.
Since our present concern is poetry, I may add a fourth manifestation,
taking the words from a poem of my own addressed to Whitman called
"Poetry: The Art." The relevant line is "The poetries of speech / are
acts of thinking love." That is, a poem is an act of thinking love. For
any poem worthy of the name is a bodily act that bears the life of a
creature onward, *lifeward*, as I said when discussing the use of the term
Loving.

And now let us turn to the opposite theme: Dying. We're familiar
with all the varied ways in which our *culture-bound* poets have talked
of death. To put it grossly, death has been either defied or welcomed;
and each of these polar attitudes exhibits variety—though mainly the
second. Some of them speak out of faith in the bliss that God will
give to the worthy (Dante et al.). Some have welcomed more secular
joys (Browning in "Prospice"). In Alfred de Vigny's monologue, the

speaker Moses, exhausted by his achievements and the pain they have brought, asks but for respite: "Let me sleep the sleep of the earth." And Miguel de Unamuno, in our own day, cries, "For human life is sickness / And in living sick, I die." One can cite related attitudes, from Whitman's "Come lovely and soothing death" to the Emily Dickinson poem that domesticates death and dying. "A wife at daybreak I shall be" concludes

> Softly my Future climbs the stair,
> I fumble at my childhood prayer—
> So soon to be a child no more!
> Eternity, I'm coming, Sir—
> Master, I've seen that face before.

No earlier poems about dying had been so intimate, so confessedly autobiographical. And yet, in the last decade, we have all been exposed to death-poems which go even further—those on suicide and death made popular by Sylvia Plath and Anne Sexton. I, for one, recoil from what seems to verge on a tragic flirtatiousness, but I hold a minority view.

Moreover, one ought to avoid the autobiographical fallacy in any discussion of verse, for a poem, as we know, is a dramatized experience in which a speaker speaks for himself or herself and not for the author. When we say that Dickinson thinks thus-and-thus about dying, we mean the speaker in the poem. And yet in poems about dying, autobiographical attribution seems difficult to avoid. Yet avoid it, we must. Shakespeare's sonnets immediately come to mind with their proud assertion of art's power to frustrate death. The procedure varies but the end of Sonnet 18 is typical—

> But thy eternal summer shall not fade . . .
> Nor shall death brag thou wander'st in his shade
> When in eternal lines to time thou grow'st . . .
> So long lives this and this gives life to thee.

This mode of defiance was, of course, a Renaissance convention—one of the accepted kinds of rationalization, which takes many forms: Herrick's "Gather ye rosebuds" is one, Donne's "Death be not proud" is another . . . and one so familiar that even a candidate for President quoted the opening in a campaign speech. It's also a culture-bound poem *par excellence*, and I know of no keener reaction than John Crowe Ransom's. Donne begins, as you know:

Death, be not proud, though some have called thee
Mighty and dreadful, for thou art not so:
For those whom thou thinkst thou dost overthrow
Die not, poor Death; nor yet canst thou kill me.

As Ransom says, "Donne sets up a figure, a metaphor, proceeds to go through an argument and as a result of the argument—which in reality applies only to the figure—calmly informs death that it's dead." Ransom calls it absurd and indeed the logic is shaky. But shaky or sound, such an attitude is at farthest remove from Thomas' cry to his father, "Do not go gentle into that good night," with its "Rage, rage against the dying of the light" repeated again and again. No rationalization here. A creature's cry but—and this is essential to remember—*not* a self-accepting creature's. A creature who rejects his fate.

Are there actually any creature-poems about death? Let me read from Robinson Jeffers' posthumous volume his "Ode to Hengist and Horsa." They were brothers—Jutes—who invaded England about 450, and they aided the British king in his war on the Picts. Hengist is said to have ruled Kent, Horsa was killed in battle—

Recently in the south of England
A Saxon warrior was found in the rich earth there, old
    hero bones
Of a man seven feet tall, buried with honor
Under his shield, his spear beside him, and at his hand
The Saxon knife: but every bone of his body was broken
Lest he come forth and walk. It was their custom.
They did not fear the living but they feared the dead,
The stopped-off battle-fury, the stinking flesh.
They honored and perhaps had loved him, but they broke
    his bones
Lest he come back.
             For life, the natural animal thinks,
    life is the treasure.
No wonder the dead envy it, gnashing their jaws
In the black earth. He was our loyal captain and friend,
But now he is changed, he belongs to another nation,
The grim tribes underground. We break their bones
To hold them down. We must not be destroyed
By the dead or the living. We have all history ahead of us.

A poem by one writer rarely evokes a counter-reply, but this one did —from Czeslaw Milosz. He contrasts two "opposing" human societies.

Part 1 depicts his Lithuanian background in affectionate terms; Part 2, the world of Jeffers; Part 3, his charge and conclusion. The title, "To Robinson Jeffers."

If you have not read the Slavic poets
so much the better. There's nothing there
for a Scotch-Irish wanderer to seek. They lived in a childhood
prolonged from age to age. For them, the sun
was a farmer's ruddy face, the moon peeped through a cloud
and the Milky Way gladdened them like a birch-lined road.
They longed for the Kingdom which is always near,
. . . .
And you are from surf-rattled skerries. From the heaths
where burying a warrior they broke his bones
so he could not haunt the living.
. . . .
Above your head no face, neither the sun's nor the moon's
only the throbbing of galaxies, the immutable
violence of new beginnings, of new destruction.

and so for ten more lines, then:

What have I to do with you? From footpaths in the orchards,
from an untaught choir and shimmers of a monstrance,
from flowerbeds of rue, hills by the rivers, books
in which a zealous Lithuanian announced brotherhood, I come.
Oh, consolations of mortals, futile creeds.
And yet you did not know what I know. The earth teaches
More than does the nakedness of elements. No one with impunity
gives to himself the eyes of a god. So brave, in a void,
you offered sacrifices to demons: there were Wotan and Thor,
the screech of Erinyes in the air,
. . . .
Better to carve suns and moons on the joints of crosses
as was done in my district. To birches and firs
give feminine names. To implore protection
against the mute and treacherous might
than to proclaim, as you did, an inhuman thing.

No attitudes could be more dissimilar, yet both are culture-bound, each reflecting a specific human society. Milosz "implores protection against the mute and treacherous might." The preliterate world of Hengist proposes to break the warriors' bones . . . so they cannot come back. But neither work, gentle or violent, is a creature-poem.

There is, however, a lyric by Thomas Hardy which accomplishes the impossible on this subject. It consists of words that a dead dog, Wessex, supposedly speaks to the people he used to live with:

Do you think of me at all,
    Wistful ones?
Do you think of me at all
    As if nigh?
Do you think of me at all
At the creep of evenfall,
Or when the sky-birds call
    As they fly?

Do you look for me at times,
    Wistful ones?
Do you look for me at times,
    Strained and still?
Do you look for me at times,
When the hour for walking chimes,
On that grassy path that climbs
    Up the hill?

You may hear a jump or trot,
    Wistful ones,
You may hear a jump or trot,
    Mine, as 'twere—
You may hear a jump or trot,
On the stair or path or plot;
But I shall cause it not,
    Be not there.

Should you call as when I knew you,
    Wistful ones,
Should you call as when I knew you,
    Shared your home;
Should you call as when I knew you,
I shall not turn to view you,
I shall not listen to you,
    Shall not come.

The poem imagines what a nonhuman creature might say to his mourners. "Wistful ones," he calls them: those who feel or evince yearning but with little hope. Do you think of me, the dead dog asks? Look for me? Hope that I haven't died? So, at times, you may almost believe, but I shan't be there, even if you should call as you used to call when I shared *your* home—*your* home, not *ours.* The distinctions are unmistakable, and what follows makes them deeper. If you should call as "when I knew you, / I shall not turn to view you, / I shall not listen to you, / Shall not come." Not a touch of wistfulness in the final speech. He has grown away from them. That's how it is. Creature-acceptance.

I've touched on LOVING and DYING; what of SEARCHING? It includes almost anything an inquiring mind might pursue or consider—a huge territory. But I've only two creature-poems to offer, each taking a different view of searching. The first is Frost's "Neither Out Far Nor In Deep":

> The people along the sand
> All turn and look one way.
> They turn their back on the land.
> They look at the sea all day.
>
> As long as it takes to pass,
> A ship keeps raising its hull;
> The wetter ground like glass
> Reflects a standing gull.
>
> The land may vary more;
> But wherever the truth may be—
> The water comes ashore,
> And the people look at the sea.
>
> They cannot look out far.
> They cannot look in deep.
> But when was that ever a bar
> To any watch they keep?

What are they doing? In expectation of something? Is it some faith that holds them there, looking out as into infinity itself, out of which occasionally something emerges—something finite, familiar, a ship . . . or are they waiting for something else to rise up suddenly—an *unknown* something? How account for this waiting, this patience, foreknowledge, though they can neither look out far nor in deep? Theirs is not the only reported case of unexplained human behavior. As J. Z. Young, the biologist, has said, from very earliest times, *Homo sapiens* developed the habit of gathering in great assemblies—"he tends to come together at intervals in huge swarms," tends to form great gatherings on hills. We can't explain such behaviors without resorting to words like rite and ritual, which do not explain at all. Yet a purpose, we feel, must be present. So we have no choice: we accept this creature-strangeness, which ultimately means accepting ourselves as we are. This is what Frost's short poem impels us to do, and, to borrow Keats's phrase, "without any irritable reaching after fact and reason." The people standing there seem most strange till we recognize them as ourselves.

Frost pictures a human action, but Hardy, in our next poem, enlarges the roles. I'll read the seven stanzas slowly; careful listening is needed. The title is "Nature's Questioning."

> When I look forth at dawning, pool,
>   Field, flock, and lonely tree,
>   All seem to gaze at me
> Like chastened children sitting silent in a school;
>
> Their faces dulled, constrained, and worn,
>   As though the master's ways
>   Through the long teaching days
> Had cowed them till their early zest was overborne.
>
> Upon them stirs in lippings mere
>   (As if once clear in call,
>   But now scarce breathed at all)—
> 'We wonder, ever wonder, why we find us here!

The poem imagines that field, flock, pool, tree once asked aloud the questions that follow:

> 'Has some Vast Imbecility,
>   Mighty to build and blend,
>   But impotent to tend,
> Framed us in jest, and left us now to hazardry?
>
> 'Or come we of an Automaton
>   Unconscious of our pains? . . .
>   Or are we live remains
> Of Godhead dying downwards, brain and eye now gone?
>
> 'Or is it that some high Plan betides,
>   As yet not understood,
>   Of Evil stormed by Good,
> We the Forlorn Hope over which Achievement strides?'
>
> Thus things around. No answerer I . . .
>   Meanwhile the winds, and rains,

> And Earth's old glooms and pains
> Are still the same, and Death and Life are neighbours nigh.

By hearing nonhuman speakers ask the same unanswerable questions that confound people, the poem unites all members of creation into one mystified family. Not only men and animals, but pool, field, and tree are bound together in our helplessness to explain why we are here. Is life the work of some Vast Imbecility which abandoned it to caprice? Was it fashioned by an Automaton oblivious to our pains? Or are we living vestiges of a failed divinity—"live remains / Of Godhead dying downwards, brain and eye now gone"? Or is there some lofty but imperceptible plan in which the Good may destroy Evil? The poet-speaker doesn't presume to reply. "No answerer I," he says. Meanwhile —"Earth's old glooms and pains / Are still the same, and Death and Life are neighbours nigh."

The poem calls to mind the quite different view of Fernando Pessoa, the Portuguese poet who died not long ago. He wrote under four different names. I quote from the one he christened Albert Caeiro:

> What does a river know of this, what does a tree know,
> And what do I know, who am no more than they?
> Whenever I look at things and think of men's thoughts about them
> I laugh like a brook coolly babbling over stones.

> For the only hidden meaning of things
> Is that they have no hidden meaning at all.
> It's stranger than strangeness itself,
> Stranger than the dreams of all poets
> And the thoughts of all philosophers,
> That things really are what they seem,
> So that there's nothing to understand.

> There! That's what my senses learned unaided:—
> Things have no meaning: they have being.
> Things are the only hidden meaning of things.

This predates the philosopher Whitehead, who asks "whether nature does not in its very being show itself as self-explanatory."

Nonetheless we keep looking for answers, marked as we are by traits peculiar to our species, as others are marked by their own. Some of the latter are more like ours than we formerly thought. The exploratory drive displayed by various creatures is a striking example. Another is play, common to numerous animals, at times resembling elaborate, organized games. Ethologists go so far as to name "nonspecific arousal" as "conscious effort." As for culture itself, once thought our unique possession, its presence in certain species is well confirmed. And for all we know, other creatures may carry on acts *comparable* to ours when we muse or question. *Comparable* must be stressed. Only lately have we learned that communication in parts of the nonhuman world is effected by odor, vibration, or sight. Again I stress the word comparable as I think of the ultraviolet hue that a bee can see in a flower which we cannot see, but also of colors *we* see that are missed by others. Facts of this kind foster man's self-acceptance. They neither diminish nor exalt him but clarify our knowledge of what we are with our own capacities and limits while compelling us to grant the same in all other creatures. Once we look from this vantage point, the world opens up to reveal realities, affinities, that could never be seen through the narrow, distorting lens of the human culture.

These thoughts call to mind the Italian, Umberto Saba, and the closing lines of a sonnet he wrote as a soldier in World War I. "Today my eyes see the earth / In a way I think no artist has known it. So beasts see it maybe." At the end of his life, he wrote of nonhuman creatures who—I quote—"by the simplicity and nakedness of their lives . . . are close to the truth . . . that can be read in the open book of creation." Joseph Cary, the critic, remarks that Saba found among animals "*his* quintessential creatureliness, a consciousness of a common ground of elemental life shared with the whole of creation. Men, like the beasts, are creatures, therefore *fratelli* [brothers]."

Could Saba have heard of Christopher Smart's poem on his cat, written two hundred years earlier? . . .

> For I will consider my Cat Jeoffry.
> For he is the servant of the Living God, duly and daily serving him.
> For at the first glance of the glory of God in the East he worships in his
> way.
> For this is done by wreathing his body seven times round with elegant
> quickness.
> For then he leaps up to catch the musk, which is the blessing of God upon
> his prayer.
> For he rolls upon prank to work it in.
> For having done duty and received blessing he begins to consider himself.

and so on for seventy-four lines. Surely Saba never read "Of Jeoffry" nor of Theodore Roethke's poems. Where Saba observes from a distance, Roethke sees from as close as his eyes allow: "I study the lives on a leaf: the little / Sleepers, numb nudgers in cold dimensions, / Beetles in caves, newts, stone-deaf fishes, / Lice tethered to long limp subterranean weeds" and so on in a poem called "The Minimal." When he studies his own kind, the perspective changes. Roethke's last book contains these self-reflecting words:

—Or to lie naked in sand,
In the silted shallows of a slow river,
Fingering a shell,
Thinking:
Once I was something like this, mindless,
Or perhaps with another mind, less peculiar . . .

And these lines

Near this rose, in this grove of sun-parched, wind-warped madronas,
Among the half-dead trees, I came upon the true ease of myself . . .
As if another man appeared out of the depths of my being . . . .
And I rejoiced in being what I was:
In the lilac change, the white reptilian calm . . .

Though neither Smart nor Roethke was known to Saba, Walt Whitman probably was. Yet I cannot learn if he'd read these words from the 1885 edition of *Leaves of Grass:*

The sharphoofed moose of the north, the cat on the house-sill, the
    chickadee, the prairie-dog,
The litter of the grunting sow as they tug at her teats,
The brood of the turkeyhen, and she with her halfspread wings,
I see in them and myself the same old law.

Saba would have warmed to these lines as to many more famous others by Whitman, who believed that "a leaf of grass is no less than the journeywork of the stars"—that "the cow crunching with depressed head surpasses any statue, And a mouse is miracle enough to stagger sextillions of infidels." The same Whitman who avowed "that every thing has an eternal soul! The trees have, rooted in the ground . . . the weeds of the sea . . . the animals . . ."

Trees rooted in the ground. Thus far our creatures have been animals. "To the Pomegranate," by T. Carmi, an Israeli, goes a step further:

Get away from here! Get away!
Go to other eyes!
I wrote about you yesterday.

"Green", I said
To your branches bowing in the wind
And red red red

        [Echo: Holy, holy, holy is the Lord]

To the drops of your fruit,
And I brought your root to light
Your moist, dark, stubborn root.

        [Literally: "I released into the
        light your root"—poet has
        creator-power]

Now you no longer exist!
Now you block off the day from my view
And the moon that hasn't yet risen!

        [But this troublesome tree, though
        commanded to disappear,
        persists!]

Come, my love
(I wrote about you the day before yesterday
And your young memory
Inflames my hands like nettle).
Come and see this odd pomegranate tree:
His blood is in my soul, on my head, in my hands
And he still stands where he stood.

All creatures—poet, tree, girl—are taken for granted as equal. And despite the poet's power to create things *into* existence and as readily make them vanish, this tree that he orders to leave *refuses*. It will not go. It's there in the eye of the speaker as much as himself and the girl.

A creature-poem involving the world of plants can go further. Kenneth Rexroth heads his poem "Lyell's Hypothesis Again" with a sentence from Sir Lyell's text on geology: "An attempt to explain the former changes of the earth's surfaces by causes now in operation." Rexroth's words compose a love-poem in which man, woman, and the lignite rock of a cliff are joined in an earthy kinship. The first lines give the setting. Scarlet larkspur flowers glitter in the April morning sun where the couple lie in the lee of a cliff of lignite, the brownish mineral, half-coal, half-peat, beside a waterfall. Here—I'm quoting— "insuperable life" is "flushed with the equinox" and the selves of the lovers seem "As passionate, as apathetic, / As the lava flow that burned here once: / And stopped here; and said, 'This far / And no further.' And spoke thereafter / In the simple diction of stone." Let me now read on as the man speaks to the woman:

Naked in the warm April air,
We lie under the redwoods,
In the sunny lee of a cliff.
As you kneel above me I see
Tiny red marks on your flanks
Like bites, where the redwood cones
Have pressed into your flesh

You can find just the same marks
In the lignite in the cliff
Over our heads. *Sequoi
Langdorfi* before the ice,
And *sempervirens* afterwards,
There is little difference,
Except for all those years.

Here in the sweet, moribund
Fetor of spring flowers, washed,
Flotsam and jetsam together,
Cool and naked together,
Under this tree for a moment,
We have escaped the bitterness
Of love, and love lost, and love
Betrayed. And what might have been,
And what might be, fall equally
Away with what is, and leave
Only these ideograms
Printed on the immortal
Hydrocarbons of flesh and stone.

The woman and man are beyond the petty contentions, the human self-centered concerns. "What might have been / And what might be, fall equally / Away with what is, and leave / Only these ideograms / Printed on the immortal / Hydrocarbons of flesh and stone." The marks of the redwood cones on *both* the woman's flesh and the lignite rock join two presences of earth: animate woman, "inanimate" rock.

I began with a poem by a high-school girl of Uganda, a poem of discovery. I close with another poem of a girl and discovery, but here the girl, a woman, sits at a dinner table with others. Quite casually she asks for a piece of bread. As the man offers it, something happens. Bread and woman appear as part of the cycle of earthly sustenance. But let the man speak for himself in this poem called "Bread" [The complete text of this poem appears on p. 224.]:

This that I give you now,
This bread that your mouth receives,
Never knows that its essence
Slept in the hanging leaves

Of a waving wheatfield thriving
With the sun's light, soil, and the rain,
A season ago, before knives
And wheels took life from the grain

That leaf might be flour—and the flour
Bread for the breathers' need . . .
Nor cared that some night one breather
Might watch how each remnant seed

Invades the blood, to become
Your tissue of flesh, and molests
Your body's secrets, swift-changing
To arms and the mounds of your breasts,

To thigh, hand, hair, to voices,
Your heart and your woman's mind . . .

Possibly some of you wonder at my intent. Do I propose that most or
the best of poems to come will be creature-poems? Hardly. Poets be-
long to the human culture: *what* they write cannot help but reflect the
concerns of that culture. Hence it is not a question of theme or subject
but point of view, change in the point of view.

As I hope my examples have shown, writers of creature-poems do
not see the world in an anthropocentric vision. They do not look at
life through the lens of the culture: rather they look at culture and life
through the lens of earthly existence.

As he gazes from a kind of planetary vantage-point, *Homo sapiens* no
longer appears as Nature's king, its master, the center of all. He sees
himself as one of a host of beings . . . Inevitably relationships change,
values change, meanings change. Having accepted their quintessential
creatureliness, men know that they share with the whole of creation a
common ground of elemental being.

Does the world become a more comforting place to live in? The
pained realities on which we could shut our eyes, ignore, or condemn
as aberrant evils now must receive acceptance as components of earthly
existence. Planetary maturity, the inevitable next stage in man's evolution, is in no respect a more soothing state that reconciles kindness
and cruelty. But maturity never is.

NOTES FOR EXPANDING LECTURE
INTO AN ESSAY

1. "Planetary maturity"—needs expansion with regard to the difficulties of accepting the griefs that call to mind Hardy's "Vast Imbecility," e.g., random horrors: infants born without spines, autism, etc. Discuss anthropocentrism as example of human infantilism. Relate planetary maturity to danger of destruction of earth by nuclear explosion; responsibility for the safety and survival of the planet and all its creatures has become man's.

2. Meaning of "inanimate" according to current scientific position.

3. Counter-reaction to creature-acceptance as shown by kinds of self-condemnation of man as a species. Examples from Robinson Jeffers and others. These must be followed by examples of remarkable human accomplishments in the form of matters not very well known—best example, Fibonacci series; of numbers as related to opposing spirals in daisies, pine cones, etc., and to the Golden Section in art (architecture, painting, etc.). These in turn must be followed by examples of remarkable "capacities" of nonhuman creatures, such as migratory patterns of birds, fish; animal architecture (see Frisch volume); crow's capacity for abstraction; etc. (See *The Seamless Web*, 198ff.)

4. Discuss religious beliefs as a human phenomenon, so far as we know, and their existence in many poems that exemplify creature-acceptance as well.

5. Discuss the unexplained way in which *Mimosa pudica* responds—"process not well enough understood," say botanists. The fact that plants lack nervous systems offers no final answer, since other systems, to date undiscovered, may possibly exist and account for the *Mimosa pudica* response.

6. Added examples of self-condemnation by human beings, based on the many unspeakable ways by which animals are made to suffer for the greater glory of science—Draize tests on rabbits' eyes for cosmetic research; breaking dogs' feet to determine threshold of pain; strapped-down primates in NASA programs, etc. Growing movements against such victimization of nonhuman creatures.

Robert Frost Himself

From *Robert Frost Himself*, copyright 1986 by Stanley Burnshaw and reprinted by permission of George Braziller, Inc. Identifications: Alfred C. Edwards ("ACE"), senior vice-president of Henry Holt, Inc.; Kay, Mrs. Theodore Morrison; Edgar T. Rigg, president of Henry Holt, Inc.; Lawrance Thompson, Frost's official biographer; Wade Van Dore, author of *Wade Van Dore and Robert Frost*, Wright State University Press, 1986; Elinor, Mrs. Robert Frost.

November 12th, 1958, about 11:00 A.M. Office of Alfred C. Edwards: "Robert just called. He's taking the train around noon. Joe Blumenthal will pick him up at the Westbury Hotel and deliver him on time for the reading. I'll meet you in the New School lobby with tickets, and I'll introduce you to Kay—Kay Morrison—then I'll leave. Robert knows why I won't be able to stay tonight. Now, you won't see Robert till after the meeting—at Joe's apartment—433 West 21st. Robert's planning to see you tomorrow at one. Call him from the Westbury lobby. The people from Sarah Lawrence will be there with a car at five, so keep your eye on the time. Any questions?"

A few: Would Thompson be there? Almost certainly no. Where would Frost have dinner? At the Blumenthals: always the same wherever he is —two raw egg yolks. And then? Always the same schedule: He remains alone for an hour, maybe longer; comes out about seven, then taxis with Joe and Ann to the lecture hall. On the way, no conversation, though he might ask Joe if he had in mind a particular poem he wanted to hear. After the reading, Joe taxis him back for his supper: sandwiches, salad, cold cuts. Then special guests, fellow poets, and friends arrive. After a while, Robert appears. But how long the evening lasts no one can know. It depends on Robert . . .

I was able to reach the New School lobby in time. Edwards hurriedly introduced me to Kay, apologized, and fled. Feeling neither at ease nor ill at ease, after a moment or two, she drew herself up and announced that alas she would have to go off—her friends in the hall were waiting. But, oh we two had so many things to discuss! We should make a date for a talk soon—before Florida. Mid-December? She would check her Cambridge calendar and telephone.

Like everyone else in the hall, I expected that Frost "any second now" would come striding down toward the podium. We were wrong. But by failing to start on schedule, he provided me time enough to try to order my thoughts of my new acquaintance. I had heard almost nothing about her beyond a few parenthetical facts that Edwards and Louis had mentioned in passing. The first: 1918—Frost had given a reading and talk to a group of Bryn Mawr poetry students to which she belonged. The second: 1936—on five of the six evenings after his Harvard "Norton" lectures, she and Ted had invited Frost and a circle of friends to their Cambridge home (for the last of the series, Elinor held an evening event of her own). The third: 1938, six months after Elinor's death—Frost, "in need of someone to pull his life together, pleaded with her" (Kay's words) to become his managing secretary. She consented, gave up her part-time publishing job, and went to work for the poet. Now a woman of sixty, she was strikingly quick in speech, clear-eyed, determined, yet, at moments, signs of an undercurrent of strain broke through her prudent composure. Was it fear? Was she striving to come to terms with the recent death of her son?

Frost's arrival, signaled by loud applause, interrupted my reverie. The face gleaming beneath its veil of age looked, from my distant seat, much the same as the one I had seen up close decades before. He moved his head and gestured more slowly, but his talk, as Louis had said, was "as lively as ever and peppered" with anecdotes, comments, cryptic stories, playful remarks. He seemed to take greater delight in his prose obbligato than the poems. Most of them he read at too fast a tempo to allow the words to spread out and ignite one another in the listener's mind. But—how many hundreds of times had he "said" the lines of "Reluctance," "Design," "After Apple-Picking," "Mowing"?

I knew from Edwards's account of the after-lecture routine that I need not hurry to the Blumenthals on West 21st Street. Once inside, I was introduced to the earlier guests, one of whom, I saw with surprise, was Marianne Moore. Our relationship went back to 1928, when, as editor of *The Dial*, she had *telegraphed* her acceptance of a poem I had offered. Recently, from an intimate letter written soon after my last book of verse appeared, I learned that her passions included not only poetry-writing and baseball but also printing, book design, and typography. We were speaking about our respective troubles in French translation—hers with La Fontaine, mine with the modernist poets—when we both saw Frost quietly enter the room. "It's twenty-four years since we talked," I remarked half to myself. . . .

When at last I walked to where he was standing, he took my hand and enclosed it with his own. "Isn't it fine, our coming together after all those years! Let's see—how long is it since we first became friends? Was it 1924 when you were in Pittsburgh?" I was too startled to speak as he went on naming my college, the steel mill where I worked, my August visit "when Wade was putting The Gulley into condition." After some minutes, he pointed his finger at me. "Al says that you're careful to come on time. So am I. Tomorrow, then, we'll have our first long talk again, just you and I." He glanced at the guests scattered around the room. "Oh, Marianne, down there! I must talk with her. Now remember, the Westbury Hotel. We won't have time for a talk tonight with all these friends of mine waiting, but we will tomorrow."

He preferred to stand and move from person to person, group to group, asking questions but doing most of the speaking himself while appearing to analyze his listeners' faces. Of the score of people, Blumenthal was the only one I had met a number of times before, and then rather formally, as a fellow-director of the American Institute of Graphic Arts. I was eager to hear the tale of his friendship with Frost but he thought that had better wait for another time. . . . Our conversation stopped the instant we saw Miss Moore beginning to say goodnight to Frost. I looked at my watch—1:40 A.M.—and approached them.

"I must go *right now*, Robert," she said, then turned to her hosts. I told Frost I also was leaving—to see her home. Leading her down the stairs, I remarked that a cab would be easy to find on 23rd Street. "Yes, of course. That's where I'll take my subway."

"At 2:00 A.M.? Not while I can prevent you. I'll hail a taxi."

We argued as we walked the two blocks north, but at last she relented: "I'd be happy to have you accompany me on the train, but oh the thought of your waiting, then riding all the way back!"

I whistled to a roving cab. "Take us to Brooklyn, please." I smiled. He shrugged, but when I added "260 Cumberland Street," he instantly shook his head.

"Not 260! You know where that is, mister? Right near the Navy Yard."

"I think Miss Moore knows where it is. Please, let's go."

He opened the door, glowering, then tested all four locks. "260 Cumberland! Whew!" repeating the number twice. When the cab reached our destination, he braked and instantly turned off the lights, waiting for me to pay. I explained, "I'll be out in a second, then take me back to Manhattan."

I opened the iron grill door. "Oh, won't you come in?" she asked. I shook my head, raising my watch to her eyes. "Oh, of course you must leave at once. But thank you for being so generous. Good night, then."

The driver, snapping the locks, switched on his lights and raced so fast that the car careened around corners. Not till we came into well-lighted streets did he drop his speed. "You *know* that lady, mister?"

"Know her?" I laughed. "Miss Moore's not only a famous poet but the greatest woman baseball fan in the world."

"What?" he shouted. Then more quietly, "Okay, if you say so. But why if that lady's so great does she live in *that* place? Didn't she tell you two people were shot on that street last week? It was all over *The News*. I guess you didn't know or you wouldn't have—oh well, we're out of there now, thank God!" Then: "You told me Manhattan but didn't say what street, mister."

I entered the Westbury lobby minutes before the proper time, only to catch the poet eyeing the clock. Remembering from Van Dore how Frost felt about shaking hands, I swung my arm over my head to greet him. He grinned, pointed above to the clock, and, without speaking, waved to me to follow him outside to Madison Avenue.

"A good day for a walk—a long one, if you're up to it," he said slowly. At the first corner—67th Street—we moved west toward Central Park. I caught a glimpse of his profile—with the lower lip jutting forward. And the face?—mottled with age spots, and the hollow close to the right cheek, and the pursed lips . . .

From all that Louis had said of his recent visits with Frost, I expected that, instead of a two-way exchange, our "talk together" would become a steady monologue. Hence my surprise when he started out with a series of questions. What *really* had made me surrender the freedom I had in running a press of my own? Had I any regrets? Did Rigg know the *names* of the people I'd published, and the ones I wanted to take to Holt?—I tried to be brief, also to answer all that he asked. He pressed me for specificities. Who were the others I hoped to take in addition to Lionel Trilling and "the art-man John Canaday" and "maybe Saul

Bellow and Delmore Schwartz"? What were the names of some of the best books I had published? Had I set aside some "extras"? Could I spare a few? I started naming: *The Negro Caravan, White Collar Crime,* Fitts's *Greek Plays,* Van Doren's anthology, the *Botany* by Carl Wilson —"The Dartmouth man?" he asked. "I know him. I'd be glad to have it." I promised to send him a copy.

"You told Al Edwards you needed more time for writing, but then you took on this extra teaching work at your Graduate Institute." Knowing by now that a terse account would never suffice, I told the whole story, based on the Pennsylvania School of Social Work plan that my wife had followed. Our students work in publishing houses from nine to one, then take technical courses from two to five, and some evening classes. All I had to prepare were five or six lectures; the rest would be given by visiting writers: Fitts, Trilling, Barzun, Gassner, Ciardi, Van Doren, Rexroth.

"Your friend Rexroth won a thousand-dollar prize at the Poetry Society in January."

"And they gave you a gold medal for coming back to the fold after seventeen years."

"How did you know that? Were you there?"

"The *Times* had the story. It had another from Washington last month, on your opening speech as the Poetry Consultant."

" 'Poet in Waiting' it ought to be called."

"But you go there only twice a year—May and October."

"Oh no. I had to be there to free Ezra." He looked at me, wondering. "Do you know how it happened?" I waited. "Archie MacLeish told me in April that I *had* to go down to see the Attorney General, Rogers. I'd met him before. A month or so after our talk, Rogers spoke to the press. That made Archie *insist* on my visiting Rogers again. He was at his desk when I called. 'What's your mood?' I asked him. He knew what I meant but, just to be sure, I added 'in the case of Ezra Pound.' 'Our mood is your mood,' he answered. 'Well, then, let's get him out right away,' I said. And that's how it ended—except for the lawyers and so on. Thurman Arnold asked me to write a statement to read in the court. It took me most of the night, and then I went home. But Arnold wanted me back. 'Do I *have* to appear in court?' I asked. No, he said, he would read what I had written. And he did. Three days after my talk with Rogers, Ezra was freed."

It had been thirteen years since the time they had indicted him and locked him in St. Elizabeths. Pound must have known what Frost had done to get him released, yet I'd heard that all he said was, "He ain't been in much of a hurry."

"Ezra's still pretty crazy. Eliot thought so too when we talked last year." He paused. "People think it was Pound who discovered me. It was Frank Flint," he shouted. "Someone I'll never forget." He was now well launched on the Pound subject, shifting about in time, unfailingly thoughtful—grave, grim, at moments; at others, earnest, humorous, generous, sharply critical, troubled, relieved. . . .

"The last time I saw him was forty-three years ago. I suppose I acted out of sentiment for a good poet in trouble with himself, the world, and the law. He wrote some fine verse, rimed and free, when he was young. But those *Cantos!* I hear there's an annotated index, 300 pages. Lengthy things, those *Cantos.* Nobody ought to like them, but some do. . . . Funny, he was sometimes a good editor—for *others.* You know he cut out half of Eliot's original *Waste Land.* . . . And oh, the flashy dresser he was when I knew him—Byron collars, dressing gowns from Japan—out to impress people—with his learning too, though he's not a scholar. . . . But we have to remember Ezra's done enough poems to earn a place in the story of American literature." He sighed. "It's a funny world. . . ." Then back to "the Pound Case," to the Bollingen Prize "awarded to him while adjudged insane," that Archie tried to justify by separating loyalty to art from loyalty to society—"odd position for Archie, considering where he stood in the thirties." Frost talked on. Archie knew that Pound despised his poems; but he went to work last January with a letter to the Attorney General signed by Eliot, Hemingway, and Frost and *he made him* promise to talk to Rogers. He had misgivings but hated to see Ezra die "ignominiously in that wretched place for a crime that couldn't have kept him all these years in prison." Frost and MacLeish called together on Rogers, who told them Pound was tied to a segregationist-poet, so-called. Archie agreed to act on that and Frost agreed to work for a monthly advance for Ezra from his publisher, James Laughlin of *New Directions.* Laughlin consented. Then Archie made Frost go again to Washington. He talked with Rogers and when he got home, thanked him. Things remained at a standstill. Then Frost "had an idea." Eisenhower sent him a telegram of greetings at the Poetry Society evening. Frost asked Sherman Adams at the White House to arrange for him to thank the President in person and expressed "the hope" that Rogers would be invited. "After that

White House dinner, things moved fast—by Washington standards." At Archie's urging, Frost made his fourth and last trip on behalf of Pound, who at last was released, in his wife's custody. They sailed to Europe in June. When the ship landed at Naples, Pound gave the "Fascist salute and called the United States 'an insane asylum.'" We looked at each other. But Frost hadn't quite finished. "Archie," he repeated carefully, "deserves a lot of the credit.* He knew that Pound hated his poems but that didn't matter. He made up his mind after seeing him there—at the hospital. That's when he started writing letters and talking around— three years ago—and he never stopped. He did all the work he could but it wasn't enough and he knew it."

"Two summers ago in France I saw an early letter from Pound to André Spire, the poet I've told you about. They were friends. Pound was also an admirer. His letter graciously asked permission to bring a friend to a party at Spire's—'a promising Irish writer,' he called him. That was where Joyce met his future publisher: at the home of a French Zionist, introduced by the antisemite-to-be."

For the first time since our walk began, Frost kept silent. I proposed that we now turn back. He would need some time alone before people would come to drive him to Sarah Lawrence for his speaking engagement that evening.

He waved his hand. "Time enough!" We quickened our pace slightly. "Some people tell me my readings get better; others, that I go too fast. What do *you* say?"

"Last night, you mean?" He nodded. "For me, at times, a bit too fast because I like to hear the words play on each other. But half of your audiences—maybe more, I suspect—already know the poems, so they know the words. Maybe saying them quickly doesn't matter too much."

"Then it shouldn't have mattered to you but it did . . . It's hard, you know, to hit on the timing. I'll think of it tonight when I read.

---

*The New York Times, April 18, 1958: "The person most responsible for today's announcement of the dismissal of the indictment against Pound was Robert Frost." Quite typically, Frost's official biography states that "Anyone who was aware of the behind-the-scenes efforts of Archibald MacLeish might well have said that it was he, not Frost, who was 'most responsible' for today's announcement" (Vol. III, p. 258). Compare: MacLeish's letter to Hemingway: "I think Frost gets a large part of the credit. The old boy despises Ez for personal reasons but once he got started nothing could stop him and I think Rogers finally gave up out of sheer exhaustion" (September 30, 1958, in *Letters of Archibald MacLeish*, ed. R. H. Winnick, Houghton Mifflin, 1983).

Mostly women, I guess . . . And I guess you have to be leaving now."
He stopped, looked at the pavement. "Which is worse—too fast or
too slow?" I threw up my hands. "Both. To be continued, then, next
month." He smiled. "Al will know when I'm coming. Kay will tell him."

Some weeks before March 26th, Frost's eighty-fifth birthday, Rigg
summoned me to his office. At once he announced, "I've been thinking
about our party for Frost and the man to deliver the speech. I know you
agree that we have to get someone important." I nodded. "Well, I've
found the answer. I've talked with my Washington people and they're
sure he'd be willing to come. Want to know his name?" Rigg beamed.
"Richard M. Nixon."

"Oh no! You can't *do* this to Frost. It's impossible!" I could hear
myself shouting.

"What? Impossible? He's the vice-president of the United States!"

"But what does he know about *poetry?* This is a *literature* banquet.
All the guests will be writers, critics, reviewers, professors—people involved in the *arts*." I stopped for breath. "If Nixon's invited, *I* won't
come and I doubt that—"

Rigg lifted his hand to stop me. Pushing a pile of papers aside, he
leaned back, folding his arms. "Okay, then. Who do *you* want?"

"Someone who knows Frost's work—a critic of stature—respected—
well known. If possible, a man who'd have something refreshing to say
about Frost and his work."

"For example."

"Trilling." The name leaped out of my mouth on its own.

"Trilling? Who's Trilling?"

"One of the country's best critics—a professor as well—Columbia.
I'm certain he's never yet published a line about Frost. It took him some
years to appreciate his work, but I *know* from our talks how highly he
values him now. And I'm sure that the guests would be more than eager
to hear what Trilling would say. And you would too."

He sighed wearily. "Then go ahead and get him!"

I telephoned at once. Shocked at first and also pleased, Trilling asked
for time to consider the offer. Whereupon I reported the Nixon danger. Impressed, he promised to let me know in an hour. I replied that I
wanted to nail things down before Ed Rigg could change his mind. Ten
minutes later Lionel called: He accepted. I blessed him, adding how

eager I was to know what he'd say. He would not be a jot less eager, he said, to hear my reaction, and he'd send me his typewritten speech "in plenty of time."

He failed to do so. On the morning of March 26th, he phoned to say that his typist would make the final copy soon after lunch, and would give it directly to me. It would be in my hands by 4:00 P.M. at the latest. Right now he was busily polishing. As I hung up the phone, a flood of reviewers and news reporters poured by my door en route to the president's office.

The conference began as the thirty or more correspondents might have expected. "Poetry has always played a lesser role," said Frost. "When you're in college, half of all you read is poetry. When you're out, not so. Funny, isn't it? Out of all proportion." Though most of his views had been aired before to the press, one or two thoughts, he insisted, were new. He was starting to "hate the word 'peace' for the way it was being thrown around." As for people being "the same," "in the arts we want all the differences we can get. . . . In society too, we really want people to be different, even if it means a risk of fighting with each other." The great surprise came after one of his listeners asked if New England was now in decay!

> People ask me that on my travels. Often they ask me in the South. And I ask, "Where did you go to school?" And they say Harvard—or Yale. And then I say the successor to Mr. Dulles [then Secretary of State] will be from Boston: Mr. Herter. And the next President of the United States will be from Boston.

Pressed for the name, Frost shrugged. "He's a Puritan named Kennedy. The only Puritans left these days are the Roman Catholics. There! I guess I wear my politics on my sleeve." So far as the press was concerned, the conference was over. Headlines appeared all over the country—"Frost Predicts Kennedy Will Be President."

News of a different sort, but equally controversial, was still to come. The birthday dinner at the Waldorf-Astoria began in the usual manner—cocktails and drinks—for a hundred fellow-poets, critics, and friends. Rigg seated himself between Frost and Trilling. My name card had been placed six settings to the left, next to Van Doren's. "Lionel speaking on *poetry!*" Auden scoffed beside me. I muttered a word about wishing to know what he'd say. Mark, overhearing me, asked why I hadn't been given the text. Trilling was still revising, I said, when he entered the hall, and I hurriedly led him to Rigg and some people he recognized, Barzun among them. After his second drink, Trilling looked much relieved.

He began his speech by confessing a certain diffidence in approaching his task at this "surely momentous occasion." After a playful sketch of how archaeologists of the future might describe this evening's ritual, he referred to the myths about Frost. "We have come to think of him as virtually a symbol of America." But "the manifest America of Robert Frost's poems is not the America that has its place in my own mind." This "manifest America . . . is rural in a highly . . . aggressively moralized way," thus representing "an ideal common to many Americans" who share "a distaste for the life of the city and for all that the city implies of excessive complexity, of uncertainty, of anxiety.

> I do not share this ideal [he went on], though I know . . . how intense can be the pleasure in the hills and the snow, in the meadows and woods and swamps that make the landscape of Mr. Frost's manifest America. . . . But these natural things . . . are not the ruling elements of my imagination of actual life. Those elements are urban—I speak here tonight incongruously as a man of the city. . . . Of course . . . I know all that can be charged against the restless, combative, abstract urban intellect . . . [yet] I also know that when it flags, something goes out of the nation's spirit, and that if it were to cease, the state of the nation would be much the worse.

He paused, then proceeded to say that "but recently" had his long "resistance to Frost's great canon of work . . . yielded to admiration." He had more to confess:

> I have to say that *my* Frost . . . is not the Frost I seem to perceive existing in the minds of so many of his admirers. . . . He is not the Frost who controverts the bitter modern astonishment at the nature of human life: the opposite is so. He is not the Frost who reassures us by his affirmations of old virtues, simplicities, pieties, and ways of feeling: anything but. [At the same time] I believe that he is quite as American as everyone thinks he is, but not in the way that everyone thinks he is. . . .

> I conceive that Robert Frost is doing in his poems what [D. H.] Lawrence said the great writers of the classic American tradition did . . . [whose] enterprise was of an ultimate radicalism. . . . So radical a work . . . is carried out by the representation of the terrible actualities of life in a new way. I think of Robert Frost as a terrifying poet. Call him, if it makes things any easier, a tragic poet. . . . The universe he conceives is a terrifying universe. Read the poem called 'Design' and see if you sleep the better for it. Read 'Neither

Out Far nor In Deep,' which often seems to me the most perfect poem of our time. . . .

But the *people*, it will be objected, the *people* who inhabit this possibly terrifying universe. . . . It may well be that ultimately they reassure us in some sense, but first they terrify us, or should. We must not be misled about them by the curious tenderness with which they are represented, a tenderness which extends to a recognition of the tenderness which they themselves can often give. But when ever have people been so isolated, so lightning-blasted, so tried down and calcined by life, so reduced, each in his own way, to some last irreducible core of being. Talk of the disintegration and sloughing off of the old consciousness! . . . [of] 'the post-Renaissance humanism of Europe,' 'the old European spontaneity,' 'the flowing easy humor of Europe.' . . . In the interests of what great other thing these people have made this rejection we cannot know for certain. But we can guess that it was in the interest of truth, of some truth of the self. This is what they affirm by their humor, by their irony, by their separateness and isolateness. They affirm *this* of themselves; that they are what they are, that this is their truth, and that if the truth be bare, as truth often is, it is far better than a lie. . . . The manifest America of Mr. Frost's poems may be pastoral; the actual America is tragic. . . .

Mr. Frost: . . . I hope you will not think it graceless of me that on your birthday I have made you out to be a poet who terrifies. When I began to speak I called your birthday Sophoclean . . . Like you, Sophocles lived to a great age, writing well; and like you, Sophocles was the poet his people loved most. Surely they loved him in some part because he praised their common country. But I think that they loved him chiefly because he made plain to them the terrible things of human life: they felt, perhaps, that only a poet who could make plain the terrible things could possibly give them comfort.

Applause followed. Before it died, I muttered to Mark, "Lionel's going to be jumped on fiercely for all that he's said."

"He was right! To hell with them!" I had never heard any such burst from the imperturbable Mark.

Frost rose from his chair. He was blocked from my line of vision, facing the people before him. Though I found it difficult to follow all that he said, there could be no doubt that the Trilling speech had upset him—not only the words but also the angered faces of some of the guests. Donald Adams kept shaking his head in fury, as Frost said something about his having "enjoyed" being looked into "more penetratingly" than ever before. When, after uttering some rambling words —among them "But *am* I terrifying?"—he began to "say" some poems, the measure of his disturbance became apparent. Lines he had spoken numberless times jumbled in his memory. "I'm nervous tonight, very nervous." The sentence came through sharply. He started another poem, which he prefaced with jittery lightness, "as having a happy ending." It was all too obvious now: He was in no state for any sustained performance. Before concluding, he assured his guests that he "usually knew" the poems, "but I'm a little nervous tonight." I was able to hear his closing words: "I'm still investigating myself . . . I'll be investigating myself for a week. . . ."

Prolonged applause at last gave way to an odd commotion, as scores of guests gathered in groups. Others stepped close to the poet, several speaking at once. Trilling, clutching his keepsake, *A Remembrance Collection* of new Frost poems, quickly excused himself and departed for home. Edwards and Rabbi Reichert, Frost's "summer Methodist minister," stood at one side as the hall started to empty. I wondered why the poet's official biographer, Lawrance Thompson, wasn't there.

At Frost's signal, the four of us walked to the elevator lobby. No one spoke as the car sped up to the Bridal Suite. Edwards, stepping out first, followed by Reichert, led us into a drawing room. Suddenly Frost turned on me: "Do I terrify *you?*" he barked.

"What do *you* think?" I nodded, holding his glance.

"Where?" he barked again, head jutting forward close to my face.

"*Fiat nox.*"

"Ohhhhh," he grunted. Wheeling around, he resumed the walk. We chose our places. Frost, seating himself at the table, motioned to me to pull up a dining chair at his side. Reichert, off to my left, lighted a large cigar. Edwards gazed at us both from an armchair six feet away. At the sound of a knock, he opened the door. The waiter lost no time in arranging the large cold supper prepared in advance for the poet.

"*Fiat nox*—it was just a way"—Frost said mildly—"of putting together some of the poems I had saved for the book," as though no time had passed since his grunted "ohhhhh."

"Should I wonder why you bothered to group them under a special title: *Let there be night?* And coming right after 'Acceptance'? Could any reader have missed the point?"

"I did that only in *West-Running Brook*," he retorted. "Not in *Collected Poems*."

"Were there no 'Fiat Nox' poems in the earlier books? 'An Old Man's Winter Night'?—'House Fear' from 'The Hill Wife'?—'Out, Out—'?

What would you have me say about 'Desert Places'?" His piercing glance carried a meaning I couldn't construe, but I owed myself the right to go on: "And some of your eclogues—'Home Burial,' 'A Servant to Servants'?"

He had started his meal. During the sudden silence, I reamed my pipe, blew out the stem, packed the bowl. "Here," said Frost, "have something!" He pointed to one of the platters. I shook my head, lighting my pipe.

"All this—that was said tonight"—his tone had an odd satisfaction —"it's *good* for me. It will take me time to get used to it, but it's *good* for me." He had started to speak as his old articulate self. Edwards said nothing. Reichert lighted a fresh cigar as Frost plied me with question on question. How long had I known Trilling? What had he written? . . . I heard myself putting together a capsule biography, from the year I had met Trilling at the old *Menorah Journal,* through his teaching troubles at Columbia, his spell at Madison, Wisconsin, then back again, and finally his *Matthew Arnold* book that won him astonishing praise from Columbia's president, Nicholas Murray Butler. "Trilling thinks of himself, not as a teacher: as a man of letters. He's published a novel and two remarkable short stories. One of them, 'Of This Time, Of That Place,' is a gem."

"I'll read it. I'd like to *read* his speech."

"So would I." All six eyes looked at me in amazement. "He had promised to get it into my hands by 4:00 P.M. He telephoned instead —needed more time. I reminded him that he'd sworn to give it to me *before* the festivities. He was still making revisions when he entered the hall."

I started to talk of Trilling's unusual role as a critic—an intermediary looking two ways at once: at literature and society, standing somewhere in between and explaining them to each other. He had dedicated his best-known book to his friend Barzun, who had been there tonight.

"What's it called?"

"*The Liberal Imagination*—but he's often very conservative. Can't abide Franz Kafka, at least not yet—maybe in time . . ." I had probably said much more than he wanted to hear. "Time to be quiet," I warned myself, hoping that any minute now, Frost would take off on a monologue—which is just what he started to do, while the three of us marveled: Was this the man who had lost command of himself?

Confessed he was "feeling nervous tonight"? Stumbled on lines that he knew as well as his name? The lightning change was too much to believe. It threatened to keep us listening there till dawn.

"Yesterday Trilling, today the New Critics. No more worlds to conquer, Robert!"

"Many, oh many, many," he chided playfully, as we went to our places, guided by Robert Penn Warren and Cleanth Brooks. Frost had agreed to be interviewed on some technical aspects of prosody, the tape to be used with the new edition of *Understanding Poetry*. Though neither Warren nor Brooks had invented the term "New Criticism" or its methods for studying poems, their book had become the bible for schools all over the country.

Nothing that Frost hadn't stated before came forth in the course of the interview, though his stress on the "tune" of a poem, on the defects of "true" free verse, on the test he relied on for sound—"something my ear refused"—struck me as quite at odds with New Critical scripture. But Brooks and Warren were more than pleased, they assured him, as we made our way to the nearby Century Club. Lunch would be served in about ten minutes at most in a private room. While Frost, Warren, and Brooks were chatting, I spied a familiar figure enter the check-room at the farthest end of the hall. Hurrying there at once, I called out, "Lionel! Lionel! What wonderful luck! Frost is here." I pointed to where he was seated. "We're lunching with Brooks and Warren. You know you created an international incident last night."

"Who, *me?*"

"Well, at least national. But come with me, come with me *now*. He's *there!*" I pointed again. "And tell him how much you love him!"

"Gladly. Of course! Gladly, gladly . . ."

The two of them greeted each other with an almost loving embrace. I tried to make out what they said, but the most I heard were phrases from Frost about joining with us at lunch and Trilling's "regret—an engagement with Edgar Johnson," followed by Frost's "we should see something more of each other. . . ."

During our leisurely lunch not a word was said of the night before. Frost was too busy recounting his earliest meetings in England—with Yeats in particular, whom he took delight in mimicking for "his talk of the agony each of his lyrics had cost him." Then, mockingly, praised him. I had never heard him speak with more ease or high animation, not since that first long afternoon on the porch of his Shingle Cottage some thirty summers before. Had the shocks of the banquet evening carried him up to some higher summit of self-acceptance? Or was it that I, grown used to the easefulness of our private talks, had only to hear him converse with others to feel anew the spell of his speaking presence?

"Then nothing new has gone on at 'the Holts,'" Frost asked as the waiter left with our order, "or you would have told me? Nothing bad, that is."

I offered a quick summary of the one item of consequence: a promising editor from Doubleday would arrive May 1st as the new head of "the trade." "He's fully forewarned: I told him all about Rigg, but he shrugged it aside. Thinks it a challenge." Frost gazed at me, waiting. "I also asked John Ciardi to join in a literary advisorship—something easy to do since he lectures from coast to coast and hears what writers are doing. John roared at my notion. Nothing could make him take on an added commitment—and neither should I, he warned. A week later he called me to say he had hit on a great idea for a brand-new book. It was on its way to me in the mails."

He was full of ideas about Ciardi, more than his most assiduous hearer could hope to remember. John was not only clever, charming but sharply perceptive. . . . "You know why he couldn't afford to keep on teaching? Says that it interfered with his lecture traveling."

"The birthday story he wrote about you after his Florida visit told me things I never had known. For one, the name of your next book of poems, *The Great Misgiving*. I must ask about that some time. When Ciardi quoted you, I felt I was hearing your words."

"We had a good time together. He sent me the article. It's one of the few about me that I've read." He stared at the window. "Uncannily accurate." The phrase didn't sound like Frost's. He used it again before going on with: "Didn't you say he's printing your piece from your foreign-poetry book?"

I nodded. "He's also named it *The Poem Itself*. I don't suppose you looked at the—"

"Why don't we wait till we see what comes out of it all as a book?"

He gazed at the plate of cakes he had ordered. "Some dessert?" I shook my head. "Then we ought to begin our walk."

"Funny, your living in France and reading their poets didn't affect your work as it did some others'—Eliot, Pound, MacLeish."

We were off on discussions of influence, living abroad surrounded by foreign sounds, and the loss to a writer's ear. In defense of Archie, I said that a kind of international traveler's aura marked a few of the best of his poems, though his famous "A poem should not mean but be" was unfortunate nonsense. As for his latest work, *JB*, I hadn't read it. I'd *heard* it. That was enough. Heard God's voice coming over the loudspeaker.

"Heard it? Where?" Frost wanted to know. I described the evening at Yale when my wife and I had been asked by our friend John Gassner of the Drama School to attend the gala premiere. "Your former Amherst colleague Canfield did the directing. A lavishly staged spectacle! Just a year ago this month—but you know the rest."

"No, I don't," he said in an unconvincing tone. Nonetheless I obliged by stating facts that were public knowledge, after a word on the party honoring Archie at the president's house. " 'Not quite the same as it was twenty-three years ago,' I said to Archie when we were alone, 'or don't you recall the post-performance symposium that we held for *Panic*?' He smiled. 'Do you think I could ever forget it?' I wasn't sure what he meant but it didn't matter. In any case, it wasn't till last December that *JB* came to New York—at a terrible time: the middle of the newspaper strike. No one could read the advertisements or the critics' reviews. Nobody thought the play could survive till lo and behold! radio and television came to the rescue with broadcasts of rave reviews from the *Times* and *Herald Tribune*. They made *JB* a major success."

Jealousy flashed from his face. "Archie has power, hasn't he? Power." My nod was the obvious answer. Elia Kazan, erstwhile Left-wing theater thunderbolt, had staged *JB* with the best available actors, setting, costumes, and music aimed to achieve, as the *Times* declared, "theatre at its highest level." The jealousy went back to his "days of badness," months after Elinor's death, to the night of Archie's much applauded Bread Loaf reading when Frost, unable to bear it, downed a tumbler of whiskey and embarrassed the audience. And now, twenty years later, *JB* was "the only" poetic drama on Job: for serious playgoers, critics included, no such work as *A Masque of Reason* existed.

"You and I know," Frost pondered, "Archie has always been a derivative writer." Had he read one negative critic's remark that the play not only made use of masks but itself was a mask? Or had he been thinking of Archie's echoes of other poets? Neither, as his next remark explained: "Did you catch the end of *JB*—the resolution through love? People think that everything is solved by love, but maybe just as many things are solved by hate." He pondered for a moment. "Part of Archie's thought may be traced to his inheritance. Think of his folks— big merchants in Chicago. Always had money. Lots of it. Also a place in the West Indies to run off to when he needed."

"Antigua? Beautiful island. Some time ago I learned from one of my friends who's known him for years that when Archie lived in Paris trying to write, in the twenties, his wife helped to support them by her singing."

"My!" he shouted. "Never heard about *that*. I'm glad you thought of telling me." I assumed by now that Archie-as-subject was done with, but he couldn't leave it alone. . . . "Things seem to come his way— always have." He spied me taking a hurried glance at my watch. "Time to travel? Did you say you'll leave me at Joe's on your way to teaching?"

"Yes. I'll look out for a cab. Wish I could hear you read, but I too have to speak tonight. I can be there later."

As it happened, there were too many guests surrounding Frost to enable us to continue. While I talked with Joe of my coming Midwest trip with my daughter, Frost came over to join us. What kind of college was right for a girl who had always been a painter *and* an avid reader? Frost stood quietly listening. Maybe, I sighed, it's only a matter of luck and the student can make the difference? "Don't ask me," said Joe. "Ask Robert! He's the expert on colleges." "And I'm still learning." He chuckled. "Last month I heard that the girls at Radcliffe read more books in a week than I do in a year. Does that help?" Before the evening ended, he led me into a corner. "Make sure you're back in time for my Washington party. Al will tell you the day. I'm counting on you to be there. . . ."

I had more than enough outside my duties at Holt to keep me busy in the weeks that remained before my July trip to Europe with my wife and daughter—correspondence with nineteen men and women at work on *The Poem Itself*; lecture notes to prepare, and guests to invite for my

Institute classes. Meanwhile Trilling had called: He'd received a letter from Frost; he would send it at once. I showed it to Rigg and Edwards: "Read the final word from Frost on the Trilling affair."

Ripton, Vermont
June 18, 1959

Dear Trilling:

Not distressed at all. Just a little taken aback or thrown back on myself by being so closely examined so close by. It took me more than a few minutes to change from thoughts of myself to thoughts of the difficulty you had had with me. You made my birthday party a surprise party. I should like nothing better than to do a thing like that myself—to depart from the Rotarian norm in a Rotarian situation. You weren't there to sing "Happy Birthday, dear Robert," and I don't mind being made controversial. No sweeter music can come to my ears than the clash of arms over my dead body when I am down. We should see something more of each other. I wish the Holts hadn't let your trade book get away from them.

Sincerely yours
Robert Frost

A few days later Frost called Edwards to say that Quincy Mumford had "made" him Honorary Consultant in the Humanities for a three-year term. Two weeks passed before he accepted the offer. By then he had surely received the three verse manuscripts we agreed to review as part of our scheme for expanding Holt's poetry list. Dudley Fitts, who had led me to all three writers, "almost had chosen" the book by Maxine Kumin for his Yale Series of Younger Poets. I passed this intelligence on to Frost. Though my letter offered qualified views of my own on all three manuscripts, we agreed that to publish or not to publish would be his decision. He had made his choice before I returned from Europe in mid-September.

Finished copies of *You Come Too* [a selection of Frost's poems for children] had already been mailed to reviewers. Would the title lead them to *North of Boston* in which "The Pasture" had first appeared? I hoped that *Robert Frost: The Trial by Existence*, the soon-to-be-issued biography by Elizabeth Shepley Sergeant, a longtime friend of the poet, would remind readers that Frost had made this lovesong for Elinor the introductory poem in all his collections. The announcement of the Sergeant book led me to wonder about the poet's endorsement of Thompson, who had been his official biographer for twenty years. I asked a few innocent questions. I could learn nothing beyond the fact that Thompson had been disgruntled enough to evoke from Frost a reassuring response.

A note on my desk at the end of September read: "Robert anxious to see you today. Important!!! Hasn't much time, so be there by three. If you can't, let me know at once.—ACE"

I explained to myself: He wants to talk about Kumin's book since he's probably had his fill of "The Future of Man" symposium. Possibly not, since surely three of the speakers would be worth hearing—Bertrand Russell, Julian Huxley, Hermann Muller.

"I started off with a statement," said Frost as we seated ourselves, "so they'd have an idea of how I was taking the future—give them a hint of my thought about science and Darwin, eugenics, even Karl Marx. They were startled a bit when I said at the end that people perhaps were just superstitious enough to leave their directions to what I like to call passionate preference—passionate preference for something we can't help wishing were true."

"I always thought that a wonderful phrase, though—"

"Always?" His questioning face jutted forward.

"Well—years ago I copied it out of a book by a man you dislike: George Santayana, *The Sense of Beauty*. He's discussing Whitman, democracy's beauties, and 'the charm of uniformity in multiplicity'— without quotation marks. Everywhere in Whitman, he says, 'it greets us with a passionate preference.' And then he starts to demean democracy as a 'terrible leveling.' The paragraph ends in confusion."

"I'm not surprised. I would puzzle over his meaning when I sat in his class at Harvard." But the man, he added carefully, was a "beautiful speaker" and he also wrote "good poems."

"Good sentences, too," I said, "that refute his official philosophy. 'It is not wisdom to be only wise . . . But it is wisdom to believe the heart.' Can't recall where he said it. Or where he declares that it's *probable* that the supernatural exists—decidedly probable!"

Frost shrugged. "I went back to Harvard a second year hoping to study with William James. He was away—sickness." Frost enrolled under one of his pupils instead: Santayana, who not only had taken "a different turn" but was sometimes scornful of James's ideas. "I could tell—I had read his *Psychology* in another class." Santayana would talk about history, saying the way that people behaved proved they were not believers, because when confronted with danger, they dealt with it *practically*, for all their praying! "It seems to me"—Frost quoted the words slowly—" 'those who are not materialists cannot be good observers of themselves.' He leaves out the *other* part of ourselves, and the other part is *there*. James knew it. So do we all."

"And so did Santayana," I said, "for all his words on illusion. He talks down mind or spirit so much—art, morality, religion—yet the worst he can do is to say they entice us away from material truth—for him the only reality. Reconcile that with the poet he was! 'And some are born to stand perplexed aside / From so much sorrow' . . . note where he places 'aside' after 'perplexed.' "

"You know a lot more about him than I thought you would. Why?"

"I was carried off by his way with words, verse, prose, cleverness: 'There is no God and Mary is his mother,' and so on. When I first came across his term 'animal faith,' I said 'a kindred spirit.' Then I read more. Something similar happened to me with Emerson, till I learned to ignore what I couldn't accept while holding onto the best."

"You've heard what I think of 'Uriel'—the greatest Western poem yet, I call it. And so much else in Emerson but not all. He could see, as he says, 'the good of evil born,' but there he stopped. He couldn't bring himself to say the 'evil of good born.' You know from my *Masque of Reason* that evil is real. It's in your part of the Bible."

"Yours too, if you really are an 'Old Testament Christian.' "

"I'm just as strong on badness as on goodness."

The *Masque* led me again to think of Thompson's review. I asked if he "had been in" on the Future of Man? "No," Frost grunted, adding casually, "How do you feel about Larry?"

"I haven't seen enough of the man to say. Obviously he has charm and wit and apparent brightness. I never thought much of his *Fire and Ice*, but it's almost twenty years old. Your *Masque of Reason*, I felt after reading his comment, seemed to be out of his reach as a critic. I'm eager to see the pamphlet he's just published. One thing I liked —the tone of his birthday piece in the *Saturday Review*. It helped me understand why you chose him to be your biographer."

"That's *all* of it?"

I thought a moment before confessing my shock at Thompson's rushing away the night of the Trilling affair. "How could he let himself stay away after what happened?" Frost looked at me quietly, and so I continued, "There must have been some emergency to make him run off, and he must have told you the reason." Frost looked to one side. "By the way, have you ever read Randall Jarrell's essays on you? I'll send the book if you'll read it."

My words were lost or he wilfully shut his ears. After his long silence, he raised his head and gazed in my eyes. "I'm counting on you to protect me from Larry."

I lurched at him in amazement. He nodded steadily. "But he's your official biographer! *You* picked him."

"I'm *counting* on you," he repeated gravely. "You will be here. I won't."

"If you need protection, simply undo what you did."

"Too late now."

"*Anyone* has the right to retract for a valid reason."

"I gave him my word."

"You gave him your word how many years ago? Twenty? You gave yourself up to a person you thought you could trust. How could you *know* he would change? He *must* have changed or you wouldn't be asking for protection."

"I want the truth. I need protection from lies, all sorts of lies."

"Edwards ought to hear about this. Have you told him?" He shook his head. "Edwards should know."

"Maybe—in time. But now: you and I only." He grasped my hand. Moments later he rose to his feet. I followed him to the door. "And to think"—he wrinkled his forehead—"I haven't even asked you about your daughter! How rude of me, all this talk of myself! Where is she now?"

"Carnegie School of the Arts," I said uneasily, "at least from my last account. Six girl-strangers sharing whatever the rooming-place calls it —having to like one another. From her voice on the phone, she's not too pleased."

"Why don't you go there to see her? Sometimes a talk can help a child—sometimes, at least." The words led me to Carol Frost, to the night of talk between father and son, to the tragedy three days later. "Be sure to tell me about her when I come next month." He turned around to explain. "The poets' big Academy dinner. Don't you know of it? Their twenty-fifth something . . ."

The something was the twenty-fifth anniversary of the Academy of American Poets, on November 4, 1959, at the Waldorf-Astoria. Frost appeared, after his train arrived, for a short visit at Holt, following which I drove him to his hotel. "You won't rush back, I hope," he said, closing the door. "We probably won't have time to talk after that party, with all the poets crowding about."

In case Ciardi were to ask what he thought of his plan, I'd better tell him now: an anthology of thirty poets born since 1900 to be made, he said, "objectively" by the *vote* of a large group of critics, reviewers, poets, and what he calls experts. Each of the thirty winners will have three hundred lines of his own and will write an essay on what he considers himself to be doing as a poet. The book was to be the successor to John's *American Poets at Midcentury.*

"Objective, is it?" Frost glowered. "Choose the best of the poets by *vote?* Count me out of it! Count yourself out of it too!"

John was excited by the project—"for once an anthology free from an editor's prejudice." I had liked it too, for a while, but its very virtue made it inhuman. I took a long breath. "John may not be there tonight, but Maxine Kumin, the poet we agreed to publish, will sit at my table. If your crowd thins out at the end, I'll lead her over to meet you."

"Where's your daughter now?"—my words on Maxine may have led him to ask. I summarized quickly: Before I could "go to see her," a bad hepatitis had literally sent her flying home.

"She wants to look at the Boston Museum School. I'll drive her there in May, which should give me a chance to come to Brewster Village, then on to visit with Fitts—who, by the way, asked if I thought he might lure you to Andover to speak to his charges. I hope you'll agree. You'd be taken there by car. Fitts is the Emerson of that Concord."

"He should telephone Kay. Tomorrow I go to Wellesley; Friday to Bread Loaf to meet with some Middlebury alumnae. Will you visit me there next summer?"

"I won't have time to leave my Poundridge place. I've all I can do to keep up, and I can't find help on weekends. But it's all worth doing even when I'm not sure. It was last July, for example, while walking around, admiring our handsomest apple tree, that I noticed half the trunk at the base was rotting away. I dug out three full buckets, then filled the hollow with Sakrete cement. You should look at it now! I'm waiting to see it break into blossom in May. When I worked on the wound, I thought it was probably hopeless."

"Hopeless? One time at my farm in New Hampshire—can't remember which one—I came on a little birch that had fallen across the road where a wagon wheel had run over it. When I saw how crushed it was —half broken, lying there—I wasn't sure there was anything I might do that would save it. But I lifted it up, slowly, as high as I could without breaking it off, then bound it with splints, drove in stubs, and tied it up. Later—I forget how much later it was but it couldn't have been very long—I found that nature had helped me out. The tree was taking on life, new life: The sap was running; leaves coming out. . . . The birch never quite straightened up, but it *grew*—grew tall, sturdy, and strong. . . . More than once I've seen how nature reasserted itself." He paused. "You've heard me say this before and I'll keep saying it: Nothing is irredeemable." Noting my quizzical glance, he went a step further: "Least of all the human race."

After introducing my out-of-town guests (Maxine Kumin, Cleanth Brooks) to my friends from Holt, I mentioned my earlier visit with Frost, and his birch-tree story. "I half-suggested he tell it tonight, but then I had no idea how huge this party would be. Six hundred? More? Plus those on the three daises?" At the scheduled time, Mrs. Hugh Bullock, the president, awarded two prizes to poets Léonie Adams and Donald Justice, with a trio of speakers to follow. Hindsight shows me I ought to have known that Detlev Bronk, the scientist; Sir Pierson Dixon, United Nations Ambassador; and Arthur Flemming, Secretary of Health, Education, and Welfare and former political science advisor at Dryden, would outdo one another in lauding the virtues, the glories, the numberless marvels of poetry. Mrs. Bullock was doing her gracious best, yet I couldn't suppress my dismay. This twenty-fifth banquet, despite the finest intentions, was becoming too grand, too sumptuous, too magniloquent—something was needed at once to tumble it down to realities. It was up to the closing speaker, Frost, who began not an instant too soon: "Poetry has always been a beggar. Homer was a beggar. He begged through seven cities. He ate at the table of the patrons—I suppose in those days he sat at the foot of the table instead of up where I have been sitting tonight. He sat probably under the table." Mixing jokes with barbs and ambiguous side-remarks, he proceeded to add: "My own idea of poetry isn't of its climbing on top of the earth, nor of its standing on top of the earth, but of its reclining on top of the earth and giving way to its moods. Like a spoiled actress, you know, the day after she has been on the stage, reclining on top of the world and giving way to her moods. . . ." Having blown the hall clean of the early orators' pieties, he ended with four of his poems, including the prayer that was now his signature: "Forgive, O Lord, my little jokes on Thee, / And I'll forgive Thy great big one on me."

A copy placed on my desk of a letter from Edwards to Dag Hammarskjöld was the first news I had of the March 17, 1960, United Nations luncheon arranged so that Frost could "exchange greetings" with a group of Soviet writers. A State Department official, two interpreters, Edwards, and I would attend. My request for information on each of the delegates yielded nothing more than the names of the leader and his cohorts. Thanks to my wife's coaching, I was ready to help the poet pronounce the names, but as soon as we'd started, he shook his head; he would never be able to speak them decently anyway, and besides, the interpreters could do whatever was needed. Then, nodding to me, he "thought we might try out one of the names, maybe the leader's." *Shéviakoff*, I repeated over and over, mimicking the Russian my wife had spoken last at the age of four. Ten pained minutes of repetition were enough. *Krushchev* remained *Kerchief*. Frost walked to the window. Rain dimmed the facing buildings. "Why are we going there anyway? They don't care about us, and besides . . ."

The trim United Nations official who greeted us sped us at once to the topmost floor, then led the way through a room-wide corridor hung with enormous paintings, some of which I'd viewed at loan exhibitions. "Our guests will be here presently." He bowed as we entered the empty hall. Standing in front of a window, we stared at the rain graying the streets below. Frost's face seemed gloomier than ever. All at once a band of chattering people strode through the open door. Shéviakoff, trailed by his three underlings, quickened his steps toward Frost and, in what was intended as English, spoke about feeling greatly honored to meet with "Mjeester Frustum." Frost, beaming, grasped his hand. "And to think"—he nodded, gazing into his visitor's eyes—"to think that you came all the way from Russia to see *me!*" Gloom had turned into brightness. What if the puzzled interpreter hesitated before attempting to speak? Much relieved, Andrew Cordier, Hammarskjöld's assistant, urged us all to be seated. With the help of six interpreters, he set out at once making introductions and placing guests at the U-shaped table. Frost sat in the center; Cordier at his left; Shéviakoff at his right. My place, to the right of the latter, faced the Soviet's chief United Nations interpreter.

Just as the waiters entered bearing the main course of the banquet, Shéviakoff snapped to his feet. He was moved to recite a poem right now, said his own pretty, dark-eyed interpreter. The poem, in its English version at least, was a typical propaganda piece that stirred none of his hearers. At once he recited another poem. Apparently better, it was given long, sympathetic applause; whereupon he called upon Mjeester Frustum to read a poem of his own. Frost smiled and, shaking his head, announced that he much preferred to "put" a few questions and to do some talking instead. After polite applause, he eyed in turn each of the Soviet writers. "Do you sleep at night?" The interpreter, nonplussed, gave me an icy glance before undertaking his duty, following which the four writers answered, one by one, with bewildered *Yes, yes, of course.* Frost snapped, "I thought so. We do too, and that is because *our* revolution was over a long time ago. Yours is over now too. People can't sleep when there's a revolution going on." Uneasy silence ensued as the chief United Nations interpreter strove with the poet's thought. Frost quickly entered the breach, stating that he profoundly and unalterably opposed the current idea that "all the peoples of the world ought to be alike. We are ourselves and you are yourselves," he added, pointing his finger. "We're each different. That's the way it should be. And I *love* you for your difference."

This was the second shock, and before the visitors absorbed it, Frost had begun "some thoughts on religion," in the middle of which he recited his well-known prayer "Forgive, O Lord, my little jokes on Thee, / And I'll forgive Thy great big one on me." From the tone of their whispers, it was clear that they hadn't expected anything even approaching such irreverent utterance from the quasi-official American poet. But before they had time to regain their balance, Frost had returned to his views on the difference among the world's peoples.

Then came another couplet, written, he explained, about a huge lump of iron sent by the King of Sweden, a meteor fragment fallen from the sky, which everyone could gaze at later: It was on exhibition in "a Meditation Room" below. "A symbol. It stands for unity. But even as you look at it, it seems to split. You think of the tools that can be made of it, and the weapons: 'Nature within her inmost self divides / To trouble men with having to take sides.' " From the look on his listeners' faces, he could tell that the point he was trying to make had escaped them. He recited "The Objection to Being Stepped On"—an "innocent pastoral poem, which should be familiar to Russians, who have always been a great agricultural people:

At the end of the row
I stepped on the toe
Of an unemployed hoe.
It rose in offense
And struck me a blow
In the seat of my sense.
It wasn't to blame
But I called it a name.
And I must say it dealt
Me a blow that I felt
Like malice prepense.
You may call me a fool,
But, *was* there a rule
The weapon should be
Turned into a tool?
And what do we see?
The first tool I step on
Turned into a weapon.

The interpreter facing me threw up his hands. "Hoe? hoe? Did he say 'hoe'?" Frost turned on me suddenly—I was now his authority on the U.S.S.R. "Is there *no* word in Russian for hoe? I thought you told me the Soviets have millions of farmers!"

On the back of the menu I made a sketch which looked enough like a hoe to show the interpreter what was meant. He studied it quickly, then handing it back to me, cried out, annoyed—"I'm an intellectual. *Why* should I know about farm tools?"—whereupon he broke into Russian. I had no idea what he said, yet he must have explained the point of the poem, for the visitors applauded heartily. Before we left, Frost took care to bid a warm goodbye and thanks to everyone present, and especially to congratulate the United Nations interpreter on having enlarged his command of our tongue with "one of my favorite non-intellectual words."

While I was busily planning my coming January trip to Israel, Turkey, and Greece, Edwards dropped by my office: "Exciting news"—Frost would recite "The Gift Outright" at the coming Inauguration. "Fine!"

I replied. "Short enough and perfect for the occasion. Best of all, it's not an occasional poem. Lucky for Robert he hadn't been asked to write to order. It's the 20th, isn't it? I'll try to make sure to see the tee-vee broadcast while I'm abroad."

. . . Not once in all the hours of talk in his favorite Boston restaurant did Frost mention his forthcoming trip to Israel. Kennedy's invitation and "the great event" were his opening words. When, he asked, had I learned of the invitation and the name of the poem? Did I know how it came about? First time in our history—asking a poet to play a part in a President's inauguration. "When I heard who'd won the election, I called it a 'triumph of Protestantism over itself.' Nobody seemed to know what I meant, I could see; but I didn't explain . . . Now, when do you go? And only to Israel?"

"After Jerusalem: Istanbul, Ephesus, Pergamum—my stepdaughter's surgeon-husband runs the Air Force Hospital in what we used to call Smyrna. Athens next, and Delphi, then London for a day or two. All but the last are new to my eyes, not to my head. Countries of the imagination."

"And maybe that's what we ought to let them remain" Frost argued. "But we don't allow it. We can't." Not in this age when it's much too easy to circle the planet. "All we will ever see are the leavings of what used to be Jerusalem or the Parthenon. Not the same thing at all, but once in a while"—his eyes brightened—"somebody—no tourist-traveler—stumbles against a treasure. Do you know of the archaeologist Sukenik? I met him accidentally ten years ago when I called on Freddy Adams. He had taken four of the Dead Sea Scrolls from Israel to the Morgan Library to have them make some infrared photographs. What a sight they made! Think of it—they were written by scribes in the first century. They're a thousand years older than any biblical manuscript known—and in almost perfect condition! Sukenik and I became friends quickly; we understood each other. He wanted me to come to Israel; he'd take me to special places. Now that I'm finally going, he won't be there. His son is an archaeologist. I plan to see him."

The Scrolls may have made him remember that I broke away from our last visit to call for Mary Ellen Chase, who would speak to my class on the Bible. "Did you learn any thing that you hadn't known?" he asked rather sharply. She had come, I explained, not to enlighten me but the students, yet I learned enough that was new to be able to answer yes and to give him examples. First, about "feet"—their unsuspected importance. And to judge from some of the lines she quoted, "feet" were exalted. Second, the crucially different "function" of each of the Testaments.

Frost thought for a moment. "Victor says that everything found in the New was there before in the Old. Victor, of course, is religious. What about Mary Chase?" I admitted the question hadn't entered my mind. "What would you say if someone asked about me?" Nonplussed, all I could do was stare. "Oh come, it's easy." He chuckled. "All you need do, if your questioner's up to it, is to make him compare me with Eliot. He's a pessimistic Christian. I'm an optimistic pagan. That's what I always say when they try to corner me."

Who, I wondered, had tried? Surely not Rabbi Reichert. Thompson, perhaps? In fact quite probably, considering his *Times* review of *A Masque of Reason* and Frost's enraged response. "Larry," he mused —was he reading my mind?—"didn't seem as much surprised as I thought he'd be when I talked of going to Israel." Pause. "He'll have a class at the university—important business—of his own."

"I've been thinking"—I tried not to stammer—"with a bit of hope —of your trip together. Not knowing the language, both of you may be forced to depend on each other more than you'd like. It will offer the chance for—dare I come out with it?" Frost gazed at me steadily. "Mending fences, frank talk of the way things changed—why and how to go back to what they had been at the start."

"Too late. Couldn't go back if we wanted." He stared at the tablecloth, unaware of the waiter beside him. "You are the only one I can count on now and I know you haven't forgotten." I nodded, pointing a thumb toward the waiter. Frost looked up. "Now the desserts." The young face broke through the wrinkles.

We had time enough to parry a dozen subjects and to lay them neatly at rest. In fact, he had never seemed better, though one of the questioned words—"play" in "Two Tramps in Mud Time"—had to be left unsettled. "Only where love and need are one, / And work is play for mortal stakes"—what he wanted of "work is play" was the gambler's word. "A punctuation mark isn't the answer. Something we'll have to return to after we both come back."

"I plan to be your advance scout when I get to Israel. Any instructions?"

"One—and very important." His hand covered a smile. "Tell them how bad I can be if they're not careful!"

Few events in my twenty-four days in Israel involved Frost. . . . I briefed a number of writers, professors, public relations people, and others eager to learn whatever might make Frost's visit "all it should be." They asked about food and drink ("his favorite is ginger ale, with rum if possible"), his hearing ("slightly deaf, but unpredictably"), his physical endurance ("seemingly limitless, but needs to be held in check"), his attitude toward well-intentioned praisers ("he hates apple-polishing"). Other questions, about his likes and dislikes and "things to watch for," demanded care. I spoke of his playfulness—light, and serious, often baffling—of his special interest in Israel's archaeology. As for religion, they knew, I supposed, Cook's discussion,* also the *Masques*. His dislikes? I advised against praising other living poets. And I urged them to choose a first-rate guide to show him the country: "Someone who knows the names of all your trees and flowers." Frost might even decide to "go off botanizing" on his own. . . .

Welcomed home three weeks later by Edwards, Rigg, and their aides, Cecile Daly and Frances Keegan, I rolled up my sleeves and attacked the mail hiding my desk top. A swift hour passed, then Edwards called for "a short talk" that was long enough for him to say how happy he was at my having arranged for a book by the Prime Minister. And what sort of person was Ben Gurion? How could he find the time for writing? Robert, I said, ought to meet him. They'd understand each other. Besides, the Jerusalem hosts would stand on their heads to please him. "Robert," Edwards reported, "phoned from the Coast while you were away. No message, no question. All he said was: 'I want to hear myself praised.'"

I wondered how much praise he could take after the recent event, with the "eyes of the nation" watching him. The night before, my wife had described the Inauguration. Frost, I realized, in spite of himself, had written a poem-to-order as a prelude to "The Gift Outright." The rites began at 10:00 A.M., with Cardinal Cushing's benediction; Marian Anderson next, with the national anthem; another prayer;

*Reginald L. Cook, *The Dimensions of Robert Frost*, Rinehart, 1958, pp. 188–94 especially.

Vice-president's oath of office taken by Lyndon Johnson; then another prayer. Frost, next on the program, walked through the bitter-cold air to the lectern. "First, the dedication," he announced, holding wind-blown pages. Brilliant sunlight glared on his head. He stumbled over the opening word, but after five or six lines, he stopped: "Not having a good light here at—" Not all the words came through on the small television but the picture was clear. Frost struggled on, then stopped: "Can't see in the sun." When Lyndon Johnson tried to cut off the glare with his hat, Frost pushed it aside, uttering something that made the audience roar and applaud. Then he set the typescript aside. "This was to be the preface to the poem I can say without reading. It goes like this." Another round of applause and then, without hesitation, he re-cited "The Gift Outright" in a clear, full voice. At the last line, after mentioning a change for the present occasion, he finished the verse and added at once: "What I was leading up to was a dedication of the poem to the President-elect—" He was still speaking but the words were lost to my wife. They were not lost to the people at Holt. In his nervous state, Frost had said "to the President-elect John Finley," sub-stituting a Harvard professor's name for Kennedy's. The blunder—he had dropped his voice—must have been missed by most listeners, who rounded out their tribute to him with long applause.

First on my list of tasks after jousts with my mail was a detailed let-ter to Frost provoked by the plans prepared by his hosts. Three packed typewritten pages were needed to show why the places they failed to in-clude *had* to be visited—Megiddo (*i.e.*, Armageddon), above the cara-van route to Damascus; King Solomon's copper mines in the desert; the mad-looking Arab townlet Jaffa (Joppa of Jonah's memory); the farm kibbutz on the Galilee. I mailed a copy to Thompson, adding a note on the archaeological remains of the Nabateans and the Dead Sea "sculptures" of Sodom above "Chez Mme Lot."

Larry, who had come to New York for a business talk with Edwards, called at my office afterward. He had read each word of my letter; he wanted to see every last place I had mentioned. But, alas, I was much too hopeful: Frost would never agree—if it smacks of rubber-necking. "Curious word to apply to the Galilee, Joppa, Megiddo," I said. "Be-sides, he told me quite firmly that he's planning to talk with Sukenik's son . . . Nothing in Israel means more to Frost than its archaeology." Larry smiled, shaking his head for moments. Was he mocking my innocence?

"What a time you had!" he mused. "At least I can try to match it."

"You'll probably go me one better. After all, I missed the Inauguration while you and Kay had a perfect view of it." His forehead furrowed. "What a terrible time for Robert," I said. "Bungling his lines—blind in the sun—unable to see what he'd written—forced to give up in front of the crowd—to throw himself on their mercies. Lucky he did so well with 'The Gift Outright.' "

"You really *believe* that story!" He nodded, half-smiling.

"Story?"

"Frost had it planned from the start. Everything—down to the oversize typewritten pages Stewart Udall had made when he said that the regular ones would be hard to read in the sun."

"Are you saying he really *could* read them?"

"He never intended to—not with the wonderful chance he had, with the eyes of the crowd on *him*—Frost, not Kennedy—watching for what he'd do next. So he tricked them all, pushing the papers aside with a canny apology, then with the limelight all to himself, he recited at the top of his form 'The Gift Outright,' which he'd spoken hundreds of times."

I stared at him. "Are you going to say *that* when you write the biography?" I asked quietly.

"Maybe"—lifting an eyebrow.

"I shouldn't if I were you. Readers will think you're mad." He laughed in scorn, shaking his head. He waved goodbye from the doorway.

More than once I had wondered about Frost's fears: He had never offered proof of his need for "protection from Larry." Now I could stop wondering. Thompson hadn't bothered to try to reconcile his claim (that Frost had planned each move "from the start") with the blundering of "Finley" at the close. Would a person in full control of "everything" ruin his crowning moment? Too unlikely even for Thompson, who had long before arrived at the stage at which he found it impossible not to *believe* the worst. The distorting lens through which he saw the poet by now had become his eyes. How protect anyone from the havoc of warped vision? By resolute efforts to question, modify, temper? Offer interpretations that Thompson would wave aside as foolishly wrong?

What of the etiology of this deep and grave distrust? Hints were all I had heard, and not of the still redeemable sort that suggested answers. In the eyes of the public the two were friends, while the truth! . . . I should probably learn the reasons in time. Meanwhile what mattered most was the course to choose.

What if Frost were to break the relationship? Thompson would then be free to write whatever he pleased, to paint the alarming picture he considered true. Frost would surrender all constraints that his publishers and his friends might conceivably force on the man he no longer dared trust. Yet Thompson, once deprived of the seal of official biographer, could not venture too far in his vilifications for fear of portraying himself as the spiteful avenger. Frost would have to choose between two risks, and to me the decision was clear, since no amount of constraining could cleanse the official biography of its author's bias. This is what I should have to propose, now that Thompson had forced me to see his vision of Frost.

Toward the "Knowable" Frost

"My poems—" Frost said in his early fifties, "I should suppose everybody's poems—are all set to trip the reader head foremost into the boundless." Thirty years later, when questioned about some proffered meanings of "Stopping by Woods . . . ," he replied, "Now, that's all right; it's out of my hands once it's published," which didn't stop him from saying of its being a death-poem, "I never intended that but I did have the feeling it was loaded with ulteriority." He often talked of specific poems, occasionally of how they were written, most often of when or where. Did the comments help? To speak for myself only: A poem is a virtual object added to the landscape—virtual because it cannot be touched or seen; the experience it offers is never actual as the warmth of the sun is actual. The poem speaks to readers indirectly in a mode of dramatized speaking addressed to their own experiences, their own desires. Response depends on what they bring to the poem and what they are able to "hear." At best they may think that they hear it all. If they hear little, they may search for help. . . .

Frost's poems, as everyone knows, are sometimes difficult, always subtle, and in some degree elusive. By saying that "The poet is entitled to all the meanings the reader can find in his poem," he not only stressed the likelihood of clashing interpretations but also proposed its rightness and, by implication, fostered repeated encounters with the very same poem. He could sometimes play a game by keeping readers off balance. Of "The Most of It" he might say dryly, "It's another one people have bothered around about—the meaning of—and I'm glad to have them get more out of it than I put in. . . . I do that myself as the years go on." Throwing dust in the eye was almost a pastime, Cook implies, quoting some of his comments—"Neither Out Far nor In Deep" was a "rhymy little thing," "a joke on microscope and telescope." And although with "Kitty Hawk" he took great care to state what it meant, most of the time he chose to insist that his poems were clear if rightly taken—if he had wanted to make them clearer, he would have used different words. And, in any case, a poem should not "be pressed too hard for meaning." True, certain ones had to be "taken doubly," others singly (as he wrote in *A Further Range*); but most of his poems could and would be taken in multiple ways. At times the most perceptive of critics and readers emerge from identical poems with thoughtfully differing judgments—with apparently irreconcilable recognitions.

Which amounts to saying in a somewhat oblique paradoxical way that much of Frost is "obscure." That "His subject was the world that is so familiar and that no one understands"*—true though it be—doesn't lead to an answer. Nor that his poetry fails to be helped by the kinds of explication that help readers of Eliot, Yeats, or Stevens. There are no adducible fixed-and-findable treasures at the end of the analytic rainbow: no Eliotic neo-Christian myths, no "systematic" Yeatsian *Vision*, no ascending steps on Stevens' stairway of imagination. Frost's poetry calls for more than the tracking down of allusions, ambiguities of language, echoes from other writings, and the other "strategies" which, once exhausted, end the need to explore. Eliot, Yeats, Stevens (as others also have found) are "easier" writers than Frost. There would be no imperative point in saying of them that "The poet is entitled to *all* the meanings that the reader can find in his poem"; whereas with Frost this seemingly evasive remark showed the way toward "the answer." Read, for example, "I Could Give All to Time," then see what such thoughtful critics as Poirier, Jarrell, Brower, Pritchard, and Cook have to say. Does any one of these comments satisfy a reader avid to know the meaning of *every line?* Hyde Cox, with whom Frost often discussed his work, waives the question aside: "The poem suggests more than one can specifically nail down, and that is as it should be." Which leads

---

Frost: Centennial Essays III, ed. Jac Tharpe, University of Mississippi Press, 1978, p. 101.

back to Frost's assertion that poetry was "the one permissible way of saying one thing and meaning another" and the risks it entails, for it presupposes being "rightly taken," which cannot be counted on when a crucial part—or parts—of the rest of the meaning is missing. ("Don't work, worry!" he had once advised his Harvard students, only to be forced to add weeks later: "I meant worry about ideas.")

"Rightly taken"—Frost "explains"—holds the key to his meaning. "They say the truth will make you free. / My truth will bind you slave to me." What does the couplet say? "You can talk by opposites and contraries with certain people because they know how to take you," he told a college audience. What if they do not know? What happens to the meaning? And what led Frost, within a month, to hint at the couplet's missing part by urging a different audience: "Having thoughts of your own is the only freedom"—*telling* them how to take his poems. One might hope that everyone knew by now. But more must be taken into account than his talking by opposites or omitting parts of implicit meanings. To understand a Frost poem calls for putting together *"all* the meanings that the reader can find"—those that are clearly stated, others plainly or even vaguely implied, still others only suggested— then drawing out of all that is found, intimations of the *poem's* intention. For the meaning itself rises out of the mixed totality which most surely includes the seeming contrarieties that themselves form much of the "message," as they well might do in the work of a poet for whom "everything written is as good as it is dramatic." To take rightly a poem by Frost is to open one's ears, eyes, and all other senses to the indefinably subtle ways with which he played his language in the hope that the "thought-felt thing" he created would find continuing life in the life of his reader.

A thought-felt thing: "Poetry is the thought of the heart. I'm sure that's what Catullus meant by *mens animi.*" Though "feeling is always ahead of thinking," "poetry must include the mind as well. . . . The mind is dangerous . . . but the poet must use it." Use it with "fear and trembling"; use it with full concern for the limits of knowledge: "there is nothing anybody knows, however absolutely, that isn't more or less vitiated as a fact by what he doesn't know." Granted—yet thinking is a gift to treasure. "No one can know how glad I am to find / On any sheet the least display of mind." No one can know how he felt by "gradually [coming] to see" that in his poem "Give All to Love," Emerson meant "Give all to meaning. The freedom is ours to insist on meaning." On meaning and more. On the freedom to "stay" as Emerson stayed throughout his life: like the hero of " 'Uriel,' the greatest Western poem yet," to look with "cherubic scorn," with "contempt for a person that had aged to the point where he had given up newness, betterness." One could—and should—remain immune from cherubic scorn without forgetting that few blessings, if any, come unmixed.

Those of science—to take the clearest case of Frost's concern with thought and its ceaseless searching—"It's the plunge of the mind, the spirit, into the material universe. It can't go too far or too deep for me." Lost in admiring science, he let nothing stop him, given his lay limitations, from learning enough to be able to follow some of its great explorers. Niels Bohr went out of his way to tell the host of a dinner discussion that the poet's questions were more incisive than those of any professor-scientist present. Frost not only was overjoyed by all that science had learned; he also mocked the fear of its possibly robbing existence of mystery or romance—at the same time, loathing the smallness of mind, the arrogance, the "cocksuredness," of many professional scientists he encountered. "It is not given to man to be omniscient." After so many years of remarkable searchings, they're still unable to do much more than ponder three great questions: where we came from, where we are going, what the steering principle of human living has been. And Darwinism, great as its founder was, seemed in its fixed determinist form to be marked by an all-explaining pretentiousness ruling out everything else—"passionate preference," Bergson's *élan vital*, Jamesian free will—that made of our lives far more than mechanical applications of ordained behavior. Evolution itself, moreover, confirmed the basic belief in progress, about which Frost held strong reservations: "The most exciting movement in nature is not progress, advance, but the expansion and contraction, the opening and shutting of the eyes, the hand, the heart, the mind."

If science, with its ceaseless testing of all it learns of the world outside, brings no light to the three great questions, what of philosophy, which is based on nothing beyond our mind's self-knowledge? "Logical systems [are] nonsense," Frost maintained, for "even the most impersonal processes [are] determined largely by influences controlling the logician but altogether excluded from the system and ignored." Thus in 1915; twelve years later: "I'm less and less for systems and system-building. . . . I'm afraid of too much structure. Some violence is always done to wisdom you build a philosophy out of." For example, the systematization of science which proceeds by assuming it possible to find all the answers when the most it can find are "pieces of wisdom," grains of truth. Much the same for politics, for here also the answers, if any exist, lie past the reach of the human mind—which didn't keep him from weighing the proffered solutions. "Communism, democracy, socialism . . . all complex problems of our time . . . have to be examined seriously." "A deeper understanding of socialism" was what he was wishing to "get" in Russia, he informed *Izvestia* in September 1962. Eight years before, after attending the World Congress of Writers in Brazil, he declared: "I'm a nationalist and I expect other people to be." Yet during World War II, he had called himself "a Lucretian abstainer from politics."

Frost's beliefs on politics appear to some as a model of contradictions. But to others his contrarieties result from observing the same phenomena from differing points of vantage, each of which leads to a different perception possessed of its own validity. . . .

With what seemed like a quip, Frost refuted the charge that he contradicted himself: "I'm not confused; I'm only well-mixed." "I *am* the conflicts, I *contain* them." He was deep in his eighty-fifth year, having often in letters and talk and some of his best-known poems given the source of his contrarieties. For example, on the meaning of "Mending Wall," he denied that he had any allegory in mind other than "the impossibility of drawing sharp lines and making exact distinctions between good and bad or between almost any two abstractions. There is no rigid separation between right and wrong."

. . . If "Frost appears to contradict himself, the explanation," says Jac Tharpe in *Centennial Essays*, "is simple: he tried to tell the truth. In the everyday world, a thing appears at times to be true, and at times its opposite appears to be true." Though such contrariety was an ever-beckoning mystery and necessity, it was not beyond transcending. In 1926 he wrote to Sidney Cox:

> Having ideas that are neither pro nor con is the happy thing. Get up there high enough and the differences that make controversy become only the two legs of a body, the weight of which is on one in one period, on the other in the next. Democracy monarchy; puritanism paganism; form content; conservatism radicalism; systole diastole; rustic urbane; literary colloquial; work play. . . . I've wanted to find ways to transcend the strife-method. I have found some. . . . It is not so much anti-conflict as it is something beyond conflict—such as poetry and religion that is not just theological dialectic.

We are into a subject that needs a book in itself. What did he *really* believe? How far did his faith take him? We have bits and pieces from others, as well as his works to guide us. Do they offer enough? To avoid being wrongly taken, he took unusual care, at times, in his public use of "spirit" and "soul," equating the first with "mind" and the second with "decency" or "integrity." But "God" he used unglossed, in spite of or maybe because "The thought it suggests to the human mind," as Shelley had warned, "is susceptible of as many varieties as the human minds themselves.". . .

By the time that Frost was arranging poems for his first book, *A Boy's Will*, he had come to a view of faith and God that prepared the pattern of all that he later learned through seeking, questing. He defined himself as "an Old Testament believer." He confessed having had revelations: "Call them 'nature's favors.' An owl that banked as it turned in its flight made me feel as if I'd been spoken to. . . ." Although he publicly called it "a curse to be an agnostic," he feared that certain remarks he had made might be misconstrued as a skeptic's; hence, he "commissioned" an intimate friend to convince Thompson that he truly believed in God. The couplet-prayer "Forgive, O Lord, my little jokes on Thee . . ." would probably only seldom be wrongly taken, but what of his shrugging off sectarian theology, churchly trappings, even some venerated Christian tenets as "froth"? How many people would know that his kind of belief drove him to draw the line "between trivialities and profundities"? Yet there can be no doubt that at times he felt less than sure. Seven months after Elinor's death he suddenly turned on his friend Professor Robert S. Newdick: "Where is this God I hear so much about? Where *is* he?"

Frost defined a religious person as one who "can say he aspires to a full consent"—"All I do in [*A Masque of Mercy*] is reach for something." Aspiration: strong desire. "To believe is to wish to believe," wrote Unamuno, "to believe in God is, before and above all, a wish that there may be a God." More than once in intimate moments, Frost dwelt upon Mark 9:23–24: "Lord, I believe; help thou mine unbelief." One thinks of his credo: Belief is "best when rapt, above paying its respects to anybody's doubts whatsoever." Doubts were as much a part of his trial by existence as his faith, aspiration, and all-too-human moods. "Play me some great music, something you think is great," he asked Hyde Cox in the course of a visit. His host played part of a Handel *Messiah* recording. As it closed with the aria, "I know that my redeemer liveth,"

Frost listened intently. "Hyde, do you know your redeemer liveth?" he asked half-teasing. "Sometimes I think so," came the reply, "do you?" "Oh, I don't know," Frost answered, "but I do know there's such a thing as redemption." In the autumn after his trip to Russia, at a party in Rabbi Reichert's Ripton home, he asked out of nowhere, "Victor, what do you think are the chances of life after death?" "I teased Frost by reminding him that when you ask a Jew a question, you don't get an answer; just another question: 'What do you think?' I asked. He became deeply silent. Then he said to me, 'With so many ladders going up everywhere, there must be something for them to lean against.' " His words, echoing James ("The mutable in experience must be founded on immutability"), cannot be heard apart from all he had sought in his life of seeking. So Marice Brown—like others close to the poetry—sees Frost as "a spiritual explorer . . . not only driven to understand the *how* of God's ways but . . . also deeply concerned with the *why*. . . . The thread that runs through it all is the quest itself."

In his *Letter* of 1935 to *The Amherst Student* the ostensible subject was the special badness of the present age, but the heart of his message was "form." The "evident design" in the situation facing people "may vary a little" from age to age. Its background has always been "in hugeness and confusion shading away from where we stand into black and utter chaos." But . . .

> There is at least so much of good in the world that it admits of form and the making of form. And not only admits of it, but calls for it. We people are thrust forward out of the suggestions of form in the rolling clouds of nature. . . . When in doubt there is always form for us to go on with. Anyone who has achieved the least form to be sure of it, is lost to the larger excruciations. I think it must stroke faith the right way. The artist, the poet, might be expected to be the most aware of such assurance. But it is really everybody's sanity to feel it and live by it.

For the maker he was, ever "seeking, questing," much that he learned became the stuff of poems and of other writings and talks that are virtual poems-in-prose. "Any little form [he was able to] assert upon the hugeness and confusion [had] to be considered for how much more it [was] than nothing, [also] for how much less it [was] than everything."

The thoughts foretoken "The Figure a Poem Makes," the preface to his 1939 *Collected Poems*. No words by Frost on "the poem" are so widely quoted: "It begins in delight, it inclines to the impulse, it assumes direction with the first line laid down, it runs a course of lucky

events, and ends in a clarification of life—not necessarily a great clarification of life, such as sects and cults are founded on, but in a momentary stay against confusion." The last five words lead us to James
("if a reader can lapse back into his immediate sensible life at this very
moment, he will find it to be a big blooming buzzing confusion") and
to Frost's paraphrase ("The present / Is too much for the senses, / Too
crowding, too confusing— / Too present to imagine"). Besides this assault on the senses, "There is always tragedy. That is what life is. . . .
[N]othing," however, "is so composing to the spirit as composition. We
make a little order where we are. . . . We make a little form and we
gain composure." "Each poem clarifies something. But then you've got
to do it again" "because confusions keep coming fresh." Will there be
no end? Can "what seems to us confusion" be "but the form of forms,"
as Job supposes in *A Masque of Reason?* "Directive" offers a promise:
"Drink and be whole again beyond confusion." Moreover, "the good
of the world" not only admits the making of form but demands it—"it
is really everybody's sanity to feel and live by it." This is the human
lot: to be called to achieve some form, some order out of the hugeness,
buoyed upon faith in assurances that may bring acceptance.

The Poem Itself: Discussing
Poems into English

From the introduction to *The Poem Itself: Forty-five Modern Poets in a New Presentation*, edited by Stanley Burnshaw. First published by Holt, Rinehart and Winston in 1960; currently available in an edition published by Simon and Schuster, 1989. Copyright 1960, 1988 by Stanley Burnshaw.

Thirty years ago in *This Quarter*, I published "A Note on Translation" which suggested that the only way one could experience the poetry of a language one did not command was by learning to hear and pronounce (if only approximately) the sounds of the originals and "simultaneously" reading literal renditions. Since the poetry inheres in the tonal language (the sounds of the poem in its original tongue), how could one possibly experience a Spanish poem in any language but Spanish, a French poem in any language but French? The "Note" appeared at a time when translators felt free to do anything: they were "re-creating originals"! Bilingual editions had not yet become familiar —nor had Frost's definition of poetry as "that which gets lost from verse and prose in translation." Before long a publisher expressed interest in my notion, and I embarked on a small anthology. But then he insisted that verse translations also be included, despite the danger of confusing and distracting the reader. And so for the time being I abandoned the project, certain as ever that mine was the only means by which a reader could begin to experience the poetry of other languages.

But my method had not gone far enough, as I discovered many years later when I found myself working on some poems by Mallarmé. My literal renditions were scrupulous, yet in certain key places a single French word could not be rendered by a single English word—pieces of two or even of three might be required. Other words, with double denotations in the French, had to be halved in English or equated by impossible compounds. And certain phrases that looked easy in the dictionaries carried quite untranslatable connotations essential as meaning. As for syntax, the reader would have to untangle it for himself. And the allusions—though at times they might hold the key to the poem, they could not even be considered, since they stand outside the purview of all translation.

What sort of experience, then, did my confident method offer? Obviously a most inadequate one: a great deal more would have to be added before an English-speaking reader could begin to experience Mallarmé. And if this were true of so familiar a poet, then it must be true of other "difficult" moderns, such as Rilke, Vallejo, Montale; it must be true to some degree of every participant in the poetic revolution of the last hundred years. The method had to be expanded, the line-by-line rendition enriched, at least with alternate equivalents where necessary and with leads where ellipsis and syntax might frustrate a reader. Other clues had also to be given: to telescoped images, private allusions, specialized symbols, systems of belief, and similar problems. And what of the poem as a work of sonal art? For a reader who wishes to hear and pronounce the original, however approximately, any number of interesting points might be signalled; not only of rime, assonance, meter, and strophe, but of graces, stops, turns, and the sonal felicities of the whole. To be faithful to its intent, the method had to be enlarged into a literal rendering plus commentary—into a discussion aimed at enabling the reader both to *understand* the poem and to begin to *experience it as a poem*.

The result of these thoughts—which can be read on pp. 100–101—fell short of its maker's ideal, yet it served to show others how a somewhat "difficult" poem in a foreign language could be made accessible to English-speaking readers through a new type of presentation. The first to examine "Don du poème" not only approved the theory and the practice but also made fruitful suggestions. When the specimen was next submitted, to other scholars and to poets, the response took the form of immediate offers to collaborate. One poet-critic thought that the discussion should be made twice as searching, but he soon saw the unwisdom of trying to analyze too much. For once the reader begins, he can plunge as deep as he wishes. The aim is to help him *into* the poem itself.

There are, of course, various ways of approaching foreign poetry; when a writer uses one, he does not thereby surrender his right to use others.

Those of us who are drawn to particular poems in other languages will always be free to revivify them with English verses—and as one of this group, I applaud the practice and hail the occasional achievements. But these are personal preoccupations, and translation is of public concern. English versions of foreign writings abound, but the reader who wants to experience the poetry of other literatures must look elsewhere; the vast stock of verse translations provides no answer.

It provides no answer for several reasons. First, and overwhelming, a verse translation offers an experience in *English* poetry. It takes the reader away from the foreign literature and into his own, away from the original and into something different. The instant he departs from the words of the original, he departs from *its* poetry. For the words are the poem. Ideas can often be carried across, but poems are not made of ideas (as Degas was informed by Mallarmé): they are made of words. Regardless of its brilliance, an English translation is always a different thing: it is always an *English* poem.

In this fact about words lies the source of all the slanderous remarks that have been made about translators, from Frost's sentence quoted above to the notorious Italian pun *traduttore-traditore* ("translator-traitor"). Says Poggioli: "Both original and translation deal with a single substance, differentiated into two unique, and incommensurable, accidents"; and Nida: "There can never be a word-for-word type of correspondence which is fully meaningful or accurate."* When Coleridge proposed as "the infallible test of a blameless style" "its *untranslateableness* in words of the same language without injury to the meaning," he took care to "include in the *meaning* of a word not only its correspondent object, but likewise all the associations which it recalls." For every "meaningful" word is a unique totality—unique in sound, denotation, connotation, and doubtless much more.

But the order that words make is no less crucial to the translator than the words themselves. For when they appear in a sequence (as in a poem) they begin to mean in a special way—their uniquenesses act, as it were, selectively. The position that each word holds in relation to the others causes parts of its content to be magnified and other parts diminished. Yet even though some meanings recede as others come to the

*On Translation, ed. Reuben A. Brower, Harvard University Press, 1959; Renato Poggioli, "The Added Artificer," p. 138; John Nida, "Principles of Translation as Exemplified by Bible Translating," p. 13.

fore, all of them are to some degree also active—whence the multiform richness of feeling and thought conveyed (the "suggestions, ambiguities, paradoxes, levels of meaning" of current terminology). These facts may be read into Coleridge's definition of poetry as "the best words in the best order," especially into his famous remark about "a more than usual state of emotion, with more than usual order." Today we talk of the "affective" phrase or sentence, whose word arrangement differs from that of prose; we say each poem is an organization of such phrases. But some critics go further: each affective phrase is a rhythmic metaphor—a poem is a series of rhythmic metaphors which evokes a physical response in the reader's body, in his internal and external muscles. Not only the mind, but the total organism moves with and "mirrors" the rhythmic pattern of the words. For a translator to evoke this response by different words and word order would of course be impossible. But, all corporeal concurrences aside, could a translator even think of trying to carry across into a different language the "more than usual order" of the original words?

And yet, with all its limitations, verse translation has given us almost all we know of the poets of the rest of the world. And from what we have been given we have formed our judgments. Can they be trusted? The only works we could read have been those that happened to appeal to translators who happened to succeed in turning them into English poems that happened to get published. This fortuitousness should be enough to make us suspect that the picture has been skewed; but there is more. We naturally judge the quality of a foreign poem by the quality of the English poem it inspired, even though we know such correspondence is rare. As a result, verse translation being the poorest subdivision of English verse, we must continually assure ourselves that the originals are much better—which is safe enough, but only a wishful assumption. And what of all the poetry that has never been carried across because it seemed too long or too compact or too difficult or too delicate to fashion into an English poem?

The method of *The Poem Itself* should overcome all three obstacles we have noted in verse translation. Because each word of a foreign poem is unique in itself and in its order, we ask the reader to read the original along with our English approximations (usually set in italics, with alternate meanings in parentheses and explanations in brackets). Our comments on allusion, symbol, meaning, sound, and the like will enable him to see *what* the poem is saying and *how*, though the poem itself is an unparaphrasable totality. As to how much the reader will hear of the sound of the poem, this depends on what knowledge he already has and on what effort he is willing to invest in learning to hear. This book, then, offers poems and the means toward experiencing them.

But the means vary, for each work is a unique problem: how can it best be presented in terms of this book? The extent to which each author has differed from my Mallarmé "model" may be judged in the varied approaches of the other 140 commentaries. Each author has, of course, been free to write in his characteristic way, and to emphasize certain things in a poem and pay little attention to others. Individuality of response is no less apparent in our way of presenting a poem than in a verse translation. Indeed, most of the poems in this book were chosen by the contributors themselves. But the editors have also been free to respond in their characteristic ways, and to do more than was ever intended, entirely (I like to think) out of necessity, in a collaborative undertaking dedicated to a new method.

"Don du Poème" as it is presented in *The Poem Itself* appears on the two pages that follow.

STÉPHANE MALLARMÉ

DON DU POÈME

Je t'apporte l'enfant d'une nuit d'Idumée!
Noire, à l'aile saignante et pâle, déplumée,
Par le verre brûlé d'aromates et d'or,
Par les carreaux glacés, hélas! mornes encor,   4
L'aurore se jeta sur la lampe angélique.
Palmes! et quand elle a montré cette relique
A ce père essayant un sourire ennemi,
La solitude bleue et stérile a frémi.   8
O la berceuse, avec ta fille et l'innocence
De vos pieds froids, accueille une horrible naissance:
Et ta voix rappelant viole et clavecin,
Avec le doigt fané presseras-tu le sein   12
Par qui coule en blancheur sibylline la femme
Pour les lèvres que l'air du vierge azur affame?

(*Poésies.* 1887)

"Gift of the Poem" this is entitled, and the specific poem is identified in the first line: "I bring you the child of an Idumean night." For a year Stéphane Mallarmé (1842-1898) had been working upon a verse drama for the stage, named for a princess of Edomite (Idumean) ancestry. "*Hérodiade*" was to embody a new poetic theory: "To paint, not the thing, but the effect it produces"; and though the undertaking filled him with terror, he could scarcely foresee that it would remain uncompleted at his death thirty-four years later.

The setting appears in the first eight lines. The writer has been laboring at his desk throughout the night, the lamplight glistening on the window, the images of Hérodiade's world all about him. Finally at dawn something has taken form, has been completed—a poem, such as it is, has been born. He takes this child of his thought into the adjoining room where the child of his body lies sleeping with its mother. He presents it to her and asks if she will give it nourishment.

Except for the indefiniteness created by the punctuation, the setting can be literally transcribed thus: (1) *I bring you the child (offspring) of an Idumean night!* (2) *Black (dark), with wing bleeding and pale, [its feathers] plucked,* (3) *Through the window burnt with spices and gold,* (4) *Through the icy panes, alas, still bleak (dreary),* (5) *Dawn hurled itself upon the angelic lamp.*

The word *Palmes!* suddenly appears, an exclamation whose import we are left to imagine; then the description continues: (6) *Palms! and when it [dawn] showed that relic* (7) *To this father [who was] attempting a hostile smile,* (8) *The blue and sterile solitude trembled (shuddered).*

(9) *O singer (of lullabies), you who rock the cradle, with your daughter and the innocence* (10) *Of your cold feet, welcome (greet) a [this] horrible birth:* (11) *And, your voice recalling viol and harpsichord,* (12) *With your faded finger, will you press the breast* (13) *Through which in sibylline whiteness woman flows* (14) *For the lips made hungry by the virgin azure?*

This poem, like a number of others by Mallarmé, dramatizes the birth-process of art. But why does the solitude tremble? why is it sterile? And why does the father look on his offspring with animosity? Both the actions and attitudes of this poem cannot be perceived apart from Mallarmé's lifelong obsession with his own creative impotence, with his fear and his struggle against it, and with his seeming horror of the birth-process itself. The child of this nightlong labor, a pale, bleeding bird born in the icy dawn, will die if it is not nourished. But the one who gave birth to it can do nothing more for it.

It has been a strange, almost sterile birth, such as might bring into the world the strange poem of the princess Hérodiade, who rejects all human contact and for whom barrenness is the burning ideal. "Yes, it is for myself, for myself that I flower alone. . . I love the horror of being virgin . . . I want nothing human / O final joy, yes, I feel it: I am alone. . . ." Denis Saurat points out that the kings of Edom were supposedly able to reproduce without women. The poet also—and in this instance it is a blood-soaked, horrible birth. But once born, the offspring of the mind must be nourished in order to live. Brought into the world, it must be welcomed and sustained by the world.

Certain English "equivalents" in our version of this quasi-sonnet are too bare.

"Plucked" (2) is too concise for the broad, slow sounds of *déplumée*, a word which carries the further implication that a pen has been removed. "Spices" (3) lacks the exoticism and aroma of *aromates*. *Ce père* (7) means much more than "this father": it implies pity for the poor, exhausted poet with his faint, ambiguous smile. Similarly *la berceuse* (9) carries overtones of intimacy and tenderness toward the wife and mother. It might also be the lullaby itself.

A number of other elements are curiously evocative. *Noire* paired with *pâle* (2), and *lampe angélique* with the other ecclesiastical touch *relique* (5-6). The "innocence of your cold feet" (9-10). The change from the intimate pronoun *ta* (*fille*) to the more distant *vos* (*pieds*). And the breast of the nourisher-and-sustainer —it will be pressed by a finger that is "faded," "withered."

A number of the images in this poem occur elsewhere in Mallarmé, almost as his signatures (*bleue et stérile, viole et clavecin, vierge azur*); but what shall we make of *Palmes!*? A French critic found a line in Virgil containing both *palmas* and *Idumaeas*, but does this help? To some American scholar-critics the exclamation symbolizes both martyrdom and victory. Other readers suggest that the dawn threw itself suddenly, like elongated, irradiating palms, or Homeric rosy fingers—and that the very sound suggests something broad, spread-out flat, like a bird wing, to which dawn has been related implicitly (2). But perhaps *Palmes* simply occurred to Mallarmé and he retained it because he felt that he had to—much as he introduced in another poem the word "ptyx" because this pure invention struck him as being both right and necessary for his purposes.

Thomas Mann Translates "Tonio Kröger"

From the introduction to *Varieties of Literary Experience: Eighteen Essays in World Literature*, edited by Stanley Burnshaw, New York University Press, 1962. Copyright 1962 by Stanley Burnshaw.

The title of this volume [*Varieties of Literary Experience: Eighteen Essays in World Literature*] calls for explaining, especially the first part, with its echo of William James. By dropping the definite article from *The Varieties of Religious Experience* and changing the adjective, I intend neither depth nor mystery. A reader prone to pry may smile at my disclaimer, that I simply could not find more faithful words for describing this assemblage of eighteen essays—on writers, novels, plays, poems, movements, themes, ideologies, approaches—each of which embodies a set of assumptions, a style, and a method of its own. Such variety, deliberately sought for, seems worth adducing at a time when every critic is supposedly enrolled in one of a handful of "schools."

So much for the main title of the book. The five words that follow are another matter, and though they might lead to a variety of questions, they particularly suggest that we ask ourselves what we mean by the term "world literature." If it denotes a library of volumes, each section of which contains the complete published writings of a specific language, then "world literature" has only academic interest: it could be experienced by few if any living persons, for one can *experience* only as many literatures as the languages he commands. Most readers (including most scholars and critics) can never be truly at home in more than a very few foreign tongues. Hence "world literature" *as it is read* is by no means the totality of writings produced by the peoples of the world—not the alien originals at all but domestic imitations.

All this may be obvious enough until we remind ourselves that every piece of literature in translation is a very different thing from the work from which it was transported. The domestic imitation is made of dif-

ferent words. We "know" this, of course; we "know" that every translation is a new work; and yet we approach it not as we approach a new
work originally written in our own language but with a special and
pervasive awareness of difference. And we make charitable allowances,
even to the extent of downgrading the translation by seeing the original enclosed in a halo of imagined superiority to whatever we find in
the words before us. This curiously impeding awareness operates not
only with dissatisfying translations. No matter how affecting the words
before us, we "know" that the work they derived from must surely have
been superior, for we properly assume that something precious has
been lost. The moment we become aware that we are reading a translation, the normal relation between book and reader breaks down. The
translated book is, of course, no longer entirely foreign—but neither
is it "genuinely" English. What then can it be but a species of limbo
literature?

Though such a question would always seem ungracious, it sounds
particularly so today when translators are more productive than ever
before and publishers promise them support. Dazzled by the first revelations of a goldening age, many readers may quickly reverse their
ancient habits, and, in pursuit of the new, long-hidden joys, push aside
everything including thoughts they long held to be true. Somewhere
along this enchanted line, they may start telling themselves that all the
essential differences between first-hand and second-hand literatures
are merely a matter of theory, and then with a pragmatic wave of the
hand, dismiss these differences as no longer worth considering. Merrily
bound for the other extreme, they may even find themselves believing that the impossible has been accomplished: that the translation
"problem" has at last been solved for all time.

Other readers, however, especially those with a weakness for books
about literature, are likely to remain unchanged; for if recent criticism has contributed anything importantly new it has been to point
up the implications of the ever obvious fact that a book is a matter of
words. It is always and overwhelmingly a matter of words—as colors
are the painter's materials, so are words the writer's; but whereas colors
have no fatherland, words are stopped at each linguistic frontier. It is
Zapiski iz Podpolya for readers of Russian and *Notes from the Underground* (or *Letters from the Underworld*) for readers of English: from
title to conclusion, two structures of different words, which is also to
say: two different structures. But in all such structures we find, in ad-

dition to the words, a variety of abstractable creations. How many, we may never be able to say; nor does the arithmetic count. What matters is that certain of these creations can be carried over from language to language without decisive loss—story, plot, fable, myth, allegory, generalized analogy. Ideas can also be translated to the extent that two languages possess terms that are reciprocally appropriate. Occasionally idioms may show something like a one-to-one correspondence, as will some elements of form in the gross. But such types of equivalence are as much as can be hoped for at best, for if literature is made of language, then it is changed when its language is changed—changed for better or worse, but in every case changed.

Nobody will deny that these statements hold true of poetry—besides, given certain aids, every reader can experience foreign poems in their original words [1]—but what of prose? That the English tongue possesses some fine works of fiction in translation is beside the point; their excellence has nothing to do with their difference from what they purport and are taken to be. And it is mainly because excellence here does away with full awareness of difference that readers need to realize what can happen even to prose in the process of change.

No handier example can be suggested, I think, than the following passage from *Tonio Kröger*, since Thomas Mann himself presided at the ceremony of analysis that took place at Colorado College in the spring of 1941.[2] Some thirty teachers and students of German had been asked to translate this paragraph from the middle of the story:

> Und Tonio Kröger fuhr gen Norden. Er fuhr mit Komfort (denn er pflegte zu sagen, dass jemand, der es innerlich so viel schwerer hat als andere Leute, gerechten Anspruch auf ein wenig äusseres Behagen habe), und er rastete nicht eher, als bis die Türme der engen Stadt, von der er ausgegangen war, sich vor ihm in die graue Luft erhoben. Dort nahm er einen kurzen, seltsamen Aufenthalt.

The discussion began with the fifth word: why had Mann used, instead of *gegen*, the archaic *gen*? Was there some connection with Siegfried's trip north to Iceland? Mann explained that he had striven for a balladesque atmosphere. As for the fourth word, *fuhr*, he had used it in the sense of *zog*; hence *traveled* would be too "pedestrian." *Norden* had been intended in what Mann called "a certain symbolical sense." *Er fuhr mit Komfort* had been written with technical comfort in mind. The word *innerlich* gave rise to much difficulty. *Schwer haben* turned out to be a deliberate understatement. *Anspruch haben* was finally translated as *entitled*, though Mann regretfully permitted the omission of *gerecht* (*rightfully*) for the greater good of simplicity in translation. *Creature comfort* was too explicit for *äusseres Behagen*, he said; and as for *rastete*, there was simply no exact English equivalent. The penultimate *selt-samen* had a dreamlike or fantastic connotation for the author; but *fantastic* was a bit exaggerated, *strange* would be unmelodious. The best solution was *a brief, enchanted stay*. After eighty minutes of de-liberation, the following version was accepted by all present, including Thomas Mann, who considered it to be more faithful than any of the three published renderings of the same passage:[3]

> And Tonio Kröger went north. He went in comfort, for he always said that anyone who had so much more to bear inwardly than other people was surely entitled to a little outer ease. And he did not stop until there rose before him in the gray sky the spires of the cramped little city from which he had once set out. There he made a brief, enchanted stay.

Faced with such a demonstration in rendering so small a part of so long a story, a reader may throw up his hands. Frost was all too right!— "Poetry is that which gets lost from verse or prose in translation."—the quotation repeated again and again: it cannot be repeated too often. And yet, the "poetry" is by no means the main element contributing to the massed-up effectiveness of a foreign novel or play rendered into English. Its untranslatable charges of meaning may prove crucial only in isolated passages or they may inform every sentence from beginning to end; but even when this poetry is lost or weakly imitated, other im-portant structures may remain in the domesticated version—the many "abstractable creations" noted earlier and the new constructions (char-acter, situation) to which they give rise. All such things of course owe their existence to the original words from which they have now been cut off; but the life they lead and the power they exert no longer depend on those words.

They depend on the newfound words that compose their natures, which is to say that differences always arise. How many or how de-cisive depends on the "veil," if we think of translation as that which hangs between the original and our eyes. The veil distorts, as it must; it conceals; at times it darkens. But there is still much to be seen. The image behind it glows with curious light. And like every object viewed through a veil, it may sometimes seem to us finer than it really is. Not necessarily because we endow it with virtues we should like it to possess (as some Frenchmen have done with Poe), but rather because of the texture of the veil. Is there any reason why a prose translation cannot, as literature in a new language, be superior to the original? Is the King James Bible, for example, less great than the Hebrew? Even such exhilarating questions can only affirm the fact of difference. They should also make us alert to our limits, especially when we try to see all that a critic tells us he has seen in a work of world literature. How easy to forget that his sometimes seemingly excessive pronouncements or incredible findings, in a Dostoevski novel, for example, developed in the course of his involvement with *Zapiski iz Podpolya*, whereas we may have read only a book entitled *Notes from the Underground*, or *Letters from the Underworld*. Better to realize why such readers as ourselves must always stand outside: not only the original work but every critique it engenders will always remain not quite within reach, clad in obscuring veils.

NOTES

1. As I have tried to show in *The Poem Itself*.
2. As reported by Hans Rosenhaupt, in *The History of Ideas News Letter*, Vol. 3, No. 3 (July 1957), pp. 60–63. Reprinted by permission of Dr. Rosenhaupt.
3. The three published renderings follow:

And Tonio Kröger journeyed northward. He traveled comfortably (for he was wont to say that any one who has so much more distress of soul than other people may justly claim a little external comfort), and he did not rest until the towers of the cramped city which had been his starting-point rose before him in the gray air. There he made a brief, strange sojourn.
—Trans. by Bayard Q. Morgan
(German Publication Society, 1914)

And Tonio Kröger traveled north. He traveled with comfort (for he liked to say that anyone who was so much more disturbed internally than other people had a perfect right to a little external comfort), and he never stopped until the towers of the narrow city from which he had come rose up before him into the grey air. There he made a brief, strange stop-over.
—Trans. by Kenneth Burke
(Alfred A. Knopf, 1925)

And Tonio Kröger travelled north. He travelled in comfort (for he was wont to say that anyone who had suffered inwardly more than other people had a right to a little outward ease); and he did not stay until the towers of the little town he had left rose up in the grey air. Among them he made a short and singular stay.

—Trans. by H. T. Lowe-Porter
(Alfred A. Knopf, 1936)

The Seamless Web

From parts 1 and 2 of *The Seamless Web: Language-Thinking, Creature-Knowledge, Art-Experience,* copyright 1970 by Stanley Burnshaw and reprinted by courtesy of George Braziller, Inc. Occasional minor words have been added or changed for clarification; others have been removed along with the numbered references to "Notes and Comments" and the bibliographic references in the original volume.

"Who" Does the Creating?

In the pages that follow, I say, in the plainest prose I can command, what I believe poetry inclusively, comprehensively to be. And since my proposal differs from all other proposals, I offer its genesis at once:

Poetry begins with the body and ends with the body. Even Mallarmé's symbols of abstract essence lead back to the bones, flesh, and nerves. My approach, then, is "physiological," yet it issues from a vantage point different from Vico's when he said that all words originated in the eyes, the arms, and the other organs from which they were grown into analogies. My concern is rather with the type of creature-mind developed by the human organism in its long movement through time out of the evolutionary shocks which gave birth to what we have named self-consciousness.

So far as we know, such biological change failed to arise in any other living creature. So far as we can tell, no other species, alive or dead, produced or produces the language-thinking of poetry. We are engaged, then, with a unique phenomenon issuing from a unique physiology which seems to function no differently from that of other animals—in a life-sustaining activity based on continuous interchange between organism and environments.

How far beyond word-worn limits can such an approach to poetry lead? Before attempting to answer, one must get a clear view of the mode of thinking involved in creating a poem. Only then will it be possible to explore the essential function of poetry in human existence.

Against such backgrounds, we may also begin to recognize the implications of calling poetry an "art." . . .

In the pages that follow I shall be referring to two ways of thinking: those that seem to be involuntary and those that seem to be brought into play by the will. In discussing what happens in the course of composing a poem—the entire course, down to the last redaction—I shall limit myself to these two, bearing in mind always that "voluntary" and "involuntary" are unpretentious adjectives which correspond to two clearly dissimilar ways in which, for most of us, our brains *appear* to behave. To mistake them as substitutes for "logical" and "alogical," for example, is to abuse and misconceive. My terms have nothing in common with dualisms of any variety; every dualism, no matter where it appears, needs to be scrutinized for what it may (wittingly or not) conceal, reduce, or oversimplify. Furthermore, in no possible sense are "voluntary" and "involuntary" processes proposed as the thinking of two separate brains or minds within a single organism—which is what the Freudian view, for example, proposes ("The unconscious is the true psychical reality; in its nature it is just as unknown to us as is the reality of the outer world, and it is just as imperfectly communicated to us by the data of consciousness as is the outer world through the information reaching us from our sense organs. . . . In what is psychically real *there is more than one form of existence*"). . . .

"The Body Makes the Minde"

To believe with John Donne that "the body makes the minde" is to take into account everything that might affect the body: forces separate or in fusion, from without and from within, whose existence we have only started to recognize, whose nature and number may lie past our powers of perceiving. So immense are the possible combinations of external forces alone that it seems ludicrous to discuss them in terms of what we now know or in time hope to know. The more promising course has been to learn our bodies and then from within to look outward. And we have come upon one finding with which all that may be discovered will have to accord: *the entire human organism always participates in any reaction.* To be sure, the body is made up of qualitatively different structures, each associated with specific functions. However (to use the careful, condensed language of Dr. Kurt Goldstein), "A specific location is characterized by the influence which a particular structure of that area exerts on the total process, i.e., by the contribution which the excitation of that area, by virtue of its structure, makes to the total process." Which is to say that the particular quality which the functioning of any localized part contributes to the organism's performance does not exist by itself and cannot exist outside the total relation. . . . In fact, "it is impossible to understand or analyze the organization of highly complicated human skills, *including symbolic skills*, except in the context of multidimensionality." Often enough "psychological" and "physical" seem indispensable as terminology but unless the data they help to describe are evaluated in the light of their functional significance for the entire body, they will end up designating what simply does not exist. "We are always dealing with the activity of the whole organism," states Goldstein, "the effect of which we refer at one time to something called mind, at another time to something called body." Hence, rather than depriving the psychical or the physical of their respective uniqueness, the emphasis merely explains why uniqueness cannot derive from independent segments of the body acting independently—why kicking a football is no more a purely physical act than reading a musical score is a purely mental one.

This is not to say anything different from what poets have at times remarked, in exalted or "objective" terms. The favored example of the first is from Emily Dickinson, of the second from A. E. Housman:

> If I read a book and it makes my whole body so cold no fire can ever warm me, I know it is poetry. If I feel physically as if the top of my head were taken off, I know this is poetry.

> Experience has taught me, when I am shaving of a morning, to keep watch over my thoughts, because, if a line of poetry strays into my memory, my skin bristles so that the razor ceases to act. This particular symptom is accompanied by a shiver down the spine; there is another which consists in a constriction of the throat and a precipitation of water to the eyes; and there is a third which I can only describe by borrowing a phrase from one of Keats's last letters, where he says, speaking of Fanny Brawne, "everything that reminds me of her goes through me like a spear." The seat of this sensation is the pit of the stomach.

More significant generally—and closer to the biologist's particulars— are the views of another modern, the late André Spire, who saw poetic experience as somatic accumulation and release and the action of the organism as a parallel to the poem. Distinguished by its word-order and other expressive structures, every poem (of the kind Coleridge would call "essential") exemplifies in an especial manner the involuntary physical activities that accompany all affective speech. Hence, in the writing of verse, the order and other forms of its language—with the more or less strong stresses, undulations, sudden stops, repetitions, modulations, and the like—are an "echo" of the movements within the poet's body: the poem's language is their external and communicative aspect. Conversely, in the reading of a poem, the motions and attitudes of the muscles in all the bodily structures—not only those of the face (especially the mobile and sensitive muscles associated with responses of sight and taste) but equally those hidden from view—"translate" into physical motion the psychological impressions and ideas and feelings evoked in the reader.

Spire's intuitions, like many others', have been confirmed by the laboratory. (To quote Goldstein again: "Numerous investigations have shown that, simultaneous with the perceptual phenomenon, a great variety of additional somatic events take place. . . . [We] are justified in assuming that a certain muscle tension corresponds to every sense impression.") But Spire goes further, being also concerned with the meaning of the body's natural way of paralleling a poem. These actions set into motion by the feelings cannot, of course, be thought of as mechanically imitative since the body is not a machine. Rather, because the poem evokes an "organismic" experience which takes the form of a correspondence or parallel, it must be regarded as an internal metaphor. And for the organism it is this metaphor that constitutes the "true" poem. . . .

"WHO"?

"A man is born into the world with his own pair of eyes, and he is not at all responsible for his vision," wrote Stephen Crane, who then went on to burden him with responsibility "for the quality of his personal honesty." The extended implication—that everyone is "responsible" for what he makes of the capacities he was born with—seems unarguable. It is that indeed and imperatively more to British and American ethologists, many of whom would dispense with all notions of the "innate." By contrast, their European colleagues cling to "genetic endowment." And they put forth powerful arguments for assuming (as one of them phrases it) that "certain mechanisms of behavior must themselves be refractory to any modificatory changes for the simple reason that they *do* contain the phylogenetic programming of learning processes." Not that they would disagree, for example, with the assumptions in Camus' remark that "After a certain age every man is responsible for his face." Their experiences, rather, compel them to insist that even before an entity of protoplasm first encounters society, its responses will have been predetermined to a significant degree.

I have not encountered any possible reason for doubting that the genetic uniqueness of every newborn organism makes for differences in response and *consequently* for differences in development—emotional, mental, physiological, whatever aspect be considered. This does not mean, however, that the organism can long continue to respond with the full capacities with which it was born; on the contrary, from the very beginning (in the womb) some are inhibited, others diminished, yet others lost in the natural courses of interaction with an environment that presses and modifies. Hence the organism comes to respond with the functional remnant of its original totality—the remnant made functional within the influences and accidents of all it encounters. Since for each person these are as unique as his genetic endowment when he enters the world, the nature of Crane's and Camus' "responsibility" changes: from a solidly based demand to an ethic conventionally fashioned of stern as-ifs.

Any composite of "a person" which is faithful must glow with elements conveniently ignored by our habit of making each "I" the master of all it was given. For the organism, participating in every action and reaction, working toward continuously stable interchange with its environments, and driving to dispose of whatever disrupts its balance, always proceeds *as an entirety* "on its own," regardless of what may be happening in the structure usually looked upon as its director. Which is to say, its brain, though "the brain" is itself composed of a number of structures, some of which think by themselves (spinal cord, medulla oblongata, cerebellum, hypothalamus). Only in one small area, the six square inches of the cerebral cortex, can be found the type of thinking we describe as voluntary—and this thinking, like every other event in the universe that is the person, is a bodily process.

How can such a material event be converted into an idea? Stimuli produce biochemical changes which give rise to nerve impulses which, in their turn, produce specific responses—so runs a current explanation. Though this general picture will no doubt be replaced by another, we may remain sure that in normal human beings the sequence will always be the same as the outcome in thought will always differ. So each person, as he grows and learns and changes, makes his own ways of thinking out of the functional remnant of the capacities he was born with *and* out of all that his organism encounters. Or, if one prefers, each person is a unique constitutional entirety only some aspects of which become available for others to behold.

Herbert Read in referring to one of these aspects as "personality" was thinking of the directly perceived self of a man as it appears to his friends, which differs from the same man's self as adduced from his creations. Whether the first be known to acquaintances or only to intimates, it must be clearly more "outer" than the second. Hence, to expect in these two aspects an equivalence is to ignore the unlikeness of the occasions that bring each forward. As readily equate a certain "outer self" busily negotiating insurance contracts with the same man's (more inner) "creative self" at work on a "Peter Quince at the Clavier."

What, then, can be said of occasion and creativity? (The very question reflects what J. Z. Young remarked of the way each person organizes his brain. Westerners look at once for causal relations. Since it lies at the basis of our science and reason, we do not question causality itself, as others whose brains have been differently organized would do.) Like anyone else, a creative artist inhales the surrounding world and exhales it. Whatever is taken in is given back in altered condition or transformed into matter, action, feeling, thought. And in the case of creative persons, an additional exhalation: in the form of words or sounds or shapes capable of acting upon others with the force of an object alive in their surrounding worlds.

Such an object arises out of characteristic cycles of accumulation and release. At certain moments, words or sounds or shapes demand escape from the creative person. The organism becomes burdened. When it cannot find relief, it becomes literally overburdened. The interruption in the cycle produces an over-accumulation, a dysfunction of the organism, which manifests itself in a variety of states, from vague excitement or tension and irritability to malaise, severe discomfort, even pain. (Robert Frost speaks of "lovesickness"; Schiller, Newman, T. S. Eliot, of "burden"; Byron of "rage.") Persons other than artists may of course go through similar cycles, but with a poet the accumulation becomes associated and involved with a specific kind of verbal expression that affords relief. He may accumulate and release poems throughout his life; for a limited period or periods, regularly, irregularly; he may stop for years, then resume writing, or never resume writing.

The pattern of any single poet has no significance within the total view of a unique psychophysical constitution which cannot maintain normal balance without discharging the burdens it accumulates periodically. The poet must get the disturbance out of his system to enable it to regain the requisite stability in relation to its surrounding world until the next disturbances accumulate and reach for release. This is his normal mode of functioning, for which he deserves neither credit nor blame. Within the mass of humanity, he belongs to the creature subtype which quite literally must ex-press that which builds up within. So it appears when viewed simply as animal behavior. Creativity consists of one more cyclic excretion of the organism, having nothing to do with esthetic goodness or badness. It has to do only with constitutional need which discharges itself into what becomes a thing we call art.

Such an approach has the virtue of clearing the way for a new context in which to view creative "temperament" both with and without the eye of scientists. For while they keep repeating how little has been discovered of human thinking as detailed interreactions, scientists take for granted its involvement with individual biochemistry. And they are able to predict outcomes of interfering with normal biochemical arrangements. Meanwhile some experiments with nonhuman animals have produced impressive responses as a consequence, in one instance, of altering the organism, and in another, of altering the environment.

Representative of the first is the work of James L. McGaugh with some of the various drugs that facilitate learning. For example, an optimal dosage of metrazol, when injected into the brain of mice, was shown to produce a 40 percent improvement in learning ability. Not that specific effects were predictably the same; quite the contrary, in some subjects, it altered "attentiveness," in others, the capacity to vary the attack on a problem; in still others, persistence, or immediate memory, or long-term memory. "Different drugs work differently for different strains, different individuals, different intellectual tasks, and different learning components"—the comment comes from David Krech. Taking what may seem a complementary approach, he and his colleagues have been studying the effects of "enriched" versus "impoverished" educational environments on the brain of the rat. In accordance with their expectations, not only did the cortex of the stimulated subjects (as compared with that of their fellows) expand and grow deeper and heavier but the postulated chemical changes also occurred, showing increased levels of activity in two enzymes (the one involved in trans-synaptic conduction of neural impulses, the other found primarily in the glia cells).

What these experiments may signify for our view of creativity cannot, I think, be dismissed. And surely instead of consigning it to the dustbin of irrelevance, one does better to consider two facts: not a single rodent family has become extinct since the first appearance in Eocene times; and the rat operates basically with the same methods that are used by man. In any event, the investigations make clear that whatever interference can achieve—from without (by the action of environment) or from within (by the action of drugs)—must depend on the constitution of the specific brain that is being stimulated. It depends, that is, on specific chemical status—on constitutional uniqueness. As to whether analogous changes in human thinking are possible, for answering this question we have at least hints—negative, positive, and uncertain. We know, for example, when something obvious is lacking in the organism —when a child is born with a body which cannot produce a specific enzyme. Abnormal substances accumulate, mental deficiency follows. We also know when something obvious is added to the organism—when a substance is taken into the body which interferes with a specific enzyme. Abnormal substances accumulate; mental "magnification" follows. Finally, we know that the body itself can produce biochemical changes which lead the brain into abnormal-supernormal activity. In all three cases, the outcome depends on the specific chemical status of the person who is observed—and what does specific chemical status depend on but the "twofold matter" of genetic endowment and functional remnant of the original totality—the remnant made functional (as noted earlier) within the influence and actions of all it encounters?

One could say that this twofold matter "describes" creative temperament if it did not equally describe every other kind. Its comprehensiveness, however, has worth, for it points to creative difference as one of degree which, in its largeness, distinguishes the artist as a type. His twofold matter has indeed developed into behaviors that set him apart: the cycle of burden and release, the ability-and-need to transform the world he inhales into objects which act upon others with strange forces of thought and feeling. What potentialities he began with at birth and how they were fostered as he grew remain unknowable, though it is easy to believe that the first in some measure forms a part of every human birthright. If in his case it was present in vastly greater amounts than in most others, then artists are surely born. If, however, in the course of his development, the extent and nature of the original capacity was shaped by what it experienced, then artists are surely made. In this view, all artists are born *and* made—and both, by the workings of chance, which recovers these plain phenomena under the same sure mystery they had and will always have. Though some poets stumble on ways for releasing their creativeness, they cannot alter the fate that gave one more or less potentiality than another, as they cannot select for themselves the crucial early and subsequent influences that would foster best the gift they were born with. And to all these reasonings in terms of amount and extent, must be added that other unknowable which gives to the work of each authentic poet its cachet, setting Goethe apart from Hölderlin, Hardy from Eliot, Horace from Catullus.

Similarly these reasonings say nothing of literary excellence or of why such a thing as creativity has had to evolve. But at this point the former would lead us away on a sidetrack and the latter would force us to quote the whole of part 2 ("Creature-Knowledge"). We do better to question the passivity underlying the simplified explanations attempted above. Nothing more need be said of endowment or intrauterine influence since both (as of now, at least) stand beyond reach. It is the seeming determinism of all that ensues that may be questioned. But if poets are very much made in the course of their experiences, this making involves the identical twofold direction that controls all other makings of the human organism: the ways in which we organize our brains, our habits, our gestures, our other selves. The verbs, whether active or passive, bespeak interreaction. Nevertheless, a very great part of all that is associated with creativity bears the certain mark of involuntariness. And the fact has been recognized for centuries by poets and others, some of whom have viewed it with acceptance mixed with desperation. In any event, as it responds to the forces surrounding it, the action characteristic of the creative self is a reflex. Although, as J. B. S. Haldane points out, "Reflex, drive, and purpose shade into one another in men," many writers emphasize the reflexivity of creative processes. "My thought thinks itself," says Mallarmé. "What a delight to drown one's gaze in the immensity of the sky and sea . . . all those things think through me, or I through them (for in the vastness of reverie, the I quickly loses itself)," says Baudelaire. "One no longer dreams, one is dreamed," says Henri Michaux eighty years later. Or, as we put it today, "I do not write, I am written."

"Who," then, "is doing the writing?" The question must in part be meaningless if "awareness" (which implies a directing agent) is, as many are convinced, no more than a construct of human brains: an assumption we have taught ourselves to make as part of the picture we compose of ourselves. Certain brain scientists tell us that the "reticular activating system [an arrangement of interconnected nerve cells in the brain stem] is the source of a special pattern of electrochemical nerve impulses that must be *received* by the brain if we are to be aware of what is going on." This system, then, can regulate degrees of awareness; but what regulates the system and determines its action? Apparently at the very moment when our attention is engaged by one phenomenon, a second will come along and seize our attention, making us far more aware of its presence than of the first. Why? Because, says Dean E. Wooldridge, "the appearance of an object of overriding interest generates a new electric signal that serves to turn down 'volume control' of the nerve system registering an object of lesser interest."

Change in awareness, it would seem, is something that happens to the brain as a result of change in stimulation. Attention, awareness, is "turned on, high" by something that commands one's attention by reason of its "overriding interest." The stimulus-object forces itself upon us, literally seizing our attention. Rather than that we can always select from a field of stimuli, certain among them impose their presence upon us and fill up our awareness. Objects, events in the surrounding world can speak to us and make us heed.

But is all awareness involuntary? The notion seems absurd; from our experience we feel convinced that at least much of the time we can wilfully focus our thought and when attention wanders, bring it back and hold it there—perhaps even when something of greater interest appears. Chemists of the brain may be able in their terms to prove this false, but the brains we have created for ourselves think otherwise. And as we live, we proceed by the rules of our brains—as we must, being also their creatures.

As one of them, I have no difficulty in believing that I am being thought most of the time, that my attention is being directed, that only in between such moments do I find myself focusing my thought. For, except at such an instant as this one, I do not think about how I think, nor stop to ask what is voluntary, what involuntary, or how the two processes shuttle back and forth. When I stop to behold what is occurring, I realize that they must, my organism being what and as it is. I know when, as a consequence of my forcing, my brain has added up a column of figures and when, by no effort, it goes its own way in reverie. I know when my mind, deeply absorbed, has suddenly been pulled away by a flash of thought.

What kind of "I" is implied here? From these sentences and from all that has been said in this chapter, it obviously has nothing in common with the stereotyped notion of a directing agent in steady charge of all the activities of the organism and responsible for its action. On the contrary, much—perhaps most—of the time this thinking "I" is reflexive: how else account for what takes place when "I happen to think of an idea," when a thought "occurs to me," when a notion "comes into my head" as constantly happens? But even such an "I" may be unreal, only a manner of speaking—something we have taught ourselves to assume in order to be able to discuss ourselves. "We use the convention," says Young, "that placed in some way within us there is an agent who is said to act as we describe other men acting. This habit of postulating active creatures within bodies, the habit of animism," is directly traceable to the ways in which we have organized our brains—as indeed it must be—and for all its convenience in communicating, we might perhaps be better off without it. But as Young says elsewhere (in discussing the work of a fellow scientist who also believes "that the soul is imaginary and that what we call our minds is simply a way of talking about the functions of our brains"):

> However much we learn later, we probably never lose the modes of receiving information and acting upon it that were appropriate to our earliest communications. When we were babies the human face was the all-important source of welfare, and all actions in the world around us came to be described according to it. Perhaps none of us can completely escape this fundamental source of animism because it is the way in which our brains must work.

There is obviously much more to be learned even of this limited facet of the subject and, by implication, vastly more than is considered even in *Brain and Conscious Experience*, the compendious record of a world-wide symposium held at the Pontificia Academia Scientiarum a few years ago. For consciousness involves "the one great philosophical question that embraces all others"—as Erwin Schrödinger says—the one that Plotinus expressed by his brief *Who are we?* But have we any right, asks another philosopher-scientist, "to expect a solution to such fundamental problems when the efforts made have been trivial relative to the extreme nature of the problem?" It is easy to forget that human impotence before baffling questions does not cancel out their existence. Continuing investigations have been unable to "solve the problems" of memory, to discover a structural basis, yet nobody declares memory to be an illusion or merely a way of talking about the function of our brains. The inability to account satisfactorily for consciousness does not prove that consciousness does not exist, that it is no more than a way of talking about the function of our brains.

What should we use in its place that would serve us better? If we follow Young, we enter a plane of reality which has no room for the very machine-model on which so many proposals depend, for the organism does not maintain a static structure, as the comparison with any machine implies—the computer today or the telephone switchboard fifty years ago. In fact, as Young reminds us, "living things consist of no steady fabric of stuff . . . individual chemical atoms remain in the cells only for a short time." The cells die out. If the stuff of which the organism is made disappears, what is preserved? A pattern? Living patterns "are kept intact only by their continued activity." The "basic unit of biology is a non-material entity, namely an organization."

Organization? Pattern? Are these the best words for describing the something that is an organism which remains constant so long as the dying cells are succeeded by cells that live? Could other terms more faithfully denote this something and also suggest the uniqueness of each of these "nonmaterial entities" that make up the human species? Perhaps such a scheme as "Voluntary↔Involuntary Process" (with its arrow denoting interreaction) might suggest the range of each human being's behavior as it maintains itself in interchange with the world? But even this ungainly description lacks reality. It is only another way of talking—a form, "a construct of our brains," like every other reality that we "know." Yet if "the form that we give to the plain, common-sense world of hard material fact is a construct of our brains," this "Voluntary↔Involuntary Process" is not less real than others. Both the material world and this "I" are forms of our thinking. Whether or not they "actually" exist, we behave *as if* they existed because we must.

"The body makes the mind"—what else could make it? Yet men have been splitting themselves into two for thousands of years. Descartes was not the first, the religions may not be the last; and even those who scorn the dualism cannot quite wipe from memory the shadow of "mind active" versus "matter inert." Dealing with the latter only, scientists can hardly discern a sure line between "living" and "dead"; yet some philosophers perceive it vividly with the light of the principle of metabolism; while for others the distinguishing characteristics of man are continuous with the properties of natural objects. For philosophy is, as ever, bursting with logically proved demonstrations that destroy one another. If the body makes the mind, and what we have found can be trusted, all such irrefutable proofs are arrangements of words each of which mirrors a particular way in which the rules of a brain have been organized; they depend on the vantage point and what one is seeking.

The same must be said of the arrangements of words I offer. My vantage point—neither an angel's nor a worm's—does not rise above the levels of the earth on which we exist. I do not (like the materialists) reduce matter to something phantasized by the mind. Looking at our question "Who is doing the writing?" I proceed from the manifest fact that every poem that is born comes out of a living person, and I follow it to the action of unburdening by which his living organism releases poems. We are ready to look at the processes of unburdening.

Composition: Collaboration

For an hour, even two, a reader can be fascinated by first-hand accounts of the creative process, differing as it does from poet to poet, often from poem to poem. Yet after a time the variety fades into likeness. And the story palls as the differences begin to consist mainly in the terms for unknowns. Unable or unwilling to see a poem as the joint creation of a man and his universe, the explainers ascribe its parentage to the one or the other. So the ancients speak of the divinity without, the moderns of the power within—Greek "enthusiasm" and Roman "afflatus," Elizabethan "frenzy," Romantic "imagination," and twentieth-century "Unconsciousness." Meanwhile the act of composition remains as surprising as ever to the poet, who knows only one thing for certain: that he is *being used.*

Since no one can observe from outside what occurs in the mind, any attempt to say how or by what must depend on available reports, all of which confirm more or less what has long been suspected. In a popular current formulation: "A short poem, or a passage of a long poem, may appear in its final form at once; or it may have to go through the transformation of a dozen drafts" (Eliot). Now if "at once" means that the short poem or passage arrives in its completed form, composition exists as two different experiences: one in which the poet simply takes down dictation; another, as a process of revision. In either case, however, it begins as dictation, with the poet listening to something that speaks to him: he listens and sees the words. They command his attention. They break through and into his awareness; they will not be ignored. They are using him as their recorder.

Being thus seized, he changes his outward behavior. When Freud, busily writing the last chapter of his book on dreams, was interrupted to come to a meal, he walked, says his daughter, as if in a trance, oblivious of his surroundings. Similar behavior has been noted in any number of artists, for the concentration of such a state may be so intense as to make the worker seem to himself and to others to be in a trance. In itself the concentration, the transport, the waking dream gives no assurance of the outcome. "I imagine," said Edwin Arlington Robinson, "that the worst poetry in the world has been written in the finest frenzy of inspiration; and so, probably, has the best."

Best or worst cannot matter to the person held in this heightened excitation who knows he is being borne along in a steady unfolding. At the inception, at least, the journey is unpredictable. Inspiration has a purpose of its own of which the host becomes gradually aware, though a sudden flash may at any time reveal the course or hint at its direction. Alberto Moravia "never knows" what the work he is writing "is going to be" until he is "under way." What Yeats began as a political poem ended in "Leda and the Swan." Frost repeatedly speaks of a voyage of discovery ("I have never started a poem yet whose end I knew"). Keats could express even stronger surprise than Eliot's (the poet "does not know what he has to say until he has said it") or Ransom's (poets "later wonder what they've done and look at it to see"). To Keats, what he had written in describing Apollo in *Hyperion* seemed to be more the production of another person than his own—which points back to dictation and the language-thinking it uses. During the creative act the poet was both hearing and being "told"; both concentrating and being held in a trance-like state; both discovering and being made to discover —my verb-forms denote the reflexive character of the experience. And yet, if the poet can be said to be writing the poem while it is writing him, his active work is only a passive response to the words that command him to listen. During such concentrated moments, "It is not I who think but my ideas who think for me" (Lamartine), "Words rise up unaided and in ecstasy" (Mallarmé).

(With a reader who objects that these statements do not apply to everything called "poetry," I quite agree. They most surely have no bearing on the species that Juan Ramón Jiménez calls "voluntaria"— works composed deliberately, out of a decision to make a poem. The present book, as a serious inquiry, deals only with the type of poem that demands to be born—what Jiménez calls "necesaria.")

VISION

In his review of Shelley's *Posthumous Poems*, Hazlitt remarked that the author "mistook the nature of the poet's calling, which should be guided by involuntary, not by voluntary impulses." The sentence is almost incredible, coming as it does three years after publication of *A Defence of Poetry*, for not only did Shelley not mistake the poet's calling but he was, so far as I know, the first to have insisted unrelentingly on the magisterial role of involuntary thought in composition:

> Poetry is not like reasoning, a power to be exerted according to the determination of the will. A man cannot say, "I will compose poetry." The greatest poet even cannot say it. . . .

> Poetry differs in this respect from logic, that it is not subject to the control of the active powers of the mind, and that its birth and recurrence have no necessary connexion with the consciousness or will.

This belief was not of course new. Yet it is worth noting that for a century following (though not necessarily because of) the publication of *A Defence*, esthetic theory showed astonishing unanimity in excluding volition from creativity. Kant, Schopenhauer, Coleridge, Bergson, Croce—the list can be expanded by a great many others including the unlikely author of *The Philosophy of Composition*. Poe had fooled a generation of more than receptive French writers with his fanciful account of the writing of "The Raven" only to reverse himself later: "With me poetry has not been a purpose but a passion, and the passions should be held in reverence: they must not—they cannot at will be excited."

Strangely enough his admirers were not discomfitted, not even Valéry, the most exacting of the younger generation, whose career as a poet may also be regarded as a laboratory for examining the work of the mind in the making of a poem. The "case" of Valéry is worth mentioning not only for intrinsic interest but also because it appears at a point in time which he himself might have called the intersection of the Age of the Unconscious with the Age of Science.

In one of the brief entries in "A Poet's Notebook," he stops to deride a certain X who "would like to believe that a metaphor is a communication from heaven":

> A metaphor is *what happens* when one *looks in a certain way*, just as a sneeze is what happens when one looks at the sun.
>
> In what way?—You can feel it. One day, perhaps one will be able to *say* it precisely.
>
> Do this and do that—and behold all the metaphors in the world.

Did such a prospect attract Valéry as poet? The entry is sketched in wistful modes and, most probably, with ironies. Any answer depends on how one understands the conflict between Valéry's passion to master his mental processes and his dependence as poet on their behavior. It depends, moreover, on what one makes of all his striving, after Valéry came back to literature from his twenty-year study of mentation. Since in the years of the return he produced his best verse, had he actually remade his mind into a tool of controlling precision? Was the observer in him at last overwhelmed by the creator?

Whatever truce he had arranged between these two drives, the peace that followed was at best uneasy, for up to the last there are rumblings of resentment against the caprices of the brain. And he seems obsessed by a need to disclaim responsibility, as though the poems bearing his authorship were not entirely his own. His remarks about "The Graveyard by the Sea" are typical. "Thus, it was by *accident*," he declares with italics, "that the form of this work was fixed [because an editor] coming to call on me, found me at one 'stage' of my *Cimetière marin* [and] he did not rest until he was allowed to read it and, having read it, until he could snatch it away." The editor took it, and that settled the matter. Hence, Valéry was able to say that the poem "*as it stands*, is *for me* the result of the *intersection* of an inner labor and a fortuitous event." (Coleridge, in another context and without recourse to the language of geometry, conveys comparable detachment about "Kubla Khan"; but who would insist here on kinship between an exemplar of Romanticism and its dedicated foe?) "Spontaneity," says Valéry in the same passage, "even when excellent or seductive, has never seemed to me sufficiently *mine*. I do not say that 'I am right,' but that that is how I am. . . . The notion of Myself is no simpler than that of Author: a further degree of consciousness opposes a new *Self* to a new *Other*."

A lifetime of maturing thought had elapsed between the foregoing statements and Valéry's early essay (1889) "On Literary Technique," yet the direction of the writer's desire is the same. The "totally new and modern conception of the poet" holds the wonder of an ideal for the writer of eighteen anticipating the almost religious bias-to-be of the scientific twentieth century. For young Valéry, the poet was "no longer the disheveled madman who writes a whole poem in the course of one feverish night; he is a cool scientist, almost an algebraist, in the service of a subtle dreamer." Much of the faith in the omnipotence of science drops away as the man grows older, yet the passion to dominate the disheveled processes remains as strong or grows more insistent. And although Valéry never succeeds to the point where he can dispense with what lies (as he says) "at the depth where treasures are always buried," he disparages inspiration at every opportunity. So he carefully explains that "our personal merit—after which we strive—consists not so much in feeling these inspirations as in seizing them, and not so much in seizing them as in examining them." Why? Because "the true value of such inspirations does not depend on the obscurity of their origin, or on the supposed depth from which we are simple enough to believe they came, or on the exquisite surprise they cause to ourselves; it depends rather on their meeting our needs, and, in the final analysis, on the conscious use we make of them. . . ."

The emphasis and insistence are typical—and so pervasive as to have led Eliot to remark that of all poets, Valéry has been the most completely conscious of what he was doing. True or not, this is the picture given us to believe—and composed by the same Valéry who elsewhere declares that "there is no theory that is not a fragment, carefully prepared, of some autobiography."

The warning will not be ignored by anyone aware of the seemingly willed complexity of Valéry's statements. For although their effect has been to put overwhelming emphasis on testing and conscious revision, on conscious judgment and analysis, they never actually deny the sources of involuntary thought. An example:

> those imperious verbal illuminations which suddenly impose a particular combination of words—as though a certain group possessed some kind of intrinsic power. . . . I nearly said: some kind of *will* to live . . . a will that can

sometimes force the mind to deviate from its plan and the poem to become quite other than what it was going to be and something one did not dream it could be.

One wishes to hear more, so attractive is the passage and also characteristic, though not of his treatments of this uncontrollable aspect of creativity, which normally bristle with deprecations. Valéry is of course compelled to acknowledge the existence of—and his dependence upon —inspiration, but he seems to take contemptuous delight in couching his admissions in nimbly subordinated clauses ("after being charmed by those divine murmurings of the inner voice") or phrases ("in the service of a subtle dreamer") or in florid irony. What posture could be more respectable, what tone more congenial, to an Age of Science? No wonder that Valéry's mind, viewed from where we stand, seems to epitomize the prevalent attitude of his era with its true-believer's faith in achieving ultimately self-conscious control. In his own way, Valéry fought as desperate and doomed a battle as the different one of his master, Mallarmé. Hence it is but occasionally that one stumbles on a total confession of his poet's dependence on involuntary thinking: "We must simply wait until what we desire appears, because that is all we can do. *We have no means of getting exactly what we wish from ourselves.*"

If the passage seems to cancel the effect of his contrary protestations, it is not unique in so doing. Yet the weight of each word bears down with enough finality to make of these sentences an emblem for "conscious artistry." But before considering this "secondary" stage of creativity, one must look at specific examples of the "first."

"We get a new song," an Eskimo poet, Orpingalik, told an ethnologist, "when the words we want to use shoot up of themselves." Orpingalik made no mention of the source other than to say that "songs are thoughts sung out with the breath when people are moved by great forces." The thoughts "are driven by a flowing force—they can wash over him like a flood, making his breath come in gasps and his heart throb." But then, he adds, something may "keep him thawed up. And it will happen that we, who always think we are small, will feel still smaller. And we will fear to use words. But it will happen that the words we need will come of themselves."

The Eskimo poet was explaining himself to a person who may have remembered similar sentences, such as: "The idea simply comes" (Eliot); "It will come if it is there and if you will let it come" (Gertrude Stein); "A poem upon Mount Meru came to me spontaneously" (Yeats).

The whole of "Cargoes" came into Masefield's head one Sunday morning "on the spur of the moment." "My ideas come as they will, I don't know how," said Mozart. Frost's "Two Look at Two" and "For Once Then Something," were "written with one stroke of the pen." Wordsworth "began ["Tintern Abbey"] upon leaving Tintern, after crossing the Wye, and concluded it just as [he] was entering Bristol in the evening. . . . Not a line of it was altered, nor any part of it written down till [he] reached Bristol." A few words "floated into my head," says Siegfried Sassoon, "as though from nowhere. . . . I picked up a pencil and wrote the words on a sheet of note-paper without sitting down. I added a second line. It was as if I were remembering rather than thinking. In this mindless, recollecting manner I wrote down 'Everyone Sang' in a few minutes." And so on and so on.

Some reports contain warnings—direct or indirect—against forcing or other interfering. "When your Daemon is in charge, do not try to think consciously. Drift, wait, and obey" (Kipling). "All truly poetic thought begins to sing by itself, unless the poet is clumsy enough to prevent it from singing" (Spire). The thing to do is "to let each impression and each germ of feeling come to completion quite in itself . . . beyond the reach of one's own understanding" (Rilke). "Conscious writing can be the death of poetry" (Marianne Moore). And so on and so on.

At times there is stress upon trance, generally when the writer has been greatly surprised by its power. But not always. Tennyson frequently experienced a kind of waking trance; his "individuality itself seemed to dissolve and fade away into boundless being." It was "not a confused state, but the clearest of the clear, the surest of the sure, the weirdest, utterly beyond words." Contemporary remarks sound more matter of fact, with concern for broader aspects. Though "The nucleus of every poem worthy of the name is rhythmically formed in the poet's mind during a trance-like suspension of his normal habits of thought" (Robert Graves), the trance-like suspension may occur in all shades of intensity. "In a light trance" (to continue with Graves) "the critical sense is not completely suspended; but there is a trance that comes so close to sleep that what is written in it can hardly be distinguished from ordinary dream-poetry; the rhymes are inaccurate, the phrasing eccentric, the texture clumsy, the syntax rudimentary, the thought connexions ruled by free association, the atmosphere charged with unexplained emotion." But the very opposite can also occur in the sleep-like state if we are to believe Coleridge's preface to "Kubla Khan."

Whatever the degree or nature of trance-like suspension, a poem is rhythmically formed in the writer's mind. The poem itself—which is to say, the language-thinking—begins as rhythm and often only as rhythm. At least two of Valéry's poems came in this wordless compulsive form:

> "Le Cimetière marin" began in me by a rhythm . . . of 10 syllables, divided into 4 and 6. . . . I had as yet no idea with which to fill out this form. Gradually a few hovering words settled in, little by little determining the subject. Another poem, "La Pythie" first appeared as an 8-syllable line whose sound came of its own accord.

"I know," declared Eliot, "that a poem, or a passage of a poem, may tend to realize itself first as a particular rhythm before it reaches expression in words, and that this rhythm may bring to birth the idea and the image." Goethe said much the same thing; Schiller speaks of a "musical mood." A documentary complement to these avowals is reported by J. Isaacs, who found in one of Shelley's notebooks an entry where the first draft of one of his finest poems consists only of a rhythmical scheme held in place by a sequence of completely meaningless syllables.

"Involuntariness" has been so marked in the foregoing discussion that the word itself seldom was called for. At some point, however, its use is essential: no other phenomenon is significantly common to all reports of creativity with their differing manifestations and personal hosts. "Involuntary" epitomizes the testimony of the philosophical positivist George Eliot and the mystic Blake; of the painter (Picasso), the composer (Mozart), the scientist (Poincaré). The novelist did her best writing when something "not herself" possessed her and made her feel "her own personality to be merely the instrument." The poet took down "from immediate dictation, 12, or sometimes 20 or 30 lines [of *Milton*] at a time, without premeditation and even against [his] will." Creativity arrives, it "simply comes." It comes in the sudden flash that gave James *The Ambassadors*, in the fleeting vision that brought Stravinsky *Le Sacre du Printemps*, in the visible dance that resolved for the half-sleeping Kekulé the atomic structure of the benzene ring. . . .

This dependence, while acceptable to some, inspires others to experiment with stratagems. Goethe (like Bertrand Russell) finally learned the futility of trying: "My counsel is to force nothing and rather to trifle and sleep away all unproductive days and hours, than on such days to compose something that will afterwards give no pleasure." Herrick entitled a poem "Not Every Day Fit for Verse." Burns observed that on the two or three times in his life when he "composed for the wish rather than the impulse," he failed, just as Frost was never able "to worry" any poem into existence. "What is one to do when thoughts cease to flow and the proper words won't come?" asked Freud; "one's productivity depends entirely on sensitive moods." Yet dependence may at times become unbearable and anything seem better than waiting. One writer puts his feet in ice water, another lies down on a couch (Heine), a third exposes his head to heat (Shelley), a fourth dresses in the robes of a monk (Balzac), a fifth makes regular use of a pint of beer (Housman), a sixth tries jazz and liquor (Hart Crane), a seventh tobacco (De la Mare), an eighth the odor of rotted apples (Schiller). Mozart finds it easier to compose after eating a good dinner, Prudhomme after abstinence. . . . These methods (if the word can be used) would have been arrived at inductively, only later becoming an act of choice, like the taking of drugs. And of the latter, nothing need be said, so renowned is its use among artists. Yet I have heard of few well-known works other than Henri Michaux's poems and drawings which were actually created while drugs were controlling the mind. On the other hand, Utrillo is reported to have painted some of his best landscapes while in a perpetual alcoholic haze; the more he drank, the greater his productivity.

Roughly comparable in outcome is auto-suggestion according to some who have used it with effect. Nowadays the subject cannot even be mentioned without citing Rimbaud and his "Alchemy of the Word":

> Poetic old-fashionedness figured largely in my alchemy of the word.
>
> I grew accustomed to pure hallucination: I saw quite frankly a mosque in place of a factory, a school of drummers made up of angels, carriages on roads in the sky, a parlor at the bottom of the lake; monsters, mysteries. The title of a vaudeville conjured up horrors before me.
>
> Then I explained my magic sophisms with the hallucination of words!

Sometime later he remarked to his sister: "I would have become crazy and besides . . . it was bad." The Surrealists, on the contrary, saw nothing wrong with auto-suggestion, whatever the form. And I see nothing essentially different from their behavior in the kind of self-preparation undertaken by Valéry, who used to rise very early indeed: "Sometimes I find myself (at dawn) in a state of intellectual [mental] availability and general preparation. Like a hunter ready to pursue the first prey that comes along. . . . Delectable sensation of being ready. . . ."

"RE-VISION" AND "CONSCIOUS ARTISTRY"

If at the outset of this book I had not forsworn psychoanalytic language, at this point I should probably be quoting Ernst Kris where he talks of the "driving of the unconscious toward consciousness [which] is experienced as an intrusion from without." But I should also be adding the statement from John Locke that defines consciousness simply as "the perception of what passes in a man's own mind." Locke's formulation still serves so long as one realizes what it is that can pass and usually does pass in a man's own mind. The what is not limited to thoughts he intended to think or chooses or wishes to follow. On the contrary, it includes—in addition to the thoughts he attends to—many other kinds of thinking which flow into his perception uninvited by his will. To put it concretely, one can sit down with the intention, the hope, and the wish to complete an unfinished poem and before long perceive that what passes in the mind are ideas that "simply come" interspersed with other ideas drawn out of notes, books, and other premeditation. And that all these various kinds of thought will keep flowing in and out intermittently. As a consequence, one discovers as he sees what he is doing that the process by which a poem is revised comprehends vastly more than is generally conveyed by the curious term "conscious artistry."

The quotation marks are essential. Even a makeshift—such as "unconscious↔conscious artistry"—is not adequate. As Graves remarks in "A Poet's Investigation of Science":

> Objective recognition of the poem as an entity as a rule induces a lighter trance, during which the poet realizes more fully the implications of his lines and sharpens them . . . (granted the truthfulness of the original draft, and the integrity of the secondary elaboration).

Rather than soberly controlled deliberateness, "conscious artistry" denotes a state of heightened feeling during which the writer concentrates on his poem as it changes toward enhanced self-expression. The fact that it changes while the writer perceives what passes in his own mind tells nothing of who or of what does the changing. But this question cannot be asked without first considering its context.

All poems, before they are released to the world, including those written whole at one stroke, are subjected to "conscious artistry"; whether everything or nothing be altered from the original, the work is given "objective recognition as an entity." It is tested by the author and, if found wanting, changes may be made—to be supplanted by yet other changes including, occasionally, the very words that at first had seemed wrong. Testing-and-altering may be completed in time or may continue indefinitely without ever bringing the wanted satisfaction. The poem may be abandoned, or part of it kept as a fragment, or the whole reluctantly acknowledged at some later moment as the best that might ever be achieved. *The outcome of "conscious artistry" is no more controllable than that of the trance that created the draft.*

Secondly, the poet who at one time writes original drafts in final form may at another write original drafts that come to demand innumerable re-visions. Blake, who said about one of his Prophetic Books: "I may praise it, since I dare not pretend to be any other than the Secretary; the Authors are in Eternity," showed a meticulous capacity—in the poems preserved in rough draft—for making alteration upon alteration, rearrangement after rearrangement, deletions, additions, and inversions. Of the 396 poems in the final *Leaves of Grass*, more than nine-tenths had been subjected to some sort of re-vision ("The Prayer of Columbus" to almost twenty). Moreover, certain lines that now ring for the reader with the inevitable sound of inspiration were not given at their first dictation in final form. The "Ode to a Nightingale" originally began: "My Heart aches and a painful numbness falls." "Out of the cradle endlessly rocking" was "Out of the rock'd cradle" (in both the 1860 and 1867 editions). . . .

If one must say of "conscious artistry"—as of the creative process as a whole—that it differs from poet to poet and from poem to poem, a few examples can readily show why. According to Symonds' *Shelley*, Trelawney found the poet alone in a wood near Pisa, holding in his hand a manuscript of one of his lyrics:

> a frightful scrawl, words smeared out with his fingers, and one upon another, over and over in tiers, and all run together. . . . On my observing this to him, he answered, "When my brain gets heated with a thought, it soon boils, and throws off images and words faster than I can skim them off. In the morning when cooled down, out of the rude sketch, as you justly call it, I shall attempt a drawing."

Rafael Alberti, at the period of composing *Sobre los ángeles*, gradually withdrew from friends, coffee-talk, the city he lived in:

A "guest of the clouds," I fell to scribbling in the dark without thinking to turn on a light, all hours of the night, with unwonted automatism, febrile and tremulous, in spontaneous bursts, one poem covering the other in a script often impossible to decipher in broad daylight. . . . Rhythms exploded in slivers and splinters, angels ascended in sparks, in pillars of smoke, spouts of embers and ashes, clouds of aerial dust. Yet the burden was never obscure; even the most confused and nebulous songs found a serpentine life and took shape like a snake in the flames.

The opening lines of "Oenone" as printed in 1833 had apparently satisfied Tennyson:

There is a dale in Ida, lovelier
Than any in old Ionia, beautiful
With emerald slopes of sunny sward, that lean
Above the loud glenriver, which hath worn
A path through steepdown granite walls below
Mantled with flowering tendriltwine . . .

Nine years later, however, he republished them as follows:

There lies a vale in Ida, lovelier
Than all the valleys of Ionian hills.
The swimming vapour slopes athwart the glen,
Puts forth an arm, and creeps from pine to pine,
And loiters, slowly drawn. On either hand
The lawns and meadow-ledges midway down
Hang rich in flowers, and far below them roars
The long brook falling thro' the clov'n ravine
In cataract after cataract to the sea . . .

Re-vision has at times added an entire passage long after a poem had been published as complete. Five years went by before Allen Tate made the wind-leaves refrain part of his "Ode to the Confederate Dead," eight years before Wordsworth inserted a second stanza into the 1807 printed version of "The Daffodils" ("Continuous as the stars that shine . . .").

To take a quite different example. Three years before his death, while conversing with Frost about "A Minor Bird," I happened to ask when he had revised the final couplet. It had never been different, he assured me; it was always

And of course there must be something wrong
In wanting to silence any song.

Having by chance saved the tear-sheet from a 1925 issue of the students' magazine of the University of Michigan, where Frost had been in residence, I was able to show him the earlier version:

And I hold that there must be something wrong
In ever wanting to silence song.

Frost shook his head, wondering. He could willingly forget other revisions: " 'Birches' was two fragments soldered together so long ago I have forgotten where the joint is." Here, however, was something else; for although any alterations in some degree reflect the life of a writer's mind, certain ones among them reveal the shift in direction of his total vision.

I entitle this section of the chapter "Re-vision," with a hyphen that might have been placed there by Bryant, who spoke of the poet's need "to summon back the original glow." Perhaps if the word were taken with due stress on the prefix, writers would not at times feel constrained to fight off confusions:

There's no way to revise a poem [said John Crowe Ransom] . . . without taking the very same situation, shutting our eyes, and submitting it again to the imagination to see what's there: To see if better little aspects, little angles, of that experience won't turn up. It's hopeless if you go out into the woods, say, and say well, I'll rewrite this poem. You sit down and ponder but the thing won't come back, and you don't know what you're looking for, really.

Ransom's spontaneous answer to a question, together with Graves's more studied statement, should be enough to lay the ghosts that conceal the actualities of "conscious artistry." But they live on, especially in the bland superstition that creativity requires two qualitatively different stages, the second one practically dominated by the will.

Except for those fortunate works composed in final form at one stroke, every poem is a draft demanding two types of action: (1) creating pieces and entireties of language to replace or to add; (2) judging, choosing from the existing "givens." That both actions also may occur during the initial session of composing is unmistakably evident in any number of original drafts. We ask, then, whether any qualitative differences result from the differences in their times of occurrence. One answer appears in the statement of Graves that (the subsequent) "objective recognition of the poem as an entity as a rule induces a lighter trance, during which the poet realizes more fully the implications of his lines." He is, at least at the start of a session of re-vision, not oblivious of his surroundings: he is alert to perceive what passes in his own mind. Yet the moment he gets back into the poem, he will again be suffused by the "original glow"; though the trance be lighter, it will still take charge of his mind.

In the course of reconstituted vision, how does he create what is needed? The "most objective" poet ought to supply the "least subjective" answer—Valéry, whose own poems, as he declared, were composed of both lines that he was given and lines that he had to make. How was he able to make what had not been given? After typical digressions, he comes to the point (my italics):

> When we think we have completed a certain thought, we never feel sure that we could come back to it without either improving or spoiling what we had finished. It is in this that the life of the mind is divided against itself as soon as it sets to work. Every work requires acts of will (although it always includes a number of components in which what we call the *will* has no part). But when our will, our expressed power, tries to turn upon the mind itself and make it obey, the result is always a simple arrest, the maintenance or perhaps the renewal of certain conditions.
>
> In fact, we can act directly only upon the freedom of the mind's processes. We can lessen the degree of that freedom, but as for the rest, I mean as for the changes and substitutions still possible under our constraint, *we must simply wait until what we desire appears, because that is all we can do.*

His master, Mallarmé, had said much the same thing more briefly, and if literary history is dependable, no one devoted more time or zeal to "conscious artistry." To quote Robert Greer Cohn, who quotes Mallarmé's key phrase:

> Like an over-eager huntsman, the greedy grasp of the will could only frighten the delicate prey, get in the way; the best chance of success was to gently stalk and lie in wait, "céder l'initiative aux mots."

To yield the initiative to the words—what better definition of involuntary language-thinking in obtaining what is needed in re-vision. Might it also play a part in the other act—in the judging, choosing from existing givens? The participles point to a slow, cold process epitomized by the word *analysis*. But the direction misleads. Analytic thought can determine what the words, whatever their syntax, are likely to say to a reader; it can signal the need for change—and that is all. Analysis takes things apart. To judge and to choose calls for more than a talent for dissecting.

What is required? Jacques Hadamard, in *The Psychology of Invention in the Mathematical Field,* approaches the subject with essentially the same assumption I stated a few pages back: that every composition demands two types of action: creating and choosing. The key question —it applies equally to scientist and poet—consists in asking *How* such choice *can* be made? Hadamard, like other investigators, leans heavily on the analyses of Poincaré in the celebrated essay on "Mathematical Creation":

> How can such choice be made? The rules which must guide it "are extremely fine and delicate. It is almost impossible to state them precisely; they are felt rather than formulated. . . . The privileged unconscious phenomena [the givens that are chosen] are those which, directly or indirectly, affect most profoundly our emotional sensibility. It may be surprising to see emotional sensibility invoked à propos of mathematical demonstrations which, it would seem, can interest only the intellect."

But in fact it is not surprising in the least, says Hadamard, adding:

> That an affective element is an essential part in every discovery or invention is only too evident, and has been insisted upon by several thinkers. . . . But with Poincaré, we see something else, the intervention of the sense of beauty playing its part as an indispensable *means.*

Choice is "imperatively governed" by the sense of beauty.

If neither mathematician attempts to define the components ("the feeling of mathematical beauty, of the harmony of numbers and forms, of geometric elegance"), it is obviously because (as Poincaré emphasizes) there is more to this "true esthetic feeling that all real mathematicians know than [can be] formulated"—just as there is more to its analogue in poetry than can be analyzed. In both fields (to keep to the words of creative scientists and poets), the governing criteria are felt; they cannot be stated; they are known by the results they bring. Which at once calls to mind Frost's remark: "If the sound is right the sense will take care of itself." And Valéry's refinement of the statement: "An intimate alliance of sound and sense, which is the essential characteristic of poetic expression, cannot be achieved except at the expense of something—which is none other than the thought"; "a true poet will nearly always sacrifice [thought] to form (which, with its organic necessities, is, after all, the end and the act itself)." Choice, to sum up, is determined by "emotional sensibility," by "esthetic criteria": *by responses that make themselves known*, that "govern imperatively." We can go no further—nor need we, having learned, as Valéry elsewhere declares, that "direct volition is useless." . . .

If poetry does not come as naturally as leaves to a tree it had better not come at all, said a poet (Keats) whose worksheets are a monument of "conscious artistry." Anyone for whom this still holds the slightest contradiction is unlikely ever to understand the creative process.

COMMON AND OTHER KINDS OF SENSE

To understand the ways by which poetry speaks, the brain has to wrench itself out of the grooves it has been using throughout the last 2,000 years. It faces the troubling necessity of trying to realize how it can think when it is free to draw on all its capacities, which is to say that poetry's universe has room for all that is possible for the mind to think. Hence, in place of two reconciled contradictions, for example, we may expect to find in a poem together with the one type of thought called common sense every other that may be called noncommon (whether nameable or not). . . . In a word, pluralism in modes of thought, a number of which any poem might contain and the reader accept quite naturally. . . .

METAPHOR: NARROW AND BROAD

[Moreover,] it is easier to identify the presence of poetry than any force or quality responsible for bringing it about. Nothing is gained, for example, by referring to poetry as *emotive* discourse when "all mental phenomena are modes of feeling" (Suzanne Langer); or as *alogical* when rational utterances abound in poetry. Most identifications of this kind fall down because they rise from shaky dichotomies which turn out to be contrasts of degree, and of doubtful validity.

At a certain point—upon having reached completion—a work of art automatically takes on attributes peculiar to any self-sustaining entity. Everything within its "closed system" intensifies for the perceiver— hue, shape, pattern in a picture; the mere fact of their being framed in for attention endows them with force and significance. Equally in a poem: whatever powers the words possessed unconfined are heightened by the concentrating pressure of the frame. Equally obvious is another enlarging effect. "A word in isolation," to use L. B. Salomon's phrasing, "has only the potential meanings codified in a dictionary, but it takes only a little context to start it vibrating with overtones no lexicographer would venture to divine." Mallarmé, thinking of the ideal movement of words within a poem, hoped that his own would "light up by mutual reflection." But all words in all poems reach out in all directions, influencing everything around them, both near and distant. Their order alone compels them to mean in a special way, their uniqueness acting selectively. The position that each word holds in relation to the others causes parts of its content to be magnified and other parts diminished. Some of the meanings recede as others come to the fore, stirring in the mind of the reader a commingling of overtones that no analyst could venture to divine with anything approaching comprehensiveness.

Full fathom five thy father lies

begins the "Sea Dirge" from *The Tempest.* If it were humanly possible (as it is not) to deafen your ears to everything but the bare denotation, you might come away with a straightforward piece of fact. True, the overtones vibrate incessantly, every word "acts up," yet the thought conveyed when abstracted from the line is very ordinary. What immediately follows, however:

Of his bones are coral made

is part fact, part fancy. And line 3 makes anything but common sense:

Those are pearls that were his eyes

Yet the three lines that follow are defensibly rational, including the bias of the last:

Nothing of him that doth fade
But doth suffer a sea-change
Into something rich and strange

And then the closing lines swing off in yet another direction:

Sea-nymphs hourly ring his knell:
Hark! now I hear them—
Ding, dong, bell.

Every line of the tiny poem is charged with overtones. Even the "rational" first and fifth vibrate with more than can be heard in the "purely" informative fragment from *Little Gidding* when read without context:

> There are three conditions which often look alike
> Yet differ completely . . .

But I have assumed the ears to have been theoretically deafened to everything but denotation; and Shakespeare's dirge exemplifies with simplicity some of the complex ways by which a poem quite naturally flows out of one kind of sense and into another and yet another, and the effortless ease with which a reader moves out of one mode of thought into another and so on. Advance preparation would be the last thing needed by a mind that can "participate," that can respond upon the freedom of all its processes. *La Pensée sauvage*—the mind in its untamed state—is, as Lévi-Strauss discovered, at once the mind of the primitive and of the civilized. If it has evolved, it has been largely in learning habits for diminished response when the codes of the culture demand it. With a poem the fullness of the mind's capacities can come instantly into play because they are always there, and always ready.

Ordinary mixed with extraordinary, common with uncommon sense —Joseph Jastrow said years ago that "some thinking and some dreaming enter into every mental procedure." He said nothing about tension created by opposites for the good reason that these two are not opposites but dissimilars. Norman Mackenzie's point—that we think in a great variety of modes—bears repeating. Poetry's universe reflects this great variety: a poem is made of a number of things . . . which somehow hold together. What keeps them from tumbling apart? Obviously the question cannot be handled without knowing what the pieces consist of. Words? Clusters of words? The linguistic unit of a poem, the irreducible component, may be as small as "Palmes!" in Mallarmé's "Don du Poème" and larger than "The lights in the fishing boats at anchor" (Stevens) and "I will show you fear in a handful of dust" (Eliot). In each instance the essential effect is an indivisible image, regardless of origin as extraordinary or ordinary utterance. Such is at least their impact as isolated entities, in contrast to their miraculously magnified aliveness the instant they vibrate from within the poem. Once restored to their native context, they reach out in every direction, exerting on one another a force whose effect is to intimate complexities of resemblance. As certain parts of each recede and others come forward, new entities begin to emerge very much as new relationships emerge in a metaphor.

Hence when I now use the last term for describing the basic force or quality that holds a poem together, I ask that it be taken in its broadest possible conception. Which is to say, without regard for technical terminologies. Thus both "My luve is like a red, red rose" and "My luve is a red rose" are metaphors though the first is defined as a simile. For my purposes it makes no difference that Traherne's metaphor "Boys and girls tumbling in the street, and playing, were moving jewels" becomes a simile when "like" is inserted before the last verb. Whether a metaphor be called a simile-compressed, or a simile a metaphor-with-a-preface, every such figure of speech results in an image, a verbal copy, a likeness, a picture which stimulates more than the "organs" of sight:

> And many a rose-carnation feeds
> With summer spice the humming air   [Tennyson]
> The unplumb'd salt, estranging sea   [Arnold]
> The slow smokeless burning of decay   [Frost]
> His helmet now shall make a hive for bees   [Peele]

or the last two lines of Ungaretti's elegy which (in English) evoke the "Wild, dogged, buzzing / Roar of a naked sun." A single verb can at times have the force of a file of adjectives: Robinson's Richard Cory "Glittered when he walked," Yeats's rough beast "Slouches toward Bethlehem to be born." Also a single noun: Herrick indites the "liquefaction" of Julia's clothes.

Such images, with their seemingly unalterable rightness, exemplify Aristotle's observation that "a good metaphor implies an intuitive perception of the similarity in dissimilars." No better statement has ever been made despite all attempted improvements: that a metaphor (for example) is a comparison for presenting resemblances or differences; an analogy for stressing attributes or resemblances; a juxtaposition of hitherto separate elements; that it is tension; fusion; and so on. Some of these definitions include not only intuitive perceptions but commonplace comparisons and analogies of everyday discourse. A speaker joins two familiar elements so as to make one of them more emphatic or certain ("then you come to a hairpin curve"; "the next thing you will do will be something like this: . . ."). In general these comparisons or illustrations, with their practical purpose, add nothing that is striking or new. Essentially visual aids to understanding, once used they can promptly be forgotten—unlike an imaginative metaphor, which tends to cling on, whose fused elements sternly resist separation. Writers quite naturally emphasize the inexplicable, organic, the spontaneous aspects. The poetic metaphor is "a powerful image, new for the mind, [produced] by bringing together without comparison two distant realities whose relationships (*rapports*) have been grasped by the mind alone" (Pierre Reverdy). A poetic metaphor is "the use of material images to suggest immaterial relationships" (Ernest Fenellosa). It is "the expression of a complex idea, not by analysis, nor by direct statement, but by a sudden perception of an objective relation" (Herbert Read).

That some metaphors are poetic whereas others are not, no one questions. Function in itself, however, cannot make the distinction, relevant though it sometimes is—for example, to Augustan verse, with its abundance of low-keyed figures that clarify and compare; point up a moral or a satire; describe, contemplate, reason, embellish, explain. Dante also makes wide use of low-keyed figures which also clarify and compare. The fifteenth canto of *Inferno* has a well-known example:

> Already we had got so far from the wood that I should not have seen where it was if I had turned backward, when we met a troop of souls who were coming alongside the bank, and each looked at us as men look at one another under a new moon at dusk, and they puckered their brows on us like an old tailor on the eye of his needle.

After experiencing this passage even through literal translation, a reader will find it difficult to visualize this crowd except as peering in the dim light, each member knitting his brows "like an old tailor on the eye of his needle." The metaphor (technically an extended simile) has disclosed a sudden perception of a strong objective relationship. The crowd has become transformed by the image. It is no longer a crowd but a particular crowd marked by and bearing the tailor's presence.

A different kind of extended comparison appears in Canto 5 (the frequently cited Paolo and Francesca passage) which introduces the shades of the carnal sinners whirled ceaselessly about in tormenting winds. Lines 46–50 tell what the speaker experienced when he beheld them:

> And as the cranes go chanting their lays, making of themselves a long line in the air, so I saw approach with long-drawn wailings shades borne on these battling winds.

The picture of the shades wailing while being borne on the battling winds that torment them is so insistent as to push the image of the cranes to the background. The cranes have not transformed the shades as the peering tailor transformed the crowd. The cranes look out from the background, but they are there and they will not leave the mind of the reader who feels them as disturbing presences which are now no longer separable from the picture of suffering. The joyous sight of the birds singing as they curve through the serenity of the heavens has become part of the grief of the shades. The torment and terror magnify as the image of suffering bears down against the image of bliss. The one can no longer be experienced apart from the other.

It is the relationship between the elements in a metaphor that over-whelms any fact of rhetoric or function. Both passages from Dante are comparisons in structure, but they do not act for the purpose of com-paring or clarifying. Whether the elements within them press forward or remain in background, they have fused into a viable totality that no longer can be sundered.

The last quatrain of Shakespeare's sonnet 29 closes on a poetic meta-phor of another structural kind:

When in disgrace with fortune and men's eyes
I all alone beweep my outcast state,
And trouble deaf heaven with my bootless cries,
And look upon myself, and curse my fate:

Wishing me like to one more rich in hope,
Featur'd like him, like him with friends possess'd,
Desiring this man's art, and that man's scope,
With what I most enjoy contented least:

Yet in these thoughts myself almost despising,
Haply I think on thee,—and then my state,
Like to the lark at break of day arising
From sullen earth, sings hymns at heaven's gate . . .

The final figure, a small poem in itself, sweeps up with suddenness all that preceded. The speaker's "state" is no longer compared with that of other people, as has been done up to this point; it *becomes* the lark singing hymns at the gate of heaven. "Like" loses its force in the actualization of the image of soaring. The elements blend together in the new con-fusion that names a feeling which cannot be named by other means.

Ordinary, unaffective discourse never calls for language of this kind. Low-keyed arrangements of words suffice. Hence the bald impropriety of imaginative figures of speech in practical situations, for example. Only certain specified modes are acceptable by agreement too clear to need stating, and if someone breaks the rules, communication wavers or halts. Each plane of discourse is its own pattern of expectation, many of which demand only rational utterance. Hence no one is prepared to hear in a commonplace conversation, a newspaper account, or a lecture on politics that the earth now lies "all Danaë to the stars" or anything remotely like it. A nonpoetic figure, however, can be taken in stride, even a farfetched comparison, explanation, or illustration. It will not "fly in the face of reason" as any poetic metaphor by its nature must.

For the elements in the newly perceived objective relation both retain and surrender their integrity. In Wordsworth's "The sea that bares her bosom to the moon," the primary term "sea" evokes the total variety of the meanings it can bring to the reader as does also the second term "that bares her bosom to the moon." At the same time, certain members of these varieties come forward while others recede. Those that come forward prevail to establish the fusion of resemblance; the others establish disparities and, though subordinate in effect on the mind, they also remain there. This amounts to saying that while the reader is affected by the likenesses embodied in the metaphor, the disparities also act within his response.

For I. A. Richards, the peculiar power of a poetic metaphor derives from both kinds of verbal content. Citing "What should such fellows as I do crawling between earth and heaven," he says,

> When Hamlet uses the word *crawling* its force comes not only from whatever resemblances to vermin it brings in but at least equally from the differences that resist and control influences of their resemblances. The implication there is that man should not so crawl.

Difference of this kind is simply the obverse of the coin of resemblance: a negative asserting of likeness. It is not the kind that can make poetic metaphors fly in the face of reason. Wordsworth's line, to be sure, will not make a reader stop with questions of other meanings of sea—becalmed to a level flatness, tossing with breakers that shoot up in angular waves, and so on. Nor will Eliot's fusion of an abstraction with a concrete object—"I will show you fear in a handful of dust"— make him ask which dust is referred to—pollen? house dust? a pile sweeping over a road? But, as Richards adds, "In general, there are very few metaphors in which disparities between tenor and vehicle [primary and secondary terms] are not as much operative as the similarities." Quantitative questions aside, in a great many poetic metaphors, disparity exerts a powerful counterpull away from resemblance.

I have cited one instance in passing without looking at this aspect: Tennyson's remarkable line with the figure of Danaë, the beautiful daughter of a king of Argos who had been told by the oracle that she would bear him a son who would kill him. The king imprisoned her in an underground bronze chamber watched over by guards. Its roof remained open to provide her with light and air. Zeus visited her in a shower of gold, embraced her, and in time she gave birth to a son. I have never heard of anyone familiar with the myth who failed to be moved by "Now lies the earth all Danaë to the stars," and yet there is something incongruous in the womanly figure of earth as a virginal young girl, not to mention the conflict between the image of the underground enclosure in the myth and the infinite expanse of earth under the sky. The reader's mind, however, draws out of a metaphor as little or as much of the disparity as the objective relation demands, and without any straining. For the mind when free to respond cannot help doing two things to whatever confronts it: it connects and it animates. It joins to the object or event or idea, other objects or events or ideas out of all it possesses. It projects on whatever it beholds traits of aliveness analogous to its own and to the organism it is part of. These natural drives do not operate in a void but at a particular time, in a particular place, and under the influence of a particular context of beholding. The courses they take are thus directed by the force of their surroundings into identifications of likeness, unification. The verbal contents of the metaphor that might logically destroy the objective relation simply fall into place.

If this did not happen quite naturally and without strain on the mind, any number of the mixed metaphors found in poetry would fail. What could analytic reason alone make of Milton's

> blind mouths
> That scarce themselves know how to hold a sheep-hook.

How could it, by its widest standards, accept the figure, even when furnished with the plain meanings of the references—to the clergy, corruption, the cleric as pastor-shepherd, and so on? Or the couplet from Addison:

I bridle in my struggling muse with pain
That longs to launch into a nobler strain.

"Bridle" will not easily combine with "launch," even after logic adduces the necessary creature implied by the second word. Or another kind of figure from Shakespeare which occurs very often, especially in the later plays:

Was the hope drunk
Wherein you dress'd yourself? hath it slept since
And wakes it now, to look so green and pale
At what it did so freely?

If the mind that responds to a poetic metaphor had to go through the logical steps of visualizing the terms, Shakespeare's

O how can summer's honey breath hold out
Against the wreckful siege of battering days

would be rejected as hopelessly mixed. No amount of analytic gymnastics can put it in order. When, as Wellek and Warren admit, "one tries to fit together neatly in one image the battering siege and the breath, one gets jammed up. The figurative movement is rapid and hence elliptical." Perhaps; yet this misses the question. For if the pieces actually are there, it should be possible to fit them together—as of course the mind of the reader, acting upon not logic but the freedom of all its processes, can do. Acting upon a restriction—and with a process that does not think in the mode of thought that thinks in this figure—it fails. As Marlowe's "Was this the face that launch'd a thousand ships?" would also have to fail—if ordinary logic prevailed in the response to poetry.

Ellipsis pertains not to the mixed but to the telescoped metaphor. Here the tenor and vehicle together do not offer the reader's mind the process of objective relating that took place in the writer's. And when the reader is unable to imagine the intervening omissions, someone else will have to do it for him. So Hart Crane, in response to the questions of the editor of *Poetry*, filled in the ellipses that had mystified her in his lyric "At Melville's Tomb":

"The dice of drowned men's bones he saw bequeath
An embassy"

in the first place, by being ground (in this connection only, of course) in little cubes from the bones of drowned men by the action of the sea, and are finally thrown up on the sand, having "numbers" but no identification.

These being the bones of dead men who never completed their voyage, it seems legitimate to refer to them as the only surviving evidence of certain messages undelivered, mute evidence of certain things, experiences that the dead mariners might have had to deliver. Dice as a symbol of chance and circumstance is also implied [etc.]

A good many totally untelescoped metaphors, however, can also contain ellipses, but of another kind, which reader (and writer) may forever remain unaware of. In the opening of Shakespeare's sonnet 77:

That time of year thou mayst in me behold
When yellow leaves, or none, or few, do hang
Upon those boughs which shake against the cold,
Bare ruin'd choirs where late the sweet birds sang.

The quatrain, one of the finest in the language, has been praised as much for its imagery and sound as for the way by which the "season" is named by three different images of leaves and boughs, which enlarge into the memorable fourth line. Explanation would seem preposterous. Nevertheless, as Press points out:

"Bare ruin'd choirs where late the sweet birds sang" takes on a richer poignancy when we reflect that the England of [Shakespeare's] day was strewn with the wrecks of abbeys and monasteries, their inhabitants martyred, or comfortably ensconced in fat livings, their altars desolated, their music silenced.

All that a reader possesses in his mind is, of course, unknowable; hence a poet cannot tell what will happen there when the lines as he has to write them are given unglossed. For example in a poem on the imagined life of Mallarmé (see below, p. 251):

Even flesh can be burned
To the whitenesses of a song.

One of the terms, "whitenesses," calls up an entire aspect of Mallarmé's writings which are themselves metaphors. The lines will bring something to a reader unaware of all that is condensed in the "whitenesses" here combined with "burned" and "song," but he will not experience what a reader familiar with these referents in the career of Mallarmé will be able to hear or see.

Nevertheless, it is everything that a word can call up in a reader that finally determines for him the meanings of individual words in themselves and in relation to the others. I say "can" call up because the meanings he possesses before entering into the poem are fated to undergo some changes and enlargement developed by the suggestions of context. As he participates in the poem, he can respond with all his capacities: to what the words evoke and express as both rational and emotive utterances, since they can never be wholly one or the other in a discourse which arises from and draws upon the freedom of the mind's processes. Changed and enlarged signification results inevitably from the ways by which the presences bodied forth become known. But not exclusively in a poem and not exclusively to a reader of poetry. A person who reads none at all participates in a related way whenever he dreams.

CONDENSATION (VERDICHTUNG)

Frederick Clarke Prescott, a literary scholar, first published his thoughts on this subject in 1912 in the *Journal of Abnormal Psychology*, to expand it ten years later as part of his comprehensive work on *The Poetic Mind*. Basing his study on Freud's description of "dream work," he pointed to similarities in the ways by which the language in poetry and the pictures in dream condense. Both are "overdetermined," that is, overloaded with meanings, with a variety of references which embody meanings too elusive to identify and ultimately impossible to talk about clearly. If dreams tend to condense into a single picture a multiplicity of references *ignoring the limitations imposed by the demands of logic,* poetry tends to do the same thing. (The astonishing extent to which it can do so is apparent in the sources J. L. Lowes tracked down in *The Road to Xanadu.*) The italicized phrase of Freud's is the ground of the relation: both poem and dream condense by processes wholly alien to analytic thought.

Freud's (German) word for condensation, Prescott carefully remarked, "encloses" the word for poetry. The French psychoanalyst Jacques Lacan, however, goes further:

The *Verdichtung*, or condensation, is the structure of the superimposition of signifiers, which is the field of metaphor, and its very name, condensing in itself the word *Dichtung* [poetry], shows how the process is connatural with the mechanism of poetry to the point that it actually envelops its traditional function.

Prescott illustrates the principle of condensation with a line from the "Eve of St. Agnes." The figure is technically ordinary enough (neither telescoped nor mixed), yet, as he says, it has probably given critics as much trouble as any other in the work of Keats. It represents Madeline, in "her soft and chilly nest," as "Clasp'd like a missal where swart paynims pray." Leigh Hunt explains it as "Clasp'd like a missal in a land of pagans,—that is to say, where Christian prayer books must not be seen, and are, therefore, doubly cherished for the danger." Another critic, calling it wrong to make "clasp'd" mean "clasp'd to the bosom," claims the true meaning to be "fastened with a clasp." Another: "Clasp'd missal may be allowed to suggest holiness which the prayers of swart paynims neglect." Still another: "Missal, a prayer book bearing upon its margin pictures of converted heathen in the act of prayer." Finally: Jules Jusserand: "A string of beautiful words, suggesting, at most, a meaning rather than having any."

> I should think [writes Prescott] most if not all of the puzzled annotators were right, including the last. At least the line has all the meanings that an intelligent and imaginative reader, if not a puzzled annotator, will attach to it. The precise critic will of course note that in this line Keats first wrote "shut like a missal," and that this is final as to the meaning of "clasp'd." But the matter is not quite so simple. The fact that Keats tried this line in three different ways before he settled on the text in question shows that he wrote it, as indeed he did this whole passage, with thought and care. Why, then, did he change the original "shut" to "clasp'd"? Partly perhaps because he wanted "shut" for the last line of the stanza but partly also because "shut" is here a prosaic rather than a poetic word. "Clasp'd" not only says all that "shut" would say; but secondly it goes better with "missal," to fit the mediaeval character of the piece and to "suggest holiness"; and thirdly it admits the very meaning of "held closely and tenderly," which Leigh Hunt was too much of a poet to miss. "Clasp'd" was adopted by Keats, in other words, precisely because it meant two or three things instead of one, and was accordingly more suggestive and poetical.

Note the last sentence: precisely because it has condensed two or three meanings into one and is accordingly more poetically evocative. As Prescott points out in prescriptive fashion, "Whereas in true prose words should have one meaning and one meaning only, in true poetry they should have as many meanings as possible, and the more the better, as long as these are true to the images in the poet's mind."

There is more to be said of condensation, and not only in a poetic metaphor but equally in the irreducible units of a poem:

> Each image seen by the poet's imagination is a *complex of many images* and tends to involve the associations—thoughts and feelings—of each of these

constituents, so that the language of any poem recording this imagination has many roots in the poet's mind; and therefore this language and *even each word* of it has not single, but manifold meaning and implication. [my italics]

For these meanings "run on into the manifold meanings which are beyond analysis, and," he is careful to add, "the latter are the commonest." Taking the apparently simple

> We are such stuff
> As dreams are made on; and our little life
> Is rounded with a sleep.

he considers it

> useless to analyze the meaning of such lines. Dreams are surrounded by sleep; and likewise our brief life is surrounded by the greater sleep, which is constantly compared by poets to the lesser one. But is life also *rounded out* and fulfilled by this sleep? And does life go on in this seeming oblivion, as dreams may go on in what seems dreamless slumber? The expression is beyond the understanding, but it goes on sounding in the imagination. . . . The principle applies to all expressions of the imagination—to every word of poetic value in every imaginative poem.

Which is to say, to every working unit in every authentic poem.

Condensation, however, accounts for more than the dream-like reasoning-reasonableness of these units within their context. It points to their emotional power. It explains why analytic thought cannot go far in tracking down their meanings—"one has only to listen to poetry to hear a true polyphony emerge," says Lacan. Condensation does still more. It denotes the nature and the burden of a poem as an appeal to the mind, hence also the imaginativeness in which it asks to be experienced. For the poem as a whole is a metaphor of an all-enclosing kind, condensing all the elements, large and small, that existed apart, to identify a newly enclosing relationship, one which is memorable and meaningful in the same way that individual metaphors are meaningful and, ultimately, every unit of expression within the poem: through manifold meaning, reference, and implication.

The statement is cumbersome, attempting as it does a comprehensive view of how condensation applies to all poems. For if Lacan is right, if *Verdichtung* is connatural with the processes of poetry, then it provides the master key. But each poem is a door and each door has a different lock.

Simpler statements tend to generalize at arm's length, all figurative language being metaphor in essence. There are, moreover, pithy sentences about the "purposes" served. One of the best was minted by Frost: "Poetry provides the one permissible way of saying one thing and meaning another." (As it stands it is large enough to apply to allegory and fable also.) I shall return to this sentence with a question, for at this point some other refining is in order, since I have been using "metaphor" and "image" and similar terms interchangeably and all as imaginative figures.

A comprehensive view of metaphor takes in its extra-literary range: "All nature," says Emerson, "is a metaphor of the human mind." If the maxim is valid, we should find metaphor in all expressions of the mind—and of course we do, for language is ultimately traceable to metaphor, as writers since Vico and Shelley keep discovering. One has only to break up such a word as "symbol" (*syn:* together + *ballein:* to throw) to know the physical relationship out of which they arose. For most people most words are metaphorically dead, not only etymology's transferred abstractions (often a marvel to behold) but the everyday pictures they talk with—"mouth of a river," "arm of a chair," and so on. Such metaphors are as invisible to their users as the strikingly imaginative creations of unknown Miltons. But however vibrant "going off half-cocked," "Dry up!," or "Get lost!" may reappear to an innocent eye, they do not perform as metaphors do in a poem. Tossed back and forth and never *seen*, they are lifeless coins.

The domain of images, though appropriated by psychology, spreads wider than any science could contain, even one that takes in man's entirety. As for its native extent within poetry, it is enough to nod at the "types" into which they supposedly divide, adding to the proverbial five all sorts of refinement, such as pressure, color, temperature, and reminding ourselves that synesthesia is a given within a biological universe which thinks and feels by likenesses. For a likeness is all that an image can be; it is never exact. Edith Sitwell's "The morning light creaks" implies and demands no more than does "a sweet voice" (that a reader can taste a sound).

"Every spontaneous image," a psychologist informs us, "is to some extent symbolical." By blurring distinctions, the statement clarifies, for metaphor, symbol, and image run into one another. "One cannot long discuss imagery without sliding into symbolism," says Kenneth Burke; "We shift from the image of an object to its symbolism as soon as we consider it." Why, then, separate them? The reason may seem arbitrary since "symbol" has simply come to denote something more significant than the other two because of the frequency with which it appears in a writer's work. "Strange fire," says Tate, is Poe's "leading visual symbol." "Caves," says Yeats, is a "ruling symbol" in Shelley's verse. To some readers, however, great recurrence may seem mainly an obsession which the poet was unable to resolve (the clock for Vigny, for example); to others, his fascination by a specific significance he could never seize yet continued to reach for. Thus a symbol may rule in dissimilar ways. For Baudelaire, the word "vast" often stands for the "infinity of infinite space," says Bachelard, at other times for "the highest degree of synthesis." Some writers make a great point of their symbols (Mallarmé, Bridges, Yeats). Others show no such need: the largeness is there in the presence of Moby-Dick, in the settings of Poe's stories, in the characters of the later Henry James.

Of the assertive force of a symbol, I know no plainer example than "The Idea of Order at Key West." The reader soon realizes that Stevens' girl singing by the sea is more than a metaphor, and the singing as well. The girl and the song and the sea rise up as symbols—the girl as singer-poet, the song as verse, the sea as the source, the life from which song rises.

PHASES OF TOTALITY

If poetry by its metaphorical character says one thing and means another, what composes its "body"? Luckily we can see all we need of the poem's anatomy without murdering to dissect. Its body, as we never tire of disclosing, is made of words, and each word speaks with incomparably more than the unambiguous denotation that science seeks in its terminology. But the words are not the linguistic units and a poem may contain propositions, questions, statements, exclamations, and other expressive groups which when read outside or in isolation prove very like prose. It goes without stressing that a poem may also—and commonly does—contain images, similes, metaphors, symbols, and other figurative expressions *as well as* propositions, questions, statements, exclamations, which in or out of context are unmistakably imaginative.

Not all expressions of this order appear in every poem. Not even figures are needed. Not a single figure can be found in all sixty-nine lines of Wordsworth's "We Are Seven." The only passage that might be called heightened occurs in the opening stanza:

Her hair was thick with many a curl
That clustered round her head.

But the heightening, if such it be, is followed by a dialogue so plainly textured as to exemplify what Mark Van Doren in another connection calls a "poetry of statement." Figurative language is absent from Bridges' "I love all beauteous things." Not a single metaphor can be found in a great many excellent Chinese poems; in the following, by Emperor Wu-ti, there is only one ("dust grows"):

The sound of her silk skirt has stopped.
On the marble pavement dust grows.
Her empty room is cold and still.
Fallen leaves are piled against the doors.

Longing for that lovely lady
How can I bring my aching heart to rest?

The ubiquitousness of metaphors and similes in Western verse makes them seem indispensable, yet they seldom appear in the great body of Scottish ballads. They do not appear at all in a number of recent admired poems—such as W. C. Williams' "The Red Wheelbarrow" or H. D.'s "Lethe" or Cavafy's "Waiting for the Barbarians." In Wu-ti's poem, each "picture" acts as a term of a multiple fusion, and much the same can be said of non-figurative verse in general. Each such poem is a total unification formed of smaller unifications. Through its fusions of resemblance, it identifies a relational unity, producing the effect of figures but without their presence.

Turning now from a poem's materials to their sequence, we note at once that they move in the "more than usual order" that Coleridge proclaimed and everyone echoes. And how could such arrangement of words appear otherwise alongside the predictable, step-by-step manner by which common sense logic tries to order its ideas. Even in poems that develop propositions, dis-order bristles. One might suppose, then, that some analogous principle had been found to encompass the multiplicity of alogical ways in which poetry arranges words. Nothing that has been proposed tells us more than what poems do *not* do—which we have known all along. And the only other offered truth invokes "unalterableness"!

Any hope of discovering an all-inclusive "order" evaporates in analyzing a handful of varied poems, such as Marvell's "To His Coy Mistress," Wordsworth's *Prelude*, Shelley's "Ode to the West Wind," *Hamlet, Paradise Lost*. The internal arrangement of each is as unique as the word-materials with which it emerges. The order is there, but only as an attribute projected by looking at a poem with order in mind. It is there, to be sure, but as an outcome.

Of what? Of an over-all logic that controls all elements in all poems? If so, what type of elements? Such things as, for example, in *The Ancient Mariner:* subject matter (a specific ocean voyage), theme (call it crime), sonal pattern (of recurrent meter and rime), and further meaning (implied rather than stated)? These are elements we elect to draw out of the totality embodied by the language. Does some all-inclusive logic hold it together? Do the words hold themselves together? When we look at a number of poems, we find as many subject matters, themes, sonal patterns, further meanings, and orders as there are poems—and as many logics. To see *how* differently each poem does *what* it does, one has only to look closely at a random few—one expressing a state of mind that moves from despairing confusion toward clarity and hope (Shelley's "Ode to the West Wind"), another from distress or despair to an emotional resolution (*Lycidas*), a third that proceeds by argument (Marvell's "To His Coy Mistress"), a fourth by narration (*The Ancient Mariner*), a fifth by exposition (Pope's *Essay on Man*), and so on and on. . . .

Despite, if not because of, such manifest dissimilarity, writers, critics, and readers have maintained that one all-subsuming law or logic must exist. Coleridge learned from his headmaster that "Poetry, even of the loftiest, and, seemingly, that of the wildest odes, had a logic of its own, as severe as that of science. . . ." Kant, in his study of art, had already proposed an analogy to "an organised product of nature in which every part is reciprocally purpose (end) and means." But, as Meyer H. Abrams points out, Kant's immensely influential contribution was qualified by the author himself as "merely a philosophy of as-if." It is a compelling fact that none of the assertions of the existence of an all-subsuming logic defines what it is. Its failure to be born is at least suggestive. The nearest we come to a definition is in Coleridge's remarkable description of varied characteristics:

> This power . . . reveals itself in the balance or reconciliation of opposite or discordant qualities: of sameness, with difference; of the general, with the concrete; the idea, with the image; the individual, with the representative;

the sense of novelty and freshness, with old and familiar objects; a more than usual state of emotion, with more than usual order. . . .

Readers to whom Hegel is more than a name may not instantly think of the German philosopher despite the associations (which Abrams also points out) between the "reconciliation of opposite or discordant qualities" and the Hegelian triad of thesis-antithesis-synthesis. If any association arises in the poetry-reader's mind, it will no doubt be with metaphor, "opposite or discordant" recalling Aristotle's "dissimilars."

To follow the results of this passage from Coleridge is to be taken far from the logic that Coleridge affirmed. To follow Elizabeth Sewell, for example, is to learn that the organization of language in poetry is dual in a different way. Sounds are affected in one manner, meanings in another. To be more precise, the organization of what she calls the "sound-look" of words is in the direction of order, the organization of their "reference" in the direction of disorder. These are the discordant opposites that the language of poetry expresses simultaneously. "The aim of poetry is to create from Language a closed relation system by resolution of the two forces of order and disorder . . . by utilizing each so that each may cancel the other out and a momentary equilibrium be formed." We are deep in the woods of structure, whose infinitely varied growths invite us to gaze and gaze, forgetting what brought us there. . . . And we have yet to locate *the* logic. Can it be found somewhere in a composite of all the ways in which good poems think? Perhaps. In any event, we shall never know, because all the possible "ways" cannot be flushed out of the too many good poems in the world.

We can, however, add to "condensation," discussed earlier, three other unignorable ways. Like condensation, they are familiars of the world of dream and just as alien to practical thought.

A poem can establish the significance of something merely by presenting it, and the reader, without an instant's doubting, will respond to its presence as both knowledge and feeling though nothing is argued to prove the twofold import. Presence in itself is enough, in poem as in dream. Perhaps, as Whitehead believes, "the sheer statement of what things are, may contain elements explanatory of why things are." Whatever the explanation, such assertion in the poem amounts to proof.

This happens even when accompanying words deny the presence, as in Keats's

The sedge is withered from the lake,
    And no birds sing.

The reader experiences a presence not only in the first of these lines but also in the second, for the "no" cannot stop him from feeling and knowing what the negation tries to remove. "No birds sing," however, is not the same presence as that embodied by "And birds sing." The "no" casts a darkening veil which, as it were, causes the presence to recede—to recede in brightness, not to disappear; for it remains there, fully visible, its veiled significance bodied forth by the negative naming. Such strangely affecting presence cannot be evoked except in a poem and by the poem's power to place it there while saying it is not there.

A poem can present even polar-opposite embodiments—of love-with-hate, of joy-with-sadness—and the watcher will take from them meanings not otherwise understood. As the world knows, the nightly occurrence of such presences led Freud in his study of dreams to a thesis of ambivalence. But the "inseparableness" of opposites is no recent discovery as a principle. "In the seasons of the year, in the life of plants, in the human body, and above all in civil society," Plato had remarked, "excessive action results in a violent transformation into its opposite." Shelley said somewhere that love is the reverse side of hate. At times roughly analogous terms are used by scientists for phenomena in the physical world. But uniquely for the world of the poem, in the reader's response some degree of ambivalence colors every feeling; for in that world a feeling comes forward in freedom as *whole*. One of its selves bodies forth some sense of its opposite—much as "And no birds sing" comes forth as a whole, its self with its opposing self, though not always strangely veiled.

Other characteristic ways of the imagination might perhaps be added, but this composite is inclusive enough—condensation; asserting by merely presenting; evoking while negating; ambivalence. With discursive ingenuity, one might draw out of it some definition of Poetic Logic. But what purpose could it serve? Would it add to what we know? That *the* logic is metaphorical? As much demands to be declared of everything else, however present, in any authentic poem; even of those words which if spoken outside or alone could affect us as prose. Hence a poem is not only a grand, all-encompassing image "composed" by individual images but a self-containing field of reciprocal forces in which each element is suffused with and suffuses metaphoric influence. This condition bears witness to the transformation that occurs within what is seen from outside as a framed-in universe of an extraordinary sort. It explains why the relation there among words changes as they quicken one another, and why they pulsate with interresponding, intensifying life. Only when we keep steadily in mind such simultaneously quickening forces can we be willing to characterize a poem with our inevitably static term "metaphoric totality"—and to speak again of an all-enclosing metaphor that produces a new relationship out of elements hitherto existing apart, one that is memorable and meaningful in the way that individual poetic metaphors are meaningful: by "saying one thing and meaning another." (The foregoing sentences, like our earlier ones on condensation, are cumbersome, finical; but to write down even the comprehensive little that may surely be said of a poem and to convey its indispensable at-onceness would require a book-long sentence.)

The words quoted earlier from Frost—"Poetry provides the one permissible way of saying one thing and meaning another"—has been something of a refrain in the last pages, crying out that the poem is a symbol, not more. Yet for the reader, both during and after it has said one thing while meaning another, the poem-as-a-presence remains. It has not been lost or submerged or destroyed in the meaning of the symbol. It is steadfastly there as a structure for contemplation, knowledge, pleasure, surprise: an artifact of words that stand before the eyes and sound within the ear. If one wishes to think of the two as the presence "within" that is meaning and the presence "without" that is saying, the Frost refrain enlarges into symbol-and-more. In any event, every poem will be saying one thing while meaning another thing and also *itself*.

Or, brushing aside these remarks and thinking of the presences as feeling-knowledge, we can take one kind from the meanings of the sayings and another from those of the artifact. Two inseparable presences, then, and reciprocally alive. But not forever, surely not in a reader's forever. The words of even a profoundly affecting poem may with time diminish into memory, whereas some part of their meaning will remain in the reader as an embodiment into which they change. Poetry, says MacLeish, "gives knowledge of the chaos and confusion of the world by imposing order upon it which leaves it still the chaos and confusion which it really is," yet some sense of that order may have entered the reader, leaving upon him a trace or a wound. With poems of slight emotional meaning for him, the trace may diminish and lose force. Poems of profound emotional impact, on the other hand, may so "wound" him as to make him thereafter perceive related experiences of the chaos and confusion with altered sight. The experiences evoked by the poem, thus incorporated, will if sustained as embodiment alter his living response. And the words that gave birth to this event for his mind may recede as the change they fostered emerges as the "real" poem. I can best document these statements by my own "Poetry: The Art," subtitled "In the form of an Apostrophe to Whitman" (see pp. 216–220 below). At the time of its writing I was unaware that Whitman had said: "The words of my book nothing, the drift of it every thing."

THE "INCOMPATIBLE" FORCES

Of the various actions that a poem is said to resemble, the closest is a mode of dramatized-speaking-to-some-other, involving an object, an event, a time, a place, a condition. Neither speaker nor listener plays a role. Rather the poem's presences form the characters created for self-enactment within the reader. There they spring to life as an interior drama of human feelings and values, and there the meanness or richness of the coming alive but partly depends on the poem. I mention this evident limitation not only because of the differences among what each reader possesses and is, but equally because of those within the same reader, varying as they do with mood, place, and with time as it ceaselessly widens or narrows his capacities for response. So it is no tricking up of Heraclitus to say that the same person can never step into the same poem twice. The poem is unchanged, the person is not. Yet while the poem itself remains identical, in the reader it relives as innumerably varied experiences. " 'Cap and Bells,' " Yeats said, "has always meant a great deal to me though . . . it has not always meant quite the same thing."

Though the powers inhering in an authentic poem assault and compel the well-attuned reader with manifold meanings, when you ask him to say all that they are he throws up his hands. If pressed, he may start telling how the poem makes him feel, even why; but his description soon bumbles, as it must. The facilities of discursive language can take him to a point, not beyond. The subject flies out of hand; this hand lacks the organs to contain it. Yet something remains in its grasp which suggests what has fled. The poem "still seems to be trying to express something beyond itself," as A. C. Bradley observed long ago. Its meaning seems "to expand into something boundless which is only focused in it," nor can its creator explain what it is. Goethe could not tell Eckermann what the "idea" of *Faust* was: "As if I knew, as if I myself could tell! From Heaven, through Earth, down to Hell,—

there's an explanation, if you want one; but that is not the idea, that's the development of the action." So Blake might have replied about the "idea" of his four-line "Auguries of Innocence," much also as the Greek poets whom Plato had addressed in vain. For every authentic poem, as Jacques Maritain aptly remarks, "will make present to our eyes, together with itself, something else, and still something else indefinitely, in the infinite mirrors of analogy." I take this final word in its widest implication, recalling Bacon's great remark on "the footsteps of nature" and Anaxagoras' (as quoted by Lucretius): "everything is latently involved in everything else." I take it also in the sense of Eliot's reflection on "the song of one bird" and other humble subjects, where he says that "such memories may have symbolic value, but of what we cannot tell, for they come to represent depths of feeling into which we cannot peer." We are urged to magnify our widest conception of the subtleties and ranges of the human organism's response and to accept our limitations as we search them.

From the foregoing pages and the examples we have followed, a number of observations emerge as virtual axioms. Poetry, far from being a field of discourse governed by a single aspect of the mind—far from being "emotive" or "alogical," for example—is an open area, the human mind unbounded, the only field of discourse in which thought can participate in its entirety. Poetry draws thus on the fullness of man, enveloping all partial capacities of his thought. It is as though its modes when waking and when dreaming are present with all their potentialities ready to participate in the object, the event, the ideas embodied in the words. As in the miniscule "Full Fathom Five," the mind of the reader shifts effortlessly back and forth from the most commonplace to the most exalted, from the most palpable to the most fantastic, and at intermediate levels. My analogy here to polarity is, as always, inadequate. More faithful is a picture of breadth, fullness, and not with contrasting extremes but, as I have taken pains to emphasize, a plurality of possible modes of thought existing together in harmonious, unimpeded participation. It is the miracle of the mind that when it thinks as it does in poetry—whether in creating or responding—it operates upon the freedom of all these processes, moving easefully, naturally, from one to another as it discovers the presences that mark its voyages. . . .

Do "rational" and "emotive" utterances retain any degree of "ordinariness" and "extraordinariness" when they are read *within* their contexts? To say that they do—to insist that every line within a poem is at one and the same time filled with both ordinary and extraordinary meanings—might seem to deprive poetry of its claims as "imaginative discourse." It is the narrow conception of such a term that creates the confusion; for even the most imaginative figure of speech retains, in addition to its utterly unparaphraseable meanings, many traces of ordinary signification. "Ripeness is all," "Mine, O thou lord of life, send my roots rain!," "How can we know the dancer from the dance?"— you cannot read such imaginative passages, which send out endless subtleties of evocation, without also having a sense of what they mean on the most ordinary plane of understanding. For the human creature when confronted with anything strange—and these passages are supremely strange—instantly, almost by a reflex of the organism, begins to assimilate it to the known, to his world of the familiar; to make ordinary meanings from the messages. Humankind, unable to bear much uncertainty, must relate them to what it knows.

This is not to say anything more than that both ordinary and extraordinary meanings are present in poetry simultaneously and in the same passages. If you prefer, you may say that "ordinariness" is tied to the "actual," and the "extraordinariness" to everything else. But whatever the terms for these two significations, their presence accounts for the difficulty of saying what poetry is. For if it can be said to be anything at all, poetry is a complex of seemingly incompatible forces of meaning that are nevertheless quite compatible—forces to which we respond without any concern for the fact that the poem is simultaneously both actual and non-actual, real and imaginary, that *it makes both common and uncommon sense together.* This is not to say that in the poem the two can exist on a parity. Ordinary meanings are limitable whereas we cannot even begin to define the ranges of shape, substance, suggestion, and evocation that arise from passages which evoke the worlds of the extraordinary. Moreover, I am not suggesting that the two modes of meaning in poetry can in any sense exist separately. As A. C. Bradley might have put it, any such separable aspects of a poem lie only in our analytic heads—which is equally the only place where "form" and "content," for example, might be said to exist. But just as you cannot talk of how a poem or any other work of art is formed without also talking of what is being formed, ordinary and extraordinary meaning exist as a seamless phenomenon. Finally, there is no possibility of seeing any modes of meaning as acting on the reader in any ratios of their forces. They are simply both there together forming part of the sum of the meanings experienced in any authentic poem, along with meanings of sound, of the bodily mimicry, and others, which depend on the time and the nature of the reader. One can never go far in enumerating all the forces of meaning that a good poem is. Nor need anyone try.

Complex and multiple though they are, all the types of meaning touched on in the foregoing pages nevertheless constitute only one order of human experience: the one that a human being lives as a part of the culture he has evolved, seeing himself and his experiences within the terms of this culture. All such meanings, therefore, arise out of the relationships and resemblances of feelings, ideas, objects, events embodied in the poem to those he encounters and knows in this world he has made in which he moves. There is, however, another order of meaning mediated by every authentic poem. It derives from the ways in which the poem structures language. This action draws us into areas of man's existence as a creature inhabiting the earth. [It forms the subject of part 2, subtitled "Creature-Knowledge," which consists of three chapters: "Poetry versus the Culture," "Divisiveness," and "The Seamless Web." The pages that follow present the closing words of the second chapter and selections from the third.]

EDEN

Or is it rather the fate of a creature which had been somehow impelled to teach its brain to regard its owner as an other-than-itself? At a certain time, says Loren Eiseley, ancestral man entered his own head. All that our kind has become goes back to this crucial moment, for to see oneself, to feel, to know oneself as an other is to do as much with the world. To break through the seamless web—no longer to be part of all that one senses and knows—is to enter a strangeness from which there is no return. Paradigms of the fate can be found in ancient myths which compress to a single moment long ages during which men slowly came to realize what they had "done" and lost. If the drama of Eden is more explicit about disobedience-punishment-pain than sin, no one can doubt that the latter stands for the sense of loss, uneasiness, and fear that accuses a creature stranded outside the paradise-web. Nothing is so much as hinted of the wonders he may find there, the marvels he might achieve. The tales of the race's childhood are songs of paradise lost, of homelessness, helplessness: the lament of a creature aware of his alienation from the whole of living creation.

Though the fate of Eden is also the fate of every child, countless generations would pass before men and women could perceive this fact and their helplessness before it. As Trigant Burrow makes clear in "The Strifeless Phase of Awareness," the rudiments of human mental life

lie in the organic reactions of the unborn child. At first merely vegetative, later physiological, there develops within the embryo a synthesis of function which we may call primary, organic life. Here, in this preconscious mode, is embodied a phase of development in which the organism is at one with its surrounding medium. Here primitive consciousness is in a state of perfect poise, of stable equilibrium. Here, at its biological source within the maternal envelope, this organic consciousness is so harmoniously adapted to its environment as to constitute a perfect continuum with it.

With birth, everything changes, though in the infant's earliest stirrings of consciousness, its sensation and awareness still remain subjectively identified with the mother organism. Nevertheless, with his "forcible expulsion from the paradise of peace and plenty,"

he enters a totally different world of experience. Into the original, simple, unitary, homogeneous matrix of organic consciousness there now enter those gradual deposits of extraneous experiences caused by the organism's enforced adaptation to the external world, and these experiences constitute the nuclei of adult consciousness. The child has now entered a world of stubborn solidarity and can maintain life in consistent comfort and security only on a basis of relative adaptation to outer circumstances.

It is quite needless to add to what was said earlier on the subject of "outer circumstance" as it acts upon the child, beginning with the group of surrounding creatures who form his first reality. But "relative adaptation," on the other hand, demands some attention in view of Burrow's remark that the process of adaptation is "essentially outward-tending," that it is inherently a process of "objectivation":

With increasing objectivation, this outer rapport [between the organism and the external world] is later established in respect to the organism itself. Objectivation returns upon the very self from which it set out. The self becomes its own object, and consciousness is, as it were, infolded. Being thus turned in on itself, the organism has attained a state of mental development which distinguishes the human species from the rest of the animal world—the stage, namely, of self-consciousness.

The development proceeds by slow, irreversible stages, for consciousness of the "I" is not inborn. It grows very gradually within the human mind; it is something the child has to "do"—the "I" is not a fact but an act, said Fichte; it is something he has to learn. He has to learn it if he is to survive in the world that has brought him to birth. And the more civilized this world, the greater its demand that he think of himself as "subject" and all other creatures and things as "object." That this subjective-objective dichotomy of his experience is in fact illusory —that, in Sir John Eccles' words, "every observation of the so-called objective world depends in the first instance on an experience which is just as private as the so-called subjective experiences"—cannot matter to him or to his world. For both "know" where the boundaries lie: where *continuity with* ends and *looking at* begins. In the unreflective view of our own culture, the self is a discrete unit, something we can name and define. Such naming covers more than agency; it also includes possession. Each of us *owns* a self, an "I," about whom we sometimes think, with whom we converse, for whom we plan, and so on. More often than we realize, each of us watches this self as it behaves, observer and observed. Phrases of this sort do more than describe our thinking. They testify to the concomitant divisiveness within each individual that arose as the species gradually divided itself from its creature environment, rupturing the seamless web.

One cannot grasp the significance of any development in man's mind without also considering linguistic development, ignorant though we are of how language emerged and the forces that propelled its direction. We know only that something unprecedented occurred long eons ago, during man's phyletic infancy, when he lived in a natural continuum with everything around him. As Burrow writes, the entire experience of his common perception of the surrounding objects and creatures was a sensation—a physiological aspect—of man himself. And just as sensations and impressions were experienced by all men and women, so were their instinctual drives, their interests, their motivations. All their actions and responses were physiological in nature: organic behavior, arising from their needs, and common to all members of the species. Hence man's "compactness" at this time: compactness of man and environment, of individual and kind. It is here, in this bond between man and man, in this continuity between "objective" sensations and "subjective" feelings—between man's own physiological processes and the earth—that we see the primary pattern of human awareness and consciousness: the unitary condition of the species—man in a seamless web of relationships. What set in motion the forces that brought about change is as huge a mystery as any that can be conceived. All we may hope to gain are rudimentary notions of the process that developed *within* the organism. So, with our present modes of thought that reflect its altered course, we construct a model which at least does not hinder belief. It allows us to imagine that

> Through the modification of a segment of the forebrain, man was enabled to produce (at first unconsciously and later consciously) symbols or signs in substitution for actual objects or situations. In other words, there developed the faculty of language, through which men not only responded to the same thing with the same symbol, but through which they ultimately came to *know* that they responded in a like manner to the same thing. Through an unprecedented miracle of nature, our organism contrived to take the universe of its surroundings into itself, as it were, to incorporate it in its own neural tissues. A tree or a stream became a vocal sound. It became a spoken or a written word, and a mechanism emerged that related us to our universe of external matter and energy through an entirely new system of receptivity and response. We now became related to the world of external objects and to one another through an entirely different system of neural reactions.

This step in biological evolution, this miracle of nature, opened up unimagined spheres to human behavior. One need consider only one of its numerous gifts—the economic gain in communication—to appreciate the enormities of power it brought for man to deploy. They were and still are unforeseeable, hence almost beyond any strength of restraining.

From the very outset, danger inhered in the emerging part-function. By its sheer range, efficiency, and momentum, the capacity for forming symbols tended to overwhelm other part-functions of the organism and to take control. As a result of its ever-increasing emphasis and dependence on word-sign-symbol, human behavior began to lose contact with the medium of actuality, "the good earth." In this physiological transition from action to symbols of action, Burrow continues, "the human species, unaware of what was happening, gradually lost touch also with the organic origin of the word and therefore with the organic source of its own behavior. . . . Our feeling-medium of contact with the environment and with one another was transferred to a segment of the organism—the symbolic segment, or forebrain. . . . What had been the organism's whole feeling was transformed into the *sym-*

bol of feeling." Moreover, "with the increase of symbol usage and the coincident transfer of the organism's total motivation to this linguistic system, man developed a self-reflective type of consciousness."

Viewed from where we now stand, the series of events-and-consequences seems to have driven forward with the inexorable logic of organic power. What begins as a highly advantageous part-function gradually attains over-all domination. And because of the intermediate position it holds between effectors and receptors in the bodily system, between stimuli and responses, the new symbolic-linguistic capacity finally remakes the organism's entire mode of relationship. *Continuity breaks up into divisiveness in the three crucial areas simultaneously. Man becomes alienated from the rest of living creation, from his fellow human beings, and from himself.*

Ideally all the discrete paragraphs of this chapter I have called "Divisiveness" should compose a single sentence to suggest how man's new acquisition has transformed his life. As compared with other creatures, says Ernst Cassirer,

> man lives not merely in a broader reality; he lives, so to speak, in a new *dimension* of reality. There is an unmistakable difference between organic reactions and human responses. . . . No longer in a merely physical universe, man lives in a symbolic universe. . . . No longer can man confront reality immediately; he cannot see it, as it were, face to face. Physical reality seems to recede in proportion as man's symbolic activity advances. Instead of dealing with the things themselves, man is in a sense constantly conversing with himself. He has so enveloped himself in linguistic forms, in artistic images, in mythical symbols or religious rites that he cannot see or know anything except by the interposition of this artificial medium.

Which is to say that more and more of the time, he lives in indirectness. No longer part of the seamless web of the natural order, he stands outside, thanks to what has been at least in part his own achievement —an achievement from which he cannot escape: his divisiveness.

Can he ever recapture the sense of creature at-oneness, the organic tradition in which he lived for millions of years?

The Seamless Web

Although everyone knows that humanity is only one strand in the web of creation, one can rarely speak about man's condition as a creature without eliciting defensiveness and confusion. Part of the problem grows out of language. "At-oneness," for all its plainness of statement, carries a portentous ring. "Seamlessness" is a wholly negative abstraction. Still more difficult to envisage is the "mixedness" of man's condition. Though physical reality recedes from him as his symbolic activities advance, man obviously does not live in indirectness all or even most of the time. Moreover, the innermost tendencies of his organism regularly insist on obtaining satisfaction: he is still very much a creature of earth despite all he knows of control. Indeed one of the largest mysteries in his behavior is the source of the balance he is able to maintain between his learned restraint and the needs that propel his organism.

Those needs, drives, instincts cause endless problems for the expert who would classify and define them and chart their courses. But whether they be presented as the "dominant" few (nourishment, reproduction, aggression, flight) or as more numerous "inborn behavior patterns" does not matter at all. For the experts totally ignore the organic tradition of man's biological evolution—of his drive to regain, to recover, his primary organic unity with the rest of creation: his "seamlessness," which endured through his millions of years, whose heritage is inscribed in his myths, his religions, his arts, his rituals. One is strongly tempted to explain the omission, but the reader can readily do this for himself, aware of the mind's self-protective way of "forgetting" things which might threaten its balance. Besides, at this point a more productive paradox beckons. The very capacities of the mind that were and are involved with man's divisiveness act toward fulfilling his drive toward unification. A part of the sickness itself must work toward the cure. . . .

The foregoing pages of this book have focused on the creator; the rest of the present chapter is concerned both with ourselves as participants in what the creator has made and with the creature-drive for unity instinct within us. Analogies may be difficult to find, yet it would seem that if the reproductive drive can fulfil itself when it finds release through union with another human body, this other human-creature necessity, when it finds its release through imagination's symbols, can unite us with the "body" of the world.

How is such a statement to be justified? What is there about the creative symbol that makes possible any union with the world? In all that has preceded I referred to various kinds of creative productivity, but in facing this new question I limit myself to the art I know best, which is poetry, while continuing to assume the essential nature of all creative imagining to be the same.

FUSIONS OF RESEMBLANCE

A poem is made of words as a musical composition is made of tones: words are the public materials composing the private, irreducible entities—the metaphors, similes, other figurative structures; the questions, exclamations, propositions, other statements—and the terms denoting their relationships. No single one of these expressive units is itself a *sine qua non*. If Western readers show surprise at discovering that a poem can be effective without any figures of speech, it is because they have grown used to regarding metaphors and similes as indispensable. And, of course, the metaphor is not only the commonest figure in verse; as the naming of an imaginative fusion of resemblance which has already occurred in the poet's mind, it is emblematic of the poem itself. Personifications and imaginative similes (basically varieties of metaphor) are also functions of resemblance. As for the so-called "tropes of connection—the synecdoche ("blind mouths"), the metonymy ("When I consider how my light is spent")—though technically fusions of contiguity, they are obviously also expressions of resemblance, and of a highly compressed kind.

One might expect that figure-less verse must, by contrast, be weak in impact. So narrow a notion of poetic condensation can be tested by trying to bluepencil Goethe's "Wanderers Nachtlied, II," the poem by Wu-ti quoted on page 150, H. D.'s "Lethe," Eliot's "Rhapsody on a Windy Night," or longer works such as Cavafy's "Waiting for the Barbarians," the best of the Scottish ballads, some of the *Cantos* of Pound. Structure proves as various in figure-less verse as elsewhere—as poetic logic itself. And if, as noted earlier, each picture in Wu-ti's poem acts as a term of a multiple fusion, much the same can be said of figure-less poems in general: each expressive unit holds together with the force of resemblance to the totality they form, as a part of the work or as the whole. That is, each poem is a total unification composed of smaller unifications; through its fusions of resemblance, it identifies a relational unity. To say that a poem which fails to do so fails as a poem is a circular way of reaffirming the demand we make that a work be a whole. So we speak of the organic unity of a successful poem, attributing to it the power of a life of its own within the reader. Can such life fail to stir in him empathetic feelings of unification, since (whatever the fusions employed) its action proceeds by bodying forth similitude?

British writers of the nineteenth century, fascinated by imagination's gift for identifying resemblances, discovered in it the essential of poetic thought. "This intuitive perception of the hidden analogies of things," wrote Hazlitt, "or, as it may be called, this instinct of the imagination, is, perhaps, what stamps the character of genius on the productions of art more than any other circumstance; for it works unconsciously like nature, and receives its impressions from a kind of inspiration." Moreover, the making of "strange combinations out of common things" (Shelley) is an act of emotion. "Imagination, purely so-called, is all feeling; the feeling of the subtlest and most affecting analogies" (Leigh Hunt). And so on. Some of these writers remarked on an accompanying disturbance; yet nowhere is it viewed as bringing on a type of assault to which the brain responds with its characteristic drive to "make sense" of it. In assimilating the new to what it already knows, it may seize on things that turn out later to make bad sense, if sense at all. The organism's resumption of balance in itself cannot assure validity. There is no telling what its headlong action to contain the assault may lead to. Indeed no pathways conceal so many pitfalls as the ones that the mind may take in its "intuitive perception of hidden analogies." The distinguished French *philosophe* J. B. Robinet declared that life's principal effort is to make shells, and his *Philosophical views on the natural gradation of forms of existence, or the attempts made by nature while learning to create humanity* was for a time regarded as a scientific contribution. The world's recorded verse must be populated with images of every range which are as valid as this large one of Robinet's, and since the same doubtless holds true in other provinces of creative imagining, it makes all viable intuitive perceptions the more astonishing and precious. Moreover, the drive toward similitude reflects itself not only in linguistic fusions of resemblance but in countless other actions within the poem—obviously, for example, in parallelism, refrain, antithesis. Poems in fact are steadily engaged in the work of con-fusing, for the paradigm of poetry—metaphor—pervades its every act.

If, as Oliver Goldsmith remarked, metaphor is a kind of magical means "by which the same idea assumes a thousand different appearances," it is also the means by which the same appearance stands for a thousand different ideas. The two actions are simultaneous and indivisible. We "understand" by perceiving/feeling likenesses and unlikenesses, by bringing some things together and, in so doing, setting other things apart—assimilating/distinguishing. This amounts to regarding likeness and difference as reflexive parts of the process of relational thinking, the one implying the other. They are aspects, not antitheses. That likeness is not identity nor difference always contrariety, is generally—and curiously—ignored despite the glaring fact that much less than we suspect in experience can be fitted into neat little packets of black-and-white. The engulfing universe exemplifies variety in uniformity, as Plato had discovered long before British poets and critics rediscovered its significance for art. Coleridge said "poetry produces two kinds of pleasure . . . the gratification of the love of variety, and the gratification of the love of uniformity," which correspond to the "two master-movements or impulses of man." Wordsworth, in pointing to the second ("which the mind derives from the perception of similitude in dissimilitude") as the drive at the center of poetry, anticipated the view of the contemporary scientist. "A man becomes creative, whether he is an artist or a scientist," says Bronowski, for example, "when he finds a new unity in the variety of nature . . . finding a likeness between things which were not thought alike before. . . . An innovation in either field occurs only when a single mind perceives in disorder a deep new unity." For Wordsworth the necessity for such perceiving flows out of the depths of the organism. It is "the great spring of the activity of our minds, and their chief feeder. From this principle the direction of the sexual appetite, and all the passions connected with it, take their origin. . . ."

What of anterior causes, what of the great spring's sources? Man's actions and thoughts could hardly be impelled by and drawn toward the interrelatedness of all that surrounds him unless at the depth of his organism he believed in its unity and felt and knew it to exist, as ancestral man had felt and known it in his capacity as a participant. At these innermost creature levels of feeling and knowledge, the arbitrary cannot find room. Nature's "buzzing, blooming confusion," to quote William James' memorable phrase, that engulfs our senses is not suddenly ordered and unified and interinvolved in all its parts merely because post-Eden creatures would wish it to be. Such statements as Anaxagoras' (that everything is latently involved in everything else) or Emerson's (that everything is convertible into every other thing) are but feeble and partial intuitions in latter-day symbols of the primary organic unity of a creature who himself had been part of the seamless unity of the "All."

If the sciences, like the arts, are busy with new unifications, in their encompassing physical laws as in minor equations, every such enactment of the imagination is a mirror-image of the all-involving unity whose existence it affirms and toward which it reaches out with the only means we possess: the microcosm of a symbol. The passion impelling such creations underlies not only transcendent dramas and murals of paradisal grandeur; even in casual-seeming sculptures assembled from industrial debris its forces are at work, manifesting the same uniquely human need for perceiving kinship among the disparate, wholeness beneath the chaos. And if every such created object is a unification, it is so not only in its totality but equally in the smaller fusions that make it one. So it happens that when, in experiencing a poem, we respond within us to such large and small embodiments of language, we participate in a re-enactment of unification, whether we know it or not —and by the means (the symbols of language) provided by the very capacities of mind that were and are involved with divisiveness.

That only certain types of imaginative creation can impart a sense of cosmic identification has sometimes been insisted on by philosophers and poets in particular. The greatest of all of poetry's attempts "to say one thing in terms of another," writes Frost, "is the philosophical attempt to set matter in terms of spirit, or spirit in terms of matter, to make the final unity." The duality is quite as plain in Karl Jaspers' remark that "We call great art the metaphysical art which reveals, through its visuality, Being itself." The differences in the terms employed by Frost and by Jaspers count less than the common belief that both statements avow:

Poetry begins in trivial metaphors, pretty metaphors, "grace" metaphors, and goes on to the profoundest thinking that we have.

—Frost

Fundamentally, just art and therefore skill bare of philosophic significance is the non-transcendental manner of representing, of decorating, of producing the sensuously attractive, in as much as it exists in isolation and has no metaphysical bearing.

—Jaspers

In a conversation with Wilhelm Furtwängler, the philosopher was still more insistent. "In art there are two layers: one is metaphysically sincere, the other, while showing vital creativeness, can at best please but it cannot impress itself in an essential manner. This sharp division cannot be made with objective certainty, but I consider it of fundamental importance."

Division of art into a hierarchy may also grow from quite different thinking—from a "new ontology of the imagination," for example, as described by Gaston Bachelard in *The Poetics of Space*. Renouncing both his earlier "objective" method and his "interpretation through depth," the French philosopher-historian of science distinguishes formal from material imagination, the second of which bodies forth poetic "purity." In an attempt to help others recognize in the image *being is round* "the primitivity of certain images of being," he pursues "the phenomenology of roundness" with the addition of statements on roundness collected from La Fontaine, Michelet, Van Gogh, Rilke, and others. Bachelard's "pure imagination"—which he names "metapsychological"—is neither the "profoundest thinking" of Frost nor the "revelation of Being" of Jaspers but the experiencing of being itself ("we find ourselves entirely in the roundness of this being").

For each of these thinkers there are two different species of poetry, variously defined. Yet how would one go about separating poems which fuse spirit with matter, matter with spirit, from those which do not? Or poems which are metaphysically sincere from those in the underlayer which show vital creativeness only? Or poems which are metapsychological from the lowlier others? In all such cases, two different species presuppose two different births or sources. Are there, then, two different creative processes? Or, at the level of sources, two different sets of impelling needs, drives, compulsions? Furtwängler rejected Jaspers' dichotomy as a misconstruction of the genesis of art. Even the most insignificant tune, he assured him, originates in the same indivisible source of creativity. Both musician and philosopher clung to their convictions, neither succeeding in proving that the other was wrong.

Proof in matters of this kind seems all but unreachable. (How validate Auden's assertion that "every poem is rooted in imaginative awe"? As Mark Van Doren "answered," in a similar discussion, "If you have to prove it, then it can't be very important.") Furtwängler, however, might have added that any attempt such as Jaspers' to rank imaginative works into a higher and a lower species rests on a misconception of subject matter in art. To look, with Jaspers, for the metaphysical—or with Matthew Arnold, for the solemn-serious—is to ignore what a poem *does* in favor of what it seems to be "about." As remarked many times in this book, the experiencing of a work of art is indivisible; hence any thinking about, any focusing upon, a partial aspect of the whole can take place only within our analytic heads. Nevertheless we have no instruments for dealing with matters of rank except for our analytic heads; and when we use them to cope with this question a number of conclusions confront us.

First, every successful poem, regardless of whatever else it is and does, embodies similitude. It embodies it, as we have noted, through the action of its language, through its fusings of resemblance, in the whole and in the parts, irrespective of how each happens to be formed grammatically and irrespective of the experiences, objects, events, and/or ideas in the culture to which it happens to refer. This is to say that regardless of what any poem may happen to be "about," all the resemblance-making actions begin and end with unification. Furthermore, we may even conceive of these unifications of poetry as composing a generic mode of love. This would be doing the kind of thing that Plato, Jean Baptiste Lacordaire, and Freud, for example, have done in attributing its multiform manifestations (love of woman, of parents, of a cause, etc., etc.) to a single generative force. For the Greek philosopher, it was mind; for the French theologian, love of God; for the Viennese psychoanalyst, instinctual impulse. To conceive of each poem as "an act of thinking love" (see below, p. 218) implies an even vaster emotion, one which takes these three great forces as themselves but partial expressions of man's organic desire for reunion with creation itself.

RESONANCE AND REVERBERATION

Whether all human feelings flow out of a single source, whether, as Otto Rank believes, "every emotion which is admitted in its totality manifests itself as love," poetic thought, no matter which aspects of reality it embodies, proceeds by enacting union. Viewed thus in terms of what it *does*, every successful poem is a binding-together. And since binding-together is fundamentally what every poem is "about," we meet a seeming paradox. The substance or referents of a poem appear to serve as the vehicle for the making of unifications; or, in more familiar terms, it is a poem's "form" (structuring) that constitutes its ultimate "subject" (unification)—the act of unifying forms the poem, its referents subserve this action. But it is in this sense only that every poem must embody the identical theme, for "form" is always a structuring of particular referents. And *what* a poem binds together are elements drawn from the writer's private experiences, elements possessing public meaning and interest, which are therefore able to resound in the experience of the reader.

These *resonances* depend on and evoke the world of their culture, its events, ideas, objects, and so on. Unlike the "ultimate subject," which transcends human time and place, the resonance-world is walled in always by the specific culture it arises from and speaks to. A less apparent limitation inheres in the speech it is borne on. "In a symbol," says Carlyle, "there is concealment yet revelation"—and for this reason it is a "wondrous agency." One of the sources of the conflict was noted earlier, in the disparity between the terms of a metaphor and the counterpull away from resemblance (p. 142). A second relates to one of the modes of desires-and-needs discussed earlier in this chapter. That an impulse to reveal encounters an impulse to conceal is an axiom of behavior within the culture. And that the poet may be unaware of their effect upon his thinking also may be taken for granted, as well as their conflict, for the characteristic ways by which poetry speaks make its presence plain. We have already noted the tendency of poetic language to obscure the directness of reality, to throw over it a sort of half-consciousness of unsubstantial existence—to reveal the fervent emotions of the mind under certain veils and disguises. Revelation yet concealment—and, as a consequence, a tension which marks the very nature of poetic resonance, adding to the other forces it exerts upon the reader a further power: that of a message which "still seems to be trying to express something beyond itself."

What can be found of the reader's response to the poem's *act* of uniting? Hopeless though it may seem to ask where or how, some light yet glows from the crucial fact that this action does not address itself to bits and pieces of nameable cultural experience. It speaks purely as a force of feeling. And when this force "sounds" upon the feeling-capacities within the reader, his organism vibrates with responsive aliveness; it fills with *reverberations.* F. W. H. Myers, like a good many others, acknowledges the apparently "mysterious power by which mere arrangements of sound can convey an emotion which no one could have predicted beforehand, and which no known laws can explain." And despite the great attention given by scholars to the linguistic structures of poetry, one essential effect—if not the profoundest—has been ignored. That a poem embodies rhythm together with other patterns of recurrence (rime, assonance, parallelism, antithesis, and so on, as the case may be) has been taken for granted. But taking for granted totally misses the emotional symbolism—and consequent import—of recurrence, associated as it is with other cycles of recurrence, with diurnity, the seasons, and the deep creature reassurance that they bring. Similarly, taking for granted fails to appreciate what the presence of these expectation-patterns implies for the reader as structural reflections and embodiments of uniting in the over-all action of uniting that is every poem.

None of the foregoing observations so much as implies any possible notion of separating the meanings of any word in a poem from its sounds. So far as I can see, every attempt to do so has greatly confused by suggesting, when not asserting, that a word actually leads two separate lives. At times the sequence of sounds in a poem of an unknown tongue can be so "musical" as to delight a listener who has no idea of their meanings; and if the word "musical" can ever be applied to verse, it is here: to a sonal pattern with no denotation at all. A special kind of meaning, however, is held by some writers to exist in certain words. F. E. Halliday, for example, speaks of an "aural symbolism lying deep in the unconscious and fully operative and evocatory only when experienced in the semi-hypnotic condition induced by verse, and to a lesser degree by rhythmical prose such as that of the Bible and Sir Thomas Browne." This "elemental significance" would be possessed by only certain sounds and sound-combinations "which are echoed and partially reproduced in words like *lie, light, foam, sea, beat, grave, stone, day, glory.*" But even agreement with this writer that "Far more words are onomatopoeic in origin than is generally realised" could not affect the fact that every word is a complex of sounds and of meanings which acts upon the reader as an indivisible totality—just as his response to a poem is an indivisible experience of what I have called resonances and reverberations. In the same passage (on the "poetic state"), Valéry gives his own characterization of the first:

> Under these conditions familiar objects and persons somehow undergo a change in values. New affinities are felt to exist between them, new relationships never observed in ordinary circumstances.

and of the second:

There is a tendency to discover a complete new system of relationships in which men, things, and events . . . also seem to have some indefinable though marvelously exact relation to the modes and laws of our general being.

The most telling and neglected aspect of the reverberative process must now be considered, one which was foreshadowed in the opening pages of this book. As Collingwood in his *Principles of Art* says of "psychical expression," it consists in the doing of involuntary and perhaps wholly unconscious bodily acts, related in a peculiar way to the emotions they are said to express. Not only are the two "elements in one indivisible experience" but "every kind and shade of emotion which occurs at the purely psychical level of experience has its counterpart in some change of the muscular or circulatory or glandular system . . . which expresses it." Thus, "the mere sight of some one in pain, or the sound of his groans, produces in us an echo of his pain, whose expression in our own body we can feel in the tingling or shrinking of skin areas, certain visceral sensa, and so forth."

This involuntary expression of "sympathy" by the organism is central to Spire's massive study of the biological foundations of poetry, *Plaisir Poétique et plaisir musculaire*. By its organization of rhythm, says Spire, which is so different from that of the verbal structure in a typically logical sentence, and by its more or less strong accents, the affective word-order of verse "echoes" the internal physiological motions of the poet during composition as well as those of the reader during his experiencing of the poem. "Indeed, it models itself on these internal motions; it is their external and communicative aspect. The movements and attitudes of our muscles—those hidden in our organs and in the rest of the body as well as those of the face (especially the mobile and sensitive muscles associated with responses of sight and taste)—*translate* the ideas and feelings experienced in the poem." ("I read sentences of Goethe as though my whole body were running down the stresses"—Kafka.)

Since the poem produces patterns of motion in the body which parallel those set forth by the words, one might almost be tempted to say that in its own way the organism "reads" these motions. In any case, it clearly participates in them. As counterpart, as psychical expression, they are re-presented—and therefore "known"—by the organism in ways that antedate by millennia the life of the culture. For reaction-with-the-body is an archaic type of identification; hence to be expected in the expressions of a type of person who is (as Eliot calls him) "more primitive, as well as more civilised, than his contemporaries," one whose imagination can draw him toward the very depths of his creature nature—and his reader with him.

KNOWLEDGE

To respond to a poem is to know its resonances-reverberations—but do they equal knowledge? The question touches on categories, leading away from all knowledges which complete themselves in abstractions whose validity must be verified, regardless of the thinking processes out of which they had been born. Science, of course, is the exalted example. Every truth it proposes must survive testing by "value-free, objective" analytic procedures before it can gain acceptance. By contrast, certain types of knowledge become true or untrue according to criteria which are "subjective." And here the exalted example is religion—toward which our question of knowledge is inevitably magnetized.

So often and so surely has the closeness between religion and poetry been stressed that most people who think of the relationship probably suspect that the two must ultimately be one. Or agree with Arnold that most of what passes for the first will in time be replaced by the second. If all poems are rooted in imaginative awe, so are all religious experiences, the most voluble witnesses to which are the mystics. But as they never fail to avow, the feeling-knowledge that they behold in their ecstatic visions simply cannot be conveyed. Though poetic inspiration may already be on the decline when composition begins (as Shelley maintained), great poetry nevertheless succeeds in affecting readers profoundly, even if it is (as Shelley added) only a feeble shadow of the poets' original conceptions. This basic difference in capacity to impart does not in itself clear up the question of knowledge. To do so, one has first to define religion—if one can.

Sir James G. Frazer's definition, which was generally shared—that it is "a propitiation or conciliation of powers superior to man which are believed to direct and control the course of nature and of human life" —has been despatched for filing in the dustbin of history by replacements both legion and ingenious. Yet while the new verbal arrangements may rule out the supernatural, even the type that proposes "an expanded new religion based on the new materialism" makes room for a kind of divinity—for example, one that is "not truly supernatural but transnatural," growing out of ordinary nature but transcending it (Julian Huxley). Thus the poetic knowledge conveyed in Wordsworth's Immortality Ode and numberless other intimations in verse of cosmic-identifications-cum-beneficence must be nothing else or more than religious knowledge. Although this reasoning does not lead us quite back to archaic cultures, where poetry was at one with prophecy and other rituals, it dismisses all the distinctions that emerged when the single personage who was a poet-possessed, God-smitten seer gradually split into the specialized figures of the prophet, the soothsayer, the mystagogue, and the poet as we know him. We should have to shut our eyes to the outcome: to the fact and all its compelling implications that the primordial composite type, the *vates*, evolved into different persons who must use different means for achieving their ends. For a person who believes that means and end are ultimately inseparable, that the one cannot help but condition the other, the relation between poetry's knowledge and religion's knowledge is decisively settled. The road available to poetry is not a road available to religion. Nor is it necessary to belabor differences in interest and temperament. "I cannot answer for the experience of others," wrote Ruskin, "but I have never yet met with a Christian whose heart was thoroughly set upon the world to come, and so far as human judgement could pronounce, perfect and right before God, who cared about art at all."

Though poetry's knowledge (no matter how viewed) is neither trans- nor super-natural, some of its advocates, constrained to make it respectable, try to prove it able to compete with or even exceed the knowledge of science. A critic sets out to establish "the empirical status of the work of art" (Read), a poet argues the basis for teaching poetry (MacLeish), a philosopher analyzes the "truth-value" of art (Feibleman) or art as knowledge (Ross). . . . With their dependence on analytic reasoning, some of the demonstrations make a curious spectacle since science itself is unable to justify its existence by analytic reasoning. While value-free, science is based on values, freedom from value-judgments being one of the first, as Eric Weil points out. And since, he adds, "science and consistency are unable to justify fundamental values, and particularly themselves, as necessary," "logically, scientific thought seems to have undermined its own basis." Moreover, unless the theorems of Kurt Gödel and of Alfred Tarski do not hold, the very ideal that science pursues will continue to be hopeless. As for complete objectivity, one of its most precious principles, it is now acknowledged to be unattainable even in the segment of existence to which science applies. The apologists for poetry's knowledge may lay down their arms.

The understanding that poetry brings I call by the name of "creature-knowledge" in the hope of suggesting the entirety and profundity of the reader's involvement with the All. The poem's resonances-reverberations submerge the aspects of divisiveness that qualify his ordinary thoughts and feelings. Nor can future or past, of time or of place, exist in this here-and-now. "All possible objects of the ordinary world, exterior or interior, beings, events, feelings, and actions, remaining normal as far as appearances are concerned, suddenly fall into a relationship that is indefinable but wonderfully in harmony with the modes of our general being" (Valéry). For the poem as a whole and in its units is, above all, an act of uniting. And to respond by experiencing its act of uniting is to relive, for the duration and with the whole of one's being, an indefinable sense of organic creature unity such as pervaded our creature-existence when it "knew" itself part of the seamless web of creation. That a man is an alien, that divisiveness burdens his nights and days, that his organism is instinct with the drive toward primary unity, make his need for re-living acts of this kind more crucial than he can know. For isolate man, as he lives ever more in himself, from others, and apart from the world that contains him, creature-knowledge has become no less than a necessity for his survival.

Moses "Invents" God

From *The Refusers: An Epic of the Jews* by Stanley Burnshaw, Horizon Press, 1981. Copyright 1981 by Stanley Burnshaw. The action begins at the foot of Mount Sinai, to which Aaron has traveled from Goshen in Egypt to meet with his brother Moses.

"But I've rested enough, I say.—Can you hear me?—Come back, Moses! I say, Come back! . . ." Each shout echoed the next as it struck the mountain. "It's Aaron your brother calling. Hear me! I say, Moses, you, not I, should rest. Come back, lie down!—Answer!—How much more must you climb for your sheep? . . . I say, Moses, listen! Where have you gone? Come back now!—rest your feet—" He gave up shouting. Silence covered the lower slope of the mountain. Sprawled again on his leather pallet, he closed his eyes. By the time his brother came down from the crags, he had sunk to sleep.

Half unsure, Moses studied the face. Bursts of afternoon breeze ruffled the stalks of a wormwood bush that glinted beyond the pallet. He stepped toward it slowly, bent down, broke off a flower. Holding a petal against his mouth, he glanced at his brother. *How will I teach this stranger? How much more will he sleep?—Questions. No more questions.*

Wheeling around, he sprang toward the cleft where the plain sloped up to the mountain's base. Scattered shrubs—acacia, thornbush—flickered with amber light. One of them seemed an arm's length higher, brighter than others. Holding it in his gaze, he circled it slowly before moving close to finger the leaves and bark. Then he swung about, fixed his eyes on the ground. Lifted, they could have observed the older man peering about for a waterskin. He found one, held it against his mouth. Before he had finished drinking, Moses called, "Did I wake you? You slept a very long sleep."

Aaron sighed, "They said the way would be hard but to travel your land with—"

"*My* land, brother? This isn't Midian."

"No? Then why have I come so far?"

"Sheep. I could hold them in sight from a crag the last four days while I waited, till your shadow appeared with the guides I sent," he smiled. "And now we go on to Midian. Soon you can bless my wife and son, rest in the green country, feast in our tents. On the way we can learn each other."

"The guards at the gate let me leave for a sacrifice only. 'If you're late,' they warned, 'you'll never see Goshen again.' They said the same to my Levites."

"I saw no Levites."

"They stopped when your messengers led us in from the coast."

"Stopped?" cried Moses in horror, "Abandoned their leader?"

"From the land," Aaron ignored the charge, "we could see the barrens. When your guides told us we'd have to cross, the Levites argued."

"Priests of the Lord were afraid?"

Aaron shook his head. "Your messengers mocked them: 'Tender feet bleed on the fiery stones, chests shrivel like the shrunken trees'—yet my Levites marched behind me. Hours later your pitiless sun battered their backs. They stumbled, fell on the sand. 'That's not the sun,' your tall guide roared, 'It's the desert's curse from Egypt. You're walking on top of the sacred home of their dead.'" Aaron glowered. "Why did you choose that guide, Moses?"

"To give you a hardy protector. Be thankful, brother, you're here."

"Here, here," he echoed, gauging the distance, then the mountain. "Why here?"

Moses glared. "You can't have forgotten my message!"

"No, but what if Merneptah will soon be Pharaoh?"

"What? He's the weakest prince at the court."

"With coldest flint for a heart?"

"But cursed with a mouth that sputters in rages. Cursed, I say." Aaron covered his ears. "I tell you Merneptah's cursed with a sickening brain and a stunted son. The tower of Egypt will crack when the Ramses dies. We can topple his son Merneptah."

Aaron's hands dropped to his sides. Avoiding his brother's glance, he took a step backward, gazed at the mountain, nodded, shook his head. Moses, watching him, reasoned silently, *The neck shows age but he holds it erect. The eyes have been burnt yet they look with calm. Whenever he speaks he's certain! Can it be faith in his god?*

"I have one day only: this day," Aaron said drily, "and your message spoke of a saving sign for the Hebrews. Where is that sign?"

"There's *more* than one," Moses sputtered, "and there will be others. You and our people and I—as I promised—we'll *all break free!*"

"When, brother?" the words came wearily.

"When? When we stand up together like *men!* When the Hebrews—"

" 'Change what they are' "—half-mimicking—" 'stand up like men!' You said it before." He fisted every phrase. "My people tell their hearts it must happen in time, the deliverance—in the time of God."

"No, no—*now!* While they suffer! The people—"

"You shout of the people. What can you know of the people? Do you think that you've only to tell them they seethe with power and they'll leap from the ground? Slaves can't suddenly rise to the stature of men —except in your dreaming. Bodies chained, they drag through the days in weakness . . ."

"Weakness? Was it weakness that raised up the stone colossus at Tanis fifty-four cubits high? I saw their strength at Ramesseum. Who was it lifted the rock of a thousand men's weight to the sky?"

"Whips force backs to strain till they break."

"But theirs didn't break. Such men burn to be helped to help themselves up, for they are the Lord's. *He* commands them."

Rocked by the challenge, Aaron lashed, "By what right does Moses of Midian say what their God commands them?"

"By the will of the world's Creator!" He struggled to tame his anger. "Do your arms paw over the ground like an animal's? Don't shake your head at me! Look in my eyes! They've seen more than once in the north how a freeman who'd lived among slaves came to think like a slave; but you—you're their leader, the priest of their God! And I shall keep close. We shall—"

Aaron backed from him. "Where is the sign you promised?" he muttered. "Show it instead of bellowing!"

"You and I, Aaron," Moses roared on, "*together* we'll lead—we'll wipe out the wrongs that they're suffering. Never forget that our God is Justice, and—"

"Stop, stop, stop!" With slowly despairing voice he addressed the distance, "I ask for a sign. He gives me speeches. My ears listen to words—whose words? My brother's raging words of a desperate man who lured me here with a vow: to show me the sign, the sign from On High. He gives me nothing but angered cries and demands." Gazing at Moses, he dropped his voice. "Loneliness and this sun have cindered your brain. You're living a desert mirage. Remember what they are, my people: bodies bent to the ground—eyes emptied of light: sons of the fourth generation—prisoners cowering, lost, till they've lost the hope of hoping."

"Why, then, haven't they turned to their ruler's gods?"

"Never"—the outcry thundered.

"But why? when *their* God forsakes them? Why do they laugh at big-eared Seth, the donkey storm-god? at Hathor, the cow-headed love-god? These gods seem to favor their masters. Why do the Hebrews cling to an ancient absent god who refuses to listen? Is it because you compel them, Taskmaster Aaron?"

"They know that pain is their trial sent down by the Ever-Mighty. They must cleave to the Patriarchs' God and wait—for their children's sakes, even their children's children's."

"Wait? Do nothing but wait!"

"They know what happens when men strike back."

"Do you also tell them groaning will help: groaning the prayers?"

"Their fathers learned that rebellion doubles the punishments. Our backs know the taskmasters' whips, the clubs, the knives of the rulers. Our eyes know whenever a man stands up, he'll be slaughtered."

"I also know," Moses paused, "what you *cannot* know in your hovels. I know what the dying Pharaoh feared in our people: their sleeping fury. We've only to rouse them—show them their strength. You'll see how it quickens them."

Aaron sighed. "When my brother murdered a guard, did they fly to his side and rebel? When he fled, did they run out to save him?—My brother's hot-headed 'justice' hardened their hopelessness."

"But when this hunted avenger—this Hebrew who killed their abuser —stands again in their midst unafraid of their masters? . . . bringing them words from their God? . . . What then, Priest? For so shall I stand, and with you at my side."

"Do you think they'll open their ears to a stranger's demands? If they answer at all, they'll say, 'Where were you reveling, Moses, when we sweated bricks in the mud of Pithom—where were you resting? Did you beg your Pharaoh to ease our pain while we staggered at Luxor under his murderous pillars? Did you fly to Karnak to free us after they shackled our chests to the falling columns? How will you answer them, brother?" Flinging his hand to cut off reply, he walked toward the pallet and reached for a waterskin. "If you tell them you come as a Hebrew" —he wiped his lips—"they'll laugh and mock you. I've heard their envy. 'Does Bythia's son prefer our huts to her palace?'—Our women serve at the court: all Goshen knows what they've seen by the water-pools streaked with gold, planted with lilies, streaming with colored fish, the lagoons trilling with songbirds, tables loaded with honeyed fruits 'in the halls where the cool wind blows.' Goshen mothers sing to their babies of Pharaoh's home 'where the cool wind gently blows as the harpists play and the eager maidens read to the listless men the marvel-stories of Egypt's heroes . . .'—Moses," he warned, "If you come, our people will scoff at you: 'Look, he's here: the Levite loved at the court.'"

"Goshen knows I was nursed in my father's house by the mother who gave me life. You saw—you will *make* them remember and *show* them—" . . .

Moses swung his head to the north. Shielding his eyes, he crouched as though he had sighted movement across the distance. Minutes later he lowered his hands, faced his brother as though there had been no pause.

"The time is the choice of the Lord, Who already prepares the time." Aaron winced in confusion. "Tell the Hebrews," Moses cried, "that their Lord has declared the moment is now. Take that message to Goshen, Priest, from His mountain: the time of our God is *now!*"

Aaron fell back. "Who speaks for the Lord?" his jaws trembling. Before he could cover his mouth, it was screaming, "The sign, the sign!" Moses listened, unsure. Aaron moved back, half-fearful, then lunging suddenly. "Show me the sign, the sign!"

The two stared at each other. The late sun, reflecting the light of the granite cliffs on the lower rocks, flooded the plain. At times it came rolling in waves across the plateau that rose to the mountain. Both men glimpsed at the reddening light on their fingers.

Moses looked toward the summit. "Are your eyes pure, my Priest? Are your hands clean?" His voice tightened. Given no answer, he walked toward the rock-sheltered pallet. "Approach that tree," he ordered, "Turn your face from me: look at the thornbush—the highest! Gaze at it!" Aaron obeyed. "Approach it and keep your eyes on it, gaze at it, gaze at it!—And now walk forward!—Go, I say!"

As though pulled back by a cord, Aaron's head swung round toward the speaker's face, then forward again toward the thornbush. He started to walk as ordered.

"Watch the highest one only, Priest!—Gaze! You're nearing it. Move closer!" Aaron obeyed. "Look at it carefully!—look at each leaf, each branch!—Is the tree *whole?*" Aaron, unsure, kept silent. "Are the veins of the leaflets seared? Look close and answer!"

Aaron bent down, his forehead brushing a twig. Unnerved, he drew back. Rubbing the glare from his eyes, he replied, "No, the leaves aren't seared, but why the question?"

"Now look at the boughs and the trunk! Gaze with care, with *care!* Are the boughs and the bole charred?"

Aaron examined the trunk, then the boughs. He circled the tree. Turning to Moses, "I see no scar from a fire. But why these questions?"

"Because, because—" Moses stopped. His eyes rolled "Because"— he stopped again, then pouring out words in a whisperlike chant—"because when I stood where you stood, the leaves of this tree and the branches flamed with so fearsome a light that I covered my face. I fled up the rocks to shelter my skin from its heat. Dreading to look, I waited —for leaves and boughs and bole to crumple to ash. When at last I was able to look, the tree hadn't changed: it was whole. The blinding fire hadn't eaten the boughs. The trunk was erect, the leaves as green as before—as now. I hurried down from the rocks, but as I came near it a voice commanded me, 'Stop! Stay back! Do not move closer! The ground you tread is holy. I am your God.'"

Aaron sank to the sand.

"'I am the God of your father, the God of Abraham, the God of Isaac, the God of Jacob—the same that Abraham knew at Beersheba: El-Olám, the Eternal El; that the people have called El-Shaddái, God of the Mountain, God the Mighty, for I am the Rock of Refuge: El-Elohé-Yisroél, the God of Israel. I have come to deliver my people from Egypt. Hear me!—I shall send you before the new Pharaoh and stay at your side.'

"I had no tongue but the Voice went on, 'What shall you say when the Hebrews ask Who is the One that sent you? Answer them: I am sent by Him who has never revealed His Name but utters it now. You will say to the Hebrews'"—Moses gasped—"you will say to them *Éhye ashér éhye* has sent you—"

"*Éhye ashér éhye,*" cried Aaron, "I shall be what I have been? I am that I am forever?"

"I had no tongue to ask but the Voice had heard and answered,

'Aaron, your father's son, the Levite, will be My mouth to the people. When at last they know My Name, they shall rise and follow. Send for your brother at once and tell him all I have said. Now take your rod and get with your Priest before the new Pharaoh! As you led with the armies of Egypt, so will you lead the Hebrews out of the land. Go, go! *Éhye ashér éhye.*' "

Aaron's face, soaked with tears, rose from the sand. Lifting his head to the summit, he moaned, "May His Name watch over his Priest and his messenger—El Shaddái, Rock of Refuge, *Éhye ashér éhye!*"

"And His people"—Moses declared slowly—"will break their chains; will strain; will tear; will gnaw at them, even—"

"*Éhye ashér éhye,*" Aaron called to his brother, searching each sound for its meanings: "I shall be what I have been—*Éhye ashér éhye*—I am named after my actions—destroyer of evil—merciful judge, giver of life to the righteous. I shall be as I was to Joseph in Egypt.' Blessed be His Name." His sobs called to the summit, "As He was, so may He be forever, forever—"

Stretched on his belly, his right hand clenched to a crag, Moses kept watching the far-off shapes as they moved toward the barrens. In spite of the noonday heat, he persisted, squinting at times through lightholes formed by his fingers. He had reached his lookout soon after Aaron had left with the guides. Now they were shifting west, out of range. Closing his eyes, he sank his weight on a rock, murmuring, "Soon he'll be there to alarm them—Aaron believes my eyes." He waited for minutes, listening. Jumping erect, he sucked in the wind, gazed at the north, then moving quickly, began the descent. "So will the Hebrews believe, Great God," he cried, "when he tells them Your Name."

He had reached the sands at the mountain's base when, as though a wall had risen to block him, he stopped. For an instant his body reeled. Jerking his head to the summit, he screamed, "Did I lie to my brother? deceive him as You deceived me, God, if it was deceiving? . . . How many times have I come here, again to beseech You? How many more since I fled from the flame to this shelter, my witness stone?—And You never answered me, never! Will You answer now? or make me repeat to myself it was all my desire—nothing more than my sick heart's need to discover Your sign, any sign that could make me hear for an instant The Presence whispering out of the eyeless flame in the boughs, then thundering into my ears the cold, half-meaningless words 'I shall be what I have been' . . ." His head drooped, his half-closed eyes on the thornbush. As his sounds fainted, he cried them again—hurriedly, loud, with a sting of scorn, "I shall be what I have been—*Éhye ashér éhye! . . .*"

He lowered himself on the sands, turned on his back, bent arm shielding his eyes. For minutes he heaved in sleep. Waking abruptly, chiding, "How can you rest while—" he leaped up angrily, walked, hands taut, toward the thornbush. "Flame? Dream? Did you hear it, tree?"—moaning—"What else to remember now but hunger's mirage? —yet I keep on begging 'One more dream,' 'another such dream,' and 'again the dream.' My feet come back to this ground, my fingers trilling your leaves." He plucked a handful of tendrils, stared at the greenness, scattered them over the sand. Instantly turning to save them, he crouched, waiting—shook his head, left them to strive with the heat.

Suddenly tightened with rage, his head popped skyward. "Is this how Your justice ordains that I live in the wastes of uncertainty, so You can mock at my creature-helplessness—toy of Great Yahweh's caprice? Answer me! Throw down Your answer!" Demands gave way to snorts of scorn as he ambled back to the place where his pallet had lain.

Reaching a stool of rock, he leaned on it nervously, forehead clasped in his palms. Minutes passed. The mouth curled into a tight grimace, then burst into laughter. Fitful echoes sent from the rock-slope lengthened into a roar, then stopped as he jumped to his feet in triumph. He was shouting now, his right arm punching the air with each charge. "Your speechlessness sets me free—and we're all of us free, free, free! Oh where have You fled, Great God of Abraham, Isaac, and Jacob, now that the sons of Your Covenant howl for Your help?—for Your Strong Right Hand and Your Mercy?—Where are You hiding, Great One? Have You no ears, You, the All-Mighty? . . ."

He stood there, trembling, peering about, waiting. Echoes rankled his ears: his fingers covered them. Noting nearby a bulge of sand, he cupped a palmful, studied it, tossed it away . . . *Sand—dust—clay— creature—words—what use is thought to a man when the high questions he asks it can never answer? If a god exists, can we know his purposes?* Spurned in his answerless flights, he invoked reason: aloud again and direct to the summit "Whether or not You stood with them once, God of the Hebrews, You surely abandon them now, yet these people refuse to flee You, trusting the promise You made to their patriarchs ages ago.

What kind of God are You, then, who cleaves to His worshippers once, then mocks them forever?"

With the last plea, he walked to the witness rock, his eyes, in the quiet that followed, vacantly moving over the sands till they fell on a cluster of sharp-edged stones. He seized one quickly, gazed at it, gripped it. "This is what good men use to wipe out the sinner: He must shriek to his death in a tempest of stones flung by the righteous. Who was it taught them goodness from badness: righteousness? . . ." He squeezed his head; questions were pushing his thought too fast to be bridled. "Righteous! God of mercy and righteousness—Yahweh? . . . But what can it be: the 'good' of this heavenly father who anoints some men with blessings unearned while punishing others with curses unearned? Justice? Yahweh's justice?" He shook his head. "Justice—imagined truth that men have to force on Your universe to make their survival possible. Without it: madness."

He repeated coldly, "Without it: madness," pained by pictures the words sent into his head. "But we've made our way," he roared at the sky, *without* Your merciless justice, Yahweh! In spite of You, men bear on." He stopped, thought over his words. Repeated slowly, they wrenched his brain till he screamed, "Though Yahweh abandon us, dare we abandon Yahweh? If we spit on Your name, shall our bodies, freed of Your fetters, tear one another apart?" His eyes turned from the sky to the far-off distance. Dazed by the glare, he heard his own mouth cry, "To survive, men have to fear some Power. Without Its menacings: *tohu-bohu*—the chaos again."

He jerked his head to shake out the horrors within it. Feet paced restlessly over the clearing in front of the pallet, his body beginning to stiffen: arms, shoulders, neck. Rocked to a halt, he challenged, "And what if we find no god because there's none to be found?"

The echoing question died as he thundered, "Men can create You, Yahweh! People are makers! Who but the children of men could have shaped out of rocks the temples at Karnak? Hear me! Who but Your terrorized people could polish and raise up the twelve great columns twenty-men high?—Tell me, Yahweh, who drew out of Your chaos those wonders in stone? Were they fashioned by heathen deities? . . . They were made by *men*, slaves and captors: Hebrews, Egyptians— slaves forsaken by Yahweh—men, and *without* You, Yahweh, *without* Your help! And the other marvels that dazzle the world: without You, Yahweh, without You! . . ."

He paused to recover breath. Shouting again, shaking both fists at the summit, "What if foreigners mock at the Pharaohs? Who but these heathens drew out the miracle-powers within *all* men: Magnificence!" The syllables soared like a chant as they echoed, "Magnificence!" "If Egypt out of belief in bestial gods could raise to the skies with human hands these marvels, think, Yahweh, think of the loftier marvels—the miracles!—Israel will add to Your earth as they reach toward Your *fabled* wondrousness, Yahweh—but wait!" Shifting from pained defiance to reason, he addressed in turn the distant plain and the overhead sky. Each phrase stopped with a lengthy pause, the tone growing harsher. "What do we know of this Yahweh?—Why do they call You wondrous?—Why do their voices shake when they think of You, why?—You have never made Yourself known.—You have never shown Yourself, Yahweh.—Never once have You blinded our sight with tearful joys of Your grace.—Say then, what are You made of?" The pause lengthened—burst, "You're nothing—*nothing* at all! They've imagined all that they wished You to be, O Yahweh-Almighty-Father-who-never-was." He stopped. "But hear me, brothers!"

With head thrust forward and right arm raised, he screamed to the empty air, "You shall have your god, people of Aaron! I'll place Him high on the uttermost plane of the universe, so vastly above and beyond the grasping tentacles of all other gods that He'll gaze down serene —supreme—and forever. A god like no other before Him! A god like none that was ever born of the agonized fatherlessness of men! . . . Then heed me, people of Aaron!"

He trembled, cheeks burning, hands pressed to his thighs. Doubt, fear drained from the body, his voice rising to take command, "Hear me, Israel!"—the high-pitched call was a chant. Glancing about, he mounted a wide, flat rock. Eyes steady, he gazed around and below then into the distance. "Hear me, God of Israel,"—he sang the words slowly—"You shall be not only greater than all other gods but *above* them. For all other gods can be seen, but You, my created Yahweh: You shall remain *invisible*—the god of soul yet never enclosed in flesh. A god of *mind*, You shall never take form or shape: hence, You shall always remain *untouchable*. Not even the lengthening fingers of human hope will be able to near You, O my *unreachable* handiwork: Yahweh forever unreachable."

He waited. Swinging his eye from right to left to scan his imagined listeners below, he nodded repeatedly. Certain now of assent, he prepared to speak on. The words that poured from his throat thrummed like a teacher's—patient, plain. "If you ask, People, *what* He is made of, this only God, I shall answer, 'Thought.' I shall say, 'Not only invisible thought but untouchable thought.' I shall say, 'Not only untouchable, but unreachable by all the strivings of men.' Then do not hope even to dream of His likeness, for your God has no likeness. I say to you, 'Cease trying to think *what* He is or why or when or where or whence or whenceforth. You can neither conceive nor imagine Him, and yet He will speak to His people. His command will leap from the throats of His prophets and servants.—O men and women, children of Israel, I bring you your God! Praise Him and do His commands! Rise! Worship His All-mighty Thought with the striving human thought He has given you . . . and even with all your love! So shall He live forever—and you also, His people, His Chosen, forever."

His speech ended, he stepped from the platform, nodding, eyes on the ground. Making his way toward his pallet, he raised his face to the summit. "Thought, nothing but thought"—he muttered harshly—"Invisible . . . untouchable . . . unreachable . . . unthinkable! Is this what You gave me a mind for, Lord, to contrive a Better-than-thou?"

He threw himself onto the pallet, hearing his echoes drown in the rocks: "a mind for, Lord, to contrive a Better-than-thou?" The words startled him, "Moses, child of contriving—contriving Jochebed —body's mother who taught it the way from the moment she set him into a basket used by the priests for idols . . . Jochebed: giver, preserver: how wisely you schemed, knowing the moment to point the prow so the infant would float on waters that Ramses' daughter would see—a sign, sent to her rescuing arms—ark of the water's weeping child: gift to the childless princess—Bythia's gift from her idols . . . Dear wise Jochebed, knowing your Lord. And you too: even you, my uncertain Bythia, who saw what a possible child of slaves would have to be forced to learn to survive."

He waited, the revery ended; eyes half-open, filling with light. His nostrils widened with drafts of air. Leaning back, he gazed at the sky, coldly defiant. "And you, Great Yahweh-who-never-was, you prepared me well." The outcry shrilled, "I thank you, Lord, for my mind, but you must thank me too for I have created you, Yahweh! Rise, then, and lead! They need you—the people your Israel will have to become to deliver themselves."

Sudden flashes of fear strained his defiance as he looked from the summit toward Egypt. "Israel, chained Israel, what will you choose?" He called as though the gathered tribes were standing below him. Pausing, he asked, "Will you pray to my Sacred Contrivance?" Raising his arms swiftly, he cried, "Have you wisdom enough to know what I bring you for strength? Never before have men and women been drawn to so vast a Power, greater than earth itself, high over all creatures and lands in the purest of pure serene. Ask yourselves: How could a god of matter or flesh rival your God of Idea? Flesh and matter are visible, seizable, crushable—all the gods men worshipped before could be seen, like the sun, or shattered to fragments of stone, metal, wood, or the clay they were made of. But never your God: He is Pure Idea —invisible as a wind, unseizable as a wave. Think: what kind of god could possibly rival our God of Thought? You must answer: None; for just as a person's thought can reshape whatever it touches, so does the Thought-that-is-Yahweh bend to Its Will matter, flesh, soul, all else that His world contains."

He paused for an instant. "Yahweh will reign over earth and creatures forever but Yahweh will live for Israel only so long as your minds that think Him cleave to this God. I ask: Do you hear me, people? Only so long as your minds that *think Him* do His commandments, do what He calls you to do for Israel's and Yahweh's glory and grace; for the two shall be one!" He paused again, for his last question: "Can you raise yourselves, men and women of Goshen? Will you strive to make yourselves worthy?"

He had no more words to send on the air, yet his eyes continued to plead. They gazed toward the far-off country till the lowering rim of the sun dipped toward the plain. In the failing light, he turned his face to the summit, "Where is the way? Have I a choice now, Yahweh?" Shaking his head, "Real or contrived, we must follow You now—or we die . . .

"Onward, then onward, my Yahweh. What deeds shall I work in Your name? Onward, *together* onward: our trial has begun . . ."

[After wandering through the wilderness, the Hebrews reach the gates of the Promised Land.] Standing before the multitude, peering over their heads in the sunrise, Moses intoned, "Yahweh said to His servant, 'Speak to them first of all that has passed since Egypt!'—'Lord,' I said, 'they remember these things.'—'Not enough that they know what happened. Tell them *why*—*why* I sent you to Pharaoh, carried them into the wilderness, rained down bread, gave them statutes, turned from them when they angered me. Tell them *why* I remain in spite of their murmurings.'" After a lengthy pause, he asked, "Will you hear His commands?"

Heads nodded patiently. "Treasure your God! Only to you did He give His laws and the proof of His Might in His name too sacred to utter. Therefore worship Him only! Never bow down to the sun or the moon or the stars like heathens! Cut off your hand if it lusts to shape an idolatrous thing. I summon all earth to witness: if you, your children, or children's children fashion such images, Yahweh's wrath will disperse you among the nations and parch your seed." He stopped to recover breath. "And yet in your days of wretchedness, if you crawl on your hands and knees to repent, He will listen."

He waited minutes, then raised his arms. "Now as we stand close to the gates, seal these truths in your hearts."

In the sunrise of the morning that followed, Levites carried the Ark to the place of assembly. Dazzled in light, Eleazar, the High Priest, Aaron's son, strode at its side while the people took their places. Moses entered. Lifting his hand in greeting, he spoke softly, "Yahweh said to His servant, 'Before my people move upon Canaan, speak of my statutes.'—'Lord, they've heard the laws,' I answered.—'Is it enough,' He mocked, 'that their ears have heard? You must show *why* Yahweh forbids them to live as the heathens live.'" . . .

At the last of the sunrise assemblies, Moses appeared with Joshua. He began as before: quietly, "I asked the Lord, 'How will it be with Israel in Canaan?'—He said, 'Their days will be blessed, they will be a light to the nations, if they keep the Covenant.'—'Israel has always lived apart,' I said, 'in the wilderness years and in Egypt. Now they must mingle with aliens, walk in cities beckoned by evil.'—The Lord answered, 'Tell them of Canaan.'"

He sighed mournfully, "Tell them of Canaan! Joshua's men have scoured it: east, west, north, south. Their eyes, used to the desert's bareness, danced when they first beheld the riches—cities glowing with ornaments, flashing garments, houses paved, rooms fitted with water, everywhere dazzle of colors—works of artisans skilled with metals; treasures carried from far-off lands by their trading ships. But to Joshua's men these things were as nothing compared to the place of worship: people lashing with frenzied joy, doing the acts of Ashtarte and Baal with the sacred whores—women and men—others whirling in ecstasies, pawing the ground, shrieking, fevered with wine, gashing their bodies, cutting off pieces of human flesh, even to burning children, women, and men on their altars . . .

"How can such vileness be? you ask unbelieving. Not with beasts of the field could you find such abomination. Where did they learn these things?" His body shivered. "In the uttermost depths of corruption where they serve their hideous idols."

He leaned forward, pausing after each question, "Why does your God give you a country raging with evils?" He recoiled with a shout, "To test the love, the faith, the worth of His Chosen! For years you've lived walled off from heathens: now you must mix with their world. You were put through trials in the wilderness, but the starkest, gravest trial is awaiting you there, in your Promised Land.

"You will enter armed with His laws. Righteousness is your strength, evil your weakness. When they mock at your laws that deny their lusts, raise up your heads in pride! Israel's tribes must remain the race of Refusers, sure of the way vouchsafed by the God of gods to themselves alone!"

Joshua screamed, "Hear, O Israel! The Lord is our God, the Lord is One. Blessed be His Name from this moment forever and ever!"

Moses strode away quickly. The listeners watched. He appeared to be taking the pathway south and east from the field. "On his way to Ebiram?" they wondered. "What would he find on those mountains!"

He had traveled the Moabite plain for hours, glancing west toward the stream as the pathways started to rise. When they reached Ebiram he looked for trails that might lead him upward beyond the tumbled rocks. Herdsmen had mentioned long pebbled slopes above the escarpment and ledges that formed Mt. Nebo. Between that peak and a second, they said, was a jutting cleft from which one could see distances into Canaan. Hundreds of cubits above, a hillock glowed in the sun. Moving with care, he made the ragged ascent. When he stepped from the last of the rocks, he sank to the ground.

Thoughts pressed again when he woke: *Must they follow me even in dream?*

"Head," he blurted, noting the place of the sun in the sky, "why keep looking toward Goshen?—Body calling to body, as the ancients said?"

He smiled wearily, leaned on a stone. "Speak to him then, mother Jochebed! Say that he sought out the *safest* truth for the hearts he deceived. But if Moses deceived, he too may have been deceived by a power that allowed him to act His name . . . If this Power exists, Moses honored His Name. If none, Moses freed them from all their chains." Rising briskly, he started to climb the peak.

'You may never know, Moses! He may never speak, yet you still beseech and reason.—You never cared to atone.'

"Who cries out such thoughts to my thought?—Aaron?—Jochebed? —Moses?"

He walked carefully, eyes on the scattered stones, from the hillock down toward an open crag. *The tasks will go on . . .*

He stopped, grasped at a ledge, fixed his feet in the rock. Slowly, with widened eyes, he lowered his face westward. Light, spinning the calm Jordan, dazzled his vision.

Moving toward where he had stood at the last assembly, Moses held up his hand. "Peace," he called out quietly, "Peace from the mountain!" He paused briefly. "Yesterday, from the jutting ledge at the heights of Pisgah, I looked at the Land—at the Jordan curving among green banks—at the precious country beyond. And while I looked, the Lord said, 'This is the country I give to Israel. I call you here to see it with your two eyes, but ask of Me nothing more.' I do not ask of Him more." He paused. "With His help I led you from Egypt onto this plain where you face Jericho. This was my task. It is done. And now another servant will lead you across the river into your heritage. The Lord chooses Joshua, son of Nun." He called to him, "Joshua, lift your hand from the Ark and come to the Lord's departing servant! Now you are in his care. He will lead you across the Jordan, but Priests will go first."

Taking a deep breath for his parting message, he glanced toward Joshua. "Write in your blood," he spoke slowly, "all you have heard this day. Command your hearts and your children's hearts to follow the laws, for they are your life—your life!" He paused. "Love justice and love mercy, but pray, Children of God, that justice prevails."

With head upright, he hurried his steps southeast on the path he had taken before. None of the listeners spoke. None of them dared believe that his eyes might cease to live on the summit, watching them always, judging them.

Uriel da Costa

From *The Refusers: An Epic of the Jews* by Stanley Burnshaw, Horizon Press, 1981. Copyright 1981 by Stanley Burnshaw.

Historical Interlude

"And I will give to thee and thy seed the land of Canaan for an everlasting possession," read Yahweh's pledge to Abraham (Gen. 17:18)—yet a mere three hundred years passed from the first of the Hebrew judges, who followed Joshua (ca. 1200 B.C.), to the death of Solomon, the last monarch of all the tribes. Almost at once the United Kingdom divided: Judah and Benjamin in the South, faithful to the old dynasty, the other tribes seceding to form the Northern Kingdom (Israel)—all at a time when the land was a field of war for competing empires. In 721 B.C., Assyria destroyed the Northern Kingdom and exiled its population, to be known in time as the Ten Lost Tribes, their identity never recovered. The same fate threatened the Southern Kingdom when Nebuchadnezzar captured Jerusalem, ruined the Temple, and banished to Babylon a large number of Judeans (586 B.C.). But Cyrus, the Persian who conquered Babylonia, permitted the exiles to go back to their homeland (538 B.C.). Some twenty years later a small group set out to rebuild the Temple, ushering in the Second Stage of Judaic History. In 444 B.C., under the sponsorship of two of their leaders (Ezra and Nehemiah), the people *en masse* for the first time heard the words of their Torah.

Little is known from that date until 165 B.C. apart from the complex struggles against the forces of Hellenism. A century of independence under the Hasmonean (Maccabean) dynasty (164–63 B.C.) gave way when Rome was invited in to restore order in a land torn between contending political and religious factions. A series of rebellions against Rome followed, the largest of which began in A.D. 66. Vespasian set out to suppress it, and his son Titus destroyed the Second Temple (70), capturing countless thousands, including groups for especial display in Rome in his march of triumph. Yet the Hebrews numbered some 10 percent of the Empire's sixty millions. Communities of Jews existed from southern Russia to Spain, from northern Africa to the banks of the Rhine; a million lived in Babylonia, another in Alexandria. There was "hardly a place on earth without a Jew," said the Greek geographer Strabo. What happened to these millions . . . and their offspring?

Soon enough their extirpation was well on the way. For many years Jews had vied with Christians in winning converts until the Council of Nicea (325) forbade Catholics from entering synagogues and mingling with Jews. From 100 to 1500, though Jews proselytized many, vastly more of their own people were lost to the sword, assimilation, forced conversion, apostasy, massacre, pillage, and expulsion. In France and Germany, Jews were bandied about from place to place, whipped into synagogues, and burnt alive. Within a year of the First Crusade (1095) they felt the full brunt of rising hatred.

To try to make clear sense of Jewish survival can fill even a dauntless scholar with despair. There is no such thing as sequential development, expected behavior patterns, or "reason" except by reversing their meanings. The Church, menaced by growing heresies, strove to maintain its dominion, the Fourth Lateran Council (1215) marking a turning point. It instituted a special Jewish "badge," prohibited money lending (again), and forbade Christians and Jews from dwelling together, thus paving the way for the ghetto. And although the papal letter *Sicut Judaeis* ("Concerning the Jews") of Gregory I to the Bishop of Palermo (598) repressed any effort by Jews to exceed their permitted rights while also protecting them when these rights were attacked, this theoretical safeguard of Catholic policy—renewed through the centuries —was ignored whenever propitious. It was not uncommon for Jewish communities to be held hostage until they purchased their freedom. Meanwhile the substitution of a money economy for barter opened a way for Jews, who were barred from owning land and joining guilds. Anti-usury movements still could expel them from monarchies, but frequent lack of central authority often helped them to weather the tides of adversity.

Islamic rule offered a curious contrast, having spread by 712 from India's borders to the Pyrenees. Most of the Jews under its aegis flourished. Then a fierce reversal occurred with the rule of Berber Almohad Muslims (1130–1269). Thereafter the records vary. Almost nothing seems to be barred: a Jew was free to work as a merchant, physician, poet, scientist, scholar, even philosopher. But the Golden Age in Spain failed to survive the Christian restrictions and persecutions of 1391. Many thousands accepted conversion rather than death. That countless numbers of their offspring became observant and full-fledged Christians no longer is doubted, despite the notorious tales that kept on flourishing concerning "lip service" converts and the secrecy in which the "Marranos" ("swine") continued to worship Yahweh. In 1492 all remaining Jews had to choose between embracing Catholicism or abandoning Spain.

Of the great number who chose exile, most—perhaps two thirds—proceeded to Portugal, where, after paying a poll tax, they were given the right to enter. Five years later what had happened in Spain was repeated—but with finesse: Portuguese "Persuasiveness" in itself or allied with compulsion led vast numbers of refugees to accept baptism. The mass ejection the Jews had suffered in Spain was replaced by simpler tactics of forced conversion regardless of the victims' beliefs.

Gabriel da Costa, a member of a Marrano Portuguese family who had served as treasurer of the Collegiate Church in Porto, some time before his thirtieth year surrendered to his inward compulsion to leave Catholicism. He became a convert to Moses—"As Moses declared himself to be only a deliverer of what was revealed by God Himself, I thought it my duty to make the Law the rule of my life."

He proceeded to persuade his wife, his widowed mother, and his brothers to make the Law of Moses the rule of their lives as well, and before many months had passed, the six da Costas sailed for the longed-for haven: Amsterdam. So it was that in 1615 their small band disembarked at the teeming port of the north, which already had taken its place as the world's center of exchange—in not only merchandise but ideas as well.

Upon arriving, the da Costas took all steps needed to become a part of the extant community of refugee Jews, who were now quite free to profess their religious beliefs without interference from the Dutch. Gabriel and his brothers at once fulfilled the circumcision precept, and Gabriel decided to change his name to Uriel. Before much time had passed, however, he found himself at odds with the rabbis and other religious communal leaders, who were recognized by all as the Jewish Establishment.

Three centuries later—in the mid-nineteen thirties—a widely respected writer and critic, T. S. Eliot, in his book *After Strange Gods*, declared that unity of Christian tradition is necessary for the preservation of civilization, and hence "any large number of free-thinking Jews" is "undesirable." How might men like da Costa and Spinoza have coped with this statement?

Amsterdam, 1618

"Who am I—Gabriel? Uriel? Gabriel? father, the name you christened me thirty-three years ago for the angel who brought the news to poor little Mary that Jesus was in her? Gabriel: 'Man of God'—proper enough for the eldest son of the Catholic churchman Bento da Costa, lover of Christ that you were while you lived. But now? . . ." He sighed painfully. "Who am I here at this moment, pacing my merchant's house in this misty city of trading ships?"

He moved the cushions aside and rose from his chair. Slender beams of afternoon summer sunlight crossed the rim of the coat of arms on the eastern wall. He stepped up close to it, fingered the darker rim. Nodding slowly, he whispered again, "Peace to you, father! dead in your cross-marked grave. Bear with me now as I am: still the first of your sons, though no longer Gabriel: Man of God but Uriel: Angel of Fire—Uriel, sent by my faith in the Hebrew God to join His flock in this cold north quarter of earth three years ago . . . Uriel: Angel of Fire striving to burn off the fogs that sodden the brains of His simpletons here. Fire of the Lord they spurn, scorn, hide from the light with their idiot rules and rituals."

He walked toward a window, stopping to study the tall candelabra casting a glow on the silver wine cup beside it. "Go, proud fool that you are! Peer at the street and canal below for a possible friend or cohort! Do whatever you can to save you from facing your days ahead—and the blows your reason will have to bear till at last you make them confess your truth and their lies."

Shaking his head, "Fool that I was to have yearned in our sunny house in Porto for a life of honest piety here with my own—reclaiming our birthright truths in the ways prescribed by the only man who had ever talked with the Lord: Moses, the Pure—fleeing my two-faced life there, saying one thing, knowing another. Then what if I'm *still* the sure one?"—his shout could be heard by the servant below—"making them sail with me here? None of them suffers—wife, mother; least of them all, my brothers, who'd be content as they were before I pulled them away. But how could I let them live like the blockheads around them?"

His voice softened, "No more shrinking from 'Pigs! Marranos!' screamed by some clerical spy. They're free in our free Dutch city, free of the need to question: brotherly sheep among sheep! The rabbis lead and they trail. Can these be my brothers? and these rabbis also my brothers? Hideous thoughts! No wonder Hebrews have always crawled from hole to hole, taking their darkness with them. God's plain speech to Moses was never enough for them. They had to decide what He *meant*—twist His message, wrench it, warp it, cover it over again and again for hundreds of years till they've hidden it out of our sight."

He wailed, shifted about to step to the window, but stopped at the sight of his servant, murmuring, "Reason reels. Enough, enough!" He turned to her. "Digna? Someone below? A message? Why don't you answer me?" Smiling faintly, the dark young woman moved to one side, clearing the way for the man who waited behind her. "Ah, Samuel! Friend da Silva. Good, very good. Welcome!"

"You look quite well." Speaking with characteristic assurance, the visitor watched till da Costa offered his hand. Dressed like his host, with telltale Portuguese flourishes, he appeared to be ten years older. "Well indeed," he remarked again in his even voice. "Turmoil seems to agree with you—or you with turmoil. And how are the gracious ladies?"

"Thriving, thank you."

"Your wife also?"

"Sara's blood wasn't made for this cold and damp."

"You must take good care of her."

"Oh, she never complains; she ripples gaily as ever."

"Your wife and mother were able to thrive *without* you? Good."

"Surprised, da Silva? Disappointed? Thanks to my cousin, the time passed quickly for them. You're acquainted with Abel? my partner de Cáceres? They're visiting now at his house." Choosing two slender glasses and a wine carafe from a massive dark-oak sideboard, he set them onto a tray which he placed on a low table beside their chairs.

"And your—ah—business, at Hamburg? all went well?" Da Silva teased. "The banking, I mean. Tell me about it! I'm just an unworldly physician—can't understand these money affairs, trading in bills. Bills of exchange—is that what they're called? Fascinating!"—he smiled broadly—"Remarkable, how you're able to shift from Uriel: Trader in Commerce to Uriel: Scourge of the Rabbis." He reached for a glass. "To your health!—No, to your double health!—Oh drink with me! Living isn't so hard. Honesty isn't so painful."

"You're certain of that, da Silva?" Smiling wanly, he raised a glass to his lips.

"Excellent vintage, excellent!"

"At least we agree on wine. Now tell me, dreamy physician: how many lives have you saved since your last account. Spare the names. The number?"

"Seven, I think. No. Twelve."

"Excellent doctor and benefactor—so long as you keep your scalpel away from their brains."

"Gracious as ever, my friend," he frowned. "And I thought that your —troublesome time in Hamburg might—"

"Oh," he chortled, "that ban they issued against me?"

"Didn't it teach you something, a little of something?"

"Surely. That I was wrong. That they're even worse than I'd thought."

"Tell me, Uriel, what did you think the rabbis would do when you hurled your attack? Thank you? Praise you? Make you the chief of their wisemen? Suddenly out of nowhere a certain Senhor da Costa arrives. Armed with impeccable logic, he shouts at them, challenging all their proscriptions and rites, mocking the very truth of the laws they demand of their followers. I've read your *Theses Against the Tradition.* What did you think they'd do when you spat your icy contempt on all they've zealously guarded from harm through the centuries?"

"As divine, divine," he mimicked, "though none of it's found in Scripture. Not a word, not a whisper." He dropped his voice. "Your rabbis say that God proclaimed them to Moses aloud—the 'Oral Tradition' they call it. But nowhere does Moses speak of these things though he wrote down everything else. Wouldn't you call that odd?"

"Odd?" da Silva shrugged. "Why odd?"

"There's only one law: God's law recorded by Moses. But no, say your rabbi friends, there's another that's just as sacred, sometimes even more sacred, mind you! Rites, regulations, proscriptions, commands, imprecations, devised by self-styled sages—men, *mere men* like ourselves!"

"I know, I know," da Silva sighed. "You've said this before."

"But the first set of laws"—da Costa shot out his arms—"is the word from God, the second was written by men. Oh come, da Silva, reason with me. Since the rabbis' rules weren't given by God, how can they be *His* law?—Now why are you shaking your head? Just imagine the Lord of Hosts, the Exalted, commanding your surgical hands to strap on pieces of leather before you pray and telling you never to enter your house till you kiss a scraplet of paper nailed to the doorpost—not to mention hundreds of other odd rites that defy reason. Oh come, admit it, physician: it's as laughable as the Trinity."

"Now you're going too far," he pointed a warning finger.

"I too far? It's *they* with their superstitions that cover up God. Their followers worship a foreign cult. We must raze it as Gideon razed the altars of Baal."

"Before you attempt it, better examine your own high logic—all that you prate about *proof*."

"*They* have no proof."

"True. No proof that their laws were uttered by God. Hence you declare such *absence* of proof proves that their laws are frauds."

"Exactly."

"But that's not the only conclusion possible. Other mortals have heard commands from Above—look at your Bible! How can *you* know—how can anyone *know* that these rules were *not* given by God? You have no proof. They have no proof. Proof is of no concern in such matters. Keep your logic, I beg you, where it belongs"—he patted his temple—"and let our leaders alone!"

"Hold my tongue while they poison our air with inventions about immortality? Did I give up all that I cherished to live just a different lie? Thank you, physician, but don't prescribe for da Costa!"

Rising briskly, da Silva ambled around the room. "Slowly, my friend, slowly," the sounds fell gently. "You came here an eager pilgrim; we gathered you into our arms. Then almost at once you announced that our life is wrong, our religion a sham, our wisemen deceivers. We waited, squeezing our lips. But *you* wouldn't wait, not you! Within a year you run off to Hamburg, propound your scorching *Theses*, which earned you a ban. And yet you still keep thinking our people will hear you—will reason with you—will shun the rabbis and all their laws." He stopped for a moment, chuckling. "Innocent that you are, you expect them to worry their heads with your subtle concerns for Truth. They're men, everyday men, *people*." He stopped again. "Do you think that Hebrews are better or wiser than others? Like all the children of Cain and Abel, they're creatures—creatures who eat and work and sleep and marry—and follow leaders—just as their fathers followed—with never a question, never a doubt to trouble them. A physician *knows*."

"I'm asked to believe you know what they want above all?"

"Not to be bothered," he nodded. "To plod their accustomed paths. —Believe whatever you like, da Costa, but try to impose it on others and you'll be condemned—in this city, self-condemned."

"The doctor's discovered the secret! Believe one way but behave in another. A noble prescription."

"I'm trying to tell a friend there must be a difference between one's private and public beliefs. I implore you: keep them apart!"

"My physician prescribes duplicity?"

"Survival."

"Oh, I'll survive, da Silva . . . Put off your fears!"

"Not so simply. Everyone knows that the ban sent out by the Venice rabbis is aimed at *you*. Though it speaks of the 'many sinful men,' they are you."

Crumpling the papers strewn on the chest near the window, da Costa tossed them across the floor. "I suppose you mean these idiot words."

"Your brothers admit they're afraid to be seen with you walking the street—and your friends . . . as for your friends—"

"Those cowards in Venice refused to answer my question."

Da Silva gathered the crumpled sheets from the floor. "You seem to forget, good friend: these leaders don't *have* to reply to you or anyone else. They have the *power*." Scanning the papers quickly, he read aloud:

'By order of the elders, in accordance with the pronouncement of our saintly men, we excommunicate all such persons according to both heavenly and earthly law. May they sink lower until they return completely repentant and no longer cleave to their folly and cast no more aspersions upon our law and upon the wise men, the authors of the Talmud. If they do not turn back to God from their wickedness, then they and all who defend them shall remain in excommunication.' So says the text. And we, in compliance with it, reaffirm this interdiction and include this in the resolution: any man who hears from another a word against our rabbis shall be required, in accordance with the above-mentioned resolution, to bring it to the notice of the heads and the rabbis of the town he lives in . . .

Skipping the signers' names, he added "Venice, Tuesday, August 14, 1618."

"Everyone knows," da Costa shrugged, taking the paper and flinging it over the sideboard, "my questions remain—clear, accusing. A ban might silence a person's sounds but never his charges once they're published and known. My questions are gnawing at peoples' minds."

"Oh hardly," da Silva smiled, "now that Modena's issued his answers."

"Leon Modena!"—the burst of laughter annoyed the physician. "Everyone knows what a joke he is! Whom can the rabbis of Venice find to refute me—whom do they honor to speak in the name of their faith? Modena the gambler, chief of the circle of gamblers, and worse: a devout Jew who dabbles in alchemy—and God only knows what else. Sorcery, some of his intimates say. Modena, Modena, the rabbis' spokesman for holiness. One of his sons visits a Gentile to have his horoscope read; another studies elixirs with priests! Oh these pious Venetian Jews"—he laughed at his guest—"Now, how should you celebrate Sabbath, physician? Play tennis, of course!—the game they adore in their latest Jerusalem. How can you keep from smiling with me? Admit the fraud when you see it!—And *they* lash out at da Costa! Why don't these rabbis issue a ban against all in their congregations who fill their houses with portraits, publish dramatic comedies, or act in theatres? And what of all those who break the rules of the diet, or go out publicly drinking wine with the Gentiles? And the other synagogue stalwarts who can hardly wait to go masking as women—their wives as men—in the wild Venetian carnivals? Why, why, why? *You* know why, da Silva, yet you tell me to take their threats to heart."

"Don't ask me to be their advocate!" He shot an appraising glance at his host and walked to a window. Da Costa busied his hands with the ornaments, papers, and books on a long buffet at the southern wall of the room. His guest, leaning his hand on the casement, gazed at the floor thoughtfully. Speaking half to himself, he broke the discomfitting quiet: "Who can deny what the centuries of our exile, the agonies, the despairs have done to our spirit? We've always had men among us who cried for a golden calf—we've always had Aarons to serve them— and fierce upholders of God to make them repent. True: we've come out of the desert and into cities filled with temptations. Does it matter much or at all that the—symbols changed?" He nodded grimly as Uriel watched. "It matters indeed. Yahweh's upholders are no less fierce. But those who secretly lust for all that the Lord forbids now shiver in worry. Worse—O heavenly irony!—*they* are the ones who rush to the synagogue, close up ranks with the rest, and shout the shrillest 'Heresy must be crushed!' " He stopped, appearing to weigh his words before going on. "At first it may seem very strange, yet the need is real. They've learned what all of us know: that what matters above all else is the safety Israel secures and has always secured from our laws. Some of our people would die to preserve them—*both* our laws, for they take them as one: Moses' law, my friend, *and* the rabbis'. Wherever we live, the rabbis have made them one." He moved up close to da Costa. "Open your eyes to your actions! Look at our world! Every heresy forges a counter-unity. Every heretic gives the rabbis more strength. Can't you see what a gift you've become to them?"

"Possibly . . . for a little while, 'til people see for themselves that the rules I dissect are absurd." He nodded tensely, "Aren't the rules absurd, da Silva?"

"Some of them—possibly . . ."

"*Some* of them? Just *some* of them?"

"All of them, then," he sighed, "if you'd rather."

"I do indeed—simply because they're nonsense."

"*Harmless*, harmless nonsense, Uriel, but needed."

"For what, please tell me!"

"Survival! You don't have to hear a history lesson from me. Everyone, even the Christians, know the severities of our faith, the demands, the rigidities, the mystifying prescriptions, with all these seemingly petty and troublesome rules have kept us one, bound us together as one."

"How can there be any lasting strength? any hope for—"

Da Silva shrugged at the unfinished cry, "But there seems to be. In the—"

" 'Past,' you were going to say.—Perhaps in the past but today, the need isn't here. People wake up. Can't you see what must happen? The fogs that hang on their minds will be burned away just as the mist burns off in this land. Then they'll see with the clearness of morning."

"Thanks to the Sun of da Costa's heavenly reasoning!"

"Earthy reason—the courage of common sense."

"Which will bring on the clearness of morning"—da Silva snapped at him—"Wake up, newcomer! Wake! Your dreaming is *one* thing, our real world here is another."

"And you're utterly certain where one thing ends and the other begins?" He grinned. "Why you're almost as wise as your wisemen."

"That irony's a deceitful waste. It costs you nothing right now with a friend, but how will it help in your war?"

"Oh, is it a war then?"

"You're making it one . . ."—he hesitated—"I fear for you, friend da Costa."

"Save your fear for those who are guilty of lies." Turning about, he walked to the long buffet. As he rummaged through heaps of scattered papers, he added, half to himself, "Can a simple animal lie? Only human beings were cunning enough to invent it. But why? Out of what, I wonder. Instruct me, learned physician!"

Shaking his head, da Silva gazed in the blazing eyes of his host. "My heart tightens, hearing the blast of your pride. Can nothing stop you— even the fate of our kind? A small people, always menaced by possible death and torture: how can they risk allowing a rebel to split the ranks? They must bridle him for the larger safety of all . . ." He paused. "I warn you, da Costa, no one can fight this alone."

"But I'm hardly alone. You know it, they know it, everyone knows it. Here!"—he reached for the paper da Silva had read from before— "They acknowledge it. Read their own words: 'There are *many* bad and sinful men who deny the words of our wisemen and their explanations and vigorously challenge their words.'—The bullies at least have the wisdom to be afraid."

"Of you?" he smiled.

" 'And we hear from their mouths a voice of power.'—Of *power*, they said. Here again: 'There are many who deny the words . . .' *Many*, mind you, many."

"And where are these many, da Costa? At the synagogue? In the street? Can you name them? No one has yet stood up to defend you against the ban or to join your side."

"The struggle's only begun."

"And you'll struggle alone?"

"Someone must drive out the dark and let in the light."

"Must it be you alone against their many? One lonely apostate-prophet from Porto?"

"Each does the task that he must. Yours is to heal our bodies: you follow wherever it leads. I follow wherever my reason forces me on."

"But we always have choices." Da Silva held out his hand. "Come with me now! Though you haven't known me long, you can trust me. Come!"

"Physician of flesh *and* soul?" he smiled. "I might ask you to—"

"Come with me," he pleaded.

"Is this the cry of a friend, da Silva?"

"A serious, desperate friend, who hopes to remain your friend."

Da Costa frowned in confusion. "Go with you *where?*"

"Come with me, Uriel, come! We were always a people of peace."

"Hebrews always of peace? Not so. It's you who need the history lesson."

"Very well then," da Silva sighed, "I'll change the word. A people bent on survival."

"Survival!" Uriel studied him, shaking his head. "Survive by the grace of lies?"

Da Silva stiffened. He clenched and unclenched his hands to restore calm to his body. Dropping his arms, he scowled up and down at his host. "*Nothing* but lies," he hissed, "*nothing* but lies have saved us?" His words could hardly be heard as he rushed for the door below. Da Costa, following close, attempted to call him. He stopped at the sight of Digna climbing the threshold. Wringing her hands, the maidservant stared in confusion.

Poems

The poems in this section are reprinted by permission of George Braziller, Inc., publishers of *In the Terrified Radiance*, copyright 1972 by Stanley Burnshaw. "Florida Seaside" was first published in the "Stanley Burnshaw Special Issue" of *Agenda*, 1983–84. "Talmudist" originally appeared in *Mirages: Travel Notes in the Promised Land*, published by Doubleday, copyright 1977 by Stanley Burnshaw. "The House Hollow" first appeared in *Agenda*, 1989.

The Terrified Radiance

Because there is no forever
And any bird has as much to hope for
As any man, I can look on all I have made
With coldness, with relief—

Gather the scraps and sketches,
Bundle them into somber heaps,
Hide them in closets against the ever possible
Moment of need

For trading them one by one
To a friendless hearth where perhaps their ashen
Bodies may fan a second fire with the lucky
Loveable traces

That once had forced my fingers
Holding the pen to raise up visions
They had not known. Because there is no forever
For any being,

I want no portal hollowed
Out of the equal selves of soil,

Grass, or stone to guard my breathless heap
That must one day burden

A room, a field. For I know
And wish that whatever I am, after
A season, will die from the minds of those I leave
As those I loved

Have died from mine, mother,
Father, friends of the hearth, all—
All but a cold company of strangers distant
In time and country,

Violent ones whose thoughts
Have been burning coals in my veins and keeping
My heart from falling into the lost disease
Of numbness to this eden,

That flows from the terrified radiance of our minds.

Caged in an Animal's Mind

Caged in an animal's mind;
No wish to be more or else
Than I am: a smile and a grief
Of breath that thinks with its blood,

Yet straining despite: unsure
In my stir of festering will
Testing each day the skin
Of this wall for a possible scar

Where the questioning goad of the gale
Forever trying my bones
Might suddenly gather and flail
And burst through the wall.—Would rage

Be enough to hold me erect,
Dazed in the unknown light,
And drive me on with no more
Than my strength of naked will

To range the inhuman storm,
Follow wherever it lead
And answer—whether I hear
A Voice or only the voices

Of my own self-answering scream
In a void of punishing calm?

Historical Song of Then and Now

Earth early and huge,
No eye dared hope to travel
The palette of its rage

Till, late, they learned to wind
Shackles into its veins,
Shrank it to fit a cage.

So trust contracts to fear.
The tribes give up their feuds.
All wars are now one war.

And will you indict this breed
That strained against a code
Where safe-and-fed was good?

Fled from the mothering wood,
It found in its hand the thought
To light up endless day,

Revel with sleepless eye,

Make of itself a god,
And the veins a level sun—

Now it stumbles, dwarf in the maze
That the thinking hand had spun.
Blind in its blaze of stone,

Whom can this breed indict
That its sun is a blast of darkness,
That light is always night?

The Valley Between

Man with brow in the air,
Man with the spine erect,
Forepaws hung at the sides,
Drop your head to the grass:

What can you hear down there?
Nothing, nothing.
Listen,

Man with head in the air:
Raise it higher and higher
To the plain of alarming birds:
What can you hear up there?

Nothing, nothing.
Listen,
And hear whatever they are:

Voices calling you, calling
From the grass, from the plain of birds,
And up from the valley between
Where you batter a path alone

With your new-won stifle and knees.
Head unsure of the emblems
Unlinked to below or above,

Hearing no sound but its own,
Reels on the friendless shoulder;
Eyeballs riving with fear
Leap left, leap right, for the course,

While the shanks below push forward,
Right leg, left leg, forward,
Onward, endlessly onward . . .

Keep spine erect from falling!
Face from questioning backward!
So ever ahead and onward,
Onward, helplessly onward—

Not to Bereave . . .

For James Dickey

Not to bereave is to praise the bridled
Rays that keep each body rising
     Or falling. Who can be taken
That has not called with a sign to the seizer
     "Come, I am here."

Slaking caresses blind the blood:
Few die but have felt the scorching
     Bliss of a killer's desire
In a closed house or under the chained
     Sky where an otter

Sinks to the sea's floor to gather

A stone that will break the clam he holds
        Close to his breast. While the flint
Will of the earth suffuses: forces
        All it contains,

What will you teach your veins? The bird
Trapped from birth in a cell hidden
        From any sound, on the dawn
Inscribed in his blood, bursts with the same
        Cry that his brother

Shouts from the wood. Tangled in skeins
Of will and knowledge, how can you know
        Sight as desire, who dare not
Glance at the furies that crush your sun?
        Shielding your eyes,

While the flint will of the earth suffuses:
Forces all it contains to thrive,
        Wings cry up from the dark
Singing as the clam dies in the song
        Of the preying stone.

Erstwhile Hunter

Savaging land, the killer gale
Blown by the life from nowhere finally
Reels against the indestructible
        Sea. He will shear the crippled
Trees, he will bring the scalded stalks
        And boughs the single grace

He owns: expunge caprice with fire,
That leaf and blood once again regrow
Veils of calm and dare to nourish,
        Breathe, to sleep with quiet

Eyes under an ever prowling
      Heaven.—Who of the spared

But this exiled self could scorn and exalt
The need that will make him torture his thought
On the lost? who but the erstwhile hunter
      Become a nurse to flowers
More scourges ago than hands could ever
      Uncover of axes abandoned

By the sleeping caves of the world.

Blood

Cats move like water,
Dogs like wind . . .
Only when bodies
Have shut out mind

Can they learn the calm
Motion of dream.

Would we could know
The way men moved
When thought was only
A great dark love

And blood lay calm
In a depthless dream.

Their Singing River

Sometimes, dazed in a field, I think I hear
Voices rocking the trees; then I stop, race
To the boughs, listen—and hear not even a thread
Of a wind.

        The calling voices never resound
In aftertones that would make your ears believe,
Nor is there other proof except my temples'
Shaken emptiness. Nor can I know, if my body
Had leaped to the tree in time, what they might have said,
What I might have answered. Or if some other signs
Could show their presence.

           Now I cannot regain
Even by wilful dreaming the father faces
Or the eye or hair of the ancient women who bore me
Or think to imagine how they might pull me now
Into the redness of their singing river.

Gulls . . .

Gulls
Drop their unreachable prey from the air
Till the shells
Crack on the dying stone open

        I hear
Windows opened by trees—I hear
Seeds, the sunfire,
Rain soothing and flailing,
Sandfloors pushing up from the sea—

Tomorrow—yesterday—now:
Silence: noise—I hear them
Everywhere, anywhere . . .

      Days burn out and nights
      Boil into dawns—

Under the hiding wave
Prey calm in their guardian shells live,
Wait, while the gulls seize,
Pound through unbreakable air
The stone that wears its life away into sand.

The Bridge

We build a bridgehead from here and now to tomorrow.
Can you hear the word its gesture speaks
As it towers over us, tall, huge,
Cutting the sky with its head,
Pressing the ground with its feet? *It is running*
Across the water, charging
To span the sea in a leap.

Does it say we must seize tomorrow,
Tear it out of the air, compel the future
To come to us here and now?
It says we must make eyes ready
To know the new as swift light swims
Slowly up from the darkness: wait, hope, listen.

Has it not warned: Though hungering hands
Tear at the mists, passion is not enough?
Tomorrow eludes the blind, wild will, yet silence
Waiting passive in hope can never bring forth

Creation out of the air. *It is saying: Quicken*
Your blood with enormous thought: tomorrow listens.

Our bridgehead leans toward the far horizon
To mix with a far light flooding. Look, the arms
Reach out to greet the future! Outstretched arms
On whose young strength we hang our road
Till tomorrow raises a bridgehead:
Tomorrow also stands with outstretched arms
That the two bridgeheads may meet, the old and the new
Join hands to close the ocean.

You see no light beyond? No outstretched arms?
Half of whatever we see
Glows in cells not signalled by our eyes.
If men lived only by the things they knew
The skin of their hands could touch, their hearts would wither
Of starved need. The shapes of sensate truth
Bristle with harshness. Eyeballs would cut on the edges
Of naked fact and bleed. The thoughtful vision
Projected by our driving hope creates
A world where truth is possible: without it
The mind would break or die.

Emptiness . . .

Emptiness seeps through the air, it is seeping
Into our clothes. Where it blows from nobody
Knows, yet the dangling tie clinches
The neck, the shoulders chafe. It could come,
We knew, the Unthinkable, but this cannot be
The one we saw. Shelters abound:
Nobody tries the doors. Everyone
Seems to be standing-listening as though
Expecting shrieks of a rain from a possible
Further sky.

Is it still too soon
To wonder what if the fume could burn
Through all this skin? The light widens.
Some have begun to tear their clothes
Without waiting to ask. To learn, we were told,
Is to wait and ask—nothing was said of a presence.

A Coil of Glass

Somewhere there is a coil of glass within
Whose range the fire of stars
Thousands of light-years gone gives back the gleam
Once shed from earth—
Lost light of crumpled hours.

He who finds this glass
Reclaims at will whatever sleeps in time.
Nothing that was need ever fade so long
As air floods the redoubts of space and worlds
Roll on their pivots:
All the dead years sleep
On the faces of quiet stars.

Whoever owns this glass may one day turn
The lenses toward the face
Of the farthest star and bring at last a sight
For which men grieved through lightless
Centuries: first moment
A seed of dust unloosed the multiple flowers
Bound in its atom strength, and locked the shapes
In one vast whole of interbalanced need,
And broke forever the vile or sacred sound
Of earth before men quarreled with the ground.

II

A book might be the lens of pure hard tears,
The coil of glass that sights whatever sleeps
In time—gone light of earth holding the crumpled hours.
Focus the glass at will: look at the man—
Adam, Arthur, Christ. Look at the woman—
Lilith, Iseult, Helen. Light up the brain
Of the priests and kings, the file
Of heroes set on the seeded steps of time.
Then watch these idols crash on the floor of your mind.

Mythless your heart breaks
On the edges of days revived. Nothing can heal
The wound until you learn the lens, until you know
Builders of myth were men whose hungering minds,
Cutting through shells of sense, needed to image
The fact they hoped to see.

Focus the glass at will: it may show how men
First rose up, lost in the jungle's day
And found themselves in the dim fraternities of blood-and-mind,
Only to lose themselves again in a darker
Fiercer jungle, where wind
Is scissored by screams from a lightless ground,
Where feet trample on bleeding skulls—

Our world—our father's world. . . . Our night is broken
In a coil of glass.
Look through the pure hard tears.
What do you see?
Whose hands are pushing up through the darkness? Whose eyes
Carry a flame of signs that tell how the earth's
Long fierce darkness shall be plumed with suns?

Anchorage in Time

On pavements wet with the misty wind of spring
We walk while our bodies burn
For places where hands of trees draw sleep from a brook
And the air is damp with fern . . .

If waters image cloud, a man can see
A heaven underneath, but if he change
To look up at the sky, let him remember
His anchorage to earth. Whoever stares
May see suddenly over blue pools of sky
Moving foam of cloud: at once his mind
Will fever for truth, for his anchorage in time,
Balancing earth and heaven in his eyes . . .
Then wakes from staring and puts back the sea
And sun in place, yet never again certain
Which eyes to trust, saying in voiceless words:

What is a man, who strides against the light:
A coat of flesh drawn on the bracing bones?
And the furled earth beneath his feet: a skin
Of sand muffling the burning ribs of stone?
Or is his blood an impulse of all breath:
Flesh fused with bone in one vast atomy
With sand and stone—with earth, whose ground and fire
Speaks for all breath? Which eyes to trust, which eyes? . . .

Let those who search look to their anchorage
In time, before they balance earth and heaven.

II

The vast stone trunk of mountain lifts above
The ground no more nor less than its rocky knees
Have sunk in tight brown earth, while everywhere
Water is steadily grinding down the hills;

Water will pour the powder into the sea
Until the day the suns no longer boil
The air or scorch the grass,
Blowing from the pale disc of yellow stone
Not flame enough to melt the frozen wave
Blinding the rock and sea—
Hot earth become ice-star.

Yet must the mind woven of blood believe
An imaged vision scaled to an anchorage
In time, and watch eternities emerge
Out of the baseless dust: eternal spring
Conferred on land where cubicles of flesh
And thought must name themselves safe from the ardor
That walls apart all striving unities;
Admit no future fiercer than this river
Raging over cascades of ice the winter
Sun will soon take down.

The mind believes as much
As blood believes, nor grieves for surer purpose
In the immense star-endless curl of space
Than sea's or hill's or frail ephemeras'
Of air, but takes the earth and sun for truth
Eternal in a treasured now, and love
Its anchorage in time.

Poetry: The Art

In the Form of an Apostrophe to Whitman

I used to read your book and hear your words
Explode in me and blast new passageways
Deep in my brain, until its crowding rooms
Held more light than my head could balance. Now
That the tunnels all are cut, I pace the rooms

Looking for you, though certain I shall find
No more of you than you yourself could gather
Out of the pieces of self. The years have burned
The sharpness from the edges: I can fit
The pieces, but the mortar must be mixed
Out of our blending wills. Others have tried
And failed. I too shall fail if I forget
How thought can range beyond the last frontiers
That common sense has civilized with names.

Others who looked for you have made you say
Words you might have said if they were you:
Have lost you in their passion for a phrase.
The private man's infinitude* defies
The singleness they look for when they strive
To sort your various colors to a scheme
Of thought-and-action. Desperate for pattern,
They make the key *Calamus* and they twist
Your other selves around the centerpiece,
Losing you in that love.

    And others forge
A key of social thought that cracks apart
When words and actions contradict: *Walt Whitman,*
You said you love the common man! Where were you
When Parsons'† friends were hanged? Were you asleep
Or writing more fine words about mechanics
And farmers?—How much cosier for you
To prate about democracy than live it—
You, its self-appointed poet!

    Others,
Seeking you in your plangent celebrations
Of science and the holiness of flesh
And earth, end with a fierce *You too, Walt Whitman,*

---

*"In all my lectures I have taught one doctrine, namely, the infinitude of the private man."—Emerson, *Diary*, 1840.

†Parsons, one of seven workmen sentenced to death in the Haymarket Square incident, Chicago, 1886.

You flinched, you stumbled, hankering for a "soul" . . .
The substances of sense too harsh too bitter
A truth for you to live by! Underneath
Your protest boils the soft romantic sickness
Of all the Shelleys, Heines—bright lost leaders
We hoped were men. You were afraid of the dark:
You who had thundered "Science is true religion"
Sang the groveler's wooing song to Death
And God and Spirit! . . . *Hide, at least, the image*
Revealed: the gaudy chaos of a man
Reviling his own faith!

But who can dare
To arbitrate the depths of you that anger
Against your tranquil self? I am not certain:
I have seen the signposts of contradiction
Planted by men impotent to discern
The harmony beneath the subtle wholeness,
And in their self-defence erect confusion
On quiet entities. A poet's words
Are signatures of self—the many selves
Subsumed in one profounder sense that knows
An all-according truth: a single eye
Uncovering the countless constellations
Of heart and mind. Wherefore the syllables
Reach outward from the self in an embrace
Of multitudes. The poetries of speech
Are acts of thinking love; and I must find
The thought that grows the center of your passion.

And so I say to those who precontemn
The message of *Calamus* as the flowers
Of twisted love what Plato showed of truths
Uttered by poets. And I say to those
Who spit upon your social thought *"Respondez!"**

---

*"Respondez!" was first published in 1856 as "Poem of the Proposition of Nakedness."
Other words of Whitman: "the human race is restive, on watch for some better era, some
divine war"; "A new and tender reverence."

The human race is restive, on the watch
For some new era—some divine war—
Whose triumph will entrench a brave good-will
Among the common people everywhere—
The trodden multitudes for whom you clamored
A new and tender reverence.

But for those
Who sneer because you looked for lights beyond
The planes of sense, there is no final answer
If they deny the mind its birthright freedom
To range all worlds of thought and sense and vision.
Everything that can be believ'd is an image of truth*—
The images refined to great and small
Will cluster into orbits of belief
And hold together as the planets hold
By kinship and denial, in one vaster
All encompassing circle. Let the sneerers
Proclaim your chief intent or keep their silence
Until its name is found.

It is not found,
The answer to your central search—"the problem,
The only one"—*adjust the individual*
Into the mass.† For we have just begun
To fit the world to men, men to the world;
And we shall stumble till the single heart
Discovers all its selves and learns therefrom
How singleness and multitude can live
In valiant marriage. With your hungry hope
You pierced the shells of feeling, trumpeted
Into your country's ears, and flooded strength
Into the wavering hearts of men lonely

*"Everything that can be believ'd is an image of truth."—Blake, *Marriage of Heaven and Hell.*

†Horace Traubel reports Whitman's statement: "That is the same old question—adjusting the individual to the mass. Yes, the big problem, the only problem, the sum of them all."

For courage to fulfill their need: to thrust
Their single faith against the massed-up wills
Of many. "Sing your self!" you told them. Listening,
They pledged the valors of the inward man.
And others turned from you with dull, deaf ears,
Afraid to listen, waiting to be taught
The trial-and-error way of rats in a maze . . .

A poem "is," some men believe. I say
A poem "is" when it has spread its root
Inside a listener's thought and grows a tree there
Strong enough to burst a room in the brain,
And bring its branch to blossom. Then the host
Forgets the verse and ponders on the mind
That made this seed of growth . . . as I forget
Your poem: as I strive to learn your mind,
Thinking that when I come to understand,
I may begin to touch serenities
You saw beneath the springs of pain that nourished
Your world that was beginning—dim, green world
Trembling with death-and-birth: divinest war.

Song Aspires to Silence

Song aspires to silence.
Men of defiant words
Look to the breaking moment
When blood will shed the fever,

Freed of the ceaseless striving
To fasten mountains and seas
And tame the resistless wills
Of hell and heaven defiant.

Song aspires to silence:
The fear that drones above

The rapt fury of song
Seeks its calm in driving

The blood to bury in words
The ever-unnameable love
That plunders the mind and
        storms the bewildered heart.

Ravel and Bind

Whatever: it bears a glow
Above; a seed below,
Thinking might never know
In like-unlike confined:

Lest it erupt and flow,
What can we make with mind
But sorts according to kind
From the worlds of ravel and bind.

To a Young Girl Sleeping

Into this room of sleep let fall
        The moon's dimmest bars—
Glitter might rouse her still hands lying
        Paler than water-stars;

And let the nightwind calmly flow,
        Lay but the frailest words
On her whose face is a shadow softer
        Than evening birds'.

Days

Strange to be torn away from your embrace
                In the cold dawn,
To be taken far from your face, your silence,
                To be drawn

Past streets, fields, rivers, toward a place
                Miles, miles away
Where senseless words and images clog the mind
                Till the end of day,

When, turning back to you, I wonder, moving
                Through twilight haze,
If we must live only in meeting and parting
                The rest of our days.

Thoughts of the War and My Daughter

The year you came to the world
Blood had already enflamed
The breath of a hundred cities,
Wounds of a thousand streets
Already stopped up, embalmed

In ash. This side of the sea
We were June and green. We could tell
Sleep from waking, in silence
Pure. The wind blew east
From our rock-shelf, over the swale

Of ocean, never thrown back
To save: brittle and vain
With hope. The year you babbled

The first of your words, you could play
Hide and seek with the rain

And his shadow—while we were learning
Fear, but slowly, crossed
In a weltering love. You could prance
On fern and water, a spangle
Of sunlight endlessly kissed

By our eyes. What was your thought
When you first looked overhead
And saw in a summer's field
Of night the ever-amazed
Face in a fleeing cloud?

The same as theirs, the children
With the tongueless women and men,
As they watched from the German walls
Over their death-camp cities
An ever-abandoned moon?

End of a Visit

"I am going back—now," I say and you nod
Half-sorrowing, half-smiling.
We both look at the clock.

'I'll write, of course—next week perhaps'—a bird
Grazes a screen; startled,
Flies upward, darts down.

I gather
My parcels, books, coat; glance at your face
(It is time to go from a child,

A woman now, bruised; with a place for her head,
        thought, arms, and a trail
Her body reads in the dark)

                "I must go back."

                'I know—it's time.'

Drawn to the door, I hold it,
Open it, speak, half-aware
That while I repeat my words
The earth's sphere to which we cling will be fleeing
Another countless thousand miles from nowhere to nowhere.

Bread

This that I give you now,
This bread that your mouth receives,
Never knows that its essence
Slept in the hanging leaves

Of a waving wheatfield thriving
With the sun's light, soil, and the rain,
A season ago, before knives
And wheels took life from the grain

That leaf might be flour—and the flour
Bread for the breathers' need . . .
Nor cared that some night one breather
Might watch how each remnant seed

Invades the blood, to become
Your tissue of flesh, and molests
Your body's secrets, swift-changing
To arms and the mounds of your breasts,

To thigh, hand, hair, to voices,
Your heart and your woman's mind . . .
For whatever the bread, do not grieve now
That soon a flash of the wind

May hurry away what remains
Of this quiet valiance of grass:
It entered your body, it fed you
So that you too can pass

From valiance to quiet, from thriving
To silenced flesh, and to ground:
Such is our meager cycle
That turns but a single round

For the deathless flesh of the earth,
For the signless husks of men dead,
For the folded oceans and mountains,
For birds, and fields, and for bread.

End of the Flower-World

Fear no longer for the lone gray birds
That fall beneath the world's last autumn sky,
Mourn no more the death of grass and tree.

These will be as they have ever been:
Substance of springtime; and when flower-world ends,
They will go back to earth, and wait, and be still,

Safe with the dust of birds long dead, with boughs
Turned ashes long ago, that still are straining
To leave their tombs and find the hills again,

Flourish again, mindless of the people—

The strange ones now on a leafless earth
Who seem to have no care for things in blossom.

Fear no more for trees, but mourn instead
The children of these strange, sad men: their hearts
Will hear no music but the song of death.

House in St. Petersburg

If my mother had never been the protected child
Of a dreamy scholar in a protected house,
    I would not be writing these lines—

If the sign hung in the window of that house
Had told a different lie from the lie it told,
    I would not be writing these lines—

If the bribed police who winked at the sign had lived—
If the old one had not choked in a swilling night,
    I would not be writing these lines—

If the young recruit had been briefed with the well-bribed word
By his well-bribed captain before he walked by the house,

Or if he had never tripped on a cobble of ice
And ripped his shirt as he sprawled on a gashing stone,
    I would not be writing these lines—

If he had not then remembered the house with the sign
Because of the word it had always said to the street,

Or if when he asked the service of needle and thread
Father or child could have brought him needle and thread,
    I would not be writing these lines—

If the suddenly tongueless man of a stricken house
Had dared to speak with his eyes and a bag of gold,

Or if the gold had said to the young recruit
What it always said when the hunted spoke to the law,
   I would not be writing these lines—

If the young recruit had not shouted guilt in the street
So that passersby turned round to assault the house,
If he had not screamed the name as he climbed the steps
To the barracks and flung his find in his captain's face,

Or if when the captain scanned the innocent's eyes
He had found a gleam that confessed it was not too late,
   I would not be writing these lines—

If the innocent had not shouted again and again
And again—if the captain could have closed up his ears,

Or if his major, cursing his luck and loss,
Had never signed the papers to pillage and seize,
   I would not be writing these lines—

If the child and father, clinging with dread in the snows
Of night, had failed before they reached the frontier,

Or if their boat, lost in a wild North Sea,
Had not been sighted and saved on a Scottish shore,
   I would not be writing these lines—

Or, when they voyaged again, if their battered ship
Had not groped through its trial to the promised port,

Or if when they saw the sun of a friending earth
They had not danced in the recklessness of its air,
   I would not be writing these lines—

If the father after the years of dancing and grief

Had sought his sleep on an alien hill of Home,
      I would not be writing these lines—

Or if my mother, walking in tears from his grave,
Had not returned, one April, to join his sleep,
      I would not be writing these lines—

And if she herself, before, in a long ago,
Had never told this tale to a young one's eyes,
      I would not be singing her song.

Midnight Wind to the Tossed

I glared at the wind, the wind glared back. The window
Walls us apart. Where has it gone? No answer.
Better that way. A truce is made, the issue
Thrown to a future night.—At last: *Good-night.*
But fire comes creeping out of the sky, into the room,
In eyelids. *Oh, what are walls?* "Scatter their stones!"
Why? "For your reachless roses." *Roses?* "And listen:

A free man needs no house: only a fool
Lusts in rooms for calm: only the old
And young can always sleep: only the tossed
Wrestle with shadows, striving to close fingers
On shapes of loving. Wake! To be purely free,
Speak to your hands until they drop from your arms:
Cherishing is to touch, covet, and seize."

Sonnet to the Earth

Because your flame was torn from burning skies
And spun in space to find the course or fail,
We cannot look at you with children's eyes—
For we are children of the same travail;
Nor can we let our calm become too strong
Or build contentments in the path we found,
For you must always be a moving song
And we must always follow for your sound.

Though yielded to your song's enchantment, none
In our tribe of flesh can give his heart's release
To certainties—thus do we mock or wrong
Your will, torn by our fear of stark caprice
That questions why we follow in your song
Arcs that may break us both against the sun.

Isaac

The story haunts this tribe that cannot wipe from its eyes
The flashing hill, the trembling man tying his son in his arms, the
    bewildered ram
Bearing twigs and firewood. They think it again and again
Through fifty centuries. Even now when they look at a chance hillock
Under the sky of an unmysterious day, the eyes
Of their poets hang it with flame—
                "Father, father, save Isaac!"
One of them hears his night cry out, as though the indifferent cloud
Were sown with seeds of blood bursting to flutter
Over the boiling stones.

              Even my own father
One morning of my longago childhood helplessly

Watched his thought slip through the triple Hegelian chain
With which he wrestled the world, to relieve the curse
Thou shalt not raise thy hand . . .

                    Nor yet can a generation
Die without shouting once into the air to purge its heart
Of the blind obsessive tale, as though for always unsure
Of the wrong of worshipping the blood's terror of sacrifice.

The Axe of Eden

And finally
The pure question that throbs under every facet
Of trust and bitten peace,
To ask of how and when,
Giving up all the wherefore-whys, outdistanced
Beyond all confrontation.
So prepare to enter: You must be asked,
Facing the face in the glass.

                    —There is no one there,
You expect to say; thus having clouded over
That a shape cannot break through. It is always an image,
Never yourself itself. Likeness
Is only a mask of thought, no touching fingers
To taunt you to hopefulness, madness, emptiness, sleeplessness.
You are withered enough to learn and you lack the years to evade.
What could you fear
That you have not already sustained? By now you have died
All the imagined human deaths. Who could devise
Wiser horror?—Then take your height in the glass,
Silver the back. Gaze—and joy
In our innocent birthday song
      Out of the mud
      And into a field
      Lighted with trees and stones

Earth of the paradise—fen
To Eden—garden of faultless joy,
Teeming berry and leaf and flower
And over, under, around, and across,
Birds and angels flying the air—
They yellow down from the morning sun,
Scattering home through sleeping stars
—While your God was breathing, breathing out of His tree
Beneath whose branch you slept,
His sacred fruit above your head
In the evening air: apples of God,
Glistening always over your vacant eyelids,
Cluster of suns
Ever beyond the reach of arms,
The reach of eyes, dazed
In haloes burning the clustered branch,
Clustering mystic suns
Beyond the reach of thought—

Where
Had your footsteps led? From the garden wall
Had you spied the ravine beyond? Your body
Shivered sleeping against the ground
The night you heard the branch sway down
To thrust into your hollow mind
The knowing suns, so into your veins
The birth of dream: *to seize beyond*
The reach, though seizing kill and spirit
Wail from its dying blood—to seize
His burning rose, swallow the fruit
Of God, His flesh infuse your flesh,
His sight your sight—

The sacred tree
Twists the cluster high in a sudden
Scald of wind. A fleering bird
Shakes you up from the ground. And must your eyes
Surround your body's fear, watching
Shadows out of whose coil
May leap your double of dream?

Light

Breaks on the garden, bearing into your glances
Comforting shapes of day—yet the drugging dream
Hangs on your eyes. And shall they always peer
Dreading the sudden seizing wraith,
The possible other of dream?

He is everywhere. Fly!
Save yourself! What are eyes against arms? Fly!
Hide in the cave by the wall, and think, think
A waking dream to save. Seize! Kill
If you must—all is alive in this land but the stones.
Take one! harder, fiercer. Raise it and strike! But stop—
Everything bleeds.

Now you are safe, you can walk
With this axe of stone in your hand, back toward the tree
Breathing to you as before. Shall you forget
It led you to an axe through a coiling thought
Of sleep to waking?—Before you walk,
Look at your hands.
Where will you wash the stain?
Eden's well dries up at the touch of blood. Cross the walls
To the cataract in the ravine. But once outside
Can you come back?

Go to God with your stain!
Ask who made you shed the blood. Open your voice, accuse
The clustering suns that grew in your mind the sickness of dream.
Dare you believe Him innocent, you who were cast
In His shape? You were shaped of Him by His Will in a pyre
Of yearning, lonely of God! All you have done is obey
The impulse under the image. Why be afraid?
He gave you fear. Is He in truth the God-
That-Makes? Then go in the helpless knowledge the suns
Compelled beneath your skin.

The axe cries out
Against the blight of this Eden Perfected—land

Of the paradigm void—if nothing dies
Nothing can spring to birth. The restless axe
Cries out for making. The edge that kills creates.
Who will hold back the hand straining to shape
The multiple dances?

                              —You have crossed the wall
To the cataract in the ravine where blood dissolves
Back to the sea from which you climbed
Out of the mud
And into a field
Lighted with trees and stones—
Fen to Eden's ultimate height. If anything shout
Into your ears that He drives you out of His garden,
Cry the Responsible God who prepared your flight
In the pyre that made you His double—

                              Puny creator,
Walking now with your axe beyond the ravines,
Beyond the cataract now—
Who could have ever believed this opening world of endless fields?
They would never have been believed, even from the farthest ledge
Of the garden wall. And now, lost in their midst,
How can your teeming eye and ear
Accept such oceans of grass burning a naked sun,
Vastnesses of fields and rivers and trees, rising mountains,
Magnificence of birth so wide and huge and far
And high—world without walls! trilling with cries, calls, screams,
Miracle wild of shape and wing. Leaping creation.
Infinitudes for the possible . . .

                              Does the axe
Know? One might think it reasons,
The edge bubbled with rays, breathless
With force and flight. Watch! It is thundering toward you,
Surging over your head—your guardian! Wake up,
This is no second nightmare. You are no longer the child
Who cried for help in a poem that was prayer to Eden.
Nobody listens to cries in this goldening chaos,
Except his own.

Yet scream if it brings relief,
Though yours are the only ears that turn, yours and your generations',
Milling through chartless paths that shape
The soil, multiple treading millions
Rising and dying in change and to each a pulsing
Axe, the body's stone extension that rises
To fall, to change, yet never to grow
A willing tongue of its own. Yours
Is the single voice and still it shouts from the reckless rise into
    knowledge
Forever against yourself and your stone
In wavering love and dread of both—

Though you have done no wrong. There is no evil
Except of a word you have made in fear. There is no fear
Except in the wound of wraiths borne
From your pure equation of man with axe. And are you sure
That pure is true, reasoning out of your cage
Of filaments attuned to your narrow gamut
Of voices here where the silence of night
Pounds the incessant torrent and beat, the blooming buzzing
    confusion
Past the filaments' deafness?

                          And if you burst the cage
Into the day's torrent, would you grow sure?—
Messages beating into your ears,
Morning through night, starlight through sunrise,
Howling: screaming: cries of murdered ants and dying birds and
    failing grasses: explosions
In shrieking trees: in the spilling bloods of the billion creatures
    falling, rising, seen and unknown, near you, over you, under you—
You walk the earth with an axe. Now it advances
Whirling over your head.
Acknowledge the stone, ask in the cage
Our only question: *Where?*

Though we tear at each other's tongues, we are the kindred
Of fear's confusion, given the range of a jungle

Unchartable, though the apertures of its sight
Would make of a point a sphere . . . the earth is round
And flat . . . each twilight we fall to wither reborn . . .
—Find the way through your dust,
Delusion done: Enter your tremulous wholeness:
The world is one and the world is a trillion fragments
Of touch. Grow them together, cleave them apart—
They bear no scar: It is you, their maker-and-breaker-
And-healer. Then press, cry
Against the cage of your mind till its agonized walls
Burst, and ravel and bind,
Erupt in a flow of reason and blood's dissolving sea
Sight that makes and tears with a healing kiss—
Or, mute on land with fear,
Languish under your axe!

                    The myths
Denying change advance their sanctities
To ring you in a return to a primal God outgrown
And the priests you watched by the bloodfires on the swamps.
Must you flee them again, though swamp and fire
Had disappeared, had become night-past
Voids of fear? Yet flee! For ever the rites
Of terror wake, exhuming a primal dream
To strangle time and your history.

                        Everything made
Is good and sacred. The paradise dream
Of childhood never was. You were old
The instant you crossed the wall out of Eden,
Forehead gouged by compelling will to follow the sudden self
Boiling your veins. O ancient face gorged with pain,
Beloved newborn face, look outward now and across
Your worlds within the world! Admit no sin
But grief, no prayer but desire . . . So turn eyes
With your making passion, and bear toward the multiple hills
Sight: and they shall be there as you build them there,
Though you die before or the clash of suns enshroud.
Truth is the truth of wish: direction is all.

Night of the Canyon Sun

Lying above the rim
Of this hollowed world: my sight
Held in the never-believing
Night of this dark, suddenly
Floods with love for the sun.

But you, black sun, why you
Alone of the guardian terrors?
Beneficent sun, cold warmer,
Whose flood transfused to leaf
Propels the broods on earth?

Shall mouth resist with praise—
Mouth of your tissue—striving,
Fed on yourself, green sun,
Maker-sustainer? I carry
Within the horns of my skin

The same pure arcs that listen
On the infinite's beach of fire,
The same forever wisdoms
Churning, out of whose gasps
The living and dying spheres

Unroll. Then hail, my unquenchable
Day! white sun and only
Turner of sea-bed, mountain,
And helplessly flowing waters,
Whose law's caprice compels

Breathings of ice to burst
My axe of stone and knowledge.
O mountain- and vision-breaker,
How long will the heart stay blind
To your bitterly building might?

The moon is a frozen thought
But yours is the symbol fused
With the tendrils of its sign
So vastly strewn that desire,
Scanning the lights of dark,

Passed you by in the search
Of fire. Eye of your flaming
Graces not mine alone
But drives me outward onward
To gather a calm that men

May grow when their bodies learn
To meet the guardian terrors
With unexalting prayer.
Wherefore, against all shadows,
In the hard plain light I cry:

"Consume-sustain your sun
That feeds and consumes our flesh!
Gorge on the bones for worship
And flee your dark! Oh smother
The god in the sun with his passion

Not to adore: to know!"
An echo beats through the dark

From the wailing rites of fear
To maim the words of light:
"Never to know but adore."

—Speech falls back from the air,
From the canyon, into my ears.
Who will be heard: the shadows?
My sun of the desert night?
Till words are made to utter

Reverberations of light,

No man will speak to a man
Of what can only be found
In loneliness as he moves
Unaware in search of his heart.

The Rock

Foothills of Mt. Sinai

I have looked all day for The Rock*
In this land where the grains are always seen.
I found no mark on the soil,
Sand and loam too old once more to be pressed prone or pierced
Apart. Only across the faces of scattered
Women and men are there any scars,
Rips, burrs—and these are such as a glacial mountain
Signs, roaring across dry ground to the sea
Of a younger land in the melting kill of its breath.

Talmudist

Gloat, glittering talmudist,
With your eastern eye, your northern eye, your western eye;
The days are a fog of clashing words: cleave
If you can—warp with your buzz-saw brain a light-filled
Path shallow enough for a heart to follow!

Why do you fist your words
With your merchant's hand, your scholar's hand, your toiler's hand?
Is a god you smother the dynamo of your fury

*The Rock: one of the Hebrew appellations for God.

Or a wraith you reasoned into existence in hope
It would pierce your eye with joys? Or a heartsick need

For a heaven-on-earth perfection
That drives you, though you have found there can be no right
Unmixed with wrong. Where will you go when the moment
Strikes and your arms, defying brain, reach out
To your brothers' will, your homeland's will, your body's will?

A River

For Allen Tate

Blue, windless and deep, above my head,
Above the valley, the plain, the distant trees:
    Depthless arch of a morning

September sky wherever I turn as I gaze
Upward. From these peering ledges of rock
    To which my straying feet

Have borne my thoughtless body, let me gather
A blue world overhead, a green below,
    To carry back if I find

The path to home. How did I travel here
So surely from the road through stumbling fields?
    What are those bending trees

Twisted across the slope below?—green granite
Arching a hollow? Where does that sudden river
    Come from? Where can it go?

Watched from this ledge below: see how it winds,
Sunk deep beneath its valleys, an ancient
    River. But look! it curves

East and beyond. Now it widens into a vast
Meadow of gray water? Is it water,
    That flood of vacant light,

Or a withered field? But there: it has filled the plain.
It is water.—But if water, how can it stare
    Into the deeps of the sky

With emptied colorless eyes? Or is it blind:
River too old to bear an outward light,
    To carry blue to blue?

These must be the acres I wandered across
A year ago from a road far from my house
    When I followed into the blaze

Of a setting sun an unknown hurrying man,
The loom of fleshless form that gave no shadow
    Back to the dappled ground.

These trees covet their stillness, yet I ask
Their presences to warn me against my hour
    Of flight, early or late,

Before my body can gaze with empty eyes
And love become too inward borne to answer
    Light of a sun with light.

I Think Among Blank Walls

Strive with reason under the open sky?
Landscape will spin your brain, wring your eye,
All knowledge floating weightless:

I think among blank walls
Bandied by sights whose spending clash ignites
A willing rapture, till the tongue recalls.

I Build My House . . .

I build my house to keep out vermin, damp,
Decay, and time. Poems embalm belief
With words; paintings lay out the growing brightness
In shrouds of color; sculptures mummify
Flesh softness into rock. Can a daisy think?
Whatever is learned at last, we alone can summon
Fire, can touch a match to the logs and quicken
A cold black house with locked-up light of the sun.

Once in a dream I searched a globe, holding
Candles to see whatever might wait within.
Trustful, I pried at the sphere, tore it,
Looked inside. It was empty dark:
Hollow earth of nothingness in the core.

Waking, I walked to the window; looked at the sky
Of morning overhead and the growing brightness
Below. My land was alive:
Miracle breathings of flesh and leaf joining
Voices in dearness everywhere.

There is no wasted land until we cover it
With dryness of the heart in weariness,
Deny our anchorage to a land bedded
On a basalt continent that turns on seas
Distilled from waters blown from a time and place
We can never reach or touch, propelled by light
Of a sun beyond beholding: circled flesh

Contained within a sphere, straining to tear
Through the shell, range the beyond, and flee the hollow
Nothingness of the core:

Open your eyes
To the words, the rock, the color; take what they hold
Of fever-summoned calmness—more than enough
To quicken and sustain the truce you need.
Accept them: they are all you have, though flawed
By desperate griefs and strident symmetries,
Maimed by concussive will—as all that lives
Sustains through whole con-fusion. Nothing pure
Can cope with time, unbrazed to the impure—
Look for no perfect art except in death.

Looking for Papa

All the sad young men are looking for Papa,
The sad young men who think they were bad young men,
And their fathers and their grandfathers who were young
Once and are old: all the old young men,
And the women too, and the children: every one—
They are all looking for Papa . . . burdened Papa,
Helplessly procreant Papa who never was born
Or found.
          Shall we join the hunt? Is it a game?
A wonderfully solemn game, and very sad.

Let's look for him then. In the sky, in the sea, in the ground,
Any where at all, above us, below us, so long
As we look outside. Be sure to look outside
Ourselves. . . . Poor wandering Papa,
Bright and invincible and always outside, always outside;
We must never allow him entry; we must never
          let him come in.

Clay

To a snow-world deaf,
To a leaf-world blind,
Where can you go
With your dangling mind

Save to the hells
Of joy? Then come
In your pith of fear
And your skin of numb:

The soothing tongues
Of blazing grief
May hollow your mind
Of its unbelief

In light and sound
And striving wish.
But do not covet
Your remnant ash,

Revel, or brood
In fire too long:
All thought is clay
And withered song

Whose sweet will burn
To a salt of truth
When leaf is age
And snow is youth.

Modes of Belief

For Lionel Trilling

Ever since I grew cold
In heart, I always hear
Most men that I behold
Cry like a creature caught
In tones of dying will,
Such as their eyelids bear
With cuneiforms of fail—

Where are the young and wild
Teeming in hope of power?
Though striving lifts the bud,
None can achieve the flower.
Where can the bud disperse
Within? Must every man
Entomb a withered child?—

What early hearts can store
Of sweetness still endures
Fever of flood or drought,
Till groping up from within,
A self-bereaving curse
Masses in reefs of thought,
Burns and bites the blood—

Seedling Air

I do not change. I grow
The kernel that my hair,
My thought, my blood, enflames.
I sing my seedling air:

I shout this ancient air

Into the hail of days
That washes through my skin
To pound and drench my bones.
I keep my light within:

My light burns on within

Flooding my endless rooms
Of pure and feeling brain
Till streams of wisdom-warmth
Murmur within each vein:

They chant within each vein

Will to withstand unchanged
All grindings of that air
Though torrents press down hail
Harsher than they would bear;

For what has will to bear

But outward change that strives
To enter in, and breath
But inner bloom that wavers
Under the hail of death?

Among Trees of Light

Always men on earth have sought the wondrous
Mist-shadows for sacredness; all else lay
Too far from heaven:

In the night's darkness, we said, are symbols stranger
Than ever day with all its magic and dazzle
Could hide away.

Older now with empty hands, emerged from darkness,
We move among trees of light, striving to learn
The flaming mind

That throbs in every glitter of day; we gather
Figures of light none of the dark's adept
Could find, fond

In the shadow-mists. Searching till leaves lay bare
Their sleeping suns, we dare accept as much
As fire unlocked

Can show, however the embers freeze or scorch us,
Fearful that eyes alone, or thought, or love
Alone, can capture

Nothing beyond the reaches of singleness:
Not light but the mirrored glow of a burning wish.

Florida Seaside

Every winter I saw her here, late
January, filling the same
Corner of beach alone: worn face
To the sun; then treading the sea's
Edges for minutes before the long
Glide on the water: back and forth
And back in slow, spreading spirals
Ending at last on sand—then hastily
Off again, alone as she came,
Till the next morning of brightness.

Our first four winters we neither glanced
Hello nor nodded, and then as if
Suddenly we'd been told we were sharing time,
One of us mumbled "Good to be back . . .
Better than shivering . . ." Never more;
Not even "Staying till April?"

The attendant knows each person's name and home.

"Have you seen her here? Woman about my age.
Down from the north, I think."

    "Maine. Of course I know her."

"Here this year?"

    "Not yet, but scores will be late."

"Or missing."

    "Why must you think such a thing?"

"People don't live forever."

    "Sure of it, friend? Some of us might.
    She'll be here one of these days."

"Sure of it, friend?"

    "Have to be. Happens again and again.
    Been here twenty years . . . Must run now—
    Somebody's calling . . ."

Now that it's March, I might prod him to tell me all he knows of her.
"Why?" he would challenge.
"Nothing," I'd shrug, lacking an answer
Fitted to words. He'd glance at me, shake his head,
Study my face, his eyes saying
I had no right, not even knowing her name.

Argon

Inert gas mixed throughout atmosphere soon after it is inhaled; hence all creatures breathe in part what everyone else who ever lived breathed.

So long as leaf and flesh—
Fed on each other's cast-out breath—
Nourish the oceans of lower sky: so long

As lip-sealed earth fulfils
Its sun-warmed captive circle, drink,
O drink while we may the forever imprisoned air

Of exhalations sullied
And saved, that lungs fill up their double,
Helpless inner-abyss with the strengthening gift

Of brothering air,
Undefiling, that infants, ancients,
Killers, and saints with all other choiceless share.

A Recurring Vision

Down, down, gone down,
Gone down and under the sea,
Past harbor, streets, and piers—the sun
Has drowned.

       So up with the lights,
Up, up in the streets! Let cars
Dazzle at curbs, spit light, make a flare
For whatever man or woman gropes
In the alleys home.

You must drive out black:
Remember, its fingers would reach for your throat
At the death of day. Black is cold
In a city of night or a cave.

                  Then light the stones
In all the storeys! Turn up the bells
Of fire, tier on piling tier,
Till the panes burst and ring in the comfort
Of light—which is heat. Turn on sound—
Its rays are warmth. Pour it on floors
Till they shake the walls.—Look! You live
Though the sun drowns in the sea.—Scorn!
You can tally survival, measure your miles
Of wire, tons of your stone, steel,
The heights and depths of quantified heat
That keeps your throbbing through nights of ice—

        But sometimes
In the late morning I see your same stones wearing
Wreaths. All through the day I see black webs
Hang from the towers, they sway from ledges, they are caught
In the hair of the ginkgo trees. I watch them float on roofs
And swirl down toward pavements. They crowd walls, everywhere
Watching with an unknown unknowable stare
That eats at eyes that stare back till those eyes
To save themselves fling up
From the level below to the level above, to the sky, to a colorless foam
Above. Whatever they find there
Soothes and holds them motionless.
Is it blankness of day? blankness of night?
A fiercer double disdain?

Chanson Innocente

Cast your faith in the ever-nearing
Catastrophe your brothers and I
Pull, each instant we live, down
On the mother-once sea, the nurturing sky,
The hostage acres of soil we flay
And nurse for our bread and warmth. Then hail
Catastrophe!—what else to hail
Except your terrified creature-lust

To survive? Its imminence might save,
Driving, as with the wrath from a once-
Believed-in heaven, across the water
And land our all-devouring hordes
Till none could range but a remnant shriven
Of strangelove mind and suicide hand.

The Hero of Silence

SCENES FROM AN IMAGINED LIFE
OF MALLARMÉ

The only thing a self-respecting man can do is to keep looking up at the sky as he dies of hunger.

—Mallarmé to Cazalis, 1865

DEDICATION: AN ETERNITY OF WORDS

So to compose the universe—
Killing: spawning worlds with denial,
Dragging truth through scourging laws
To earn a life in my thought.

What if the innocent blood of body's
Desire rise up in words unaided?
Even flesh can be burned
To the whitenesses of a song,

That out of oblivion ash may float
—My Orphic Book of the Earth!—
An eternity of words where naming
Creates, refusal destroys.

II. MASTER AND PUPILS

Time to lock up my brain and drudge to school.

Dare I ever cry out: "I own a glass
That sucks in eyes to the depths?"

Might they hear
If I began: "I found a curious thing
By chance—
Perhaps it came in a kind of trance"—
Thus easing the word, that they might care
This once? . . .

"A mirror, simply. Familiar—but how to use it?
        Hear!
You must more-than-glance,
You must more-than-turn
When you look: Press, burn,
Stare them out of substance, enemy-loves,
Till the sight changes to sound,
Sound to nothingness—
The indifference of the sky, a stone"—

But none of them will care to follow me, captives
Of their own dismay,
Waiting inside this fatal door

For my entering step to trumpet daily war—Yet
Might I plead with them:

"Close your book
And hear of this glass I own.
It sucks all pressing eyes, presses them back
Till gaze parrying gaze
Bursts into ice of flame, to abolish walls,
Dissolve flesh into Azure"—

But no. I am here.
Inside. Against them now.

Gravely they throb: flesh I must love. Has it overheard
My thought?

"It was only a mirror to me, to you,
Innocent glass but yet the defender of truth."

How they spurn!

"Open your pages! Safer to eye a book!"

One refuses, begins to burn
Till I must stare him down.

Who is this other who presses back? What wakes
In his eyes' answer?
What has he drawing me there
Through the mass of face dissolving? Is light the youth?
Can I gaze it out of substance, flesh that trembles?

III. SOLILOQUY FROM A WINDOW:
MAN AND FLOWERS

If flesh, then all that moves. If blood, then juices
Of ground: blood of a tree, a rock, a flower,
Of all who rise in the mist

Ever floating about a thought's secret
Abyss. Manas converge to the point of light
      Vision flees when the fires

Of seer and seen entwine.—Look at me, flowers
Beneath this window: calyx of roses, gold,
      Purple, white! Your multiple

Eyes, make me your mirror! I dive within you
Bouquet: we return one another, flower and eye
      Moving from each to each

In wakefulness, one to the other's silence:
Song. Shall we lose our flesh to dissolver-light,
      Starers become the stare?

You are shedding your faces. Where have you gone, my petals?
Go to return, vanish as you return,
      So, live in a thrust of mind!

IV. DIALOGUE BEFORE WAKING

Stare!—Stare?

When you will
You can stare it out of substance—
Not only petals.

Whatever waits
For any man answers him with a face
Uplifted, throbbing to speak and be known.

And will you know them then
For what they are as they greet you,
Or must you hide from the ecstasies
Of touch? turn dazed by the flesh
You overlove in your dark of fear?

Stare!

Since you must, at last, at whatever face moves
        toward you.

Stare while the blood drains,
Forsakes the skin.

Then stare with the ice of thought
Fired with a love that kills, and watch the skin
Curl, twist, burn like paper; the bone
To ash—

And within that face
And out of that face that offered a trembling word? . . .

A hovering fume.

V . F U M E

The air that hovered enters coldly,
Sounds in my brain suddenly—
        Nothing I heard before.

This is the silence thought can hear
From voices spoken by planets
        Scorching through nothingness—

Voice of the flame of sky! Imagined
Flower of flame! Floating
        Ideas of sound!—Listen:

They throb alone, islands borne
In azure lakes, but glowing
        Fused and pure. O Poem

Of Flight, I will you into words
From the nothingness of sense
        Through silences of sound,

Such as upon her wedding day
Cecilia, saint and blinded,
          Sang in her heart to God

Her song unheard. Yet will I sing
Entwining sky and flower
          A flame that shall be heard!

VI. INTO THE BLOND TORRENT

Whatever palpitates lives: therefore threatens.
Name them all?—If naming alone could subdue!
     One of my waiting children
     Shall call them. All the equations

Exist. With our eyes' hot destruction we lift
Covers, so all that trembles can rise to the pure
     Reaching touch of kindred
     Selves. We have only to watch

To know. There is nothing left to create. We must see!
Unravel! vanquish!—even my innocent thirst
     For the flooding naked caresses
     Of her golden hair. Cover

My eyes?—Seize! drown! till the blond torrent
Bear me on her trembling thighs to the warm
     River of calm: the sleeping
     Ecstasy of the ages

Lost, found in her golden foam. O quivering
Gulf of invisible song! She alone—from her body's
     Vessel, let me tear out
     The dream! Let the waking phantom

Blind me! body burn with her flight! I shall plunge her
—Destruction be my Beatrice!—into the death
     Of love. And out of the blackness,

Out of our blood silenced,
I may rise, victim, guarding the ash of her flame.

VII. THE WAKING

When body answered, blood
Rebelled,
Heart screeched at the ribs.

And when I uttered, vision
Burst.

And when I awoke,
I saw creation gaze on itself through me:
Infinity contained.

The dream that ravaged has remade. Nothing can harm.
I hold in me a piece of the nothingness
Of which our night is made.

Agonized earth
Has vanquished under a vacant sky.

                              O Poem
Of Flight, abolish wings!

I have no pain. My mind
The hermit of its own purity,
Cannot be touched by time, cannot be touched
Even by time reflected in ageless shadow:
Day.

     I do not seek to make. I seek
The freedom gathered, kept, and to replenish.
The finite falls about me till I die.

NOTES

I: The poem presents Mallarmé's quest: the seven scenes follow a career from the opening "Dedication" to the "Waking" out of the dream that it was: of abstracting from the world of sensation the essences that are the truth, truth of a special sort. In the first scene, he dedicates himself to this searching act: not only to find what these essences are but to create, after finding them, by naming them. "So to compose the universe," by decomposing it into its essences and then by remaking them into the "Orphic Book of the Earth," which (as he considered it) was the collaborative effort of all poets. Once found, these essences can create a universe of their own, a new "eternity of words." And so he goes forth, confronting the sensate world with the belief that "Even flesh can be burned / To the whitenesses of a song."

II: A teacher by profession, he goes to his classroom for his daily work—but worried by the insignificance of what he is teaching in the light of his quest. He dreams of brushing aside the textbooks and lessons to tell the students the great truth that he knows and is also seeking. How? He thinks of saying to his students that a mirror transforms the object it reflects into its abstract self, its truth.—And then he comes to feel it would be hopeless to try to persuade them to his thought: "Open your pages! Safer to eye a book!" But one of the students refuses—and suddenly he (Mallarmé) has become a mirror into which the boy gazes. Confused by what has happened to his own sentient self, he nevertheless knows that he has become a mirror gazing back into the boy and drawing out of this human object the essences that "mirrors" are able to draw out of the sensate world that they take in. And so he asks himself: Can he "gaze it out of substance, flesh that trembles?"

III: In a later contemplation of this experience, he tries to unravel his beliefs: a soliloquy from a window, a man gazing at some flowers. The thoughts floating into his mind as he gazes suggest some of the beliefs he had uttered about essence: the essential flowerness, that which is "absent from all bouquets." To be found, it must be removed (from all bouquets), leaving only the idea of flower. "Where have you gone, my petals?" he asks as by his force of mind he removes their presences. "Go to return, vanish as you return," he commands them now, but the second "return" is a return by living. Hence when they return to him they will not be flowers he can touch or smell but the essence-idea that will "live in a thrust of mind."

IV: The experience stays with him as he looks elsewhere on the sensate world— "Not only petals," he says. His other self answers: "Whatever waits" can stare back at the gazer to make itself known (a parallel of a kind to what happened in II, when the boy gazed back at the teacher). The scene continues in dialogue to its conclusive thoughts—that what comes out of this staring, which is a burning (I: "Even flesh can be burned / To the whitenesses of a song"), is the "hovering fume"; an essence that floats in the air (recalling the suggestion of the word "spirit").

V: And now, in Scene V, he is filled with a hovering fume—floating out of many different sensory objects. He speaks with words that signify absence, silence, nothingness, and in the fourth and fifth stanzas he cries out his resolution: in a Poem of Flight from sentience, he will create a song that cannot be heard by the ears of sense, for it will be pure flame—the flame out of which the fume of essence arises as pure idea. . . .

VI: Even out of the experience of human flesh in its inexpressibly consuming sense—of love-embrace, immolation, self-loss. Mallarmé's obsessive fascination by blond hair becomes a river of sensuous-sensual ecstasy—the "blond torrent" into which he dives and on which he asks to be borne, where he can relive "the sleeping / Ecstasy of the ages" at once "Lost [and] found in her golden foam." And then—the final desperate act: to destroy this power of the flesh, to kill at last, to plunge into "the death / Of love," so that he may rise up —from his finally silenced blood, no longer to be torn by the terrible forces of sense enflamed and enflaming; to rise up, holding the thing he has sought, the prize: the "ash of" the "flame" that is human life.

VII: He is shaken out of the dream—and the quest—for when his body answered, his "blood rebelled, / Heart screeched at the ribs," and when he spoke the words of idea-essence (I: words that had "burned / To the whitenesses of a song"), vision "burst." And he saw creation itself, the infinitely encompassing mirror, "gaze on itself through" him. Yet "the dream that ravaged has remade" —and he speaks with his familiar symbols through the remaining lines: of night, day, nothingness, purity. Waking into the transfigured reality from his dream (transfigured by the dream-into-waking), he cries out of the wakened quest, "O Poem / Of Flight, abolish wings" (thus silencing the Poem of Flight invoked in V, which bore his hope). The concluding lines of this scene are the confession: "Mon art est un impasse. . . . Ici-bas est maître. . . . We measure our finiteness against infinity. . . . [letter to a friend, Mauclair]."

The House Hollow

The house hollow. The last of our four-footed children
Dead. Fur, bones, motion, willowy footprints,
Eyes that had looked at mine stranger than all other eyes,
Lost in a palmful of ash on a cold grass.

No one now to trail my feet or hide under low forsythia,
Watching me while I call. Or late inside the house
Leap to my knees, trace on my quilt a ringful of sleep, wakeful
Eyelids closed, a quiet song in your throat through the night.

I see you move in shadows. The bed trembles.
I hear the song I could not hear, in my empty dark.

Message to Someone Four Hundred Nights Away

My dear dead loved one,
I want you to know: today I went to our house,
The one in Weston woods that we made together,
You and I—I want to tell you: the same
October afternoon sun was shimmering
Out of the trees onto the ground where we stood—need I count
How long ago?—our heads bent toward the grass, our arms
Moving through tangled boughs to shear them
Against the wintering nights of ice, our fingers
Reaching through blazing leaves for withered blooms. In the heady
Bittersweet wine of wind, we forgot hours till darkness
Blinded our hands. Holding them out for each other
We found our way to the door.

                        You remember how many times
We tried to tell our two deep friends and our words
Failed? But today I walked with them and their eyes

Showed they knew why we had lived here sheltered
Under the balancing rock.

                    Shall I try to tell you, loved one,
How it lives, our huge wild oval granite deity
On the crest of our hillock?
Gales, storms haven't loosened its root in the bedded earth
From where we'd stand watching
Its shadow tilting down the ravine on the snows
Of a thousand flowering laurel-heads in the stillness
Of sunlit mornings of May till their whiteness melted
To green glisten of leaves.

                    I want you to know,
My dead loved one, four hundred nights away: the woman and man
Who live here now were gone when I watched, letting me gather
The field, the house, the woods, the idol-rock as they were
For us unchanged, but only while I stayed. When they come back
I shall have gone, leaving no mark, taking with me
Your presence: our selves: not to return.

                                        [October 29, 1988]

Second-hand Poems

ANNA AKHMATOVA

The Muse

When in the night I await her coming,
My life seems stopped. I ask myself: What
Are tributes, freedom, or youth compared
To this treasured friend holding a flute?
Look, she's coming! She throws off her veil
And watches me, steady and long. I say:
"Was it you who dictated to Dante the pages
Of Hell?" And she answers: "I am the one."

MIGUEL DE UNAMUNO

Me destierro . . .

I exile myself into memory,
I go to live on remembrance;
Seek me, if I am lost to you,
In the barren-wild of history.

For human life is sickness
And in living sick, I die;
I go then, go to the barrens
Where death itself will forget me.
And I take you with me, my brothers,
To people my desert land.
When you believe me most dead
I shall quiver in your hands.
Here I leave you my soul—a book,
A man—a true world. O reader,
When all of you stirs as you read me,
It is I who am stirring within you.

ANONYMOUS ALBA

En un vergier soiz folha d'albespi

Sheltered beneath white hawthorn boughs,
A woman held her loved one close
In her arms, till the watchman cried abroad:
God! It is dawn! How soon it's come!

"How wildly have I wished that the night
Would never end, and that my love
Could stay, and the watchman never cry
God! It is dawn! How soon it's come!

"My love-and-friend, but one more kiss,
Here in our field where the small birds sing;
We shall defy their jealous throats—
God! It is dawn! How soon it's come!

"Still one more close embrace, my love,
Here in our field where the small birds sing,
Till the watchman blow his reedy strain—
God! It is dawn! How soon it's come!

"From the wind beyond where my love has gone,
Thoughtful, contented, I have drunk
A long deep draught of his breath—O God,
God! It is dawn! How soon it's come!"

(ENVOI)

Flowing with grace and charm is she;
Her loveliness draws many eyes,
Whose full heart throbs with a true love:
God! It is dawn! How soon it's come!

ANDRÉ SPIRE

Nudités

Hair is a nudity.—The Talmud

You said to me:
I would become your comrade:
I would visit your house without fear of troubling you.
We shall spend evenings in talk together,
Talking and thinking of our murdered brothers;
Together we shall wander the earth to find
A country to quiet their heads at last.
But do not let me see your eyeballs glitter
Or the burning veins of your forehead bulge!
I am your equal, not a prey.
Look at me: my clothes are chaste, almost poor!
You cannot even see the curve of my throat!

I looked and I answered:
Woman, you are naked:
Your downy neck is a goblet of well-water,
Your locks are wanton as a troop of mountain goats,

Your round, soft chignon quivers like a breast—
Woman, cut off your hair!

You are naked: your hands now lie unfurled,
Open in nakedness across the printed page,
Your fingers, the subtle tips of your body,
Ringless fingers—that will touch mine any moment—
Woman, cut off your hands!

You are naked: your voice flows up from your bosom,
Your song, your breath, and now the heat of your flesh—
It is spreading round my body to enter my flesh—
Woman, tear out your voice!

ANDRÉ SPIRE

Nativité

*Knowest thou the time when the wild goats of the rock bring forth? Or canst
thou mark when the hinds do calve? They bring forth their young and they are
delivered of their sorrows.* —Job

The cat lies on her back,
Tender eyed, open mouthed,
Pale curved tongue rose-tipped . . .

The cat gasps in the night . . .
A star in the midst of branches
Gleams cold, like the rings
Of a glow-worm moving through leaves.

Now tiny heads and paws swarm
On the cat's belly softly warm.

No wind. A leaf falls.

HUGO VON HOFMANNSTHAL

Eigene Sprache

As words grew in your mouth,
Now a chain has grown in your hand;
Pull the universe toward you!
Pull or be dragged!

OCTAVIO PAZ

Más allá del amor

Everything threatens us:
time, that divides into living fragments
what I was
        from what I shall be,
as a cane-knife does with a snake;
consciousness: the transparency pierced,
the gaze become blind from watching itself gaze at itself;
words: gloves of grayness, dust of thought on the
       grass, water, skin;
our names, which rise up between the You and the I,
walls of emptiness, walls that no trumpet cuts down.

Neither dream with its population of shattered images,
nor delirium with its prophetic foam,
nor love with its teeth and claws are enough for us.
Beyond ourselves,
on the border between being and becoming,
a life more than life itself calls to us.
Outside: the night breathes, spreads out,
filled with great hot leaves,
with struggling mirrors:

Second-hand Poems   265

fruits, talons, eyes, foliage,
flashing shoulders,
bodies that press their way into other bodies.

Lie down here on the edge of all this froth,
of all this life that does not know itself, yet surrenders:
you too are part of this night.
Stretch your full length, whiteness breathing,
throbbing,—O star divided,
wineglass,
bread that tips the scales toward the side of dawn,
moment of living flesh between this time and another measureless
    time.

STEFAN GEORGE

Denk nicht zu viel . . .

Do not ponder too much
Meanings that cannot be found—
The symbol-scenes that no man understands:

The wild swan that you shot, that you kept alive
In the yard, for a while, with shattered wing—
He reminded you, you said, of a faraway creature:
Your kindred self that you had destroyed in him.
He languished with neither thanks for your care nor rancor,
But when his dying came,
His fading eye rebuked you for driving him now
Out of a known into a new cycle of things.

Stanley Burnshaw: A Checklist, 1922–1989

ARTHUR D. CASCIATO AND
SUSAN M. SIPPLE

BOOKS, CHAPBOOKS, AND PAMPHLETS BY BURNSHAW

Poems. Pittsburgh: Folio Press, 1927. Ten poems published in an edition of sixty copies.

A Short History of the Wheel Age. New York: Folio Press, 1929. Prose poem published in an edition of 150 copies.

The Great Dark Love. New York, 1932. Nine poems, privately printed, with a "Note" by Burnshaw following the last poem. Edition of sixty copies.

André Spire and His Poetry. Philadelphia: Centaur Press, 1933. Includes a biographical-critical introduction, forty translations, an essay on *vers libre*, as well as a preface by Alfred Kreymborg.

The Iron Land. Philadelphia: Centaur Press, 1936. Verse narrative interspersed with sections of lyrics.

The Bridge. New York: Dryden Press, 1945. Verse drama, with an introduction by John Gassner.

The Revolt of the Cats in Paradise: A Children's Book for Adults. Gaylordsville, Conn.: Crow Hill Press, 1945. Dramatic satire in verse, illustrated by Russell T. Limbach.

The Sunless Sea. London: Peter Davies, 1948; New York: Dial Press, 1949. Novel.

Early and Late Testament. New York: Dial Press, 1952. Poems.

Caged in an Animal's Mind. New York: Holt, Rinehart and Winston, 1963. Poems.

The Hero of Silence: Scenes from an Imagined Life of Mallarmé. Poem reprinted from *The Lugano Review* 1(Summer 1965):5–14.

The Seamless Web: Language-Thinking, Creature-Knowledge, Art-Experience. New York: Braziller, 1970; London: Allen Lane, 1970; New York: Braziller, 1990 (with an introduction by James Dickey). Criticism.

In the Terrified Radiance. New York: Braziller, 1972. Poems.

Mirages: Travel Notes in the Promised Land. Garden City, N.Y.: Doubleday,

1977. Sequence of poems. Reprinted from *The Lugano Review* 7(1976):35–69.

The Refusers: An Epic of the Jews. New York: Horizon Press, 1981. Book 1: *Moses;* Book 2: *Uriel da Costa;* Book 3: *My Friend, My Father;* with historical interludes. Biographical novels.

My Friend, My Father. New York: Oxford University Press, 1986. Reprinting of the final section of *The Refusers: An Epic of the Jews.* Introduced by Leon Edel.

Robert Frost Himself. New York: Braziller, 1986; New York: Braziller, 1989. Biographical Critical Memoir.

BOOKS EDITED BY BURNSHAW

Two New Yorkers: Fifteen Lithographs, Paintings and Etchings by Alexander Kruse with Fourteen Lyrics by Alfred Kreymborg. New York: Bruce Humphries, 1938; New York: Dryden Press, 1941 (reprinted as *A Marriage of True Minds: Fifteen Pictures and Fifteen Poems*). With an introduction by Burnshaw.

The Poem Itself: Forty-five Modern Poets in a New Presentation. New York: Holt, Rinehart and Winston, 1960; New York: Meridian, 1962; London: Penguin, 1964; New York: Schocken, 1967; New York: Horizon Press, 1981; New York: Simon and Schuster, 1989. With an introduction and a note on prosody by Burnshaw.

Varieties of Literary Experience: Eighteen Essays in World Literature. New York: New York University Press, 1962; London: Peter Owen, 1963. With an introduction and a long essay by Burnshaw.

The Modern Hebrew Poem Itself. New York: Holt, Rinehart and Winston, 1965; New York: Schocken, 1966; Cambridge: Harvard University Press, 1989. Edited with T. Carmi and Ezra Spicehandler with an introduction by Burnshaw.

APPEARANCES OF BURNSHAW'S POETRY AND PROSE IN ANTHOLOGIES

"Sceptic." *Anthology of Magazine Verse for 1926.* Edited by W. S. Braithwaite. Boston: B. J. Brimmer, 1926. 59.

"Waiting in Winter." *Anthology of Magazine Verse for 1926.* Edited by W. S. Braithwaite. Boston: B. J. Brimmer, 1926. 59–60.

"Bond of Tears." *The American Caravan: A Yearbook of American Literature.* Edited by Van Wyck Brooks, Lewis Mumford, Alfred Kreymborg, and Paul Rosenfeld. New York: The Macaulay Co., 1927. 494.

"Sunday Evening." *American Caravan.* 495.

"Before Daylight." *American Caravan.* 495–96.

"End of the Flower-World (A.D. 2300)." *American Caravan* 496–97.

"Song of a Prisoner." *American Caravan.* 497.

"New Hampshire." *Modern Essays of Various Types.* Edited by Charles A. Cockayne. New York: Charles E. Merrill, 1927. 291–92.

"To a Young Girl Sleeping." *Anthology of Magazine Verse for 1928.* Edited by W. S. Braithwaite. New York: Harold Vinal, 1928. 41.

"End of the Flower-World (A.D. 2300)." *Lyric America 1630–1930: An Anthology of American Poetry.* Edited by Alfred Kreymborg. New York: Tudor, 1930. 602–3.

"I, Jim Rogers." *Proletarian Literature in the United States.* Edited by Granville Hicks et al. New York: International, 1935. 149–52.

"I, Jim Rogers." *Anthology of Magazine Verse for 1935.* Edited by Alan F. Pater. New York: The Poetry Digest Association, 1936. 13–16.

"The Driving Song." *The New Caravan.* Edited by Alfred Kreymborg, Lewis Mumford, and Paul Rosenfeld. New York: W. W. Norton and Co., 1936. 362.

"Marriage by Wind." *Contemporary American Men Poets.* Edited by Thomas Del Vecchio. New York: Henry Harrison, 1937. 19–20.

"No Words." *Contemporary.* 20.

"Rediscovery." *Contemporary.* 20.

"Anchorage in Time." *Contemporary.* 20–21.

"Strange." *A Treasury of Jewish Poetry.* Edited by Nathan and Maryann Ausubel. New York: Crown, 1957. 24.

"Nudities." *Treasury.* Trans. of André Spire. 31–32.

"End of the Flower-World (A.D. 2300)." *Treasury.* 722–23.

"Bread." *Treasury.* 215.

"Hear, O Israel!" *Treasury.* Trans. of André Spire. 277–78.

"Now You're Content." *Treasury.* Trans. of André Spire. 400–401.

"Variations on a Baedecker." *The American Writer and The Great Depression.* Edited by Harvey Swados. Indianapolis, Ind.: Bobbs-Merrill, 1966. 99–102.

"Historical Song of Then and Now." *The Experience of Literature.* Edited by Lionel Trilling. New York: Holt, Rinehart and Winston, 1967. 1282.

"Modes of Belief." *Experience.* 1283.

"Poetry: The Art." *Experience.* 1283–86.

"Turmoil in the Middle Ground." *Years of Protest.* Edited by Jack Salzman. New York: Bobbs-Merrill, 1967. 245–47.

"Mr. Tubbe's Morning Service." *New Masses: An Anthology of the Rebel Thirties.* Edited by Joseph North. New York: International Publishers, 1969. 58–59.

"The Good Angel." Trans. of Rafael Alberti. *Translations by American Poets.* Edited by Jean Garrigue. Athens, Ohio: Ohio University Press, 1970. 63.

"Individual Language." Trans. of Hugo von Hofmannsthal. *Translations.* 63.

"The Beloved." Trans. of Paul Eluard. *Translations.* 65.

"Do Not Ponder Too Much." Trans. of Stefan George. *Translations.* 65.

From "Turmoil in the Middle Ground." *Wallace Stevens: A Critical Anthology.* Edited by Irvin Ehrenpreis. London: Penguin, 1972. 99–102.

"Poetry: The Art." *Merrill Studies in Leaves of Grass.* Edited by Gay Wilson Allen. Columbus: Charles E. Merrill, 1972. 115–18.

"I, Jim Rogers." *Social Poetry of the 1930s: A Selection.* Edited by Jack Salzman and Leo Zanderer. New York: Burt Franklin, 1978. 1–4.

"New Youngfellow." *Social Poetry.* 4–8.

"Dilemma of a Dead Man About to Wake Up." *Social Poetry.* 8–10.

"Mr. Tubbe's Morning Service." *Social Poetry.* 10–11.

"A Coil of Glass (I)." *Social Poetry.* 11–12.

"A Coil of Glass (II)." *Social Poetry.* 12–13.

"Bread." *Social Poetry.* 13–14.

"Anchorage in Time (I)." *Social Poetry.* 14–15.

"Anchorage in Time (II)." *Social Poetry.* 15.

"Variations on a Baedecker." *Social Poetry.* 16–17.

"Eartha." *Social Poetry.* 17–20.

"Isaac." *Voices Within the Ark: The Modern Jewish Poets.* Edited by Howard Schwartz and Anthony Rudolf. New York: Avon Books, 1980. 433–34.

"House in St. Petersburg." *Voices Within.* 434–36.

"Talmudist." *Voices Within.* 436.

"Poetry: The Art." *Critical Essays on Walt Whitman.* Edited by James Woodress. Boston: G. K. Hall, 1983. 228–30.

POEMS PUBLISHED IN PERIODICALS

"A Winter Thought." *The Schenley Journal* 6(1922):50.

"Evening Fantasy." *The Octogonian* [The publication of the Sigma Alpha Mu chapter at the University of Pittsburgh]. 1923.

"If I Were King." *Pitt Panther* (November 1923):15.

"Eternalia." *Pitt Panther* (January 1924):17.

"Communion." *The Poet's Scroll* 3.3(March 1924):57.

"Starlight." *The Poet's Scroll* 3.4(April 1924):70.

"Dark Clouds." *The Poet's Scroll* 3.5(May 1924):95.

"Remains." *The Lyric* (June 1924):6.

"October Noon." *The Circle* 1(October 1924):61.

"After Storm: August." *Voices* 4(November 1924):12.

"Aesthetes." *Voices* 4(November 1924):12.

"Core of Night." *Voices* 4(November 1924):13.
"Blackbird." *The Lyric* 5(April 1925):10.
"Ode Before Autumn." *Voices* 4(April 1925):183.
"Sky-Girl." *International Arts* 1(June 1925):28.
"Lonely Worshipper." *The Midland* 11(15 September 1925):291.
"Sceptic." *The Midland* 11(15 September 1925):291.
"Inland Tugboats." *Voices* 5(October 1925):160.
"For Those Who Seek." *Palms* 3(January 1926):110.
"Sonnets to Shelley." *The Echo* (January 1926):n. pag.
"Wild Girl." *The Echo* (June 1926):n. pag.
"Speculation in February." *The Echo* (June 1926):n. pag.
"Sanctuary." *The Echo* (October 1926):n. pag.
"Earth Wanderer." *The Echo* (October 1926):n. pag.
"Song Before Sunrise." *The Midland* 12(December 1926):355–56.
"Still Birches." *The Midland* 12(December 1926):355.
"Song in the Snows." *Voices* 6(March 1927):173.
"Days." *The Midland* 13(May 1927):71.
"Stanzas in Spring." *Poetry Folio* 4(September-October 1927):[2].
"Your Eyes Are Blue." Trans. of Gustavo Adolfo Béquer. *Poetry Folio* 3(March-April 1927):2.
Untitled. Trans. of Spanish folk-poem. *Poetry Folio* 3(March-April 1927):[2].
"Spring Poem." Trans. of Charles d'Orléans. *Palms* 5(February 1928):136.
"Darkness and Eyes." *Transition* 12(March 1928):118.
"Spring Elegy." *Palms* 5(March 1928):202–4.
"From a Traveler's Notebook." *Poetry Folio* 6(April-May 1928):[3].
"To a Young Girl Sleeping." *Contemporary Verse* (April-May 1928):15.
"The Crane Driver." *New Masses* 4(July 1928):7.
"Three Worker Gangs." *New Masses* 4(July 1928):7.
"Saturday Whistles." *New Masses* 4(July 1928):7.
"Blood." *The Dial* 85(October 1928):332.
"These Strikes." Trans. of André Spire. *New Masses* 4(April 1929):5.
"Kisses." Trans. of André Spire. *Poetry Folio* 7(May-June 1929):[4].
"Immortality." Trans. of André Spire. *Poetry Folio* 7(May-June 1929):[4].
"When, Oh When?" Trans. of André Spire. *Poetry Folio* 7(May-June 1929):4.
"Arrival in the Country." Trans. of André Spire. *The American Hebrew* 125(5 July 1929):230.
"Lichens." Trans. of André Spire. *The American Hebrew* 125(5 July 1929): 230.
"Pogroms." Trans. of André Spire. *The American Hebrew* 125(5 July 1929): 230.
"Bird." Trans. of André Spire. *The American Hebrew* 125(5 July 1929):230.
"Body." Trans. of André Spire. *The American Hebrew* 125(5 July 1929):230.

"Sunday on the River." Trans. of André Spire. *The American Hebrew* 125(5 July 1929):230.

"Hear, O Israel!" Trans. of André Spire. *The American Hebrew* 125(5 July 1929):230.

"Exodus." Trans. of André Spire. *The American Hebrew* 125(5 July 1929):230.

"White Collar Slaves." *New Masses* 5(August 1929):8.

"Now You're Content." *This Quarter* 2(January-March 1930):419–20.

"To the Earth." *Poetry* 37(March 1931):297.

"Instead of Swords." *Poetry* 37(March 1931):298.

"Restful Ground." *Poetry* 37(March 1931):298.

"Forevermore." *Poetry* 37(March 1931):299.

"Her Crown." *Poetry* 37(March 1931):299–300.

"Blood of Earth." *Poetry* 37(March 1931):300.

"Three Vantage-Points and a Field." *Trend* 1(September-October-November 1932):90.

"Bread." *Modern Quarterly* 6(Autumn 1932):12.

"The Bluegold Day." *Trend* 1(January-February-March 1932):144.

"Variations on a Baedecker." *Modern Monthly* 7(May 1933):224.

"The Crane-Driver." *Modern Monthly* 7(August 1933):422.

"New Youngfellow." *Dynamo* 1(January 1934):14–18.

"Cold City Square." *New Masses* 10(30 January 1934):27.

"For a Workers' Road-Song." *Trend* 2(March-April 1934):71.

"A Spring Song." *New Masses* 11(10 April 1934):19.

"Mr. Tubbe's Morning Service." *New Masses* 13(13 November 1934):19.

"I, Jim Rogers." *New Masses* 14(12 March 1935):19–20.

"For a Workers' Road-Song." *New Masses* 18(14 January 1936):15.

"Toward Outer Air." *New Masses* 18(14 January 1936):15.

"No Words." *New Masses* 18(14 January 1936):15.

"Walt Whitman." *Accent* 4(Spring 1944):155–58.

From "Early and Late Testament." *American Scholar* 21(Spring 1952):150.

"Songs for Music II." *New York Times Book Review* 22 February 1953, 2.

"Blue, Windless and Deep." *Sewanee Review* 66(January-March 1958):100–101.

"Don du Poème." Trans. of Mallarmé. *Saturday Review* 43(7 May 1960):14.

"Revenant." *Partisan Review* 27(Fall 1960):726.

"Mystique." Trans. of André Spire. *Partisan Review* 27(Winter 1960):67.

"Muse." Trans. of A. Akhmatova. *Poetry* 98(September 1961):376–77.

"The White Flight." Trans. of A. Akhmatova. *Poetry* 98(September 1961):377.

"Sun Voyage." *Poetry* 99(November 1961):96.

"Seedling Air." *Poetry* 99(November 1961):97.

"Clay." *Sewanee Review* 71(Summer 1963):473.

"Bread." *New York Times Book Review* 6 October 1963, 2.

"Historical Song of Then and Now." *New York Times Book Review* 6 October 1963, 2.

"Hero of Silence." *The Lugano Review* 1(Summer 1965):5–14.

"Emptiness." *Atlantic* 222(August 1968):55.

"Seedling Air." *Tri-Quarterly* 19(Fall 1970):156.

"Retour des martinets." Trans. of André Spire. *Massachusetts Review* 13(Summer 1972):325.

From "The White Flock." Trans. of A. Akhmatova. *Massachusetts Review* 13(Summer 1972):326.

"Me destierro . . ." Trans. of Miguel de Unamuno. *Massachusetts Review* 13(Summer 1972):327.

"Mirages: Travel Notes in the Promised Land." *The Lugano Review* 7(1976): 35–69.

"Florida Seaside." *Agenda* 21–22.1(Winter 1983–Spring 1984):7–8.

"On Reading Dickey's 'Puella'." *Agenda* 21–22(Winter 1983–Spring 1984):9.

"Argon." *Agenda* 21–22.1(Winter 1983–Spring 1984):10.

"The Terrified Radiance." *The Carrell* 22(1984):20–21.

Untitled. *Agenda* 26(Summer 1988):44. Includes "A Note" from the author.

TRANSLATIONS OF BURNSHAW'S POETRY

"Les esclaves en faux-col." *Poèmes d'ouvriers américains.* Trans. by N[orbert] Guterman and P. Morhange. Paris: Les Revues, 1930. 51–55.

"Un chemin d'usine en pensylvanie." Trans. by André Spire. *Europe* 86(15 February 1930):179.

"Le sang." Trans. by André Spire. *Europe* 86(15 February 1930):179–80.

"Jours." Trans. by André Spire. *Europe* 86(15 February 1930):180.

"Fin du monde des fleurs." Trans. by André Spire. *Europe* 86(15 February 1930):180–81.

"La nuit et les yeux." Trans. by André Spire. *Europe* 86(15 February 1930): 181–82.

"Guerriers morts." Trans. by André Spire. *Mercure de france* 248(1 December 1933):305.

"Dans la nuit." Trans. by André Spire. *Mercure de france* 248(1 December 1933):305.

"A l'intelligence." Trans. by André Spire. *Mercure de france* 248(1 December 1933):306.

"Minuit." Trans. by André Spire. *Mercure de france* 248(1 December 1933): 306.

"Sang de la terre." Trans. by André Spire. *Mercure de france* 248(1 December 1933):307.

"Cycle de rêve." Trans. by André Spire. *Mercure de france* 248(1 December 1933):307.

"The Road to Delphi." Trans. by Fivos Delphi. *Delphika Tetradia* 1(April 1964):50–51.

"Guide's Speech on a Road near Delphi." Trans. by Fivos Delphi. *Delphika Tetradia* 3–4(April 1965):184.

"Song of Nothings: In the Mountain's Shadow at Delphi." Trans. by Fivos Delphi. *Delphika Tetradia* 3–4(April 1965):184–85.

"Dialogue in a Hall near Delphi." Trans. by Fivos Delphi. *Delphika Tetradia* 3–4(April 1965):185–86.

"An Eternity of Words." Trans. by Fivos Delphi. *Delphika Tetradia* 7–8(April 1966):329.

"Caged in an Animal's Mind." Trans. by Luciano Rebay. *L'Approdo Letterario* 34(April-June 1966):18–21.

"Thoughts on the War and my Daughter." Trans. by Luciano Rebay. *L'Approdo Letterario* 34(April-June 1966):20–23.

"Days." Trans. by Luciano Rebay. *L'Approdo Letterario* 34(April-June 1966):22–23.

"Bread." Trans. by Luciano Rebay. *L'Approdo Letterario* 34(April-June 1966):24–27.

"To A Young Girl Sleeping." Trans. by Luciano Rebay. *L'Approdo Letterario* 34(April-June 1966):26–27.

"Restful Ground." Trans. by Luciano Rebay. *L'Approdo Letterario* 34(April-June 1966):26.

"Into the Blond Torrent." Trans. by Fivos Delphi. *Delphika Tetradia* 11–12(1967):507.

CRITICAL ESSAYS AND NOTES

"The Golden Age of Sorrow." *Poetry Folio* 3(March-April 1927):[1], [4].

"The Birthday of French Romanticism." *Poetry Folio* 4(September-October 1927):[4].

"Vers Libre in Full Bloom (I)." *Poetry* 32(April-September 1928):277–82.

"Vers Libre in Full Bloom (II)." *Poetry* 32(April-September 1928):334–41.

"A Note on Translating Poetry." *This Quarter* 3(October-November-December 1930):343–51.

"The Student Forum." *Modern Monthly* 7(March 1933):119–21. Written and edited by Burnshaw.

"The Student Forum." *Modern Monthly* 7(May 1933):242–43. Written and edited by Burnshaw and G. M. B.

"The Student Forum." *Modern Monthly* 7(June 1933):289. Written and edited by Burnshaw and G. M. B.

"The Hotel Workers Revolt." *New Masses* 10(6 February 1934):16–18. Published under "Jeremiah Kelly."

"Notes on Revolutionary Poetry." *New Masses* 10(20 February 1934):20–22.

"We're Back in Sing-Sing." *New Masses* 10(27 February 1934):11.

"Art and Propaganda." *Poetry* 44(Spring 1934):351–54.

"Detroit Cries 'Sell Out'." *New Masses* 11(3 April 1934):11–13. Published under "Jeremiah Kelley."

"Working for the Government." *New Masses* 11(12 June 1934):12. Published under "Jeremiah Kelly, Jr."

"General Johnson, Union-Buster." *New Masses* 12(17 July 1934):12–14. Published under "Jeremiah Kelly, Jr."

"Material for a Note on Shakespeare." *New Masses* 14(8 January 1935):23–24.

"A New Direction for Criticism." *New Masses* 14(15 January 1935):23–24.

"Middle-Ground Writers." *New Masses* 15(30 April 1935):19–21.

Untitled. *Partisan Review* 2(April-May 1935):47–51. Response to Edwin Rolfe's essay on proletarian poetry in a symposium before the first American Writers Congress.

"U.S. State Department—Drama Censor." *New Masses* 18(4 February 1936): 28–29.

"The Passion for Liberty." *New Masses* 19(7 April 1936):19–20.

"Homage to André Spire." *Hommage à André Spire.* Paris: Librairie Lipschutz, 1939. 135–38.

"Vers Libre." *Dictionary of World Literature.* Edited by Joseph T. Shipley. New York: Philosophical Library, 1943. 612–13.

"André Spire." *Columbia Dictionary of Modern European Literature.* Edited by Horatio Smith. New York: Columbia University Press, 1947. 774–75.

Foreword. *The Poetic Mind.* By Frederick C. Prescott. Ithaca: Cornell University Press, 1959. v–viii.

"The Poem Itself." *Saturday Review* 43(7 May 1960):14.

"Wallace Stevens and the Statue." *Sewanee Review* 69(Summer 1961):355–66.

Telescoped translation by Burnshaw, from pp. 298, 299, and 493 of André Spire's *Plaisir poétique et plaisir musculaire.* New York: Vanni, 1949. *Understanding Poetry.* Edited by Cleanth Brooks and Robert Penn Warren. 3d ed. New York: Holt, Rinehart and Winston, 1960. 124.

"The Three Revolutions of Modern Poetry." *Sewanee Review* 70(Summer 1962):418–50.

"The Body Makes the Minde." *American Scholar* 38(Winter 1968–69):25–39.

"Modern Hebrew Poets." *Page 2: The Best of "Speaking of Books" from the New York Times Book Review.* Edited by Francis Brown. New York: Holt, Rinehart and Winston, 1969. 138–44.

"Stéphane Mallarmé." *Atlantic Brief Lives: A Biographical Companion to the*

Arts. Edited by Louis Kronenberger. Boston: Little, Brown and Co., 1971. 481–83.

Introduction. *Toward Social Sanity and Human Behavior*. By Trigant Burrow. New York: Horizon, 1984. vii–xiv.

"A Future for Poetry." *Agenda* 21.4–22.1(Winter 1983–Spring 1984):45–70.

"Seeing Ciardi Plain." *John Ciardi: Measure of the Man*. Edited by Vince Clemente. Fayetteville: University of Arkansas Press, 1987. 119–22.

"Reflections on Wallace Stevens." *Wallace Stevens Journal* 13.2(Fall 1989):1–5. Originally delivered as an address to the Wallace Stevens Society at the 1988 meeting of the Modern Language Association in New Orleans.

PUBLISHED LETTERS

"Mr. Leuba Wants to Know." *Poetry* 33(October 1928–March 1929):50–53. Concerning Leuba's response to Burnshaw's "Vers Libre in Full Bloom (I)" and "Vers Libre in Full Bloom (II)."

"The February Number." *Poetry* 38(April 1931):53–55. Concerning Louis Zukofsky's guest-editing of the special Objectivism issue of *Poetry*.

"A Poet Takes His Stand." *New Masses* 9(September 1933):27. Concerning V. F. Calverton's publishing of a controversial article by Max Eastman in the August 1933 issue of *Modern Monthly*. Burnshaw, in effect, publicly quits his position on the magazine.

"The Poetry Corps Divide." *New Masses* 12(31 July 1934):21–23. Reply to Harriet Monroe's editorial, "Art and Propaganda." *Poetry* 44(July 1934):210–15. Abbreviated form of Burnshaw's letter, "Stanley Burnshaw Protests." *Poetry* 44(September 1934):351–54.

"Stanley Burnshaw Protests." *Poetry* 44(September 1934):351–54. Excerpted from "The Poetry Corps Divide." *New Masses* 12(31 July 1934):21–23. Reply to Harriet Monroe's editorial, "Art and Propaganda." *Poetry* 44(July 1934):21–23.

"A Letter from the Poet Stanley Burnshaw about his Friend the Painter Stanley Murphy." *Art International* 16(20 May 1972):32.

"Stanley Burnshaw: A Response." *Massachusetts Review* 14(Winter 1973): 224–25. Reply to Helen Vendler's review of *The Seamless Web*, "In Review." *Massachusetts Review* 12(Autumn 1971):834–37.

"The Refusers." *Commentary* 73(June 1982):12. Reply to Ruth Wisse's review of *The Refusers*, "Jewish Dreams." *Commentary* 73(March 1982):45–48.

"Refusing." *New York Review of Books* 29(15 June 1982):45. Reply to J. M. Cameron's review of *The Refusers*, "Moses and Atheism." *New York Review of Books* 29(1 April 1982):33–34.

REVIEWS

"New Hampshire." *The Forum* 71(May 1924):704. Robert Frost, *New Hampshire.*

"Cleansing the Muse's Soul with Laughing Gas." *Voices* 4(1925):313–17. Paul Sandoz, *Legend.*

"He Who Laughs Last. . . ." *The Forum* 73(April 1925):605. e. e. cummings, *Tulips and Chimneys.*

"A Word to the Wise." *Voices* 5(January 1926):149–52. James Stephens, *A Poetry Recital.*

Untitled. *Poetry Folio* 1(March-April 1926):[4]. Langston Hughes, *The Weary Blues.*

"But is it Biography?" *New Masses* 4(March 1929):22. Andre de Hévesy, *The Discoverer* (trans. by Robert M. Coates).

"What Is Wrong With Marriage." *New Masses* 4(May 1929):21. Dr. L. V. Hamilton and Kenneth MacGowan, *What Is Wrong With This Marriage?* and Dr. Ira S. Wile and Mary Day Winn, *Marriage in the Modern Manner.*

"Poetic Suicide." *New Masses* 5(July 1929):21. Elinor Wylie, *Angels and Earthly Creatures.*

"Full Stomached Anecdote." *New Masses* 5(August 1929):21. Adolphe de Castro, *Portrait of Ambrose Bierce.*

"One of the Few." *New Masses* 5(October 1929):22. Charles E. S. Wood, *The Poet in the Desert, Poems of the Ranges,* and *Book of Indian Tales.*

"Witter Bynner—Poet." *New Masses* 5(April 1930):17. Bynner, *The Jade Mountain* and *Indian Earth.*

"Valiant Attempt." *New Masses* 9(2 January 1934):25. Robert Gessner, *Upsurge.*

"Much-Praised Poems." *New Masses* 12(7 August 1934):26. David McCord, *The Crows.*

"A New Untermeyer Product." *New Masses* 12(14 August 1934):26. Louis Untermeyer and Carter Davidson, *Poetry: Its Appreciation and Enjoyment.*

"More About the English Poets." *New Masses* 12(21 August 1934):27–28.

"Dahlberg's New Novel." *New Masses* 12(11 September 1934):26–27. Edward Dahlberg, *Those Who Perish.*

"The Theater." *New Masses* 12(18 September 1934):29. Published under "George Wilson."

"Judgment Day." *New Masses* 12(25 September 1934):28. Elmer Rice, "Judgment Day." Published under "George Wilson."

"The Theatre." *New Masses* 13(9 October 1934):28. Published under "George Wilson."

"The Theatre." *New Masses* 13(23 October 1934):29. Published under "George Wilson."

"What Happened to Stravinsky?" *New Masses* 13(13 November 1934):29.

"The Dance." *New Masses* 13(20 November 1934):27.

"Rice and the Revolution." *New Masses* 13(27 November 1934):27. Elmer Rice, *Between Two Worlds*.

"The First United Front." *New Masses* (27 November 1934):27–28. Benefit for cartoonist Art Young.

"The Theatre." *New Masses* 13(11 December 1934):28–29.

"The Most Important Play in New York." *New Masses* 13(25 December 1934):28–29. Friedrich Wolf, *The Sailors of Cattaro*.

"A Prospect for Edna Millay." *New Masses* 14(1 January 1935):37–38. Millay, *Wine from These Grapes*.

"Waiting for Lefty." *New Masses* 14(29 January 1935):27–28. Clifford Odets, *Waiting for Lefty*.

"The Dance." *New Masses* 14(26 February 1935):27.

"The Dance." *New Masses* 14(19 March 1935):28.

"Two Red Plays on Broadway." *New Masses* 15(9 April 1935):27. Clifford Odets, *Waiting for Lefty* and *Till the Day I Die*.

"The Dance." *New Masses* 15(23 April 1935):29.

"The Dance." *New Masses* 15(21 May 1935):28.

"Sklar's and Peters' 'Parade'." *New Masses* 15(4 June 1935):27–28. George Sklar and Paul Peters, *Parade*.

"Finale to a Brilliant Season." *New Masses* 16(2 July 1935):43.

"Toward a Genuine Negro Drama." *New Masses* 16(9 July 1935):29.

"Drama for Both Ears." *New Masses* 16(3 September 1935):28. Alfred Kreymborg, *America, America*.

"A Labor Theatre for Brooklyn." *New Masses* 16(24 September 1935):28.

"Turmoil in the Middle-Ground." *New Masses* 17(1 October 1935):41–42. Wallace Stevens, *Ideas of Order* and Haniel Long, *Pittsburgh Memoranda*.

"Paths of Glory Dramatized." *New Masses* 17(15 October 1935):28.

"New Theater Night." *New Masses* 17(22 October 1935):28.

"A Letter to the Author of 'Squaring the Circle'." *New Masses* 17(29 October 1935):27–28. Valentine Katayev, *Squaring the Circle*.

"Dead End Social Order." *New Masses* 17(26 November 1935):28–29. Sidney Kingsley, *Dead End*.

"The Theater Union Produces 'Mother.' " *New Masses* 17(3 December 1935):27–28. Bertolt Brecht and Hans Eisler's dramatization of Gorky's novel *Mother*.

"Five Dancers in Fourteen New Works." *New Masses* 17(10 December 1935):27–28.

"For Those 'Not Interested' in the Dance." *New Masses* 18(17 January 1936):28–29.

"Poison at the Booth—and an Antidote." *New Masses* 18(21 January 1936):28–29. James Hagan, *Midwest*.

"Serious Laughter." *New Masses* 18(28 January 1936):28–29. Lynn Riggs, *Russet Mantle.*

" 'Paradise Lost'—An Obituary." *New Masses* 18(11 February 1936):28. Clifford Odets, *Paradise Lost.*

"Questions Which Need an Answer." *New Masses* 18(18 February 1936):27–28. F. W. P.'s *Living Newspaper.*

"First 'Theatre Union Night'." *New Masses* 18(25 February 1936):28. John Wexley, *Running Dogs* and George Sklar and Paul Peters, *A Letter to the President.*

"Subsistence Love: British Style." *New Masses* 18(10 March 1936):26. *Love on the Dole.*

"Case of Clyde Griffiths." *New Masses* 19(21 March 1936):28. Lena Goldschmidt's dramatization of Dreiser's *An American Tragedy.*

"Mankind is Standing Up." *New Masses* 19(21 April 1936):26. Irwin Shaw, *Bury the Dead.*

"The Government in Show Business." *New Masses* 19(28 April 1936):27. WPA Theater Project.

"Dance Congress and Festival." *New Masses* 19(19 May 1936):29.

"Theater Critics and Audiences." *New Masses* 19(26 May 1936):28. John Howard Lawson, *Theory and Technique of Playwriting* and Lincoln Kirsten, *Dance: A Short History of Classic Theatrical Dancing.*

"W.P.A. as Historian, Reporter and Dancer." *New Masses* 19(2 June 1936):29–30.

"The Beginning of a Tradition." *New Masses* 19(23 June 1936):29–30. Mike Gold and Michael Blankfort, *Battle Hymn.*

"The Revolutionary Fringe." *New Masses* 20(4 August 1936):25–26. Published under "J. G. Conant." Christina Stead, *The Beauties and the Furies.*

"Poetry Thinking About Itself." *Poetry* 99(March 1962):387–90. Elizabeth Sewell, *The Orphic Voice.*

"Speaking of Books: Modern Hebrew Poets." *New York Times Book Review* 2 May 1965, 2.

"An Exciting Critic of the Culture." *American Scholar* 39(Winter 1969–70):177–79. Robert Brustein, *The Third Theatre.*

"Many Meanings and One?" *Sewanee Review* 78(Spring 1970):383–89. Robert Greer Cohn, *Toward the Poems of Mallarmé.*

Untitled. *Saturday Review* (23 May 1970):52, 63. Michael Hamburger, *The Truth of Poetry.*

MISCELLANEOUS

"Sixth Testament: Strength of Singleness." *Literary Recordings.* Rec. 28 November 1962. Library of Congress Archives, 1981. 157. Louis Untermeyer introduces Burnshaw.

"First Testament: Bread." *Literary Recordings.* 157.
"Cats move like water." *Literary Recordings.* 157.
"Woodpecker, hovering out of the dawn." *Literary Recordings.* 157.
"Third Testament: A Coil of Glass." *Literary Recordings.* 157.
"A book might be the lens of pure hard tears." *Literary Recordings.* 157.
"The vast stone trunk of mountain lifts above." *Literary Recordings.* 157.
"Eighth Testament: Sea Story." *Literary Recordings.* 157.
"To a Young Girl Sleeping." *Literary Recordings.* 157.
"Anonymous Alba." *Literary Recordings.* 157.
"Nudities." *Literary Recordings.* 157.
"The Good Angel." *Literary Recordings.* 157.
"Poetry: The Art." *Literary Recordings.* 157.
"Summer." *Literary Recordings.* 157.
"Ancient of Nights." *Literary Recordings.* 157.
"Thoughts about a Garden." *Literary Recordings.* 157.
"Caged in an Animal's Mind." *Literary Recordings.* 157.
"The Muse." Trans. of A. Akhmatova. *Literary Recordings.* Rec. 30 May 1964.
    Library of Congress Archives, 1981. 158. Read by Florence Becker Lennon.
"Days." *Literary Recordings.* 158. Read by Burnshaw.
"End of the Flower World." *Literary Recordings.* 158.
"House in St. Petersburg." *Literary Recordings.* 158.
"Thoughts of the War and My Daughter." *Literary Recordings.* 158.
"Pennsylvania Workers', or Millhands' Roadsong." *Literary Recordings.* 158.
"Guide's Speech on a Road near Delphi." *Literary Recordings.* 158.
"Letter from One Who Could Not Cross the Frontier." *Literary Recordings.*
    158.
" 'What Can I See from Corinth Bay?' " *Literary Recordings.* 158.
"The Heroes' Statues." *Literary Recordings.* 158.
"Eigene Sprache." Trans. of Hugo von Hofmannsthal. *Literary Recordings.*
    158. Read by Florence Becker Lennon.
Self-Portrait: Book People Picture Themselves. Edited by Burt Britton. New
    York: Random House, 1976. 156. Self-portrait of Burnshaw.
Alan Filreis and Harvey Teres. "An Interview with Stanley Burnshaw."
    Wallace Stevens Journal 13(Fall 1989):109–21.